MOTHERS, DAUGHTERS

by Carolyn See

THE REST IS DONE WITH MIRRORS
BLUE MONEY
MOTHERS, DAUGHTERS

CAROLYN SEE

Coward, McCann & Geoghegan, Inc.
New York

Copyright © 1977 by Carolyn See

SBN: 698-10837-X

Library of Congress Cataloging in Publication Data
See, Carolyn
    Mothers, daughters.

    I. Title.
PZ4.S4516Mö3 [PS3569.E33]   813'.5'4   77-3305

Printed in the United States of America

A generous grant from the National Endowment for the Arts—for which much thanks—made the writing of this book possible.

*To Lisa, Clara
and Kate,
with love*

There was plenty of opportunity for a good secretary in the early fifties in Hollywood; slowly Evie improved her life style. Her dark good looks and quick sense of humor made her popular with her office workers and the growing circle of friends. For the first time in her life she could assert herself. For the first time in her life, the burden of raising a child seemed to tie her down. For a period of seven years she punished herself and her daughter, Judy, for the responsibilities she felt she was not meeting. This was also a time when so many of her friends were marrying, divorcing and remarrying.

By the time she was in her late thirties, the guilt she placed upon herself for not wanting to be a parent was too much; she had several minor breakdowns. The need to completely remove herself from the past became too great; she changed her name back to her maiden name, moved far from her old friends and waited for her child to get out of high school. Meanwhile, she finally permitted herself to grow into a permanent relationship with a mature man.

In the fall of 1963 she set her daughter out on her own and remarried. All ties with the past were cut. None of her old friends, not even her child, knows anymore about her.

> Judy L.
> 9/24/75
> (from a classroom
> assignment on mothers)

I

A plastic horse, standing in weeds, its insides half filled with water that heaves and splashes when the horse is ridden, which is hardly ever. A patio slanting and slanting, off to the edge of a jagged sandstone bluff. Plants in pots—last year's petunias still stubbornly blooming. Lobelia. Succulents which died a little during each winter's frost, their leaves turning to mush and liquid, finally forming a soggy mulch around each plant. Weeds between bricks. The sun, every morning, coming up at a slightly different point on the ridge across the canyon from her living room. The sun, every evening, going down against an infinitesimally different wedge of green. The neighbors' house, seen from her balcony. Real horses down there—aggressively fleshy—who mated, with a little prodding help, through long summer afternoons. From the patio side of the house, another steep canyon, where leaves in flammable trees moved circularly, in patterns. A road, where another neighbor had disappeared—car and all— driving home in a flood from an art exhibit.

11

A cat climbs up against an old screen door, moaning with excitement. Her silhouette against the pink sky looks as if she's grown whiskers a foot across. Her mouth is full of hay, and locked in the hay is a weakly struggling, enormous rat.

Ruth got up, swearing, barefoot, and banged on the screen with the flat of her hand. The cat held, furious, then dropped. The sun appeared, a silver sliver. Soon the room would be full of blinding light. Ruth went into the kitchen, put water on for coffee, bent over the oven to light it, slammed the broiler door, shivered, ran for her robe and slippers, put on a record. The kids were asleep in the living room, where she usually slept; they had colds and the nights in their basement rooms were freezing.

Until the music started, the only sound of the morning was the metallic sliding of composition slippers skating across the floor. Intimations of her own mother—coffee in the morning, bourbon at night, a single box of Mallomars in an exceptionally clean and empty Frigidaire. Ruth's refrigerator right now was filled with Sara Lee cakes, defrosted; some wings left over from the Colonel, fresh fruit past its prime and, in the freezer, stacks of Celeste Frozen Pizza. Always enough to eat, if you weren't picky, usually, sometimes. Ruth drank brandy—the smell of bourbon made her sick. In the nights, lately, during the colds (which were better now, but still Reggie and Dinah commandeered her bed) she slept on the couch, and read late, drinking brandy and soda. Reggie slept with her eyes open, she had since she was a little girl, and looking from the pages of the biography of Virginia Woolf, or some other record of happier, more organized times, Ruth often met her daughter's impervious stare.

Reggie had been at summer camp during most of the divorce. Out to lunch for middle-aged bodies slammed against living room walls, surreptitious phone calls surreptitiously intercepted; Ruth's own hand had banged down on the arm of a chair with such force that the wrist was sprained and a halt called against the shouting to find Jacuzzies, ultrasonic, and an elastic bandage. Dinah was there for it all, and at the age of three had started—looking quietly off the edge of the balcony—to suck her thumb. If you have a mistress, where do you keep her? Jack's mistress was in another canyon, closer to town, the action, the beach; he traveled now with droves of little ladies down to the beach in late afternoons, his graying hair in a natural halo, and in the middle of the hairy circle, under the moustache, above the beard, a wide smile.

"What do you want for breakfast, cereal or *quesadillas*?" Her two breakfasts—the one a tortilla fried in butter with melted cheese, the other, hot water poured over a mound of processed fluff highly flavored with imitation maple. They chose *quesadillas* and sat, lined up on the couch, eating off paper plates, each with her own varicolored mound of vitamins.

"I like Ray Charles."

"Yeah."

"Except that Dinah ruined those records."

"I didn't ruin them! How could I ruin them? I was little! I didn't even know what I was doing!"

Dinah, indignant.

Reggie, repulsed, remote. The three of them in their nightgowns.

"It was my fault really." Ruth remembered afternoons when the baby hauled out the records, crying, dirty-diapered, and walked across them in baby shoes . . . *how could I have let her do that?* And tried, for a tenth of a second, to remember if that had been before she'd found out about Jennifer or not. Probably not, you know? Probably before she ever found out about Jennifer. So how could she have let Dinah ruin the records?

"You know what I want to buy this summer? I want to buy some steam curlers the first thing I get some money. I'm getting tired of this same straight hair, you know?" But Reggie looked very pleased as she spoke, and tenderly stroked her long blond hair.

13

Sun flooded into the room, the coffee was delicious. Birds sang feverishly out on the balcony.

"OK. OK. Come on. Plates in the trash, cups on the sink. Dinah, brush your teeth, wash your face. Comb your hair."

"You brush my hair, Mom," Dinah said, and didn't move.

Instead Ruth went downstairs to get her clothes. Tights, pants, sweater. Soon the spring would come, *be* here. Upstairs again, slippers clipping against bare wood.

"Come on! Dinah! Will you get *in* there?"

Reggie still lay pale on the couch, flaked out, immovable; mouth slack, eyes lidded, staring into space, into nowhere. Beneath the puffy lips, plump chin, frail collarbones, chicken pox marks from seven years ago, a perfect pair of perfect breasts . . . Boy! It wouldn't even *occur* to her to make the bed!

"Dinah! Come on!"

And only later, after Dinah left, grumbling, banging her lunch box, cadging last-minute nickels and dimes, extra raisins, nuts, managing to leave behind her math book—as later this afternoon she'd leave her jacket and mittens at school—did Reggie get up, with perfect grace, lightly freckled like an adolescent giraffe, and glide into the bathroom. Ruth, making the bed, heard her in there; slowly, slowly, brushing her teeth, caressing them as in a dream. Ruth had no nerve to tell her to *come on*, hurry up. The words wouldn't come, so after the few breakfast dishes were done, she watered the plants in the patio, fed the cats, made a couple of phone calls leaving messages with answering services here in town, and only after Reggie sloped by, round shoulders protectively narrowing over those breasts, little feet making dampish tracks across the living room rug, toes curling up disdainfully from cat hair and traces of outdoor dirt, did Ruth duck into the shower.

Sometimes she wondered about her children. Remembering her own isolation, living with a divorced mother, washing out dirndl skirts every Saturday, ironing five blouses, five

14

skirts every Sunday, listening to Jack Benny, getting up to go to school. She had learned her style from junior colleges and women's magazines. There wasn't a day in her life that she hadn't faked something. But she was even more absent from her children than her mother had been from her. So where did they *come* from, these kids; Reggie and her wine-colored jump suits, turbans, encyclopedic knowledge of thirties musicals? Other kids didn't wear turbans at Canoga Park High. And Dinah, gravel-voiced trucker, jaunty, neutered. There was no one, anywhere, like her. Was she, as they used to say in that first Beatles movie, an early clue to the new direction?

In the shower she decided for the four hundredth time what new car she'd buy when she got the money. Should she take the new noon show—but it would take more time away from the kids—do we need toilet paper? The pictures still at the framers? If she remembers to pick up the Sunday *Times*, she'll get tickets to the ballet. She didn't think of Edward, although she'd see him tonight, and she didn't think of Jack—although until a few months ago, her shower and her car had been the scenes of murderous monologues, solitary weeping.

Now she got out of the shower, *her* shower, sat on her couch wrapped in her towel, then went out on her balcony. Down there in the canyon, the horses nudged together. Right next to her a bird flew in for seed; his mate joined him. Oh, no fooling, it really was beautiful! And when Reggie came upstairs, dressed, hurrying for the first time against being late (she looks out for *herself*, God knows!) the day's extraordinary beauty was such that she gave her daughter a hug before she left, and then hustled back into the bathroom, humming. Nine-thirty.

She had been married for fourteen years and embraced the state. If her childhood had been "disorderly," why, it had been an unfortunate mistake—her parents' purely personal clash. She had chosen her husband while they were both still in college, for his bank account and his hand-tailored suits. He had been in Hong Kong, for the Korean War; he had or-

15

dered one suit a month for two years. Their first date had been at the bank. ("Hey. You want to drive down to the bank?") When they married, she discovered herself vindicated. The world was full of married people.

She threw herself into the life; the San Fernando Valley, ranunculuses in pots, and if her husband turned out to be—a surprise—well, wasn't that the subject matter of five thousand morning phone calls, the metaphor for an imperfect world? When the sixties had suggested they could ease up a little, smoke a little something at their backyard barbecues, Ruth panicked, and she had been right. In sex, recorded music, this canyon cabin, their marriage unraveled, desisted, went. And theirs had been no isolated accident; she saw its echoes all around her. How could she blame her husband, how could she blame herself? Now that the decade's tacky panorama had been struck, she was left with its consequences; "It was all a trick!" And about her marriage: "It was all a lie." The orderly world was a lie.

Ruth smiled into the mirror, sharply, showing her teeth; the skin around her eyes crumpled. She relaxed, smiled again, relaxed again. When her face was still, the face showed almost no wrinkles. Really quite astonishing, she thought. She smiled again, and there it was, the smiling ghost, herself as an old woman. If she neglected to dye her black curly hair it would turn pepper and salt, the way her mother's had. Amazing, she thought, truly amazing. Her body, which had been thin all her life, was developing a kind of life of its own. For all its exercise, her outline assumed a pear shape, the natural pull of gravity asserting itself; a gentle never-ending pull that would end in the coffin, mass straining against satin and wood, finally melting against it, maybe *through* it, who knows? Her legs looked good—they'd always been her best feature, but one night in the last months before her husband had left (no, really, *she'd* been the one to ask him to leave, the shrink reminded her to remind herself)

16

he'd looked down at her calves as she reached to put away a dish and said, "Say, you've got lumps on your shins!"

"You take that back, you bastard!" But he'd laughed and left the kitchen.

It was true, after she'd stood up for a while the skin over her shins began to corrugate. And once, driving in a sleeveless dress, she'd looked at her arm. It was living, over there on the rim of the car door, a life by itself shimmering, shaking. The arm of an old woman! A middle-aged woman. And with all of it she felt—outside the shrink or any date, or grocery clerks who said, Oh, I thought you must be sisters! while Reggie curled her lip and sighed and looked away—with all of it, she often thought, I've never looked so good.

She never touched herself.

She often went out but when she—what, made *love*?—her mind fogged out. Walled up, harmless, unable to affect, she watched rippling muscles or a rippling paunch, or once, a TV executive unveil himself with a kingly flourish and reveal something like a dead mouse. It was as though what she had received—her own days—had made her give away the nights. In the clean, interesting new days after the divorce, the freedom from tirades, from deferring to someone not stupider but maybe less competent than herself, she had lost, not the "other," because that had disappeared long ago, but something. She remembered when her husband, driving, had said, "You're all right, Ruth" and she'd pulled up her knees and braced them on the dashboard trying to look casual, pleased beyond words; she remembered a Christmas night, but why try to remember love, much less lust? What she remembered, when she tried, was that he'd given her, fifteen years ago, a toothbrush made of pig bristle, from New Zealand. They used it now to clean off the needle on the record player. The pleasure was gone, as irrevocably as the pain.

Up and out and down the hill. She noticed with pleasure

17

that the lilac was about to bloom. She heard first, then stopped to watch, two hummingbirds, fighting or making love. They wheezed in the air like broken machines.

In the car she turned on the news. She had a college friend who had made his career in classical music singing just one note. She liked the news, that one note. Walter Cronkite sounding the end of the world would sing that civilized note. A local radio announcer had taken time off once, from talk shows in the night, to sail around the world. But "around" meant back, so now he told the morning news—that another candidate for governor had walked or driven or ridden his bike the whole length of the state.

She couldn't listen to music any longer. In his headlong rush back toward adolescence, her husband had taken the scratchy remnants of the Doors, the ghost of Jimi Hendrix: they all lived with Jack and his girlfriend down in the studio in Santa Monica Canyon. He'd stolen romance, easy tears cried over handsome men, dancing in the dark—or so much later under strobe lights—and left her with nothing more or less than the grown up world.

She stopped at the post office. They wouldn't deliver to her inaccessible house. A bill, an invitation to be included in *Who's Who in American Women.* A letter for Reggie, a letter for herself. She studied the *Who's Who* application. It really was true, they didn't ask for money, they really wanted her to do it. Amazing, she thought. She opened her letter.

DEAR RUTH,
I'll be stopping down in Los Angeles next week for the first time in several years. I'd like very much to see you again, to talk over old times and maybe plan some new ones. Please say yes. Josh says hello. Come on, Ruth, do it. I'll have a nice gift for you!

MARC MANDELL
(Do you remember?)

* * *

The sprawled signature of a spoiled kid. Perfect, expensive stationery. She remembered him lying out along Connie's couch, hating Connie's kids. All of them old high school friends. Connie, Irish, affluent newly divorced, had hated him with an equal enthusiasm.

"When we go out and I ask for *rumaki* he only orders one plate of it between us. Then he tries to eat all of them, and if I try to get my half he counts them out. One two, one two! Ah, God! I hate him. You know what his *prick* is like? It's *limp,* always limp! And covered with scales! Of course what I *like,* you know, is something like *that"*—she had pointed to a beer bottle in front of her on the coffee table— " and just as solid . . ." and laughed some more and fallen back on sofa pillows.

Later Marc had gone with another friend of hers, Jewish and married, who had fallen with him into her life's one great, amorous adventure. Patrice had been too well bred at first to mention sex, but as time went on had murmured over the phone about swimming pools and Ferris wheels and back seats and vacant lots; about the two of them crushed down in beds of wild mustard while old ladies walked their dogs no more than twenty feet away. She'd left her husband for Marc, who was (behind all the tales) simply a social worker who'd worked a while with kids but got along so badly with them that he asked to be transferred to straight relief. Then, while interviewing a hippie chick about food stamps, he'd fallen into a little something extra. While pronouncing Connie's kids too whiny (well, they were no picnic), and Patty's too numerous (well, four was a lot), Marc had sold his Mustang and bought a van (as who hadn't or didn't?) and headed north with his hippie chick. Ruth had a vision of a factory or a farm where they *grew* hippie chicks, and sent them downy out into the world, to—what?—make children cry, and women beat their arms against the arms of chairs.

That shit! Ruth thought, but absently. She was thinking of

19

her husband and that secretary and generations of secretaries, and Reggie herself, walking unconcerned across the living room, soon to take typing lessons and then a bank executive from his wife. Or perhaps an associate professor of Art of the Near and Middle East, and one day late in October some faculty wife can't help but notice that her mild and scholarly husband has lipstick on his shorts. *"You shit!"* Ruth said out loud, absently, driving out again against the news.

Her job was terrific and she knew it. She was very lucky. She drove down the coast into Hollywood five late mornings a week, and by the time she drove home on Friday night she'd earned enough to keep the three of them very well. Now she drove down the smoggy, sallow streets of Hollywood proper, after the rush hour, the sun already high and hot, reflecting metallic smog off the high walls of antique movie studios. It was hot in the car, although it was only April; Ruth's blouse stuck to the back of her seat as she drove to her reserved slot in the parking lot.

She worked for an independent television station in town. She'd been in the newsroom for a while, starting before that as "public relations assistant" while she'd still been married, and then moving, with timidity, into writing the news itself, covering local events, and then infrequently reading them, her face petrified with fear behind its greasy television makeup, her eyes pleading, her mouth afraid to smile, her friends carefully noncommittal about her performance, or even lying—to say they hadn't known she'd be on that night, although they'd go on to gossip in the next sentence, to talk about the hotel fire or grisly killing they'd seen just before or after her.

She had started to work as a sixties experiment, nudged by her husband into the world of the employed. How could she know his thought was to lower his future alimony checks? And yet she thanked him more than she could say. She discovered in herself a streak of pure, unladylike ambition. She was forever meeting people who had watched her the night before. What thrills! What a pain in the neck to her husband, with his drooping moustache and his new fiberglass boat. Maybe . . . if she hadn't gotten the job he wouldn't have left. But if she hadn't gotten the job what would they live on now? And so on. The job was a handle on the world which was, like their poor social experiment, unraveling, going, gone.

She had a way of talking. She lost her fear of what to say to the men in the newsroom (balding guys in wide bow ties, who kept their hairpieces in desk drawers along with quarts of middling scotch), or what to say to the camera and her watching, apprehensive friends. She told the news as she might tell it on the phone—it was too much, just too bizarre. Then, after months of work, the dying marriage, her children going in and out of focus between sharp snapshots of the Polo Lounge, after the dramatic paraphernalia of Discovery and Confrontation and Separation, she'd sat at her desk one morning, her red eyes and swollen cheeks forgotten as she tried to get into words the exact clumsiness of a dance step she'd seen society matrons perform the evening before for some sumptuous, fraudulent charity, and Mr. Nichols had come by and asked to see her in his office. Her confidence by then was such that even against a background of children orphaned by divorce, she never considered for an instant she'd be fired, and when Nichols, his expensive shirt dampening at the armpits, his manicured fingers caressing his new push-button line, asked her if she'd—only temporarily, of course—mind taking over a weekly talk show dealing with women's events in the "community" she was able to consider and say, sure, yes, she'd love it, but she'd have to have more money, because of sitters, and extra work, and the divorce and all. And Nichols, surprised, perhaps, at not being more thanked, said, well, yes, of course, but she'd understand of course that all this was only temporary.

Of course.

She'd walked out of his office, looking carefully at the

21

plump and middle-aged typists who flanked the carpeted
path to his door. Ah, they were fat, most of them, and carefully curled, and dressed uniformly in polyester pantsuits.
They kept inexpensive plants on their desks, and pasted pictures of Snoopy or Charlie Brown on the sides of Dicta-
phones or In and Out baskets; they kept clear plastic cubes
filled in with color snaps of their daughters graduating high
school, or sons groaning under rucksacks, or grandchildren
on bikes or in bathtubs, but never pictures of their husbands
because they were all divorced. They went home at night to
children or—if they were older—to no one. They came here,
again, in the mornings, to type their days away.

Not me! Ruth thought. *Not me, not this time.* There was, at
least, a world out there, and they were going to let her see it.

"At last, she arrives." Mario Mendez, token spic, at the
desk next to hers, in charge of news from the barrio. He wavered between professional Mexicanism and his own shaky
personality. She understood it. They shared an extension
number and took each other's messages. He took more messages than she did. He hated that; she tried to make it a joke.

"Any messages, Alphonse?"

Alphonse. Some joke.

"Someone from the Women's Job Corps, the Action Com-
mittee in the barrio, someone from the County Museum and
some officious son of a bitch who wouldn't leave his name."

"I'll pull your tie . . ."

"Try it!"

She poked at him, stabbing through slats in his swivel chair
at his ribs, his youthful back. He swooped forward in his
chair and punched at (but carefully missed) her breasts.

"Come on, Mario, it's just *equality!* You take my phone
calls, I take yours, that way nobody's the *oppressor!*"

Nichols' door at the end of the newsroom opened; they
quieted down, the double row of typists had never looked
up.

"*Ai Mamacita;*" Mario said.

She called the Job Corps back, talking after that to a

housewife and self-styled leader of black women in the city, who'd heard rumors about the Corps and wanted to talk.

Ruth listened, her phone clamped by plastic to her shoulder. Without pressing, she tried to get concrete details. Trouble between the races, awful food, unannounced searching of the girls' rooms for dope and men, cruel punishments, (and here was the story) punishment by water, somehow a near drowning.

By the time she'd got off the phone Mario had gone out. The rest of the room was empty, or nearly so. Ruth ordered a sandwich and beer from the restaurant across the street. She wasn't as thin as she used to be. More than she liked, she was close to those Mexican women who sat heavily in their living rooms and gossiped their lives away.

A cup of bitter station coffee, a few moments' banter with the weatherman, who'd been trying without success or notable effort to make her for the past two years, and she went out on the road. She worked at her own pace, without deadlines, usually keeping three or four stories in her mind and working on first one, then another, keeping up several skeins of contacts and interviews and phone calls, waiting sometimes a couple of weeks until a problem was "solved," or a particular "solution" was reached, or enough had "happened" to make a "story." She generally knew what a story was, or what it meant; life did seem to arrange itself in a kind of daisy chain made up of beginnings, middles, and ends. If she worked in sit-coms instead of the news, she might think of life as a series of spin-offs—just as her teacher friends seemed to think of life as a classroom, or social workers thought of life as a catastrophe, or fraud.

She found the Job Corps at the bottom, downtown, past offices and theaters and high buildings and droves of shifty Japanese executives. Its building had been a flea-bag hotel until a few years before, and except for the American flag stuck with thumbtacks across the far wall of the lobby, might still be the flea bag it had been for the last twenty years.

"Just what is it you'll be wanting to do here?" The PR woman was pleasant, a plain-faced white lady in a sleeveless pink dress.

"Oh . . . maybe see some of your classes, talk to some teachers, have lunch in the cafeteria . . ."

"You'd have to get permission for that, of course. What would be the general thrust of the piece? Would you be able to say?"

"Not now. I'd just like to look around, really, and of course, talk to some of the girls."

"Some of the girls are very shy. I'm not sure they'd like that. They come from homes—you can't even call them homes. They've never sat down to dinner, you know? They never had a table. They—"

"What I was thinking was, if I could just, maybe, talk to a few kids who *weren't* shy, who *didn't* mind . . . It might be fun for them to be on television And other kids might see it, and think about joining the Job Corps."

She understood then that it was to be a favorable story. "Well, I don't see what could be wrong with it. But perhaps you'd like to talk to some of the supervisors first. We don't have much vocational training on the premises."

"Is there anyone in charge of recreation?" Ruth asked craftily. "That might be fun to start with."

"She won't be here until tomorrow morning. You might come by about ten. Is there anything you'd like to see today?"

Ruth looked through the cafeteria—at listless girls in soiled green aprons learning to work in "real" cafeterias. Looked into a class where girls—black and brown and discouragingly tubby—typed out *frf juj ded kik* into dreary infinity. On an impulse she took the elevator up to the top floor where the swimming pool lay gray and limp against shallow gray cement. Light reflected in clusters against gray walls. Had there ever been any fun here? Ever, in the old days?

She took the stairs down, slowly. She saw, past doors ajar, small rooms painted in cream enamel, with two made beds, and two bureaus, and college pennants from places these

24

girls would never see. Girls clattered noisily past her, starting from two or three stories above. (There was only one elevator in this hotel, run by a girl who was learning to be an elevator operator.) "Mother fucker! Listen, ain't *nobody* going to mess with . . . listen, now *you* listen!" Clattering down steps four at a time, subsiding in alarm when they spied her adult body, her grown-up hair, sliding hastily, sullenly by her, and clattering again when they hit the floor below. She looked in one room and saw a black girl, thin as a snake, holding a steam curler in one hand, a set of directions in the other.

Oh, Reggie. She'd been running in the hall of an apartment once, when she was about two, and fallen down and broken the bottle she was still drinking from. The blood and milk had mixed together on the floor. She was scared she'd get spanked because she wasn't supposed to be running. *But did I spank her?* Ruth thought. *I couldn't have spanked her, could I?*

In theory Ruth was supposed to be home by four. In practice, hardly ever. She drove out the Santa Monica Freeway to the beach, squinting into the sun behind her dark glasses. At the beach she stopped by a grocery store and called home. "Hello?" Very musical.

"It's me."

The voice ceased its music. "Hi."

"What's up, did anyone call?"

"Patty called, Edward called. He'll be working late. Your mother called. Somebody else called . . ."

"Who?"

"Oh . . . I . . ."

"Are you watching television?"

"Not really."

"You know . . ."

"Yes, yes, I wrote it down. Wait a minute. Somebody named Mandell. Who's that?"

"You remember the guy who went with Connie? And then he went with Patty? I went to high school with him."

25

Silence.
"Are you watching television? *Reggie?*"
"What *is it?*"
"What do you want for dinner?"
"Oh . . ."
"Shit, it's too hot. Why don't you just bring Dinah on down here for dinner. We'll eat at the Bellevue."

They did. An aging, motherly waitress brought Dinah a Shirley Temple and shrimp salad with no cocktail sauce. "May I try for a Bloody Mary?" Reggie asked her mother, and got it, against the law. Ruth had a brandy, and another one, and a half bottle of wine almost all to herself. Happy couples, wealthy and elderly, gathered here each night. They knew each other; they nodded some of them, to Ruth. One woman—very old—came in and had three Rob Roys in a row, drinking, finishing, snapping her fingers for more. Outside the setting sun glittered on the Pacific. Palm trees swayed on the cliffs in lacy border. Old folks walked by, two by two. "Where's Roddy?" a famous homosexual novelist asked querulously from another table. "You know he'll *hate* to be late. Roddy is inexorable!"

"Do you know what I did?" Dinah asked the table. "Today? You know what I did? I made a bracelet out of papier-mâché. You can run a car over it and it still gets its shape back, Mrs. Horka said . . ."

"You know what?"

"What?"

"She *said* so. *She* said that she ran over one just like this that she made once, and it went *squash*, like that—"

"I think I met somebody today."

"*You can bend it!*" Dinah said, raising her voice, "*and it still comes back!*"

"Lower your voice," Ruth said. "That's not true, anyway," Reggie said, in a superior tone. "That would never happen."

"It's *true!*"

26

"That's *enough*," Ruth said. "Eat your shrimp."

Dinah looked out at the aisle, offended. Her hand moved automatically toward her face.

"*Don't* suck your thumb," said Reggie, and stroked her pretty blond hair.

"I'm going to the bathroom," Dinah said. "I *have* to," she added defiantly to Reggie, and marched away.

"OK," Ruth said. "So who did you meet?"

"Oh . . . nobody."

"Come *on!*"

"Oh . . . just some guy. He sits behind me in history. I mean, actually, he's been sitting there for years."

"What's he like?"

"Oh, he's tall, you know, and he just cut his hair, he's funny, you know? He's *really* funny . . ."

"Like how?"

"Oh, you know. You know what? He told Marissa he'd been watching me ever since I went to that school."

"So, what happened?"

"Oh, you know, he sort of . . . asked me for my phone number, I guess. Actually he didn't ask *me*, he asked Marissa. But she gave it to him."

"Do you think he'll call you up?" (It was high school, all right, she the plain and cloddish sycophant with the popular girl, the popular girl answering as Reggie did now—with a vapid shrug which was as close to silence as she could muster.)

"*I* had a sort of interesting day."

"Hmm?"

And Ruth spun a few tales out of it, talking mainly to herself, to see how it sounded; the deserted lobby, the dead light in the empty pool, the gangling black girls on the stairway. She left out the girl with the curlers. Dinah ate half her salad and fell over asleep with her head in Reggie's lap. Reggie allowed it, sneaked some of Ruth's wine, ate coq au vin while

27

Ruth had scallops. They had been spoiled by Ruth's friend, Edward, who lived for restaurants and easy pleasures. Even without him they indulged themselves.

"You know what? What he told Marissa? He said he always tried to get a seat behind me so he could watch my hair in class. So he wouldn't get bored. He told *Marissa* that, and *she* has the hair of the *world*. She can *sit* on her hair!"

"Did Edward say he'd be coming over?"

"Later. After work."

"We'd better go home."

"Without a mousse?"

He was asleep on the couch when they came in. Shoes off, collar open, hair in a damp fluff around his face. His hands folded across his plump stomach, and Ruth went over to the couch and hugged him at that wide place.

"Hi, Edward," Reggie said, archly, and swayed elegantly in front of him on the way to the bathroom.

"Hel-lo, Edward," Dinah said, and sat down on the end of the couch to suck her thumb.

"My dear," Edward said, lifting his head off the arm of the couch with futile effort, "how are you? Did you have a nice day? Did you get my messages?"

"What about *you?* Can I get you anything? Would you like some coffee? With some brandy in it? Or just the brandy, plain? I have some cookies, I think, if they haven't eaten them up."

Dinah took her thumb out of her mouth. "We ate them," she said morosely.

"Nothing right now."

"You sure?"

"You stay here and rest."

"If you're sure . . ."

They could go on like this for hours. Sometimes, after Edward had gone home, especially in their early days together, Ruth would go to the mirror and examine her face, smiling and not smiling, smiling again. Strange. A far cry from the

28

worst days with her husband, when she'd locked herself in the bathroom, and watched herself cry. I mean, look at those smiles, will you? Edward had never married but he had lived for years with a tempestuous woman, who had once kicked out his windshield in an angry shower of shatterproof glass. Sometimes, holding hands and watching television, balancing plates across their laps, he and Ruth reminisced.

"How about leaving a party and screaming in the night? She used to do that. Did you used to do that?"

"Oh, sure!"

"And *lay* there on the grass, right? So then you get to go out and *look* at her, right? And she's a grown woman just howling away, making this terrible noise . . ."

"You bet!"

"And then you get to stand there and say, 'Come *on*, Georgene, you've made your point!' "

"And then people come by! And they say, 'Can I help you, lady? Is this man bothering you?' and you just lie there and sob."

"Yeah!"

"Can I get you anything? A little more wine? A little more cheese? Do you need a napkin? How about some coffee?"

"No, yes, well, maybe . . . you sit right there, I'll get it. No, really! All right then . . ."

"How about" (pouring the coffee, layering him with napkins) "how about jumping out of the car in moving traffic? Jumping out of the car and through the traffic into a big building with an elevator? I remember Jack caught up with me once in a service basement behind some laundry tubs . . ."

"Actually" (smiling sweetly, plucking a slice of carrot cake from the plate to his mouth, using his fingers, leaving a crumbly path along his brocade vest) "actually, I used to do some of that myself. It's pretty good when the *driver* does it, you know."

"No! You wouldn't do that. I just can't believe you'd *do* something like that."

29

"Simplest thing in the world. You stop the car, you get out of it. You walk away. Then the other person has to climb over the gear shift to get the car started, people are honking their horns, she has to stop crying to be able to drive, and then, you know, *she* gets to drive along in first gear and, 'Come on, get in the car, let's go home . . .' "

"I knew a couple who had a lot of trouble," Ruth might say, watching the news. "She was a nice woman, but she was frigid. She worried a lot about it, and she began to think it was because she knew her husband too well. One night she took a plane by herself up to San Francisco, and then she got a cab and told the driver to take her to the nearest brothel. She talked to the madam and said she wanted to be one of the girls for one weekend. The madam said OK. But then the first customer came in— he worked on a tugboat in the harbor—and my friend took one look at him and fainted dead away. The next morning the madam and my friend drove down to the boat landing where he worked and told him the whole story."

"Speaking of driving?"

"Yeah?"

"I knew a couple where the wife didn't know how to drive. But one night she and her husband were out in front of their house having an argument and he was yelling at her quite a bit, and she said, 'I've had enough!' or something like that. 'If you don't stop raising your voice to me, I'm going to get in that car and drive away!' The keys were in the car but he said, well, he said something like 'You don't even know how to drive!' That made her so mad she got in the car and drove away."

"But she didn't know how to drive!"

"That's what I'm *telling* you!"

A few years ago Edward had worked for the station; she had met him then. He had been foppish, hard-drinking, and cheerful; she had been shy, embarrassed to conduct her interviews against this sly, chunky presence. "Come on, Babe," he would say, "I'm ready if you are." Or in a clear, rough voice he might call out, "Are we *shooting?* Are we *shooting* this?" While she rustled her papers and blushed, and thought with hatred of the husband who had pushed her out into this or any world.

One day they had been sent out to cover a school which taught "revolutionary" driving. Pupils drove recklessly around a track littered with haystacks and constructed car crashes. She—after interviewing a teacher—was to drive around the track herself, and be "taught." Edward's gear rested on the seat behind her.

"See that haystack?" the racer muttered primly. "Try to avoid it, but don't slow down. We believe that speed and daring in moments of stress are often as effective as a sudden stop." He was terribly self-conscious in front of the camera.

At the track's first turn, when her foot had groped toward the brake, Edward, behind her, had said, "Come on, kid! Let's see you take it!" And she pressed down hard on the gas. "Terrific!" While she wrote out her story he questioned the teacher about the car; its cylinders, its wear, its mileage. Then, after he'd finished shooting backgrounds, he reached out and grabbed Ruth roughly by the shoulder. "Come on, kid," he said, and placed her in the car next to him. Around and around he drove, at dreadful speed, he all the while saying, "See *that?* Watch *this!*" That night, they had gone to bed together.

Now, as then, they conversed mainly in questions, card-castle proof (to herself anyway) that she could be as nice as the next person. As for Edward, he was civil to her parents, polite without fail to her children, helpful in emergencies, charming at the most ordinary times.

"Listen, *Reggie?*" (Raising her head from that commodious, comfortable stomach, shouting at the bathroom.)

"Yes."

"Leave some hot water for the rest of us."

A beat, and the water stopped.

31

But Dinah was asleep at the far end of the couch, so Ruth, after knocking, went into the steaming bathroom, past the slick and reproachful body of her eldest child, and into the closet which always smelled vaguely of cat shit, to find Dinah's nightgown from last night. Returning, Ruth skinned the nightgown over her sleeping daughter's head, walked her to the toilet (she kept listing to the side, sound asleep), saying *come on now, honey, let's go now.* Dinah opened her eyes once, then decided against it, so Ruth turned on the cold water in the basin, looking fleetingly at her own face in the bathroom mirror, but then to her own baby girl, her darling, sound asleep, who in a recess of her mind heard the rushing water and responded to it. Then Ruth walked her, still listing, downstairs to bed.

Why did it have to be that way? To be cut off from the child she'd like to eat if she could, never seeing her, never; and she sucks her thumb now even though she's six, and later tonight she'll wet her bed, and Reggie still sits upstairs, in a low-cut nightgown, legs loosely slipped across a chair, blowing her hair dry, ready to stay up forever. ("I *met* somebody today, Edward." *"Did* you, my dear! And who was that?") But Ruth gives her an entirely unjust look; unjust, but effective, and Reggie, after waiting ten minutes, puts away her hair dryer, and after a careful, charming "Good*night*, Edward," walks languidly downstairs. Ruth follows her down, asks if everything is OK, if she needs anything, what time shall she get her up tomorrow? To which Reggie answers in shrugs, pouts, monosyllables, and then reluctantly offers up her pale cheek for Ruth to kiss goodnight. Only in the dark does her voice follow her mother up the stairs. "He really was quite cute, you know . . ."

Upstairs it is eleven. Before anything else can happen they must watch the news. Their friends, their acquaintances; behind them, glimpses of the room where she spent her waking days, and added to it all, the comforting drone of news. Politicians lined up behind a president, while that president signs a bill. Arabs rioting, signaling wildly to each other. And every night or two a plane down in the night—not always the big ones—light planes, frail frames cracking, sliding out of the air, doing away with parents and children. Sometimes she saw herself recorded. She and her colleagues smiled away at war orphans and epidemics; they were OK.

The phone rang. Edward watched her cautiously from the couch. "Hello?" she said.

"He's there now, isn't he? Don't you have any decency at all? Don't you have any sense of property? Don't you know I own half of that house myself? I still own half of it, I *always* own half of it. I don't care about you . . ."

"I *know!*" she interrupted in tears.

"But my daughters are still living up there, I'm responsible for how they grow up, someone has to take that responsibility, has to shield them from that kind of action . . ."

If she had been alone, she would have answered, shouting. Countering with the magic weekend he'd spent in Mexico when Dinah had been in bed with a temperature of a hundred and five (how thankful she'd been, even at that moment, for that last melodramatic degree), how he'd cruelly fucked around for years—he, who'd always seemed so straight—how he'd come back from another magic weekend, which she, Ruth, had spent painting the kitchen, and castigated her for leaving paint spots on the floor, how he, fresh from the bed of that secretary—Instead, she hung up.

The phone rang again.

"Shut up! Shut up!" she screamed into it and hung up again. "I'm sorry," she said wretchedly.

"Take the phone off the hook."

The periodic buzzes started. They put the phone in a closet. The late show came on.

"What if he comes over?"

"I'll stay here. He won't come over." And of course her husband wasn't coming over. It had been too long; even their bad tempers were failing.

33

At twelve-fifteen Edward stirred himself on the couch, looked over. She closed her eyes. She was tired, *so* tired, numb to the bone.

"OK, kid."

"What?"

"I'm going home now. I'm getting up early."

Then she couldn't do enough for him, his coat on just so—a scarf around his neck, following him to the door, many hugs around his middle. Why did he have to go home?

After the door shut, she looked around. The lights in the kitchen were alive. The room glittered. She wasn't sleepy after all. She opened a can of stewed tomatoes and warmed it on the stove, pouring in a third of a bottle of Tabasco, and hunched on the couch eating. When the late show was over she read a while in a novel she'd been keeping at for a couple of weeks, and sipped at a strong brandy and soda. She'd put the phone back on the hook but it didn't ring again. She wasn't able to last very long once she'd started to read, and soon she was asleep.

II

She was back down at the Job Corps swimming pool by eight the next morning. The water's reflection sent pale freckles of light across the gray walls; the recreational supervisor, a woman in her late twenties, was cordial. "Of course they work a lot, they don't have much time to swim, they're in class all day. Realistically, once they get out of here, they're not going to have much time to swim either. They're training for regular eight-hour jobs. And that's a picnic after the kinds of homes they come from. Most of them were nothing more than baby-sitters so that their own mothers could go out. A lot of the mothers are furious at their kids for coming here."

"Do you have swimming lessons?"

"Three classes. Beginners, intermediate, advanced. We don't have any advanced yet, but we're looking forward to it. Because one of the purposes of the Job Corps is to give them at least a glimpse of another sort of world. To prepare them for the middle class . . ."

"Is that *your* job?"

"Yes, theater parties, the beach, those things. They have some tennis courts up on the top of the building, I've been giving the girls some lessons, but it's been difficult. These girls don't care about using their bodies, except for that one thing. We're always finding men in their rooms. We're trying to teach them a lot of things they don't know, but they know so much that *we* don't know that sometimes I'm afraid they don't have very much respect for us."

"Yes, well . . ." Sometimes Ruth lost her place. She prided herself on not carrying lists of questions, on not being one of those reporters who are terribly intent on the facts. Girls with men, well, sure. This woman all alone on the ninth floor of a crumbling hotel. Black men. All that. Plain little white women teaching typing. And she lost her place.

"Do you ever use the pool for anything else but lessons?"

"How do you mean?"

"Do the kids ever come here just for recreation?"

It wasn't the question she'd wanted to ask. (When am I ever going to learn how to ask a direct question?)

"They don't think of swimming as recreation! In fact we use it as a kind of social control."

There it was.

"These kids are pretty wild. The blacks and chicanas don't get along, and there are quite a few white girls from the south. It's a bad combination."

"So?"

"So they get *mad* at each other, late at night. They get homesick, they pick on each other, pretty soon they're out on the landings pulling each other's hair, or pulling knives out of their pompadours . . ."

"They still do that?"

"Sure!"

"But then—all this . . . ? What do you do?"

"We call a recreational swim."

"Why?"

"Because these kids can't *swim*! They couldn't get into

pools where they lived because they were segregated out. If they swam at all, it was in rivers or ponds or swimming holes. Almost every one of these girls has seen a brother or a sister drown. They dive in, you see, and their heads get stuck in the mud. They come up to the surface and call, they call out to their friends, their brothers and sisters, but the brothers and sisters can't swim.

"So you can understand," the young woman said, "why they're reluctant to learn how to swim, or even to go into the water. They stand by the side of the pool, and pretty soon they calm down. And then they go back to their rooms."

That was it then. Ruth talked briefly to a typing teacher and spent the rest of the morning talking to the girls. She phoned the station and arranged for a crew to meet her after lunch. Already she was dividing her story into clips, segments: the outside of the building, winos, derelicts along the downtown streets, an occasional, accidental glimpse of a beautiful black man against maybe a mailbox (why a mailbox?), the round blue shape there, the tall black phallic number beside it—and then, quickly, before any noticed, the gawky girls in their rooms, wanting it, something terrific, waiting, lounging, their hair in curlers, maybe using one of those blow dryers with that long hard shape . . . And then finish, certainly, with that pool, empty, gray with maybe some last little ornamentation, some thirties tile or an ornamental window—times past, beautiful expectations.

The Los Angeles Job Corps, she thought, over a hamburger at Thrifty Drug, *lies in some (no man's?) land made up of heavy work and light industry, the world where work, the world's work . . .* No, terrible. And she could never talk about love, or the lack of it, but the people watching should *see* it, and feel as bad as she did.

The crew was waiting for her in the lobby. Horace, who never got her name right but was a crackerjack cameraman; Buddy, the electrician, a new kid, still training; and Ron Gonzalez, for lights.

"Horace!" She hugged him. "How neat that it's you!"

37

"Did you miss me dreadfully since our last time together?" he said, and blushed. He was a big man, in his fifties. A devout Catholic with (hadn't he said?) five children. Very shy.

"More than life itself." From his chest, she looked at the kid.

"You know Buddy here, Buddy, this is, uh . . ."

Ruth waited, her head still square against Horace's chest. Smiling. Because Horace never remembered anything. And this was part of Buddy's training too. Old jokes, old friends, beloved work.

"Ah, God, honey, *you* know I . . ."

"Call me Honey. Is your name really Buddy?"

"Of course not," the kid said, getting into it. "Doesn't he call everyone Buddy?"

I wonder how old he is, Ruth thought. He's awfully cute.

They were a center of bright attention in the dark lobby. People watched from shadows, old chairs, from the doorway of the defunct coffee shop, as they laughed and chatted. "Say, listen," she said, interrupting a discussion about the lights going up in the elevator—should they unpack now, in the lobby, or wait. "Listen, don't laugh, but wouldn't you like to get the *entire world* on television?"

"Sure," Horace said. "Let's start right now. Honey, I take your picture, and you interview Buddy, and then I give the camera to him, and take your microphone, and then we get that swell little chick over by the elevator, and than *that* guy—"

"Hello, Ruth."

He had been standing there, watching them. What a terribly handsome man. Bones, above the eyes and just below them. Hell to light a face like that. You know who had a face like that? Linda Lovelace. Just hell to light. And from the security of her position—her arm, after all, still lightly across Horace's back, her companion, Buddy, who certainly did know her name, along with a sizable portion of people in this Los Angeles basin—she called out, "Hello, *Marc!* How'd you find out where I was?"

His immense, tall, shambling, rangy form was covered as it always had been by the very best. And much the same best as they had in Marshall High; soft blue shirt, soft, thick gray cashmere sweater, soft gray slacks. A watch chain, incredibly. A manicure. Perfect shoes. But all spread out, slack, easy looking, so that only his face showed any tension, the pleasing worry of someone wanting to be liked. Oh, he was so nice! He'd been terrific in high school.

"Say, kid, you're getting pretty big, you know that? Last night I saw you on television."

"Why didn't you call?"

"Why didn't I call? I've *been* calling. I called the station last night and they said you were nothing but a tape. But they said you'd probably be here this morning, so here I am."

"Well . . . Horace, is it OK if Marc comes along with us?"

"Sure."

They traveled up in the cramped elevator. Under the skylights of the top floor Ruth talked again to typists and typing teachers, to the swimming instructor, worrying, hoping Ron's lights wouldn't cancel out that dappled quality of reflected water on the walls, feeling pretty certain Horace could film that quality. She talked to the head of the Corps, a decent woman who looked like the president's wife, and then dropped down to the fifth floor, to see a girl she'd talked to that morning. The girl had taken out her curlers and wore a thick afro. Her body was throttled in a cheap flannel dress with a tight white Peter Pan collar. She sat on the side of her bed. "I want to say I am thankful for this opportunity to learn a trade, to get beyond that place my family's in," and that's what Ruth could get out of her—nothing more. The boys didn't care, they shot it, no more than two minutes for the whole segment, president's wife, poor girl, pool and everything. Ruth knew the crew didn't care, and she didn't care overly herself. She knew if they ever let her do other stuff, the good stuff, she could get the girl to say it all. She *knew* she could, and that elation carried her through last details, only vaguely aware of the men talking behind and around her.

Until she heard Horace talking—as she said goodbye to the black girl, thanking her, holding white fingers around that stocky black forearm—telling some of his work stories to Buddy and to Marc.

"Yes, in New York at that time, the sun was going down, see, and we'd been out there all day shooting—some crime series, I can't rememer who's in it. Anyway, in those days, you had to get permission from the mayor, you only got a few days to shoot on the streets of New York. So here we were, it's winter, the sun's going down early, it's our last day. We're behind, naturally. We're shooting right outside of a subway entrance on the streets of New York. So, what do you know, a guy walks up out of the stairs of the subway and falls down dead. He's dead, no doubt about it, so they want to call an ambulance but the producer's going crazy. So somebody covers the guy up with an overcoat, and we go ahead and shoot the scene. In the last scene you could see this sort of wrinkle in the sidewalk. People are walking right by it, it's this *stiff*, see? Under the overcoat."

"How terrible," Marc said.

"What?"

"That they'd do all that for something that's going to be gone the next week. Not even a movie!"

"What do you mean?"

"What Marc means," Ruth said brightly, still keeping her hold on the black girl, "is that he's not really into all that stuff. He doesn't watch television."

"You never watch *television?*"

"Marc moved away a couple of years ago, he's living up on a farm—isn't that right?"

"Yes."

"Well, *shit*," Horace said. "What are you even talking about, then?"

"What I've been trying to do," Marc said, smiling bravely against Horace's scowl, "is to get away from all that shit."

"How old you anyway?"

"You're right. I'm forty. No, listen. Social work. Television programs. White bread. I'm not kidding! I just couldn't handle it. When I drove in Los Angeles on the freeway I drove at seventy miles an hour, the same as everybody else. I was always pleasing my father . . . I've got pictures, of myself, you know, short hair, behind a desk. I was doing it all. I had a wife, well . . . It wasn't *right* down here. I mean, that was a *real* dead man, you know, under that coat."

"Yeah, sure," Horace said.

"The media," Buddy said, "has its own responsibility, doesn't it?"

"That man," the black girl said to Ruth, "is a handsome man. He your boyfriend?"

"No," Ruth said.

His perfect shirt came from money. His plum-colored Mercedes stood outside, she knew. And in the glove compartment were sheepskin gloves with their fur turned inside, to keep his hands warm. A gift from Patty, who wore, if she wore anything at all in cold weather, white cotton gloves, or mittens.

"What I think," Marc said, just outside the door to the black girl's room, "is that if we don't at least make some effort to get away from the bad things we're taught, we're going to be—*screwed,* I guess, that's it." He spoke to Horace. "If you're born with, well, what I'd have to call everything, you have to be thinking about it. My mother has a beautiful yard in the Los Feliz Hills. Do you think she'd ever go out and garden? No, she'd be ashamed, she won't do it. Because people in her class don't garden. It's stuff like that, you know?"

"He got a nice way of talking though," the black girl said.

"Come on, Buddy, you got everything?"

"Yeah."

"Listen, Ruth. You want to have a drink? I came all the way down here to have a drink with you."

"Los Feliz to Los Angeles is a backbreaking drive."

"No. All the way from British Columbia." He towered

above her, a manila envelope held rather forlornly against his chest. He was from high school, and the sixties, so she went.

"What I can't understand is why you did that to Patty."

"Did that, *did* that. That's not fair, really. I think anything anybody *did* she did to me."

They were alone, in a bar at the top of a building in downtown Los Angeles. Away from them, on every side, stretched ruins—last week's industrial bombing, cars smashed and stacked and smashed again; asphalt parking lots bounded by wire, locked and locked again.

"Because when you look at it, she was married, right?"

Ruth nodded.

"And it was basically her idea, right?"

"But still, to break up . . ."

"I didn't know what she was up to, Ruth! Until it was too late, and then I didn't know what to do."

"Couldn't you sort of, voice an objection?" She remembered her friend, crying: "I came over here, Ruth, just to surprise him, and there's pictures of this—*cunt* all over the place." Endless phone calls. In the afternoon, the night. Her own husband saying, "Can't you get off the phone? For God's sake, for once!" Because a woman with four children who leaves her husband for a man like Marc is stupid, plain stupid.

"So," teasingly, "what about Connie?"

"That was a different problem altogether. Patrice was a good woman, Constance wasn't, it's as simple as that."

"Come on!"

"It was all a mistake! I got fixed up with her, that must have been just a thing people were always doing for her . . ."

"She went out a *lot,* she had all the men she could ever use—"

"Bob Goodman fixed us up, pretty soon after . . ."

"How is Bob?"

"Fine."

"So?"

"She gave me dinner on the first date. She's got bugs in her kitchen."

"That's not her fault!"

"I wasn't having a very good time. Neither was Josh."

"You brought Josh on a first date?"

"Well, what else was I supposed to do with him?"

"Well," Ruth said, "so then what?"

"I ate her dinner. We weren't getting along, anybody could see that. So after dinner I decided to leave.

"I was putting Josh in the back of the car, he was sound asleep. I was leaning in and covering him with a blanket, when I noticed I sort of had trouble moving. Because Connie was leaning in there with me."

"So?"

"So we went back inside, that's all. But I never liked her."

"But why? You don't say why!"

"Listen," Marc said, "what ever happened to Marina?"

"She married Jim Spokes for a while. Then she got her master's degree in folklore, she made a movie about the Canned Heat—"

"What ever happened to the Canned Heat?"

"Her roommate, Mary, do you remember? A pretty blonde, she went to Ethiopia to get married . . ."

"But Marina . . ."

"Well, she got sick of all of it, so pretty soon she gave away her books, she gave away her master's thesis, she even gave away a lot of her old blues records . . ."

"I know," Marc said, "I know."

"So then she moved to San Francisco, to study yoga. I went up there one time, to work on a story, and I looked her up. She was living in a regular commune, right on the Panhandle. There was one kid there, I was there for four days, all I ever saw him eat was popcorn. He was a fiend for popcorn."

43

"Yes."

Silence. Marc is a beautiful man. It is because he is so large. He is *huge,* six-five, wouldn't he be? And utterly relaxed. He has soft eyes and long, deerlike lashes. He looks like an animal, a nice domestic animal. An ox, maybe. As strong as an ox.

"I guess you know why I came to see you, Ruth?"

"No." But somewhere in her body, around the calves of her legs, or, she hates to admit it, a little further up, she guesses.

"Listen," she said a little wildly, "how come you never asked me out in high school? I sure would have done it then."

But she knew. Because he was rich and she had been poor. Because he was a senior and she had been a freshman. Because he was really popular, and she had faked it, because . . .

"You weren't *Jewish!* You think I was going to go out in high school with someone who wasn't Jewish? Besides, I think I had four dates in high school. Not counting triple dates where your girl is looking out of the window as hard as she can."

"Oh, Marc! But you were the one! You were the only one who ever had a good time!"

He had been big, but too soft for sports. He had played the bass in a jazz trio, and told jokes from the high school stage. He had acted, and sung, and even danced—with clumsy grace. He had been their whole metaphor for a good time. She had barely known him then, naturally.

"Yeah, kid, well, I never had a real date until Katherine, and that was the last semester of my senior year."

His dead wife. She can remember, years ago, Patty ranting on the phone. "So he's got a dead wife. Big deal! I'm not impressed! He's got to come to terms with what's happening *now.* I mean, *I'm* here *now!* He's either got to see more of me or less of me, and by this point, I'll *tell* you, Ruth, I don't care

44

which way it goes!" But she'd cared a whole lot, as it turned out.

"What was Katherine like? I never knew her really." What she had seen she didn't like. A short, beautiful blond girl, creamy face, large breasts, beige sweaters. Sat on couches at parties, with her hands in her lap, waiting for men to come around. They did. Ruth, thin and dark, talking in the middle of the room, had driven away her husband.

"She was a wonderful woman, Ruth. I can't say any more than that. I always have that to contend with."

"But you were *stupid*, Marc!"

"In what way?"

"Not to stay with Patty. God, she was really crazy about you . . ."

They were, after all, talking about one of the major romances in their own popular history, the leaving of a decent man by a strong woman momentarily demented, a hundred intrigues and desperate phone calls; the husband, lying one cloudy Tuesday morning on a shag rug in what was the playroom, actually scrunched up between their pool table and one of the first pachinko games, sobbing, didactically: "I'm having a psychotic break!" And his wife, driving him to the UCLA Medical Center, and then driving home again, to pack, and leave (with her four small children) to live with Marc.

"Four kids, and they weren't even mine—that was an awful lot. I'm *sorry*, but I couldn't help thinking—that's the rest of my life, you know?"

"But you've got Josh."

"That's *one*."

"I have two."

"Two?"

"My *daughters*, Marc."

"Oh sure, no offense! You know who says no offense?"

"Who?"

"This crazy kid, this terrific kid, he plays championship

rubgy up where I live. You'll meet him. He goes into the bar, over at Nanaimo, and he says, 'I'll have a half and half, no offense!' And so they give it to him, no offense."

"How'm I going to meet him?"

"Because you're coming *up!* I've come to take you *away* from all this. I want to show you a good time, *baby.*"

"What was that girl's name?" Ruth said maliciously.

"Linda. You know what's been great for me? Just to sit here talking to you. You don't know how I've been planning. I even brought things to show you." He reached for his manila envelope. "This is Josh, now."

A beautiful boy, matte finish.

"And this is the vegetable garden."

A vegetable garden, nicely kept.

"The place. It's a hotel, really."

A long, low building with a veranda across its middle.

"The bay."

A storybook bay hemmed in on both sides of the snapshot by bright green hills.

"Our dock."

A ramshackle dock which appeared to start perhaps forty feet out in the water, continued to shore and up a gently sloping lawn that grew down just to the water's edge. Ruth couldn't help thinking of money.

"The woods out back."

Woods, storybook woods. Leaves like Roman coins. A thin silvery wash across the bottom of the print.

"You really did do it."

"Did what?"

"Just really dropped out." Another staple of endless conversations, whole mornings, afternoons spent on the phone, that staple of a certain kind of married life. Marc as a dropout. While the afternoon sun sloped down across their respective backyards, and Ruth and her friends clamped phones to their ears with their shoulders, leaving their hands free to string beans, or shell peas, or even do the ironing,

while they went on talking,   until their husbands came home.
"Yes."

But she was still looking at the picture of the woods.

"Come on," he said then. "Do you have time to walk for a while? I get restless sitting in one place for too long."

Downstairs, in the street, he sniffed the air disdainfully and looked around. "Where can we go around here? Isn't there a blade of grass anywhere?"

"You know what?" she said, as they walked, "some of the best news stories I see are those nature things our ecology guy does. We kid about him, you know, we say there's a certain class of people who love to do a story in front of a pine tree, wearing their Pendleton shirts. But there's a kind of unity there . . ."

He wasn't listening.

They had come to the library, were walking down its cement paths. Winos sat on cement benches. Big hibiscus bushes, there since the Great Depression, bloomed. What it used to be. Old ladies with shopping bags. The noise receded.

"Would you like to step over on the grass?"

"What?"

"We have to be on the grass, I think."

"What is it?" They stepped, sedately, off the cement, over a six-inch box hedge, onto thick lawn.

"Before I say anything you have to kiss me."

Together, they stepped carefully back onto the cement path. He held her hand as she stepped over the box hedge. They went on walking. Birds sang in library trees as they passed by. The smell of chili floated on the air, a boy wheeled by on roller skates. She was in high school again, and finally happy.

"We live so much on myths," Ruth said to him. "Patty really loved you."

"And Connie hated me, is that what you're trying to say?"

"No, of course not." The vision of something limp and cov-

47

ered with scales—superimposed on the kid up on stage—
danced in front of her eyes, lost its limpness enough to wave
and say hello. "No, although she certainly wasn't fond of you
in the same way."

"She hated me."

"Oh, for heaven's sake, Marc . . ."

"No, I mean it."

Meanwhile, her body subsided. At least partly. His trembling subsided, she could see him calm down. But her body
was still warm, sluggish, sunburned from within.

"It would be nice if someday you could see my place. I
know you're working, but if you could think of some kind of
a story to do, or even take a vacation, I think you'd like it up
there."

"It does sound nice. I've been working pretty hard. I take a
lot of pride in it, but I'm pretty tired. It's hard—with the
kids."

His face clouded for a minute. Then he said, "Doesn't Jack
take care of some of that?"

"Just a little, the minimum."

"But he should take care of you. You . . . should be having a good time."

"It's getting late," she said. "I have to get home."

"I'll drive you to your car."

He pulled in right behind her car where it was parked by
the Job Corps. They were downtown, in its heart. Her mother used to dress her up, on December 8, the Feast of the Immaculate Conception, and take her downtown, to see the department stores, their Christmas windows. His Mercedes
smelled clean, expensive. His body smelled as good. He
turned off the motor, took a deep breath, turned to her.

"I just bought a new camera," he said. "You know what I'd
like to do? Just take your picture, take your picture, take
your picture."

She saw, on the dashboard, the sheepskin driving gloves. It
was only the second time he kissed her. She closed her eyes,

48

and, in the city twilight, beneath floors of hysterical girls, fell back with the elite.

"I have to get home," she said. "The kids will be worried."

They weren't. Ruth passed through a kitchen where the remains of several afternoon snacks lay heaped up in the sink. It was uncomfortably hot. Reggie sprawled, watching television, her pale thighs spread wide, languidly lapping at a huge tablespoon of vanilla ice cream. When that tablespoon was done (in a matter of minutes, not seconds), she would pull her bones together, and make it out to the refrigerator, dig maybe another quarter of a pint out of the container, and balancing it, mosey back out to the couch, where her spoonful, carefully licked, might last until the next commercial. At Reggie's feet, Dinah read *Black Beauty*.

"Don't you think that's a pretty depressing book?" Ruth asked her.

"Yeah, but it has a happy ending, Grandma told me," Dinah said, not looking up.

"How are you?" This to Reggie, looking or not looking at the pink, elaborately supple tongue passing over the ice cream and over it again, barely, barely diminishing the soft white mountain . . . Ruth turned back out to the kitchen to get herself a drink. Brandy.

"OK," Reggie said, and watched the television. But there was something there. Reggie had many levels of inattention, but this evening she was quite close to the surface.

She sat down on the couch next to her daughter. They watched a rerun of *Sea Hunt* for a while, the only sound the steady whine of Lloyd Bridges's somnambulistic bubbles.

"What'd you do in school today?"

"Nothing . . . what'd *you* do?"

"I went down to the Job Corps again."

The night sank away from them, a long beach with no configurations. No real dinner to fix, no need to run the vacuum before "someone" came home. No need to worry about snapping the string beans, looking busy, not drinking too much, or drinking at all. Dinah turned her pages. Reggie ate. Ruth drank.

"I had kind of a depressing interview today."

"You know that Hollis? That guy I told you about?"

"What's P-A-T-H-E-T-I-C?"

"God! Was it depressing!"

"P-A-T-H-E-T-I-C?"

"*Pathetic*! OK? What he *has*, evidently, is sixteen perfectly living trapdoor spiders. He's *gone* out, and you have to remember he's the kind of a kid who lives in the Valley, not the kind of a kid who comes from around here, he's *gone* out, and he's found these spiders, and he digs them up, alive, and brings them back to his room and keeps them. And his *mother* is just going *crazy*."

"How interesting." But she, naturally, so naturally she couldn't, didn't think about it, heard almost nothing. She avoided the afternoon and looked, in her mind's eye, at the black girl she had last talked to. *Why do I do that?* she thought. Why don't I just leave a story when I finally *have* a story? Why do I just go on until I find something that's going to make me feel rotten, so that it probably puts something like a dark cast on the whole rest of the story, so that even if it's something cheerful, even if it's supposed to *play* cheerful, it has that bad feeling about it. It's like when Jack would be tightening a screw in the old days and keep tightening it and keep tightening it, even though I'd tell him not to, and pretty soon . . .

". . . all made of nylon, can you imagine? I mean, not even human hair, just this silly, glossy nylon? Nine of them, can you imagine! Of course, maybe he was kidding me . . ." She disappeared around the corner to the kitchen; Ruth heard the refrigerator door open.

"Not any more before dinner!"

"What's for dinner?"

"Oh, I don't know, go ahead and have some, I guess. But what do you mean, nylon?"

"I *told* you, nine nylon *wigs*! All sitting in a row out on his mother's dresser. She says she likes to look nice when she goes to work, can you imagine? In *nine different* wigs? And he says they're all different colors, *orange* and like that." She lapsed suddenly into television watching.

"But who is this again?" Dinah's teacher wore different wigs every day, dressed up in wild costumes and wore heavy perfume. She said it was so the kids could learn to like to come to school. Twenty years or so she'd been working here, up in the canyon. She'd been divorced for years, paying off her first husband's gambling debts, but she'd gotten married again, just recently, to the janitor. How strange, after all those years, to marry the janitor . . .

"I *told* you, his *mother*! He can't stand his crazy mother! She yells at him all the time, and his father's moved in with some other woman, and so this lady just yells all the time. He said he got so mad at her the other day he threw a box, no wait a minute, *she* threw it, she was yelling at him about something, and she wouldn't stop, and so he went out into the kitchen and got a box of Rice Crispies and said, *Here's what I say to you!* And threw the Rice Crispies out all over the room. Then he ran out of the apartment and just stood there in the hall. Then, he said, he thought, *what am I doing?* And went back inside without saying a word to her and got out the vacuum . . ."

"A-N-V-I-L?"

". . . and vacuumed up all the Rice Crispies while she stood there and yelled at him . . ."

"A-N-V-I-L?"

"Anvil," Ruth said. "And then what did he do?"

"What's an anvil?"

"I don't know, something—you make, make horseshoes on it. So then what?"

"What?"

"So then what?"

"Oh . . . he just *left*, I guess. He does that all the time, from what he told me."

"And she's got nine nylon wigs?"

"Yeah."

"And what does she do?"

"Hmmm?"

"For a living. What does she do for a living?"

"She doesn't really have to make a living . . . but oh! Here's one thing. She has these weekly sessions, she's like an analyst or something, these people come over to her house one night a week, and she's their leader. She gets them to hit each other with pillows, and tells them to let out their aggressions. Hollis says they feel real silly, you know? All these old guys sitting around on the couch hitting each other with pillows, and they're too weak to do it very well, and she starts yelling at *them* too. Hollis says he just puts on his earphones until they go home. He says sometimes he can hear them right behind his earphones, can you imagine?"

"Can that really be true?" Her interest was slipping again.

"Oh, *yeah,* Hollis says . . ."

But she was thinking about the black girl. It didn't have much to do with money. There was that lady with the wigs, she must have money, didn't Reggie say that kid had money?

"S-U-P-P-O-S-E-D-L-Y?"

"Supposedly. Listen, come sit up here on the couch for a while."

A half hour later the phone rang.

"My *dear!* Is it OK for dinner?"

"Reggie, is it OK if Ed and I go out to dinner? There's pizza in the freezer, or fried chicken."

"Not *again,*" Dinah said furiously, but Reggie opened her eyes wide and said, "No."

"No?"

"*No, I told* you, he's taking me *out* tonight, over to a *friend's* house, they both play the guitar, it's going to be a rehearsal, and you said OK. I asked you the minute you came in and you said OK."

And so Edward came over, with a steak, and lettuce, and a good bottle of wine, opening the door without knocking, his

52

eyes twinkling behind round grandma glasses, his paunch gently covered in red stripes or muted checks or whatever his vest of the day included; came in replete with slogans or aphorisms which he loved the sound of ("Never shoot a kestrel, Geordie!" which he loved to say ever since he had seen that movie, whatever it was, in which a member of the English gentry had explained to a peasant that it was unwise, for whatever reason, to shoot a kestrel).

"Hi there, Dinah!"

"Hi, Ed-ward," not looking up from *Black Beauty*.

"My dear! Hello there! Where's Reggie, then?"

"Out. With some boy. I didn't see him. He honked outside for her."

"Are they *supposed* to do that?"

"She just ran out of the house. I didn't get a chance to meet him."

"Did you get a look at him?"

"Yeah. He looked slick."

"I'm gonna tell Reggie you said that," Dinah said.

"I'll kill you if you do."

"What about this broccoli, then? Do you want it hot, or cold, or raw with mayonnaise? My dear?'"

Dinner on trays, in front of the television. War, acted out on the new, expensive color screen.

"There was this terrific old cameraman on the set today, right? And he's muttering around, and I can't hear him, see? Because he's pretty old, and he's just wheezing away there. But it turns out he's reminiscing about when he was down in Mexico with Bernstein. So he's talking to another guy on the set and he's saying, 'Remember that nurse on the set down there? That Mexican nurse?,' and the other guy says sure, and the old guy says, 'Well, I was fucking her.' And the other guy says, 'No!,' and the old guy says, 'Sure, I was fucking that nurse on weekends, but what I didn't know at the time was Bernstein was fucking her on the weekdays . . .' So anyway, the end of the story is she turns out to be pregnant, and she

53

has the baby, and the cameraman goes back on down there to be with her, and meets Bernstein in the hospital hall, along with this terrifically nice Mexican who is naturally the real father. Very nice."

"He went all the way back down to be there with her?"

"They *both* went *down,* they *both* wanted to see what it looked like . . ."

"Say, Mom? Did you know what Mrs. Carey said today? She said . . ."

"This steak is delicious, my dear, really delicious . . ."

"Come on, it isn't anything. What did she say?"

"She said . . ."

"No, it's *very* kind of you, you work as hard as I do, to go to this kind of trouble . . ."

"*You* bought it . . ."

"She *said,* we can't call her Mrs. Carey anymore, because her name is Mrs. McIntyre. But you can tell she still likes it when we call her Mrs. Carey. But she likes it when we call her Mrs. McIntyre."

"This guy on the set, he's up on a guy wire, see? We've got him flying around . . ."

"Can I watch *The Waltons?*"

"She can, can't she? I mean, it's OK, isn't it? Because we're talking?"

"Of *course,* my dear."

"Say, Mom?"

"Be *quiet* for a while! You've got the program you want!"

At the end of the program she hustled Dinah off to bed— no bath, no story, but many kisses: "A hug, a kiss, a love and a pat . . ."

"Will you leave the door open?"

"Of course."

And watched another drama on the television screen. "What do you *talk* about to Ed?" some of her old friends asked her, or used to. "He doesn't read anything but *Gourmet* magazine, so what do you *talk* about?" No one asked you that about your husband—not at least until it was too late. Like a big black balloon, the sad and bloated face of the girl at the Job Corps floated up in front of her, blotting out Cannon's face, or was it Bronk? Or Barnaby Jones?

"I just want to watch this for a few minutes," Ed said, and patted her shoulder. "I know a guy on the show."

She woke up for the news, blotted with sleep, went in to brush her teeth, barely washed her face so as not to wake herself up, didn't take a shower, as a signal to Ed. He waited until the end of the news, and after the very last commercial went in and took a shower. As a signal to her. She tried hard to go to sleep (because she was just so tired, that's all) but was wide awake when he came out.

"Hi there!" he whispered, cheerfully, and lay down beside her. Oh, he was a good man, a kind man.

"I didn't take a shower, I'm kind of a pig tonight . . ."

"I *know*! It's awful, really awful!"

"What if Reggie comes in?"

"She always comes in downstairs, you know that . . ."

She heard, even in the whisper, a beginning of hurt in his voice. He's my *friend,* she thought, Jesus Christ!

Afterwards, as she tried to go to sleep, as owls and shrews woke up, and sports cars caromed down the black canyon, he whispered again, directly in her ear.

"Have you," he hissed, "have you ever watched old movies on television, Palmer? It's not a pretty sight, I can tell you that."

At about five in the morning as the darkness turned gray and squads of birds began to sing, she felt Ed quietly get up, move to put on his clothes, make his slow way to the front door. He always left early because he didn't like, he said, to be there when the children woke up. Ruth, because she had an acquaintance who had been raped at six in the morning on the first day she went out to her job, always got up and locked the door behind him. Today, she went back to bed, thinking of those hours between four and six in the morning when lovers all over the city drove home on the freeways to where they should have been spending the night, and how she could put that on television.

One of their friends, a Hollywood PR man, had been screwing his usual two women by turns, one of whom drove home at six-thirty every morning in order to fix breakfast for her two children before they went off to school (why such a good mother left her children alone all night was a soft spot in the story). On the morning of the fabled Los Angeles earthquake, which happened in half-dark, at quarter of six in the morning, the PR man had gotten a call from the kids, who said that they'd gotten through the earthquake all right, but how was their mother? Except that he'd been sleeping with his other woman that night, and went through a second little earthquake of his own . . . Might there be a special for public TV, she thought, wide awake, a half hour of little stories like that? Could the center be the earthquake?

She began to think of what a woman might really do, if she could persuade them. Couldn't they see that Milt getting that phone call was (she couldn't lie in bed any longer, got up and put on the water for coffee) more important, certainly *as* important as all the statistics on divorce, or whether a sniper gunned somebody down, or even the earthquake itself? But how would you show it? Without being "cute"?

The locked door clicked, cautiously. The rapist coming in. Did she really hear that? No, it was silly. She was out on the balcony, watching the canyon, already hearing the steady hum below of cars on their way to work. But she heard it again, the dim, cautious, leaning of a key against the Yale lock. And the door opened, against all possibility. Ruth stood up, trembling. Reggie came in.

"Jesus Christ!" Ruth said. "Jesus Christ!"

"It's all *right!*" Reggie said. "I just . . ."

"It's OK! Just . . . do you want some coffee?"

"Sure." She went out into the kitchen. "Can I get *you* some?"

"Yes."

She returned, with coffee. "Did I scare you?" Her face was wild, pale. Blue smudges under her eyes. Cuts and scratches all up and down her legs. A button off her blouse. Her skirt, which usually zipped up the back, now zipped up the side. *"Jesus Christ,"* Ruth said. "Do you know what time it is?"

"Wait a minute," Reggie said. Her eyes were glittery, her tone confidential. "Just wait a minute. I know what you're thinking. But just *wait!*" (Another item for that special. The story about the comedian, could it be true? When he was caught with a starlet, explaining to his wife, "Are you going to jump to conclusions, or are you going to listen to my side of the story?")

"We went over to Rob's house, and listened to them rehearse. They were very *good!* But, *actually,* if you want to know the truth, it got a little boring for the *girls,* you know, just sitting there . . . But they were very *good!* So *then!* It was about eleven, maybe even earlier. Hollis had to go home for something, maybe it was a guitar pick, I don't actually remember, but he felt like he had to go *home* for something, well his *mother* was up, and she was just, she was just awful, as awful as he said. She said—get *this*—she was right up there, sniffing at his *breath,* can you imagine, in this negligee with feathers, and she said to him, 'Are you on *top?*' She meant *pot,* can you imagine, so he starts telling her *no,* he isn't, but then she starts *screaming* at him, why'd he leave the picture window out to the backyard unlocked, why'd he leave the mustard on the sink after he'd made his sandwich, and all the time she's just ignoring me there, I could have been the wallpaper, and so Hollis said, *well,* he said some *stuff* to his mother, and then he got me out of there, and I have to tell you it was just awful."

"Then what?"

"Well," Reggie said. Then she smiled. "Oh, Mommy! Can you believe it? If you can believe it, just listen to *this!* He works for a vet, can you imagine? Twenty hours a week, ever

57

since his father died. Because his mother won't give him his money, can you believe it? He has two pair of *socks,* only *two* pair of socks! So he was really upset after we left his house, he just felt awful, he couldn't even talk for a while, but then he took me over to where he works, and we talked to the guy on duty; and then he took me with a flashlight up and down, we saw the dogs in the cages, and the cats, there was even a snake. I saw where he used to sleep when he used to be on night duty . . ."

The alarm clock rang. Ruth shut it off.

"So then what?"

"Then what?"

"What happened then?"

"What do you mean?"

"You're in that place. You're looking at the cats and dogs . . ."

"Isn't it time to wake Dinah up?"

"In a minute."

"Well. Listen. Listen. I know I should have called you. But after that stuff with Hollis's mom, you know? I just didn't . . . I don't know. What we *did* was, oh, it was just so neat. He lives in the Valley, nothing like around here, but when his folks were together they lived in a big house out toward Thousand Oaks, *way* out. He said he wanted me to see where he used to live when things were still all right, so we drove out there. The house is real big, just beautiful, right up against a big hill with a lot of trees. So we walked up through the yard *way up* on this hill. It was just beautiful. And he showed me where he used to go when he was little, and felt bad. He calls it his secret place . . ."

I bet, Ruth thought sourly. She fingered her bathrobe. It looked terrible. Why doesn't Ed *buy* me one, she thought crossly, buy me a beautiful one? He's *around* here all the time with that wine he brings up, he gets off scot-free with those bottles of wine. Tears filled her eyes.

"Mommy?"

"Yes."

"I know . . . I mean I know that was a dumb thing to do. I really know that. Not to call, and to stay out late like that. I swear I won't really do that again. But you have to know something, even if you get really mad and ground me. It was the most wonderful time I ever spent in my life."

"Grounding? What's this *grounding*?" Grounding was for families who had a ground. "I'm not going to do anything like that. It's just . . . listen, Reggie."

Reggie listened. But Ruth had trouble finding something to say. Not to smoke marijuana? But Ruth did it herself. Not to have sex? But she hated her own mother for everything she had ever told her about sex, hated herself for not wanting sex more, and often thought with regret of the grocery clerk she hadn't made it with when she was sixteen—still remembered his hand on her breast, down at Nancy Stone's beach house. Ernie Walser, where are you now? Could it be that under that air-brushed hair this . . . *Hollis* could have that too?

Reggie waited, looking penitent. Or was it an act?

"Look, Reggie," (and remembered what her father had used to say to her, before he'd left) "I love you no matter what you do . . ."

Reggie nodded, looking sly.

Dinah trudged into the room, her face swollen with sleep, furious. "I just want to thank everybody for waking me up!"

"We thought you'd like to sleep a little late, that's all," Reggie said smoothly.

"But this is the day for the *tie-dye* class! I have to bring all this *stuff*. Say, what's the matter with you? You look funny."

And so the matter faded, like tie-dye after washing, until after breakfast, when Dinah went off to school, carrying plastic quart bottles and four old pillow slips. Reggie picked up the breakfast dishes. It was a mark of how much trouble she felt she was in that she started doing them even from last night. There were stickers in her hair; her blouse bagged

59

open to show the top of a perfectly translucent white breast.
Was it bruised? Ruth couldn't see.

"Look. Reggie." Her voice cold. But for the wrong reasons.
But how's she going to know that? Ruth thought. There's no
way she's going to know that.

"I just want to say this. I'm not going to punish you, because in the wrong run, the *long* run, it wouldn't mean much
to you if I did."

She could see the relief in Reggie's shoulders. (And how
am I going to punish you? she thought. Keep you home
when I'm not here? Keep you home at night, just you and me
and Ed lined up on the couch? Take away your allowance?
You don't even *get* an allowance.) "But I have to tell you,
driving late like that, you can get arrested."

Reggie nodded vigorously.

"And a little grass now and then is . . . OK, but never in
the car, OK?"

More nods.

"Because if you get arrested (humorously) I may not have
the money to get you out.

"And staying out late like that (firmly) is just dumb, and
thoughtless. If you like this boy, and you seem to, well, I
know times have changed, but all this stuff isn't going to
make much of a good impression on his mother."

More nods.

"So that's, well, that's pretty much all, except . . ."

Reggie interrupted. "OK," she said brightly. "I'll certainly
remember that."

"Except change your clothes," Ruth said contemptuously,
"before you go to school. You look just awful."

In the car, on the news, a fire chief explained the hazards:
"Los Angeles is a desert"—into somebody's conference line—
"we mustn't let those green lawns fool us." You wouldn't
hear it on the radio, you wouldn't see it on the tube, the black
girl sitting downcast in her room, on a single bed, on the side
of her bed, her hair screwed in big pink curlers, a black belly
hanging in one Goodrich roll over onto her torn Levi's, her

feet flat, calloused, side by side on the dirty floor. A bureau with no pictures, no pictures at all, only the furniture, the decorations nothing, nothing, although "We encourage the girls to pretty up their rooms with every little kind of personal effect," and down the hall in other rooms, there were pennants up, and pictures of rock stars, and glossy photos of a boy or two, and clothes around, red pants or green, skimpy skirts to terrorize the sexless typing teacher, but this girl sat, clean and sorrowful, her stomach there for all to see, under her fading halter top. She had a cast in her eye.

"Where do you come from?"

"Down in Alabama."

"And they sent you all the way up here?"

"Yeah."

"Are you a little homesick?"

"No."

"Really? Don't you miss being at home?"

"Nothing *to* miss."

"Do you have a family?"

"Yes'm. My mama, and my sisters and brothers, and my step-dad . . ."

"Do you like it up here? Are you having fun?"

"No."

"Do you ever think of going back?"

"No."

"What are they teaching you to do?"

"They teaching me to type, also to spell. They got me on a diet . . ."

"What do you think you'll end up doing?"

"I be a typist somewhere. I think."

"And that's what you'd been planning to do?"

"No."

"Do you have any idea what it is you might *like* to do?" (Thinking, she could be a teacher, a social worker, a nurse, she could join the Democratic party, get some idea about what's going *on* here . . .)

"I know what I want," the girl had said with great clarity,

61

her one eye looking straight at Ruth, the other staring fixedly at the painted bureau with no personal effects, "but I ain't going to get it."

"What is that?"

"Throughout my life I want just one thing. I want one person to love me and I love him, that's all." Her big dead-black face flashed forward, as on an acid trip. "I want one person to love me and I love him."

"But, my dear!" (what Ed said) "My *dear*! Certainly that's easily taken care of. You get a decent job, you meet somebody."

The girl couldn't spell, but she knew the world. "No way," the girl had said, looking at the bureau and at Ruth. "No way."

As soon as she got to work, before she had looked at her messages, Ruth looked up the Mandells' number—behind the modern digits, an old Olympia exchange. He answered on the first ring.

III

He picked her up after lunch in his Mercedes. They went out for a spin, waiting in traffic by the Music Center, riding high across the Hollywood Freeway to Old China Town, down baking, sloping streets to Union Station, back again those few blocks along what once must have been a dry wash full of rye weeds, which now held streetcar tracks, train tracks, scars of the commerce of world war; then west again, onto the Hollywood Freeway.

West through Los Angeles, a whole shallow history on either side of them, wastepaper hills, stucco houses gone crumbling down the drain. Skinny palm trees, sunbaked backyards, bleached window shades, laundry, lantana, crumpled papers in the gutter: Echo Park, heroin heaven, where children used to play on buckled pavement, and still did, drearily. Along the rim of the hills to their right, more palm trees, pretty lace. She looked out the window for a while, then at his hands on the leather steering wheel.

Carolyn See

"They have rats in those palm trees, did you know that?"
"Hmm?"
"Rats. In all those palm trees."
"I hate this city."
"I love it."

Their first disagreement. Well. She knew—she knew everything about him. That he'd been a baby on the east side, an infant in the old Boyle Heights, hundred-degree desert-dry Jewish ghetto. (Was that why old Jews went to Palm Springs now?—holding onto metal bars, stepping carefully down cement steps into stinking sulfur springs, sitting morose in shallow water up to their necks, heavy-lidded, soaking old bones, in springs, in mud, in the tule roots?) She knew he'd been an infant in Boyle Heights, even seen a picture of him once—could she remember it?—looking like himself in drag; lidded eyes, heavy nose, baby paunch, crocheted bonnet, wadded quilt, lopsided diaper. His grandmother didn't speak English, wasn't that it? That she didn't speak English? And his father, brash, a go-getter, a messenger in downtown LA during the Depression, then a—what did they call them?—a quick Jewish kid pulling and pushing racks of bright cheap clothes through LA's garment district. She knew the story; the war, the business of clothing the new poor, who were just rich enough now from their defense plant jobs to be able to buy clothes, but too shy to come into stores. Bernie Mandell borrowing money, stealing merchandise (his son said, contemptuously, to Patty, to Connie, to anyone who would listen) and setting up shop high up in a dark building down on Santee. In the streets down there you could hear the sound of hundreds of sewing machines, a thin hum through the district. Millions were made there, during the war; Mr. Mandell had made millions. Even now, as they drove the freeways, Mr. Mandell was down there, eating either at the greasy spoon on the corner of Sixth, or two blocks away at the Mexican place where he customarily ordered a double Margarita and a double order of *nachos*. A

64

heavy man, in expensive, heavy blue suits which made him sweat. Patty had told her. She had told Ruth everything; the move from Boyle Heights—where Jewish bullies had chased Marc home from school—to Eagle Rock, where Irish Catholics took their turn. And finally, just before Korea, the definitive move for every conservative Jewish family who disdained Beverly Hills, the crosstown jump to Los Feliz, *above* the Boulevard, two stories, Tudor planking, minuscule circular driveway, birds of paradise in a tortuously kept-up flower bed the length of the house. And Marc had graduated from John Marshall High, and gone east to school and his sister married (was it swimming pools that guy was in? Burglar alarms? Patty had gone to that wedding). And Marc's mother had settled back against the gold and white cushions of their never-used couch, in their never-used living room, and let out a sigh and fingered her pearls. Her job, her trip from musty slums, was over. All over now but color television evenings and worrying if the "children" smoked dope, and driving down Los Feliz Boulevard to Vermont Avenue, to patronize the few transplanted Jewish grocery stores which catered to the traveling rich. All over now, no worries. (Her husband never cheated. Marc told everyone his father never cheated.)

"I was thinking, I know a lot about you," she said. "From Patty. I wonder, do you know as much about me?"

He traveled in the fast lane, seventy, eighty. Patty had said she loved him because he drove in the summer with bare feet.

"I don't know if I can handle this," she said.

"Hmm?"

But he must be nervous too. Scared to death.

He wheeled across four lanes, turned off at Glendale Boulevard, drove up and under the freeway and on again, in the opposite direction. He dipped south on the Harbor, caught the Santa Monica, going toward the best exchange, the San Diego cloverleaf, built by a woman. Ruth reached

65

into her purse for sunglasses. He reached across her with his right hand, tipped open the glove compartment, pulled out his own. His arm grazed her breast. If he had come west, so had she too, with some little success. Soon all Los Angeles might be living at the beach.

"I don't know where to go," he said.

"What?"

"A motel is out. Don't you think?"

"Oh . . . yes."

"What about your place?"

"The kids will be home. Besides . . ."

"It's your house with Jack."

"Yes."

"You know my dad has that beach house."

"I'm sorry. I don't think I could ever go there."

"It has a pool, and a sauna, and they aren't ever there except on the weekends . . ."

"I *know.*"

"Oh. Sure. You know what I'd like to do?"

"What?" (With trepidation.)

"Ride the cloverleaf all the way around, all the way around the San Diego and come back again to where we are."

"Can you do that?"

"I don't know. Want to try?"

"Why not?"

They approached the San Diego Freeway, bisecting Santa Monica, cutting beneath and rising again. North and South, East and West, upper and lower, scalloped by on-ramps, off-ramps. Just a few minutes too soon for the rush hour.

"Hang on!" he said.

Down the sweet slope onto the San Diego.

"But how do we get back?"

"I don't think I *can.*"

"Isn't there a way you get back on?"

"No!"

He took the next off-ramp, Venice Boulevard, pulled over to the sidewalk and stopped.

"What do we do now?"

"Get back on again."

"To the beach?"

"Yes."

"Are you hungry?"

"No."

"Will you kiss me first?"

Stilted, stylized, stiff in every muscle, they kissed, sweated. A Mercedes, silver, passed them in the slow lane. "Hey, buddy," its driver said, and drove on.

"What can we do?" he said. "Where can we go?" His wife had died, he couldn't stand too many more shocks.

"It'd better be my house then."

In the end they approached the house like bandits, tiptoeing up the dusty path, holding branches for each other.

"What do we do now?"

"Wait a minute! Let me see who's there!"

He held her by the waist, pushing her up to peer into her own living room. Reggie sat with what must be Hollis, watching the three-thirty movie; Dinah crouched with a girlfriend over a board game. *"What do we do now?"* His breath delicious into her ear.

She climbed out of his arms, ducking into the downstairs part of the house, took a quilt off the foot of Reggie's bed.

"This way!"

Up paths, up rocks, past the house up to the rim of the dusty hill. The sun tilting west with no fanfare, a rock in clear jello.

"I've always wanted to do this."

"You mean you haven't?"

"No!"

He panted behind her.

They climbed up sharp rocks. She worried about snakes.

"Here."

A natural grotto, a breathtaking view. A natural place to make love. Someone else had had a different idea. A folding beach chair sat under close-locked branches, a catsup bottle with a single dead flower.

They spread the quilt. He stood up with his back to her, outside the tent of branches, to take off his pants. Hitching his belt up, unfastening it, bending awkwardly, shucking off pants. Jockey shorts. A little loose. Had he been fatter? Had his mother bought them? Linda? When he turned she looked at it/away from it/at it. Will there ever be a first time when all this goes OK? Or will this be the last first time? Might this be the last time?

"OK, here," he said. They looked into each other's faces. Her dress was off, her bra. Bikini underwear! But if the laundry hadn't come back it might as easily have been a girdle. No stretch marks, she didn't have stretch marks. But she had a belly. Drat! she thought. And remembered that when she'd done a piece on Sandstone, the free love place here in the canyon for middle-aged professionals—doctors, lawyers, writers, sociologists, all studying each other—she'd lined up with them for a naked buffet dinner. And they'd all held their plates across their stomachs.

"Here goes," he said, smiling nervously, sitting next to her, crouched down.

Does the sun cast shadows? Yes. He smiled above her. She smiled back. He shivered. His skin was rosy in the light. Then silver. The sun turned red as a tomato. She turned her head aside. Branches quivered, in motionless air. Silver. Then gray. So many times, this strange act. In furnished rooms. In rage. In love. Weeping and cursing. Thinking of something else. Thinking of *it*. The leaves smelled of sage, rosemary, common weeds, dust. Did you come yet? Did you come? Will you come? Did you come? Why, why didn't you, can you say why? (And later, recently, in these years, poor men hunkered down, peering sideways down at themselves;

fingering, surreptitiously, just a minute! A minute! Touch it! Touch it! Touch me.)

"Oh!" he said.

She braced for the question. Too old to lie, not going to lie. (But she would have lied.)

"I'm glad it's over!"

"Yes."

"Yeah."

He reached over, one side, then the other, pulled the quilt about them, rolled them in it like hot dogs in pastry. Burrs clung to the quilt. Found their way inside. "Are you all right? Wait a minute here!" He rolled them back, then over again, onto their sides. She shivered once, then began to warm up.

"This is ridiculous," she said, in her newscasting voice. "When I got up this morning I had no *idea, no* idea . . ."

A crash in the brush. They froze, together. Two hikers pushed by them, a yard from their heads.

"Dumb time to be out," he said, after a minute. "They won't be home in time for dinner."

But she had thought, against all logic, that it would be the kids. Might have been the kids. "Listen," she said, her heart pounding, "I've got to get home. What do you want to do?" The silliness of it broke over her. "Would you like to stay for dinner?"

"God! Do you think I should?" and then, "Why, yes, I'd like to very much. But . . . don't you think . . ."

"No, really, why not?" But she spoke out of crazy social obligation. Did she have enough, even, for dinner? She hadn't gone shopping.

"Listen, I think it'd be very nice . . ."

Her face was pressed against his neck. His chin cut obliquely, crosswise across the bone just under her eye. She moved down a little; her chin rested against his collarbone. One of her arms was "around" him, her hand lay across the back of his neck. Her other arm, her left one, scrounched down between them. She dismissed it. She'd been dismissing

69

that other arm her whole life. At home with her mother, at the age of eleven or twelve, she'd read one of her mother's library books, red-lined. Lovers lying together, after love, their knees pressed together "like oranges." So that's how it is? Like *oranges?* Where was his arm? Across her hips. Where was his other arm? Under her neck. Where were they now? In a canyon, on the ground. "I'm glad it's still light," he said. She didn't answer. They breathed for a while, in unison, out of unison, in unison. I have to get up, she thought, and get back and fix dinner. He was heavy against her, solid, paralyzing, a breathing block of wood. What was he like? He was tan, he had an open shirt, he stood on the back porch kissing Patty at somebody else's party. Somebody's back porch. His hand, his free hand, moved tentatively across her hips. Not tentatively. With confidence. With impersonality. Like a mower, a thresher, a radial steel tire. Very weird, was her last conscious thought. How many times, to luckless lovers, her husband, had she whined in her twenties, without a hint of parody, "All you care about is *it,* you don't care about me, at all!" *At all* was the rhetorical flourish, the last touch, the instrument of wretchedness. Now his hand was between her legs, his cock was in her . . . such words, such words! She watched *it* coming toward her, like a tank. Like that tank in that war movie. *My God! My God!* But he was unimpressed, and continued with his own more leisurely, unhurried, spasm.

Her hand was on his neck again. Her head was on his arm. Her face was buried in his neck, his chin pressed down against her cheek, she moved down, and locked in against his collarbone.

"My God," she said. "Gee!"

"So what do you think?" he said, anxiously. "Should I stay for dinner or not? I don't want to leave you with something heavy to explain to the kids."

It was almost altogether dark, as they got up, turned away from each other to dress. "It's our anniversary," her father had told her once, about her second step-mother. "I mean, our wedding anniversary. We have another one, for when we both hauled off together into the bushes, but we don't celebrate that one in public, heh, heh." Had it really been bushes? This had really been bushes.

On their way down, she held the quilt because she knew the trail. He went down first, in case there should be snakes. His leather soles scraped against sharp-sided sandstone rocks.

They detoured past the house, downstairs to the kids' rooms, to drop off the quilt. They had forgotten to shake it out. One side was covered with burrs, twigs, needles, dirt. "Wait. Don't. I can't put it back on the bed!" She searched in two closets, found another blanket, rushed to spread Dinah's quilt on Reggie's bed, put the older, ragged blanket across Dinah's under the spread. The burred quilt she placed, pushed, down on the floor of Dinah's closet behind a stack of games. They worked together, in deadly earnest.

What should they do now? For an insane moment she thought of suggesting that they sneak down the path, slide the car away, then return in a burst of motor power and manufactured *joie de vivre*. But she couldn't put the idea in words. By now he was standing near the door, arms folded nervously across his chest. She took a step toward him; he took an identical step back.

"What do you think?" he asked her in a half-whisper. "Do you think I ought to leave now, and maybe come up later?" For an instant he looked foolish, vapid, middle-aged.

"No," she answered in irritation. "Let's just go upstairs."

They walked up the stairs, silently; tried the door. It was locked, and rather than fish for the key, she knocked. He stood behind her.

Reggie opened the door, framed in yellow light. Ruth pressed in, against the light and against her daughter.

"I'm sorry about this morning," and since the girl stood in her way, she pressed up against her, kissed her cool cheek.

71

"Ma! You're late!" Dinah bellowed from the kitchen. "What'd you bring for dinner?"

A smell of cedar (from the paneling), house dust, guinea pig droppings, dead flowers, food. Somebody had been cooking something. Grilled cheese sandwiches? Soup? Somebody had been cooking something.

"You must be Hollis?" Ruth said. "Hello."

The blond boy inclined his head, lounged in the doorway between the living room and kitchen. Behind his head, over the refrigerator, she saw that it was a quarter to seven.

"Listen," she said, "I'm sorry I'm late. Listen, guess who I met today at work?" She heard a dreadful, glassy cheerfulness rising in her voice. "Marc Mandell! Dinah, you're probably too young to remember him, but Reggie, I'm sure . . . Dinah, this is Marc Mandell, Reggie, Marc Mandell. Hollis, Marc Mandell."

"Mr. Mandell. Hi!" Reggie gave him a blinding smile. She had not moved, really, from the open door, though she stood inside it now, in effect blocking their way out. "You're Patrice's friend, aren't you?"

"Ah, *Ma!* Ah, my God! You didn't bring anything for dinner!"

And Dinah's girlfriend observed—detached, unintroduced—"There's nothing at all in that refrigerator to eat."

"Can I get you a drink?" Ruth said to her guest.

"Yes, I, yes, thank you."

"Except wine," Dinah's girlfriend said darkly. "Unless you count wine."

"I can go get something," Marc said. He had not removed his sheepskin jacket.

"I'll go with you," Ruth said. She turned back around toward the door, nervously put her hand to her hair. Burrs! She had come home with burrs in her hair. She looked at the man beside her; his clothes were impeccable, but his hair was dull with dust. Ruth dared a glance at Reggie. Reggie looked square at their faces, one at a time. Smiling brightly.

"But you just got here," Reggie said.

"Yeah, Ma," Dinah bellowed, "you just got here. Whyn't you remember?"

"She was busy," Reggie said blandly, and out of the bad habit of sixteen years, Ruth sharpened her face to fix her with a *look*. But times had changed. Reggie looked back at her, blandly.

That boy lolled between the kitchen and herself. She couldn't even ask him to sit down; he had been sitting down before she'd come in. She turned around once again, completely, in the yellow light.

"Come on," she said to the man beside her. "Let's go. We'll be right back," she said to the room at large. "What would you kids like?"

They stared at her.

"You could start with some milk," Dinah's friend said.

"Some pizza, no! Some chicken!" Dinah said. "Go get some chicken from the Colonel!"

"Hollis *hates* that," Reggie said primly, and Hollis spoke up, not to her, but to the other man in the room. "Hormones. You know how many hormones they put in that chicken? You know how they raise them? In cages. Those chickens live and die without ever getting their feet down on the ground. I don't make that much out of vibrations, but that's taking too much of a chance as far as I can see it."

"You know what Kesey wrote about killing animals on his farm?" Marc was the age to be Hollis's father. "He said you could get away with killing chickens, in fact there was nothing to it, they had no consciousness to speak of, but that when it came time to kill a cow everybody on the farm felt really terrible. The cow felt terrible, because she knew what was going to happen, and all the farm people felt awful, and the Karma got really rotten. Kesey would be dropping hammers on his toe or falling down, and the day they did it would be just a terrible thing, taking a life like that."

Ruth risked a look at Reggie. Her daughter's eyes grazed

73

hers, and came to rest on her boyfriend, who responded, "Just imagine a whole factory full of *chickens.*"

"You're the only people I know around here who don't fix meals," Dinah's friend observed. "My mother goes shopping and fixes regular meals. There are a lot of dishes, but us kids take turns doing the dishes. You're the only mother I know who uses paper plates."

"I *would* cook, Jodie, I used to be a pretty good cook. But I'm working now and I don't have the time."

"So what are we going to do?" Reggie asked. "Is everyone staying for dinner?"

"Hollis, you're staying, aren't you?" Ruth said, but Reggie meant, by everyone, Marc Mandell.

"I could go home," said Marc.

"No!" Ruth said.

"Well, I could go out for something."

"Come *on!*" Dinah said in anguish. "What are we going to *do!*"

"Does everyone like pizza?" Hollis said languidly from his position against the door jamb. "Reggie and I will go out and get some pizza."

"Pepperoni!" Dinah screamed, and her friend said, low-voiced, "I don't really like pizza but I could eat it if you'd bring some milk along with it."

Reggie looked annoyed, almost annoyed, not quite annoyed, and said nothing. It was an expression her mother hated.

"What do *you* want to do?" she said aggressively to her daughter. "You and Hollis could just go out . . ."

"We don't have any money."

"Well . . . Well, Marc and I could go out, and bring back some pizza, here."

"But *we've* been here with Dinah all afternoon."

"Come on," Hollis said, dislodging himself from the door, "let's get going. What kind does everybody like?"

"Pepperoni!" Dinah shrieked.

74

"Anything," Ruth said wearily, "Just anything for me." They smell it on me, she thought. She remembered a college friend of hers who worked through her adult life at a bank. A user of a diaphragm instead of the pill, she had refrained from sex all through the week, since her co-workers claimed to be able to pick up the smell of Koromex on anyone who used it. And that's not the half of it, Ruth thought. Breathing now, above herself, she picked up hot gusts of cunt, of sperm, of sage, of weeds, of dirt. Ah, God.

"Everything but anchovies," Marc Mandell said genially. "Although any combination you get is going to be all right with me."

When Reggie and Hollis were gone, he moved to take off his coat.

"They're wise, aren't they?" he said.

"Your hair has some dust in it."

"Yours too."

They both laughed, unhappily.

"But what do you think?"

"About what?"

Now that her way was unimpeded and her home her own again, she moved into the kitchen to get them both some wine. He followed her, anxiously.

"Well, did she like me?"

"Who?"

"Reggie. That's her name, Reggie?"

"Oh . . . yes. "

"Gee, I would have thought just the opposite."

"Well, actually, Reggie doesn't like too many people, too much of the time. But she liked you, I'm sure she did."

"How old is she?"

"Sixteen. Just a year older than Joan." She spoke the name of Patty's oldest daughter.

"Yeah. Well, Joan and I always got along OK. It was the boys I had trouble with."

"Yes."

"Does Reggie go to high school?"

"Yes. She's doing very well."

"She's very beautiful."

"Stunning. And smart too."

"Not as beautiful as you are," he added, dutifully.

"How old was that girl, you know, Linda? Not much older than Reggie, was she?"

"She was nineteen."

"What's it like, being with a young girl like that?"

"Oh . . . it looks, it looks like it's going to be fine. At first it's just great, you think you're going to be young all over again. You tell her everything you know, and she listens and listens, but pretty soon you start getting your own ideas back, like you put on a cassette tape, your own ideas coming right back at you in this little girl's voice. And your ideas start sounding a lot dumber every time you hear them."

He smiled at her over his glass. She poured him a little more.

"Like Carol Knaak. Remember Carol Knaak? Just a little bit of high school is what I mean to say."

She remembered only Carol Knaak's yellow sweater, short-sleeved, nubby-knit, with shoulder pads. And laughing, going from some class to another.

"But it was *she* who left *you,* though, wasn't it? Linda?" She was pressing, she thought, just to get the facts clear, and breathed easier when he said, "Ah, it was time. She said it herself and I believed her, I agreed with her. The relationship wasn't going anywhere, it was time for her to split."

"But what," she said, interviewing him, head cocked, charming, on the air a hundred times, "was it *really* like? Being with a girl like that?" And was shattered to hear him say, "She was the acid queen, that's all."

"You mean," she pressed on, wretched, unable to stop, "that acid was all that important to your relationship?" How old I sound, she thought helplessly, how old. "Jack and I

76

took acid a few times." (How *old*, how old!) "And it was very important to us both. I think it probably was the thing that sent him off to another life."

"But what about you?" he said, his romantic amiability suddenly gone. "What would you have said it did for you?"

"Changed me from a sad person into a happy person? We had thought about it for a long time, you know, read all that stuff . . ."

He was nodding. They were on the couch, alone together, the television set was on. The two little girls knelt at the far corner of the room, playing another game of Clue.

"We were already too old for all that. But that one summer we went to see *A Hard Day's Night* a dozen times. Jack was already in his thirties . . ."

"Did you take it with Jack?"

She could see, in the lamplight, signs of Marc's age, the lines beside his eyes, a looseness under them, a looseness under the jaw. He was the kind of man who needed a shave twice a day.

"No. He said it would be bad for us to take it together. That we had too much against each other from over the years, and it might all come out. So the first time, when he took it, he took it with a friend, an old surfing friend."

"That was *his* story."

"No, I really believe him. I just think he took it with a guy, that's all. He's an athlete . . ."

"What about you?"

"With a woman friend. You don't know her."

"Was she all right?"

"What do you mean?" But she answered anyway. "Sat in a corner. Wore a red sweater. She stuck it out a whole night. Things were very formal in those days. You know."

"Did you *ever* take it with Jack?"

"About six months later. It was very nice. We laughed a lot. It was about six months before he left."

"Did you . . ?"

"We tried. He said that was the only part where it looked as if it might turn out to be a bad trip for him."

"What about you?"

"Oh . . . I don't know."

To be talking about this without pain was astonishing to her. For this was one of sixty or seventy scenes, which for the past five or six years, had been the central pain in her life. In truth she didn't remember what she had originally felt about some of these scenes; her husband lolling, as he had once, in a blue pinstriped shirt, on his girlfriend's couch (Ruth having stalked them in the night), while she and poor Jennifer had waited for a verdict, deep in the night, and he had smiled ingratiatingly, and put his feet up on the slipcover: "After all, I love you both, you both know that." Or when Ruth, distressed at the lack of sex in their marriage (Why? Had she been distressed? Because according to every rule, there should have been more, that's why), had presented him, after a month of data keeping, with a calendar which held in it the thin record of their affection, he had responded with shouting, and blows, while she wept, as usual, and the calendar dropped and heeled between them. And that night on acid when he solemnly informed her, stepping out of the shower late at night, his two eyes turning to six eyes and back again, that it was because she was getting her period, that was why it hadn't worked, and what did she expect? And an eternity later, that same night, she sitting on the toilet, winking owlishly at whitest toilet paper, *a lie!* She thought, in echoing acid caravans, but like Tom Sawyer's aunt, had thought again, *a kind lie.*

"Actually, by then, I don't think I wanted it very much either. There wasn't any pleasure in it for either one of us. We neither *one* of us wanted to do it." Amazing, she thought.

He nodded and smiled, but had no chance to talk. The children had come to sit with them on the couch. Dinah was, in fact, already talking.

"Wait a minute, Dinah, don't interrupt."

Marc Mandell uncrossed his legs, stood up with his wine glass and went into the kitchen. When he returned with the bottle of wine, smiling amiably, Dinah had hardly started.

"I turned in all but two assignments, sixteen mistakes, and pretty sloppy, and Jana turned in the *exact same thing,* all but two assignments, *sixteen* mistakes, and pretty sloppy. So you know what he gave her?"

"No."

"B minus. And you know what he gave *me?*"

"No."

"C minus. Not even a C. So you know what I did?"

"No."

"I told him about it. I showed it right to him. I said, 'Mr. Rizzo, *look at this!* You gave Jana a B minus and she had all but two assignments, sixteen spelling and mathematics mistakes *exactly,* and pretty sloppy work!' "

"Yes," Ruth cut in. "So what happened?"

But Dinah was not easily interrupted. "Never mind."

"No, now, come on. Mr. Rizzo," Ruth explained to Marc Mandell, "is a monster. We've thought of hiring a skywriter at the end of the semester . . ."

"The last day of school!"

"Because he is really unfair, he really *is* a tyrant . . ."

"Mr. Rizzo *sucks!*"

Marc Mandell put down his glass, filled it to the brim. "May I pour you some?" he asked Ruth. "Excuse me for helping myself like this."

"In the sky! That's what we're going to write in the *sky!*"

"He really is quite terrible. We've just been kidding about it. Because he really is quite awful. He actually has a board . . ."

"A *game* board!"

"Where he lines up everyone in class every week according to how well they've done their homework."

Marc Mandell listened politely.

"And that, well, in the kind of school we have up here, just isn't . . ."

"Mom thought of the skywriter. And she says she's going to do it! She even called up once to see how much it costs! Didn't you, Ma? How much did it cost? Thousands of dollars," she said, answering her own question, "thousands, and she says she's going to do it."

"Really?"

"We just thought about it one day. As kind of a joke."

"Did you call them up?" He was severe.

"Yes, but they weren't there. It was a Saturday. *Actually,*" she said to her daughter, who was sitting wedged between them now, stiff-legged, in need of a bath, her hair smelling defiantly of wet chickens, with her friend standing at her shoe's end, a dirty little shadow, "Marc has a son about your age. How old is he now, Marc, did you say?"

"Nine."

"Does *he* have an awful teacher?"

"He's doing very well in school."

"But does he . . ." Dinah was bumping now, uncomfortably, bumping in place, her legs bending and straightening in a series of bone-shattering jerks; her elbow, at least on Ruth's side, moving in time but at a different rhythm, nudging Ruth's arm, Ruth's rib, Ruth's breast.

"Calm down, honey."

"But does he have an awful teacher?"

"No."

"Mr. Rizzo Sucks, Mr. Rizzo Sucks. Mr. Rizzo Sucks."

"Dinah . . ."

"You know what the kids in the class do?" Dinah's friend asked. She too moved in rhythm, symbiotic to Dinah's but at a different speed, entirely different.

"No," Ruth said.

"They just write Mr. Sucks. Get it?"

"Yes."

"All over their papers. On the desks. But he can't get mad. Because that could be anybody. Just . . . Mr. *Sucks!*"

80

"Girls," Ruth said. "Why don't you both take a bath? And wash your hair. Jodie, are you spending the night?"

"Sure, if my mom says OK."

"You mean you haven't called her yet? Go ahead, dear, and call her right now." As if Jodie ever called her mother. Please, she prayed, please Dinah, don't say anything, don't give me away. But Dinah contented herself with a strange look, and Jodie moved, wordless, to the phone.

"You know Josh, Dinah, don't you?" Marc queried suddenly. It was the first question he had directed at her. "I think you met him a couple of years ago."

"Sure," Dinah said in her most negligent tone. "I met him." She got up from the couch, crossed closely in front of them both without asking to be excused, went into the bathroom and slammed the door. Jodie hung up the phone, glided silently after her, shutting the door in turn with hideous quiet; Ruth could hear them whispering together.

"Jodie!" she called.

"Yes?"

"Is it all right?"

"What?"

"Did your mother say it was all right?"

Silence.

"For you to stay?"

"Yeah."

"Then why don't you both *wash your hair!* And don't . . ." But the sound of bath water drowned her out.

"Well," she said.

"Tell me about your job," Marc said.

"What?"

"Your job."

"Well, it's—you saw it. It's just like that."

"Every day?"

"Yes, pretty much."

"But what do you think about it?"

"Think about it?"

"Do you like it?"

81

"Oh, *yes!*"

"Why?"

"Why, because it's—wonderful!"

"But it's the *same,* isn't it, every day? You just said so."

"But I love it!"

"Why?"

She had been hoping to talk about something else. "Because you see things you'd never see otherwise."

"But couldn't you see them on television anyway? I mean, that's where all the rest of us see them."

"But when I do a story like that one yesterday—oh, I don't say it's the greatest story in the world, but I'm *in* it, you know?"

"I don't mean to be rude . . ."

A rich man's son.

She capitulated. "Well. You went up north. Do you like it up there?"

"It's beautiful. Incredibly beautiful."

Shouts from the bathroom. "Dinah!" she called. "Quiet down!" Then, "What I do isn't beautiful. You certainly couldn't call it beautiful."

"Then why?"

"Don't you remember what Patty used to say? That she quit graduate school because there was no one to have coffee with? Where I work there's always someone to have coffee with."

"I feel very badly about Patty."

"Do you?"

"She was a good woman."

"My best friend. Well, of course, you know it."

"She's with someone else now."

"Sure."

They looked at each other. Nowhere to go in this conversation. Her canyon cabin was heated only by an oven. The gassy fumes were everywhere. But to open a window would be to chill the house.

"You know what I hate?" she said. "I hate that in this town you either live down in the Valley in some awful little house that has all the conveniences, or up here where it's beautiful and you freeze in the winter and boil in the summer. Or you live at the beach in the fog, or if you move inland you die of smog. I'm sorry it's so stuffy in here but there's really nothing I can do."

"Up at my place the air is perfectly fresh."

But she felt wretched, lousy. "How about Patty? Why didn't you come to Patty for this?"

"She's with someone else now."

"She'd go with you in a minute."

"I don't want her."

"Look." She was thinking of her psychiatrist, a beautiful woman with false eyelashes, who did needlework. "I know you don't like her kids. Well, mine . . ."

"I don't know about any of that."

She tugged at her collar. She was stifling. *"Look,"* she said bitterly, "there's something I have to say to you. I'm thirty-six. Almost thirty-seven."

"Yes." He was smiling, sweating. "Did you ever drive across the country?"

"Yes, why?"

"It's wonderful, isn't it? Maybe we could do that someday."

She had had too much wine. Maybe this was a night like a dozen other nights, since the divorce. Except that this time the best part had come first. *Get lost,* she wanted to say, *go home,* and (echoing her mother) *you only want one thing!* Except she wanted it too. "What I want to know is," and heard the sharp, belligerent tones of her mother on the phone, playing bridge, paying bills, "why didn't you go back after the woman who still loves you?"

"I don't love her?" It was a genteel question.

"Really?"

"Well, I wouldn't have left her if I did, don't you think? Not that she's not a good person."

"Hey, *Ma!*"

And at the same time Reggie and Hollis came in the front door, with pizza.

"We got one plain, for the kids, one everything but anchovies, all right?" It was Hollis speaking directly to her. For the first time.

"For *sure,*" she said, and blushed, flustered. Too old, shouldn't she remember? To be talking like that.

"Say," he said, by her side in the steamy kitchen, as she hacked inexpertly at the pizza, "my dad used to watch for you on television. You weren't ever on enough, as far as he was concerned. He said you were pretty good."

"Not nearly enough for me either."

"No *really.*" His glossy head hung, insistent, over hers. "He said you were pretty good."

"*Ma!*" It was the fourth or fifth call.

"Reggie, please! See what she wants!" It was hard to move from a shout to conversation. No wonder he left, she thought, despairing, invoking the hard face of her husband.

"Do you mind if I tell you this? I don't think he'd mind. I think he'd like you to know." The perfect little face—a nose job there? braced teeth?—was terribly earnest. "He said you shouldn't be on television, he said that was your wrong line of work. He said you had a great bod. He and my mom used to kid about it."

"You're sure he said that?" she said, thrusting a bending paper plate, already soft with grease, into his hand. "That was certainly very nice of him I'm sure. Here's a napkin to go with that."

The phone rang. It was for her. She took it in the kitchen, still cutting pizza. It was Edward, he would be working late. Thank God! There was, in the back of her head, a genuine, physical burning. Here she was, here she was; her life might be changing. Did it even matter, that her life might be changing? It had to matter, didn't it, for lack of anything else? Her life, her mind, the back of her head, was like an expensive, maybe five-dollar Christmas card for children. You send it to them on December 1 and they open a little paper door marked December 1, and there, in a drift of unglued glitter and a patch of flocking, is a partridge, or a wise man, or some such holiday prop. Three and a half weeks later, the child must have opened all those doors. Her life; but did it matter, really, that it might be changing? Was it a thing to get upset over? To blush about?

There was this man in the living room; sitting up on the couch, bending slightly over one knee, where a paper plate was balanced, putting pizza in his mouth, thinking of things to say. And if there had only been one phone call this usually dreary Wednesday night, why, it had been for her. Her face did sometimes appear on that electric screen; she rarely made mistakes, and the people who watched, if they thought about it much, might never guess her husband couldn't stand, no, didn't like, to sleep with her.

When she brought her own pizza into the living room, most of the company was ready for seconds. She saw this and waited for Reggie to notice, to say something, get up, take charge. But she didn't. Her older daughter's eyes were shiny brown porcelain, inanimate; they weren't made for seeing, they didn't see. She thought of asking Dinah, even Jodie, to go to the kitchen for the already cut seconds which were sizzling in the oven, but the two girls sat queenly, indecent; two of them in one armchair, stark naked, their wet hair wound in towel turbans, their baby genitals appearing and eclipsing as they crossed and uncrossed their legs. Besides, if she asked Dinah, she very likely might refuse to do it. I am the only one, Ruth thought, in this room, who has gone to work today, and even her enchantment with this musky luxuriant man (who had been sitting, even as she guessed, bent to his pastry, tomato, cheese, and now sat back, relaxing, only partially replete, against the couch) didn't keep an edge from her voice, when she asked, "Would anyone like more pizza? There's still plenty of it in the oven."

85

They all would.

The early news was over, both local and network. Silent, they watched thirty minutes on the English fox, the smaller children groaning as first the rabbits, then the fox met the inevitable kiss of death. At ten o'clock Dinah's favorite series came on, but Ruth, remembering that Marc hated television, voted strongly for the old black-and-white movie which came on nightly at Channel 13. After some minutes Lucille Ball and Bob Hope were discovered to be in love. "Why are we watching this?" Hollis asked.

"Because," Ruth said, "isn't it better to at least watch old movies than those terrible prime-time things? Dinah, I *wish* you'd put some clothes on!"

"It is not!" Dinah said, and her friend echoed, "It is not either."

"Listen," Marc Mandell said, "if it's because of me we're watching this, forget it!"

But Reggie said, safely within the arm of her hair-sprayed escort, "Gee, Mr. Mandell, don't I remember that you hate television? I think I remember that Joan told me that once. That they couldn't watch when you were over there, wasn't that it? Or is it just kind of a change to watch it now? Because they don't have it where you live now, do they?"

"They have it," he said. "But I don't own a television set, no."

"Do you have a farm up there?"

"Are we going to watch this or not?" Hollis complained. "As long as we have it on we might as well watch it."

"Dinah! Are you going to get dressed?" And as the two girls rose, their hair free now, tangled and wet across their necks, "Will you *please* pick up your towels and put them away where they belong?"

"No. I don't have a farm. I bought a small hotel. An inn, really. But it hasn't been used for a long time."

"How interesting that must be for you! Especially when you've spent all that time doing something else."

"Dinah!" Ruth called into the bathroom. "If you're not going to watch television, why don't you go down to bed? You don't have to *go* to bed, but you could play some game or something—Listen," she added, "you can stay up as long as you like talking. It's fine with me."

"No!" Dinah shouted, but after a whispered conference, said, "Oh, OK."

"Do you *run* this hotel, Mr. Mandell?"

Reggie, under her boyfriend's very long arm, appeared to be laboring under a hard burden, a Chinese coolie bearing water, or cement. However, she smiled as she asked the question. "Can you really make a living out of it?"

"The hotel isn't open now. I've been renovating it, a little at a time."

"But I bet when it's finished a lot of people will come there."

"It's a very small hotel," Marc Mandell said stiffly, but Hollis interrupted, saying, "We could go downstairs too."

"What?"

"Downstairs, with the kids. Play games."

Reggie looked scared.

"I mean it! Monopoly."

"It's pretty late," Ruth said. "I like Dinah to at least be in bed by now."

"That's OK. We'll stay in Reggie's room. We'll keep an eye on them."

A beat, two beats. Three people looking at one middle-aged woman. "Oh," she said finally, "I guess so." And Reggie was betrayed.

"Just," Ruth said, "just don't . . ."

"Oh," Hollis said, "we wouldn't dream of it." He smiled charmingly. "Come on, you kids! Sir, I'm glad to have met you."

Dinah and her friend came out of the bathroom, in nightgowns, their hair still wet and tangled.

"Are you sure you're going to be warm enough?" Ruth

87

said automatically. "Dinah, when you get down there, be sure to brush out your hair. In fact, why don't you brush out each *other's* hair? Be sure to, now, or it'll be harder to do in the morning. *Much* harder."

"Yeah, yeah," Dinah muttered, but came over to where Ruth sat and kissed her on the mouth. Soft lips, little lips. Then Jodie leaned in. But Dinah wanted to be the last, and kissed her mother again.

"Goodnight, now," Ruth said. "Don't forget about your hair."

"Goodnight," Reggie's boyfriend said from the doorway.

"Goodnight all," Reggie said merrily, and disappeared.

"So," Ruth said, looking at the man sitting on her couch.

"So."

Ah, she was tired, she wished he would go home.

"It's been some day, hasn't it?"

"Yes."

"Come on over here." She came, thinking that during the whole night there had only been one phone call, but that at least it had been for her.

"What are they going to do now?"

"Now?"

"Is he going to stay here? Stay the night?"

"Not that I know of."

Which was true. She was master of not knowing things. (And what had it gotten her? A lot of nights alone on this couch, eating stewed tomatoes laced with Tabasco and chunks of heavy cheese.)

"You don't even know if he's going to spend the night?"

"No, no," she hastily said, "of course not. I'm sure he won't."

With that he put his arm around her. She settled in, wearily, against his cashmere shoulder, for affection, maybe a minute's sleep. Determinedly, within the television set, Bob and Lucille argued it out; did they really love each other, were they, in spite of their shady backgrounds, fit parents to adopt a child? "Well," Bob Hope said, "we'll never know if we don't try. I'm game if you are." The feeling was, it wasn't for themselves, exactly, or even for the lost little orphan, it was for the life, the change of it, and besides, the movie was coming to an end. Something had to happen. Marc Mandell took her hand, put it between his legs. Ah! That was like all the rest of him, luxurious, affluent, thick.

"Again?" she said. "My God! I have to get up in the morning and go to work."

"Why don't you turn off the television set?"

Why don't you? she thought, but rose to do it.

There it was. All over again; through exhaustion, embarrassment, the press of events, he was able to do it to her again. And only hazily—events appearing in a crystal ball and then sinking again—did she apprehend the pantomime, the mirrored image, of young bodies twenty feet below them, and hope, as she went to sleep, finally, against this stranger's shoulder, that he had not noticed that there had been no reopening and closing of the downstairs door; that there were in this house tonight, not two crowded bodies sleeping, or even four, but six.

IV

"Psylocybin, sure, OK, yeah, it's a kind of an interesting high, I like it, but I'm trying to be more serious. You know what I found out? That acid, oh, they say a lot about acid, but I feel like, I always *have* felt like, it's mostly tricks. Making time stop, so what? Beautiful colors, so what? I *do* know that if you lock yourself in a room with a friend and a couple of hits of mescaline, you're going to find out the truth about that friend, and yourself, you have to. Not always a pleasant truth. Mescaline is a hard master."

Ruth's eyes traveled the length of the table to where her husband was speaking to another guest, then returned to the task at her hand. "Do you want a flower?" she asked a turbulent little girl. "Keep your fingers out of it! I'll do it! Do you want a flower or not?"

"A pink one, a pink one! And some extra icing."

"On the other hand, I found some pot soaked in opium a few nights ago, now *that's* a weird sensation. Like you're paralyzed. But it's good for some things, if you know what I mean."

"Do *you* want a flower?"

"No, scrape it off, I hate it."

"An old guy down in Cardiff-by-the-Sea I know, he's got a lot of groovy friends. I was down there a few weeks back, and this Italian artist he knows told me you can get a terrific high off the wild nicotine that grows around here—right *here,* in fact, right over here you can see some, that yellow flower. He took some and brewed it up into a tea, and you know what happened to him? He was paralyzed, literally *paralyzed* from the neck down. He said it cut into his social life considerably."

A dozen desperate children had spent most of this afternoon collaborating on a mural, painting on long swatches of butcher paper which Ruth and Reggie had tacked up in layers along the patio side of the house. The little girls had worked with long-handled brushes, dribbling paint in slimy scalloped wedges across the paper and onto their organza polyester party dresses. They had squabbled over the assortment of potato prints which Reggie and Ruth had carved the night before and set to soaking for them in a bowl of cold water. They had grabbed at paint jars, cruelly jostling, muttering, under the sounds of Dinah's shrill master plan, "Put in more red, more *red,* did you hear me?" They ignored the more or less continual broken sobs of little Lisa Watanabe, perhaps a foot shorter than most of the partygoers, poor Japanese tot, prodded again and again away from even the lowest strip of paper, continually left—for all Ruth's sporadic efforts—with the blurriest prints, the rattiest brush, and the one color black. But the tiny child's vision had triumphed at last. Her unequivocal statement had been a thick, ribbed slash of dumb black against the pastel wanderings of the other little girls. Then Dinah's friends had fought for Lisa's brush, and when Ruth protested, had jammed their own bright brushes into the pot of black. After another forty minutes, when Ruth and Reggie declared that game finished, and sent the children over to a galvanized tub at the far end of the patio to wash up, the three conjunct strips of paper were black, black, or smeary, unrelenting charcoal gray. Ruth would be able to wash the remains off the walls and patio, but there would be no bright souvenirs to roll up and cut off in bright paper banners to give to departing little girls—as remembrance of Dinah's seventh birthday.

"Listen, a friend of mine brought something over to the house the other night, he said it was—something funny sounding—I can't even remember the name of it, but it was the chemical equivalent of marijuana. That doesn't sound so bad, does it? In fact the guy was real apologetic about it. He said, 'I don't know if this is going to get us very high or not, but we might as well try it.' It's kind of a powder, you snort it like coke. We divided what we had, it didn't look like enough to do anything to *anybody,* and the four of us each sniffed it up, him and his girlfriend and Jennifer and me. And we went on talking, and you wouldn't believe it. About two-thirds of the way through the next sentence, old Jennifer there, she was sitting on the floor, she just rolled right over on her nose, and said 'Where *am* I? Am I on another planet?' But I couldn't even answer her. The same thing had happened to me! I couldn't believe it!"

The mother of one of Dinah's friends made her way toward Ruth, stepping carefully across the uneven bricks in the patio, ducking under the thrashed, tattered remains of a piñata, stepping sideways past the old card table which still held half-filled pots of poster paint. She stood beside Ruth, waiting until she had heard the last. Then she said, hissing theatrically, "Who is that *person?*"

"Dinah's father."

Ruth bent down to pick up the damp napkins of the few children who had already finished. *Can I help it?* she might as well have said, gesturing from her shoulders, rhetorically. *Did he look that way when I married him? Twenty-four custom-*

92

made suits direct from his Hong Kong tailor, what can I tell you! That on our first date he took me to his bank? I stood there and watched him make a deposit. Not a withdrawal, mind you, a deposit!

Her other feeling, that fugitive delight, she wouldn't stoop to explain. He was something all right, his hair in that shining albino halo, only slightly receding from his delicate forehead, his beady, crackling pale blue, insane eyes, his tiny wishbone wrists. After all the fights after parties, droning Sunday morning arguments which by the weather and the very slant of time they both knew would inexorably continue into afternoon and night; after every infidelity and tantrum, she still took pride in him; his insomnia, his sinus attacks, his tirades, his shirts. Today he had come to his child's birthday party dressed in an apricot tank top, bright green velour caftan draped rakishly across his narrow shoulders, a tight pair of faded jeans with an embroidered Japanese butterfly appliquéd just underneath the genital bulge. He wore Adidas jogging shoes, with stripes which exactly matched the caftan's green velour top. No socks, never. He ran a hundred miles a week. He was forty-four years old, and impervious. When Reggie had greeted him this morning with a tentative sneer and, "Don't you think all that's a little outdated?" he had answered her question with a question. "Do you like my new copper bracelet? It's done wonders for my arthritis."

This was a family party then, as well as a neighborhood gathering. Reggie had stayed home for it and Hollis was here too, on the balcony on the other side of the house, reading *Be Here Now*. And Ruth's neighbor, Gina, from down in the canyon, who smoked dope on weekday mornings and practiced her flute in the nude. Of the eighteen children here, Ruth had known six of them since the mornings after they had been conceived, the days they had been born. Connie's boys, Luke and Jonathan, and on the far side of the table, Joanie, Anthony, Tracey, Little George, dressed in homemade clothes, perfectly designed, perfectly stitched. Patty had driven in forty miles from the far reaches of her San Fernando suburb to be here. With the children whom Marc had hated. (Or was that really true? Was it true that "infidelity" had pried Ruth and Jack apart? One simple secretary? If it weren't true she wasn't going to admit it now.) Today, after the second chocolate rum cake for the grown-ups, after the champagne, after Jack had gone home and the piñata had been swept up, she planned to tell Patty about Marc.

She'd been in love for eighteen days. Two and a half weeks, bright, burnished, covered with glittery dust. It divided into the four actual days they'd had together—the two weekends he had flown down, lived in semi-secrecy at her house. He had brought expensive marijuana in a pigskin case, and carefully packed plastic bags of Cedar Bay shrimp. He told them about his place, the forlorn, perfect little inn by the side of the northern bay. Small, sure, real small, no enterprise about it, just one big downstairs room which he planned to make into a combination sitting room and pub, and another wing built on toward the south which might actually make him some money—a young people's drinking room, where he might sell beer to the loggers, because up in Vancouver they made a distinction in how they sold hard liquor and beer. And that *was* it, really, just a little dining room and a kitchen, and upstairs six bedrooms, for the occasional perfect tourist, just this dopey perfect place he'd bought. He'd seen an elk once, on his property, at dawn, when he had been taking a walk with his son. And you could drive at sunset every day across a tiny isthmus and buy bags of these very same fresh bay-shrimp, already cooked in caldrons of seawater right on the boat.

He told all this to Reggie and to Hollis, leaning forward on the couch, passing them joints from his ready supply, never asking Ruth if he might or might not, laughing and nodding until Hollis called him *man,* and Reggie, high and sleepy, looked more and more distinguished, tilted her regal head further and further back, until, each of four nights, about eleven o'clock, she went to sleep.

"No fooling, it's a gas up there," Marc would say to Hollis. "There's a lot of stuff up there for a man to do, I really mean it. Maybe you'd like to come up there sometime, maybe in the summer, it's a knock-out up there, it's a gas." And Hollis had nodded and Ruth had smiled each of those four weekend nights, and they had waked up Reggie long enough for her to say she was going to sleep now. Then Ruth and Marc would walk together to the door like old folks, saying good-night to the younger couple, ignoring every implication, asking them only to try to not wake Dinah up. Then, alone, or something like it, they sank into each other's arms, in rosy lamplight, against soft pillows, in love, full of plans.

"Do you think she likes me?"

"Oh, she's *crazy* about you!"

"What about him though?"

"Oh, *sure.*"

Because it was their plan, oh God, how wonderful to have a plan again, that in June, just at the end of the school year, she would bring Dinah up to Cedar Bay for a day or two, to get acquainted with Josh, and then, if that worked out—but they mustn't go too fast—in July Ruth might bring Reggie for a visit. She'd be welcome to bring Hollis with her, since he seemed to mean so much to her, and maybe—it was fool-hardy to plan too much—if the summer worked out, if Dinah and Josh got along, if *Ruth* like it up there, then (it was true that Reggie had one more year of high school, but they certainly had high schools on Vancouver Island, Marc said, although it was true he didn't know exactly where); *if* everything worked out, without necessarily committing herself to anything, Ruth might extend her two-week vacation to take a leave of absence. Hadn't she been working very hard? Hadn't she said she might like to try documentaries? Something like that? What he was trying to say, had said for seventeen, eighteen days, couldn't they *all* come up there? To green fields, hard work, good times, a new life?

Sitting on her couch, she listened and nodded. Why not? Didn't life happen like this, in accidents? Had she been any less surprised when she'd noticed her jock-strap husband had turned a new corner, become a lascivious ninny? Who was to *say* anymore? The weather girl down at the station (and she had gone to the Columbia School of Journalism!) made a fresh pot of coffee one night when her husband went out for a dozen sugar doughnuts. He had never come back; she had drunk up the coffee. The Lord who kept taking away had to give back sometimes.

After the children went to bed, the grown-ups clutched each other. "Oh, I love you," he gasped, "I think I love you! Isn't that amazing?" Looking up at him she saw no trace of the crank who had lain sideways on Connie's striped chaise, smirking, grimacing, wincing, saying, "Connie, *please,* does he have to do that? In the *living room?*" She didn't recognize the man she'd stood behind in line at theaters, nodded to at parties, heard stories of: "He sneaked me into his parents' sauna, I can say no more." She did see the beautiful senior from John Marshall High. Saw him as he sat there holding her, and then pushed her back so that he could lie on top of her, or pulled her back so that she could lie on top of him. Oh, my God, he was beautiful, *beautiful!* "I don't believe it," they assured each other, solemnly, repeatedly. "I can't believe it."

On the weeknights, he called her on the phone, late at night. "I can't believe it, can this really be happening?" And late at night, after the kids were in bed, after the late show (after Edward had gone home) she phoned back and whispered, "I can't believe it either." She hadn't told Ed. Sometimes, in the evenings as they watched the news and made their desultory efforts toward dinner, she saw, from the corner of her eyes, Reggie watching her from the corner of *her* eye: What are you going to do about this? You're not going to just let it go on like this, are you? Are you? For very long? (On weeknights Hollis stayed home too, contented himself with the phone.)

"Do you ever find it hard to believe you were married to him?" Patty stood beside her, looking past the children to Jack, the sun taking his head in a clamorous halo. She had never like him much. He was talking now to Connie, who leaned back against a eucalyptus trunk and looked seductive. For all their courtesy through the years, Patty had never liked Connie very much either. For that matter, Ruth cared little for Connie's other friends, and left most of Patty's other friends punctiliously alone.

"I have to admit I find it a little strange. But then I have to admit I never really understood why you married Dan."

"We didn't marry *them*, there's your answer. They married *us*. Think about that."

"I can't."

"Let me have that! Let me have it, let me have it, let me have it!"

"No, it's hers! Give it to her! Come on, give it up!"

"*She* had it first!"

"But she's a guest."

"But it's her party, it's *her* birthday, give it to her."

Three little girls fought sobbing over a silver whistle. No, it was a kazoo, a whistle with no sound, you had to supply the noise yourself. Dinah triumphed, clutched the silver thing to her dirty chest, blew into it, hard.

"But it doesn't *do* anything," she wailed. "I can't make it *work*!"

"How's it going?" Ruth asked Patty. "How do you like it all the way out there?"

Dinah threw down her kazoo and ran off to play kickball at the edge of the driveway. The others followed her. Little Lisa Wanatabe crept timidly to the discarded toy, knelt, picked it up, blew cautiously in, hummed. Craftily, over her glasses, she surveyed the crowd, found her mother, crossed the patio to her, stood propped against her, blowing a low, triumphant tune.

"Same as here, same as everywhere. You can get more house for your money. There's room for that big garden in the back. The kids like it. The school's OK. They can walk to it. There's a sort of a hill on one side of the street, it's the skateboard capital of the neighborhood. It's the suburbs, you know? You buy it, that's all."

"But do you like that?"

"Sure, it's OK. I've got a dishwasher, I've got two ovens. I like that stuff. I've even got a sewing room. I like things to be convenient. I don't see how you can live up here in the canyon with the drive, and prices the way they are. I like it out there."

During their divorce, Patty's husband had been stricken with remorse and guilt. If the "sin" had been hers, certainly the fault must be his own. Patty had agreed, and come out of the divorce with all their possessions and most of his future earnings. She had worked part-time for a while, with Headstart children, but really preferred to stay home with her own. "I'm having a pretty nice time over here," she had told Ruth over the telephone just after her separation. "I went out and bought some material, I'm putting up new drapes in *my* living room. I'm upholstering *my* couch." She had survived the fragmenting of her marriage tidily enough, but losing Marc had been another thing. "I went out with him last night, and you know where he took me? Over to his parents' and they didn't say a word to me all night. Do you know why he did that? He *knows* they don't like me, why did he do it? And afterward he said he was *tired,* he left me standing there like a jerk right on my own front porch. He said he was tired, my God almighty!"

"I've told him," she would say to Ruth, rhetorically, tiredly, just below panic, suppressing panic, "that he's got to make some kind of decision or other about all this. He's either got to see more of me or less of me and that's all there is to it. I'm not going to be treated like this!" When, taking her at her word, he had seen less of her, she had sobbed, late at night over the phone, to Ruth.

"He says he can't handle it! He says he needs *more space!* More space, can you believe it? Ruth, can you make that out? My God, my God, he's thirty-seven years old. Do you think there's anybody else? There has to be, don't you think? He wouldn't just . . . Do you think there's somebody else?" When there had turned out to be somebody else, Patty had gone to pieces. "I told him, I told him, *I told him* I don't care, *I don't care.* I love him, right? That's right, isn't it? All right, so if I love him, then I want him to be happy. That's right. He says he needs both of us. Well, if I can just hang on I think it's going to be OK. You know what her name is? Linda. Did you ever know a girl named Linda? I called him up the other night and she answered. She asked me if I'd like to leave a message, and I said, never mind, *I'll get him later.* I really believe that, Ruth. If I can just *make* it through this, I'll *get* him, I'll get him later. Don't you think that's possible? Don't you think that's true? Do you think I ought to call him again, and talk about this, get all this out in the open, make my position clear? Do you think he'd mind that? Answer me truthfully, try to be as honest with me as you can. I just want to get it across to him that I'll take him anyway he wants, I just want to be able to see him sometimes, I just want . . ."

Then, awful nights, she would break down, follow him home from work, crouched in her car, neglecting her children, waiting for him to emerge from "that girl's" house. She accosted him on the street, at home. She sat waiting in *his* car behind his steering wheel, pale with self-induced starvation, loneliness, fatigue. "I told him he just couldn't be doing this," she whispered to Ruth. "He broke up my marriage, that's true, isn't it? There's no way he can get out of that, no matter what he does, no matter what he tells me. *He broke up my marriage!* I told him he just has to give her up, I don't care how he does it, I don't care what he says, I *told* him! I'll go to his

99

father!" In the end she had done just that, but Marc's father had listened ambiguously and shown her the door. Faced, then, with a *fait accompli* which for once was not of her own making, she had set about to make the best of it: "I wrote him a letter, it took me all night. I told him that as far as I'm concerned he's more than my lover, he's my father, my brother, everything in the world to me, nothing, as far as I'm concerned, nothing can change that. I was looking in his car the other day—oh, I was following him around, it's just hard for me to get over that, I know where he shops, and takes his cleaning, oh, shit *you* know about that, I don't have to tell *you*, I'll get over it pretty soon, and I noticed he got himself a new cassette recorder for his car. So you know what I did? I went out and bought a tape, the Modern Jazz Quartet recorded live in Paris. He played it for me the first time I ever went over alone with him to his house. I've given a lot of thought to it. Because if he played it the *first* time he was with me that means he liked it to begin with, it isn't something he's just going to associate with me. And so no matter what kind of stuff he associates with Linda, he's still going to play those cassettes because he likes them. And every time he plays them, even if he's with her, he's going to think of me, he's got to."

And even when the inevitable happened, when Patty found he had quit his job and was going north with that upstart, that possible junkie, that impertinent hippie chick, she turned it all to good account, sailing out on her lunch hour to buy the finest pair of sheepskin gloves money could buy and dropping them discreetly in his front seat, as he stopped by the Park Lane Cleaners to pick up his shirts. "Every time it snows, he's going to remember me. And it snows a lot up there. Doesn't it? Doesn't it? No, I don't mind the expense. I think of it as an investment."

With that she had sold her house in town, gathered up her kids, her loom, her bulbs, her balls of yarn, and moved to the farthest reaches of the San Fernando Valley. She'd had it, she said, she'd never fall in love again. A marriage, children, lovers, you had to draw the line someplace. After all, she was thirty-five.

But Patty's blond hair was as glossy as a colt's, her brown stomach unblemished by any bulge or stretch marks. Soon the principal at Joanie's elementary school was passing her notes. Anthony's baseball coach came over to grease her car on the weekends, boxboys whimpered as she disdained their efforts to help carry her groceries to the car, and finally she found a man to suit her tastes, a married dentist who had capped the teeth of stars. "Twenty-five thousand for a complete set of new ones, that's what he charges them," she told Ruth on the phone. "And when they howl he tells them, 'I'm the best! Take it or leave it!' Can you imagine?" One morning she called to say, "I didn't know exactly what he was thinking of me and I didn't want him to think I was coming on too strong, after all he's married and has all those kids, so I called him last Friday and said I had to be over in his neighborhood for Anthony's Little League, and maybe it would be all right if I stopped by his office for a picnic. Because he has a great office, a regular factory with about a dozen dental assistants and nurses and some girl who teaches preventive medicine classes. So he said, 'Sure, come on over!' And I was real cool, about as casual as I could make it. I wore some Levi's, I'm down to about a hundred and five now, and I bought some wine and artichokes, *you* know. But listen! God, I can't believe it! When I got over there the place was completely deserted, the place wasn't even *open* on Saturday. He's sitting in his own waiting room just like *that,* you know? Wearing an *alpaca sweater!* So he ate the lunch and drank the wine and jumped me, right there on the floor in Thousand Oaks, I can say no more." And when Ruth giggled she continued, "I don't even know what's going to *come* of all this, Ruth, I don't even know what's *happening* anymore."

And Patty was content with her house, the basketball ring on her garage door where her suntanned children shot baskets after school, the visits of her dentist, three, four times a

101

week, her alimony check, the admiration of her sons, grocers, ex-husband, everyone. Only rarely, on harsh October afternoons, when the California weather hinted at faraway snows, did she call Ruth to rail: "I told him I don't care if his wife's crazy or not. I don't care if all his best patients are his wife's friends. That's *his* problem, not *my* problem. He's got to think it through sometime, it might as well be now. There's going to be a time, he might as well face it, where he's going to have to see either more of me or less of me, he's got to make some kind of decision about all this."

Now, Ruth turned to her oldest, closest friend and asked, deceitfully, "What about Marc? Do you ever hear from him?"

"Not for quite a while. When Linda left him he wrote me a couple of letters. That he'd made a mistake to leave me in the first place. That he was thinking of putting my kids in his will. I wrote him back. That's all."

"Do you know exactly what he's doing up there?"

"Going crazy, I guess would be about the size of it."

"Why?"

"He's got nothing to *do!* Here he made this big display, and he leaves his life and friends behind, and now he's up there without any life and friends. You know?"

"But . . . what does he *do* now?"

"He used to be a social worker, then he worked in his dad's business. He doesn't have to work, *you* remember."

"But . . ." She really felt she couldn't go on.

"Oh, *hell,* I don't know what he does up there. He paints, he always used to paint. Awful landscapes. One butterfly in the morning sunlight. He's going crazy up there. There's nothing to do."

"I've heard from him."

Patty looked at her. The afternoon sun slid past thick eucalyptus leaves, and shone directly in on the little crowd of parents and children. Toddlers threw down their ice cream and cried. Jack covered his rheumy blue eyes with an exhausted hand. A mother from Topanga Canyon Elementary School sank sideways on heavy haunches across a picnic bench. "Felicia," she said to her fretful child, "it's time to go. I mean it, I'm wasted." Ruth saw Patty's fine, clean skin turn pale as paste.

"Oh?" she said. "What'd he have to say?"

"Actually," Ruth said, "I've seen him, he was down here."

"Oh?"

"Two weekends. I wanted to ask you, I know it's over with you and him, but I told him I couldn't do anything unless I asked you at some point . . ." (which was a lie, she had never told him anything of the sort) "whether . . ."

"You want to get started with him?"

"Yes, I guess so." She felt bogus and lame. "Yes, I thought so, if you didn't mind."

"It does beat all," Patty said. "Sure, why not? Go ahead. See what happens, why not? *George!*" she called out. "Joanie! Anth! Tracey! Come on! We're going."

"Is it all right?" Ruth asked. "Is it OK? Because if it isn't . . ."

"Sure, why not? It's been years, after all. I *am* a little surprised. How long ago did this happen?"

"Two weeks."

"Well. *Kids!* Get your things. Tracey. Dip a napkin in a glass and wipe around your mouth. No, that's punch. Go inside and splash a little cold water on your face. Come on, now, it's getting late. We have a long drive."

"Patty," Ruth said, "I *told* him, I wouldn't do anything until I had talked to you."

"I will say one thing," Patty said. "You know Judy Cruzen? She got a letter from him the other day, he told her he was mounting a concerted campaign to find somebody to be up there with him. Because he'd go crazy up there if he had to be all alone."

"How long ago was that?"

"I don't know. You want me to find out for you?"

"No."

Patty moved with an abruptness through the world. Her cookies had hard edges. She had taken an extension course in Boolean algebra. Her shirtwaist dresses were cut of varying fabrics but always to the same, uncompromising pattern. Now she scooped up her dark glasses, placed them in her canvas carry-all, swept through torn wrapping paper to find Tracey's party favor, picked up Anthony's windbreaker, clipped it over her arm, took two definitive steps to go.

"Pat!" Ruth said. "Call me, will you?"

"Sure. I'll call you tomorrow. Jack! Goodbye. Connie?" She nodded, and was gone.

Later, when they were more or less alone among windswept debris, Ruth told her husband.

He had declined to work at the cleaning up and stood stiff and jittery where the patio's edge hit eroding sandstone. She and Reggie collected plastic forks, tossed red punch over the side into the canyon, scraped icing from paper plates into the canyon. Tonight the coyotes, raccoons, wild dogs, would clear it all away.

"You remember that Marc Mandell?"

"Who?"

It was his policy never to hear her, and if he could not apply that policy, never to know what she was talking about. He was a busy man, too pressed to be interested in whatever her trivia might turn out to be. He had more than once called her since their separation, and upon her answer, answered himself, "Yeah? What is it? What do *you* want?"

"Marc *Mandell*."

"Yeah?" He paced the patio in his dudish clothes, asserting his claim to where he walked. He had made, laid, the patio himself, row by row, unraveling his bricks at night after each day of sweating work, hating to end his project, dawdling as assiduously as Penelope with her suitors. Now he was a visitor only, on his slanting work of art. He had often asked her, in jest or in rage, when she would get her ass out of here, so that he might resume his just, his proper domicile.

104

"He's up in Canada now."

"So?"

Reggie stacked a pile of flowered paper bowls, thrust them deep into a paper bag. Thin paper bags—the grocer here in the canyon was greedy to the last degree.

"So? *So?*"

Reggie bent to recover the scarred piñata, looked at her father, her mother, disappeared down the hill with sacks of trash.

"I've been seeing him."

"That creep?"

"He's been coming down from Canada."

"Is *that* where he went?"

"I've been seeing him, Jack."

"*So?*"

A door slammed from the other side of the house. Reggie had gone in the other way.

"I think it's quite serious. In fact I know it's serious. He . . ."

"That Jewish jerk!"

"But is that," she said, weak with rage, "isn't that . . ."

"That fatass fag!"

A night, five years before. A wedding of some friends of theirs. Here on this slanting patio. Roast suckling pig, bought from Fed Co; skinny, all bone and hairy cartilage, lying on its side like a dead cat. A mariachi, out of tune. The marrying judge, surveying the guests in their ribboned finery. "If I'd known how it was going to be I would have worn my robes." A fine rain. A hundred people inside their little house, pushed off the patio by inclement weather, smoking dope, sniffing some of the first coke, downing Old Fed Cal by the compulsory case. The bride and groom on the balcony. Their second marriage; second marriages are made in heaven. Ruth standing in the patio, cleaning up, hearing the voice of a computer programmer: "How's Jennifer? I haven't seen her at work." And her husband's exasperated answer as he

105

stacked paper plates ringed with pork fat. One piece of college learning finally helped her in later life; Lambert Strether peering dumbly down at that French river, Madame de Vionnet with what's-his-name, rowing without his jacket: Of course! they were lovers!

"Are you lovers?" she'd asked her husband. "Why don't you tell me?"

"Oh, uh, yeah," he'd said smiling, stacking paper plates, and broken into laughter.

So, she thought now, it won't always be your way, you little shit. "I think," she said, "I may be going to visit him this summer."

"*What?*"

"Visit him. This summer."

"You can't do that!"

"I can."

"You can't do that!"

"Why not?" If that Hollis boy had not been in the house, she would be wailing now, running nimbly down the canyon path: Jack would be following, feather-footed, peppering her with blows. Their divorce had been stormy.

"You can't take the kids. I'll get a court order!"

"You want to go to court?" she whispered. "You want to trade life-styles? You want to talk about your . . ." But words failed her. Rage choked her off.

"Fags, blacks, pimps, kikes!" he railed. "That *fag* you've been seeing *now,* what's *he* going to do?"

But she was beyond conversation.

"*Little,*" she told him, "that's what you are, just a little, selfish *creep.*" She always stopped short of the last crucial insult and wondered later why she did. "You go away, you fuck your brains out . . ."

"Small-minded, hypocritical, middle-class!"

"Well," she said sweetly, "give me this chance to broaden myself," and watched him prance and caper toward her—Jumping Jack Flash.

She lay on her back, gazing at waving leaves. One bright star. "Success in television; success in love," she articulated at the center of her mind. She wished it to one star each night. One star might have it.

"Hey," Hollis's voice wavered from the back porch, "cool it, will you?"

"They drive you to it sometimes," Jack told the boy. "They drive you to it."

"Oh, yeah, well . . ."

"Why don't you call *him* one of your names?" she inquired from the ground. "He falls into one of those categories you were talking about, isn't that right? You could have killed me," she went on, careful not to get up or even move, "against these bricks. Would that be so terrific? Would you be happy then?"

"Are you all right, ma'am?" Hollis bent over her, respectfully, but didn't reach to help her up.

"I'm all right, Hollis. I'm sorry you had to see this."

"Believe me, it's nothing."

She sat up, considered her hurts, the rage of her husband, that diminutive, electric *bête noire.*

"Don't worry about it," she said to him, the canyon, the young boy, her daughters within. "I'll pick up, I'll move away, I'll move my things, then you can come back. Wouldn't you like that? You've always said, you'd *like* that. Then you can move them all in here, just the way you always said you wanted." She was referring to a time, which loomed large in their history, when he had suggested that he move in his girl-friend to live with them. It wasn't so much, she had discovered by now. Most distraught, divided husbands came up with that hopeful, if simplistic solution. There had been times since the divorce when she'd wished that for herself. A long hall, and off in separate bedrooms, a wealthy industrialist, handsome gardener, Mexican poet, black gold medalist from the Olympic Games. Life as a motel, a Holiday Inn.

"Come on, Ruth, lighten up," her husband said wearily.

"Would you all like some coffee?" Hollis said. "I believe Reggie has put some water on for coffee."

"Yes, I'd like that very much," Ruth said, sitting up. "Why don't you go inside and help her with it? Oh, and Hollis, as long as you're taking the trouble, do you think you and Reggie might make us some sandwiches? I bought some extra things for after the party." She wondered where Dinah was, if Reggie had gotten her out of sight, out of sound. *So?* she thought defensively. *Well?*

"I just want to say before we go in," she said formally to her former husband as she dusted herself off, "that this certainly isn't good for the children, as you well know."

"I was just thinking," her husband said, sitting on the picnic bench with his head in his hands, "it's been eight months. That's pretty good for us."

"Terrific!"

"What I can't understand is how you can go off with that little Jewish prick, is all. He's not a nice guy."

"I'm not sure about nice," she said, "I'm not sure that's a consideration."

"But he left Patty flat, didn't you always say? Isn't that what happened?"

"Big *deal,* Jack!"

"I would just think," he said carefully, and she could see a familiar desperation, sense of loss, Catholic guilt, beginning to grind him down, hold him safe until the next bout of anger, "that you would want to try to avoid that sort of thing, try to stay away from it if you can from now on. He's not exactly the best bet, is he? With that kind of a record?"

"If we started holding what everybody's done," she began, "if we had to look at what all of us had done, before we got a chance to start in again . . ."

"Yeah, yeah." He was starting into the house.

"But don't you feel that way?" she persisted.

"About *what!*"

"That we've got to have a chance! That just because we screwed up doesn't mean we don't get a chance."

"A chance? A *chance*?"

And she knew the worst was over. She had told her husband.

"I don't know what's going to happen exactly, but I thought I might take the kids up there for a little while this summer."

"*Where!*" he said, but his heart wasn't in it.

"Canada. Vancouver Island. He has a little place up on a bay up there."

"*What?*" he said, but she knew he had heard her.

Later on, in lamplight, in their cozy cabin, the four of them ate sandwiches and talked it all over, while Dinah played solitaire.

"I'm not sure what it's going to involve," she said carefully. "All I had thought of doing is—I don't know exactly. Maybe going up there for a little visit. It's a beautiful place. It's the kind of place you'd go to for a vacation anyway."

"You don't even know this guy," her husband grumbled. (He who had his bills for gonorrhea sent to her by "mistake.")

"But we've known him for years. You just don't like him." Five, maybe six years before, Patty had brought Marc to one of their dinner parties. Jack, an avid reader of *Sunset* magazine, and interested in budget meals at the time, had barbecued an enormous salami for part of their dinner. Marc Mandell had remarked upon this salami, and Jack had heard him.

"He did leave Patty," Reggie said.

"I *know*," Ruth said.

"What's that?" Hollis asked Reggie. He had been, up to now, absorbed in his sandwich, holding it with both hands, wiping each finger separately, down from the palm, with his napkin.

"Mother's friend. He went with a friend of mother's for a while. Then he left her. For someone nineteen years old."

"Far out! When was that?"

"A long time ago," Ruth said.

"Not so long," Reggie said. "Three years, wasn't it?"

Dinah finished her sandwich, picked up her trash, took it to the kitchen, stuffed it in the kitchen wastebasket. (Very good, Ruth thought.) Then she came out, sat on the couch beside her father, wound an arm around his neck. They looked exactly alike, as if, literally, the little girl had come from the same mold as her father, and had only been decorated differently by the artisan who had made them up; straight hair for one, frizzy hair for the other, a voluptuous puff to the lips for the little girl, the moustache which effectively hid the lips of her father. She whispered in his ear. "No," he said, "I can't. No," shaking his head, "not now." But she went downstairs anyway and came back with a pad and felt pens in different colors, and soon he was drawing with her, absently, as he talked. Ruth recognized the same drawings—line drawings of lions, cheetahs—that he had scribbled for her during their courtship. "You are a lion and a cheetah, the lynx of which I never gnu." Sure enough, he wrote it, at the bottom of his daughter's page.

"She left him," Ruth said. "He's up there all alone. *You* know that."

"So now he's come down here for you?"

"Well," she said to her daughter, "I don't suppose there're too many people up there where he lives."

"What'd she leave him for?" Hollis asked.

"She thought the island was sinking," Ruth told him.

"Far out. I really mean it."

"All it would be," Ruth said, "is a vacation. I haven't taken one since I started work. *You* go," she said to her husband. "You've been everywhere. Japan, Finland, Mexico."

"Yes, but that was for races. That was a whole different thing and you know it."

"Do you run?" Hollis asked her husband.

"Yeah."

"Far out. What distance?"

"Five thousand meters, ten thousand, marathons, mostly, now."

110

"He almost made the Olympics twice," Ruth said. "He would have, too, except for injuries."

"Tough luck," Hollis said. His airy hair in the lamplight spread diagonally across his face, obscuring all features except his nose and chin. "You kept on with it though?"

"I've been getting into other things too. I've got the boat now, and that got me into skin-diving, and of course I always do a little skiing in the winter. I've been trying to do some other kinds of things too. I've been going up to Elysium, and I just took a four-day workshop in Polarity Massage. They say it's new but I've been learning that stuff all my life . . ."

"But you still do the running?"

"Yeah."

"After all these years!"

Ruth smiled and folded her hands in her lap.

Jack refused the question. "So what do you want to do then?" he asked his wife. "Go up there?"

"*Yes!*"

"Take the kids?"

She didn't know, exactly. Take them, leave them, whatever seemed appropriate. She wanted to be lying on the ground, under trees, in dry leaves. With. His arms around her. Some such thing. The ground should be dry. The sun should be out.

"I haven't had time to think about it . . . it's only a couple of weeks we're talking about . . ."

"Don't shit me, Ruth! You wouldn't go up there if you didn't have the whole thing in mind. You think I don't know you? You think I don't know the way you talk?"

She looked across the room to her older daughter for support. Green eyes, blank face. What no one had mentioned so far was that this time was not the first. She had taken her daughters on another trip down, down, with a man in a sombrero, across desert wastes, buzzards on Pepsi Cola signs, sweating profusely, the children locked mercilessly into the oven-hot back seat of a Porsche, down, down, right after the divorce, hundreds of miles, into jungles, into cold mountain

111

wastes. Until she had woken, and it was time to come back. She still felt the shame of it acutely.

"One thing. You're not taking Dinah. I'll get my mother up here. *If* it's only for two weeks."

"Don't I get to go?" Dinah said, drawing, holding onto her father. "I never get to go anywhere."

"No!" Ruth said. "If I go, I'm taking her with me. I'm taking both the kids. It's only for two weeks. It's just a vacation. You'll like it, Reggie, I swear. And Hollis, why don't you see if you can go on up? You can get work up there, I'm sure of it. Don't you think your mother would let you do it?" Aware that she had transgressed, was transgressing, in all kinds of ways. Reminding Hollis of his own boyhood. Asking him, over her own daughter's head. Playing the fool—to have traveled 1400 miles in a Porsche, with a man in a sombrero, to have towed one's children across the Sonoran Desert, exposed them to typhoid, derisive laughter, at her age—at my age, Ruth thought. And then—even if at another level—to chance it all again. Jesus. Jesus save me.

But Reggie and Hollis locked eyes, he nodded and she spoke up. "I'd thought," Reggie said, "that since all this might be going down, I'd just stay here."

"*What?*" her father shouted, but she was used to him.

"Stay here. Right here. Hollis has a job already for the summer. Right here in the canyon. In a hash pipe factory. Can you beat that?"

Dinah put down her drawings and went to turn on the television.

"During a recent drought in South America," an electronic voice informed them all, "many wild animals, already endangered, faced the possibility of extinction. Even the armadillo, noted for his imperturbability and toughness in the face of the challenges of savannah life, searched in vain for his life-giving sustenance, water."

They turned to watch, the five of them, an armadillo rooting in cracked earth.

112

"Why don't they give them a dish full of water, for Christ's sake," Ruth's husband said irritably. "They're right *there*, aren't they? Just pour their fucking canteen water into a dish."

Silence. They watched television. Lamplight. Pictures. Books. Canyon life.

"Other animals as well, even the anaconda, suffered from this unexpected turn in fortunes, and were faced, perhaps, with death by thirst, a living death. Only a few men . . ."

"Hollis had a snake like that, didn't you, Hollis?" Reggie was sitting on the floor next to him. She was holding his hand.

"*No*, not an anaconda, a reticulated python."

"Well, Hollis had a snake though."

"The purpose here was to hunt these creatures, not for any hope of profit or gain, or even the pleasures of the hunt, but to safely tranquilize them and transport them to a safer, wetter climate."

They watched as several sullen men in red shirts and leggings thrashed through shallow mud, pantomimed surprise, then flung themselves on an equally sullen snake, sunning in slush.

"Shit!" Hollis said. "That's awful! Excuse me," he said to Reggie's mother.

Thinking nothing of it, she nodded to him, it's nothing really. By now Dinah was in her own lap. She watched snakes and dolphins over her baby daughter's shoulder, smelling sweat, cake, icing, dirt. "Does anyone want some coffee?" Reggie asked. They all did, and she went into the kitchen to put more water on for it.

"What it would be then," Ruth asked Reggie when she returned, "is that if I were to go up there, you'd stay here? Just for the two weeks?"

"Yes."

"What would your mother say, Hollis? I don't mean that you should necessarily stay here. I only mean you'd more or

113

less keep an eye . . . Of course it's only for two weeks. It certainly wouldn't be for more than that. Just a vacation. After school is out. I might not even go at *all!* You know," she went on, "I certainly didn't have any idea that things would be turning out like this. I expect your mother feels pretty much the same way. If you'd asked me even a couple of years ago what I thought, what I would have thought, about you and . . . all I'm saying is . . ."

He didn't answer. He was watching television. Her husband, beside her, was watching television. It is important not to go crazy, she addressed someone. I'm not kidding, it really is. I don't know how it happened, I don't, I swear I don't, it just got out of hand. Football games at King Junior High School. Fluffs of crepe paper on each saddle shoe. *How can I be doing this?* She was talking to her mother, just home from a day in the office, with dinner still left to cook. Kraft dinner, or a lamb chop on a slice of white bread. *It just got out of hand.* But her mother was doing the racing form, before undressing, crying, going to bed. Her mother wasn't talking.

V

They sat together, uncomfortably, on a concrete block half buried in damp grass. It had been part of a path to the kitchen garden and they leaned back, together, against the ribbed shingles of what was still a root cellar. He was reading poems. The concrete block was warm in the sun; the grass pressed down damp beneath them. His voice, a very nice reading voice, throbbed and hummed along in the sun. Behind his voice, the intermittent quarrels of chickens, the strangled yelp of Whisty, his aristocratic whippet, and behind that, the steady hum of hundreds of thousands of gnats glowing like golden dust in the yellow sunlight. Thousands of gnats humming over acorn squash, or lacy filigree of dill weed, planted between low sloping rows of cucumber pickles. Behind everything, ceaselessly, under damp layers of newspaper spread along the ground to catch them, earwigs, chewing.

She leaned her head against his arm. He was wearing a blue workshirt, clean and unironed. Her feet were cold, she

115

tucked them down under the folds of her long denim skirt. (It wasn't exactly a hippie skirt, she'd worn it to work from time to time.) She put her head back against the cellar wall and imperceptibly, she hoped, moved her rib cage so that her breast lay against his arm. She could feel his muscles move in response beyond the larger movements of his arm as he turned the pages. Ah! How lovely. He went on reading, until he had finished the sequence. Then he fell silent, the book still open in his lap. His legs were crooked halfway up, his feet, brown and broad, were bare in the grass. The sun had a few feet to go across the sky before it fell into the crease of blue-gray hills. The bay was flat as a bathtub full of water. A steamer chugged in the distance, leaving a discreet column of smoke.

"That was beautiful."

"But certainly you'd heard them before . . . "

"I really don't think so."

"But you were an English major!"

"I don't think we paid much attention to poetry . . . "

"Patty knew those poems, we used to read them together all the time . . . "

Ruth contented herself with saying, "Yes, I know."

"But really, why is that?"

"Why is what?"

"Why haven't you learned more of that? Since you were an English major. I would have thought you'd have known more of that. Except that I guess being a big career woman you don't have time for that sort of thing."

It was interesting, in all her years she'd never gone without a bra. She could have, she was small-breasted and firm enough, but it had simply never occurred to her. The second or third time they'd gone to bed Marc had smiled at her bra, and she hadn't put one on since. She was wearing a silk blouse now. She felt good. Except for the rough wood at her back. And her cold feet.

"I don't know. The people I knew didn't read poetry. I

guess we usually read novels. Do you think the kids are OK?"

"There's nothing to happen to them up here."

Up here. Only this morning she had still been *down there.* Then up in the air, with Dinah, cleaned up and crazy with excitement, beside her. Then up in the air again, in a rickety plane that made her breath stop as it took off and landed and took off and landed again, on fat green islands in a dull gray sea. In Victoria she had rented a car, nervously, then driven north, feeling put upon. *I shouldn't have to be doing this alone,* discounting the presence beside her that got hungry, asked questions, needed the bathroom. *He should have at least met me at the airport!* But he'd been waiting in the doorway of his inn, a handsome picture.

"I'm a little cold. Do you think we could go inside?"

"Yes, but if you're cold now, I don't know how you're going to stand it in the winter."

She smiled at him.

"No, I really mean it. It's very cold up here in the winter. You can go months without ever seeing the sun. It just pours down day after day. You can't go upstairs without your coat—"

She smiled again. After her first tour of the place, she wasn't too crazy about going back upstairs anyway, filled as it was with the batiks and macramé and ceramic pots of his last lady friend, Linda, the naked lady of the snapshots Patty had agonized over. Ruth wondered if he would ever roll up the macramé, fold up the batiks, put away the pots. And Linda might have worried about those drawer-pulls, made of resin filled with grain and seeds, which opened every cupboard and drawer in this entire hotel. Or the poetry. Because Ruth knew for a fact that he'd learned all that from Patty.

"Can't you just dress warmly?"

"No! Because everything is damp clear through. And I never light a fire in the daytime."

"Why is that?"

"Because! Because I'm the one who has to chop all the

117

wood! One week out of every year. Before it gets too cold. I
go out—Linda used to go with me, do you think you'll want
to go with me? I rent a chain saw and do all the wood for the
winter. It's too precious to use during the day. And if you
keep a fire going during the day, how are you ever going to
get used to the nights?"

"Do you maybe sip a little sherry?"

She knew he already thought she drank too much. But he
surprised her. "Patty used to drink sherry all day long. Did
you know that? Sometimes she'd drink a bottle a day. Then
she'd cry, if I'd ever mention it."

"I don't remember Patty ever drinking very much of anything."

The sun hesitated, seemed lightly to float like a luminous
balloon on the crest of the mountain, and slid without pro-
test, down past the somber pines.

"Well, *you*," he said lightly. "Compared to you nobody
drinks anything." What he said was partly true. Compared to
her he drank nothing at all.

They picked themselves up, gingerly and with hesitation,
and began to walk toward the hotel.

Dinah and Josh appeared at the far end of the path, heading in the same direction. They had been gone for several
hours, Josh obeying his father's suggestion to "take Dinah
for a walk."

"Josh? Josh!"

They hesitated at the end of the drive. "Yes?"

"Did you turn off the switch in the cistern?"

Hesitation, then a nod.

"Did you mail the letters?"

"Yes!"

"What about Whisty, did you take him for a walk?"

Hesitation, then "No!"

"You should have done that while it was still light, Josh."

By this time the children were close to the porch. "We'll
just take him now, Dad, OK?"

Ruth found her voice. "If you're going, Dinah, you'd better put on your jacket. It's cold."

"Where is it?"

"Hanging up in the kitchen with the rest of the other jackets."

But Dinah left the kitchen door open as she went to get the jacket, and Marc hustled over, tight-lipped, to snap it shut. Dinah stayed inside for what seemed like a long time. Marc loosened the whippet from the long chain which kept him, in the daylight hours, in the shadow of the hotel veranda. Now he held the struggling dog by the neck. Another half minute went by.

"Shall I just take him now, Dad?"

"No, she said she was coming, so wait for her."

"Maybe he could just start off and Dinah could catch up with him."

But Marc looked at her coldly. "You've never seen Whisty run. They'd be out of sight in a minute."

Josh shivered. He was a slight boy, with a pleasing unkempt mop of hair. She wished she had thought to tell him to put on his jacket too. So far she hadn't told him anything.

The door burst open, Dinah came out, cheerful and oblivious. "You know where it was? It wasn't in the kitchen at all! It was upstairs by the suitcases! So I had a lot of trouble finding it! Come on, Josh!"

Marc loosed his hold on Whisty's collar, and it was true, the dog, at least, was out of sight in perhaps a minute. The children followed after at a run, shouting and whistling. Ruth could hear Dinah's clear laugh. It sounded great, against that dimming background of pine, and bird song, and over the ridges like a gray shelf, a thick soft fall of silver fog.

Dinah had left the door open again but it didn't matter, they were going in anyway.

The hotel's kitchen was large, well-lit, fairly clean. A dish-towel hung across the handle of the refrigerator door, and another against a cupboard by the sink. Jars of dill pickles

119

were banked up against the refrigerator. On another wall, bookcases, wicker chairs, stereo equipment. A braided string of garlics hung almost from the ceiling to the floor; Linda had probably done that. The stove was electric—hardly the thing for a rustic inn, and the cupboards were full of things like granola—this again might have been Linda—and good cheeses, tinned meats, cocktail mushrooms. A painted sideboard held little stacks of produce from the garden.

"I tell you what, since we have all this squash, let's have a mandala pizza."

"What's that?"

"Linda used to call it mandala pizza. It's very good, and it's very inexpensive." (And even by now she knew this was one of his favorite themes, in spite of his gloves and his jacket and his rich dad.)

"You just take the biggest squash you can find, that one, I guess, over on the sink, and slice it in the thinnest slices you can—Linda used to slice it almost paper thin. Then you dip it in egg and then in flour, and fry each slice very crisp and brown. Then she used to arrange them in a big skillet in a pattern, an overlapping pattern, and heap it all up with grated jack cheese, and put it in the broiler until it was melted . . . "

Already Ruth had the knife, and was slicing the squash as thin as she could.

"Would you like some wine with that? I could open a bottle of wine . . . "

"Yes, please."

As soon as she sliced the squash he took the pieces, dipped them in egg, flour, browned them in two skillets, and laid them on paper towels to drain. He worked in silence. She kept slicing, facing inland, at the sink, looking out the window. The hills behind the vegetable garden were turning blue-black; already the deer were coming down the slopes, the way Marc had told her they would, in twos and threes, to make their nightly attempts at the corn.

"That's enough."

"What would you like me to do now?"

"You could set the table."

But the children had come in by now and they did it. When they had finished Josh sat down by the stove with a book. Dinah sat down next to him.

"Can you read it out loud?"

"I don't want to."

"Come on . . . "

"Josh gets to read by himself. He needs his own space . . . "

"But *why!* I want to hear what's in it!"

"Dinah . . . "

"*Yes,* Mother!"

"Look!" Marc rinsed his hands. "Dinah, have you ever used earphones?"

"What do they do?" She eyed him distrustfully.

"You can hear music in them real well. And (he looked significantly at Ruth) nobody else can hear the music." He clapped them around her head. She looked frail and sad under the phones.

"Now, you sit here . . . "

But she couldn't hear him.

"*What?*"

"*Sit there!*" he bawled into her ear, past the earphones. He leafed through records, picked out one (*The Boyfriend*), put it on the machine. Dinah winced.

"Too *loud!*"

He turned down the volume, and turned to Ruth. "Now we can have a few minutes before dinner." He took her hand and led her through the dark and tiny breakfast room to what would be the main lounge, or pub, when he got through with it. Plans (he had already told her) included an enclosed circular bar at the far end of the room, two sets of love seats facing each other over low tables, perhaps a piano, some mechanical tennis, and some summer furniture out on

121

the veranda. But almost nothing had been done in here. Rolls of carpet pushed up against newly paneled walls; there was a smell of fresh paint. Marc still lived in the kitchen, all alone; his boy slept upstairs. The only furniture in here, outside of sawhorses, tools, was a Ben Franklin stove, one couch, and in the middle of the room, a king-size waterbed. "I'm afraid to put it upstairs, for fear it'll fall right through." Outside the wind whipped at a few canvas chairs.

"Does the ocean ever come up this far?"

"I've heard that it does. But whoever put the lawn in on that side of the place didn't think so."

"Who put it in?"

"Who do you think?"

They sat together, hand in hand, on the couch, sipping wine. They spoke tenderly, desultorily. But in spite of the Franklin stove it was cold in the big room. Through two open doors, in the kitchen's yellow light, they could see Josh reading by the stove. Near him Dinah rocked violently, pushing her feet ferociously off the floor, then swinging back, then pushing ferociously again. She listened to the soundless music with her eyes closed, and from time to time would sing along with it. *Oooh,* would come to them, disconcertingly in the darkened room, far away from the firelight, and *ooooh* again. Each time Marc's lips tightened. *But that kid of his!* she thought. *Jesus Christ!*

"Shouldn't that dish be ready by now?" she asked him.

"You're right."

For dinner the four of them sat together at the kitchen table, the corner brightly lit, the eggplant crisp and succulent, the salad—made with greens straight from the garden—tender and tart. Under the lights Marc was charming; he asked Dinah about her school down in Los Angeles, she answered back, and Ruth had to remind her about her manners only twice. Josh talked to Ruth, rustily at first, hesitant, then said, "Do you like shells? *Sea*shells?"

"Josh . . . " his father said warningly.

"Yes, I do . . . "

And he was up from the table, slyly, not acknowledging his father, after excusing himself, and back in a minute with a box which he unwrapped, still ignoring his father, while Dinah leaned in next to him and said, "Golly! Josh, can I see?"

"I got these in Hawaii when I was there with my dad . . . "

And while Ruth nodded and exclaimed, she remembered that trip. Three years ago it must have been. She remembered Patty's grief that she hadn't been invited.

"And these were from the Seventeen-Mile drive, I wasn't on that one. Where is that, Dad?"

"Near Monterey."

Ruth nodded, and remembered that trip too. "Can you imagine," Patty had said, on the phone, "a person who takes a whole day, I don't mean a morning, but a whole day, just to gather seashells?"

"No," she had answered—had she already started work then?—"I can't."

"Do you like rocks? I don't mean ordinary rocks, polished rocks?"

"Josh, that's *enough!*"

But she said firmly, "Yes, I do." And when Josh vanished up the dark staircase with Dinah close behind him, Marc looked at her anxiously, and smiled. "Do you think it's going OK? I think it's going OK." She leaned over across the table and kissed him.

"It is, isn't it?" he said.

Later they all went together up the cold dark steps, into Josh's room, carefully immaculate, filled with his collections of coins and stamps and rocks and shells, and—across the room on an old naugahyde couch which must have come from Marc's marriage years before—stacks of stuffed animals, carefully arranged. On the wall an elaborately stenciled poster looked down: *Darling Josh, I walk along the beach, my toes sinking warmly into the soft sand. I am so alone today, thinking*

123

Carolyn See

*of you. I let the single grains of sand sift sadly through my fingers—
where are you, my almost son, my loved one, my little brother? I am
so lonely for you today . . .*

Marc caught Ruth's eye. "She sent that the first time she
left. That was when she thought the whole California coast
was going to fall off in an earthquake. Then she had the
nerve to send us something like that!"

Josh shucked off his clothes in silence.

"She was a pretty good artist, wasn't she?"

"Yes."

But she was gone now. Ruth stood up straight to kiss Dinah, laughing in the top bunk bed, and leaned in the dark
cave of the lower bunk to kiss Josh. He was a handsome boy,
his hair like a blond cloud off his pale face.

"Gee, I *love* this," Dinah said. "I love being in the top
bunk."

"Can we talk a little, Dad?"

"It's late," Marc said sternly, but Ruth, risking a little role-
playing, said, "Oh, it's only the first night and we're only going to be here for the weekend this time. They can whisper
for a while, can't they?"

Marc said, "I can't imagine Dinah whispering under *any*
circumstances," but in a tone which allowed the possibility of
whispering.

Ruth and Marc sat for a while on the couch in the big, un-
furnished downstairs room, watching the fire snap and shift
in its own red-gray light. "Can I get you anything?" he said
once, and, "Would you like me to read out loud to you
again?" Each time she shook her head. He sat beside her,
holding her hand.

"I'm happy," she said.

"I'm happy too."

There wasn't anything more to say. Outside the wind
plowed the pines and the bay lapped upon the gravel beach.
They sat for perhaps a half hour. Once Marc got up to put a
new log on the fire. Once he got up and went outside to chase
the deer away from the vegetable garden. She stayed inside,

124

shivering as the door opened and closed, still watching the fire.

"You know, the stove is a lot more efficient if we keep the doors to it shut," he said as he came in, but she, disregarding that week he would spend sawing wood, said, "Oh, for tonight at least, let's keep it open."

He nodded, walked softly across the room to check that the door to the front hall stairway was closed and then turned back to her.

"Stand up."

She did, and he kissed her. He was too tall for her, she was too short for him. The light made his face into planes, into gashes of light and darkness. She looked at him, with half-closed eyes, as he kissed her mouth, her cheeks, her forehead, her hair. She saw his cheekbones, his own eyes, lightly closed, his neck and the hollow just above his breastbone. His hands were large, broad, with short, broad fingers. They were rough from his work outside—his ambitious garden. His body was broad too. No fat, no fat there, but broad, earthy, stocky. Like the body of a farmer. He was all muscle—not athletic muscle, but accidental, ordinary muscle; a body that never thinks of itself. He held her breast for a minute, not nearly long enough. God, how terrific that I should like this so much, she thought, and that was her last conscious thought. He dropped to his knees and pulled up her long skirt. She felt ashamed and exposed—that he should find out so immediately and intimately how excited she already was, and expected him to pull away, to turn away, as soon as good manners allowed him, but he stayed, and stayed. His hand dropped her skirt; she held it for him, now seeing the top of his head, now not; just standing, swaying. She put out her hand to steady herself, she nearly lost her balance. He stood up, she couldn't look at him. He began to undress her. As soon as she was naked she sat back on the waterbed, again, feeling vulnerable, silly even, as it swayed under her, away from her.

"Get under the covers, it's cold in here."

She did, and watched him undress. It was amazing that there were so many bodies in the world, that most of them held pleasure for someone. He paused by the side of the bed, looking down, and she reached up her hand to caress him. But he shivered and got in beside her.

She gave herself up to feeling. There was a record playing, and she heard it, the waterbed swayed beneath them, she felt that. She hardly felt herself at all, only him. She seemed not to exist, except for pleasure. Afterward, trying to remember what exactly it was that he had done, whether he had held her in a certain way, or even looked in a certain way (for afterward, they made love mostly in the dark; he was right, it was warmer in that large room with the doors to the stove shut) she could hardly remember how he did things at all. She kept one image, past later quarrels and trivia, of their lovemaking. That night, that particular night it must have been, because the doors to the stove had been left open, he hauled himself, swaying drunkenly above the waterbed's contained waves, onto his knees. He had been between her legs again and his face was shiny, dripping. "I love your body," he said thickly, drunkenly, so beautiful that she had never seen anything so beautiful, and lay—half fell—across her again. That was it, maybe that was it; that he could say that and make you believe it.

Afterwards he went to sleep.

The morning, Gentle sun. He woke up, thrashed across the waterbed, opened the french windows along the bay-side wall, moved into the kitchen to start coffee. He came into the big room again, lit a stick of incense, which she found pretentious, embarrassing, and of another generation, but still liked it pretty well. She was certainly far from her house, her yard, her job, that plastic horse in the backyard, that line of typing secretaries. She put her hand behind her head, the bed swelled beneath her. Upstairs she could hear her daughter talking to his son, voices faintly audible and new, words tentative, unformed, shagged over with sleep. Marc moved about in the kitchen, briskly. Swallows had nested in the eaves above the veranda and swept in front of the windows in wide-angle arcs under and out again, biting insects from the shining air. She lay there, her hands behind her head. The ceiling in this room was very high. Her husband had once accused her of only looking at the ground, of only pulling weeds, for instance, instead of looking at the garden in general, and he had been right. She tended to look at the floor— those jars of homemade dill pickles clustered, oozing, against the refrigerator—or at whatever was "going on"—or at the accoutrements of any room . . . The ceiling here was far away, about a story and a half away. The walls and ceiling were painted a fresh, aggressive white. She noticed what she hadn't seen the night before, a row of posters along the far wall, mounted on cardboard covered with acrylic, something. Long lovely ladies in swirling dresses. Like something Linda might have done, Mucha posters. Here the lens in her mind closed; she really didn't like those pictures around here, not just the ones done by Linda—she didn't like any of them; too banal, too boring, too on the nose, her boss would have said. Too hammy, too second-rate. Boy! How tiresome that Yellow Submarine kind of look to someone who really is, almost, forty. (Yes, but you listen to the Beatles.) Yes, but they're geniuses. (Yes, but you listen to Little Richard.) Yes, but that's parody. The posters were an embarrassment, like the incense burning on the Franklin stove's ledge.

"Come on," he said. "The coffee's ready. You want an English muffin? I'm having a muffin with cream cheese."

"Sure. Thank you."

She got up, reaching quickly for the nightgown, in case the kids were coming, then—for the first time—made this bed. Walking around and around it, reaching down, tucking. The bedspread was covered with dog hairs.

He came out of the kitchen, carrying two English muffins, each wrapped in a paper towel. How elegant, how efficient! To not use dishes in the morning. Then there were none to wash!

"The coffee's in on the sink."

He had already gone out to sit on the warm cement steps of the veranda. She joined him. A sprinkler was already on, soaking the mint-new grass. He had the tiny morning paper, the *Nanaimo News*. He looked at it, then looked up, noticed his dog. Whisty whined and flung himself against the limits of his chain.

"*Yeah*, Whisty, *here* Whisty!" The dog writhed with pleasure. Marc returned to his paper. "You think we ought to buy an outboard motor?"

Intense quiet. The lawn continued to slope down to the bay. The air thickened with gnats and pollen and fragments of spider web, and through the air, over and over, those free-wheeling swallows zoomed in and out, right over their heads. In a minute the children came out, carrying English muffins spread with cream cheese and big mugs of hot chocolate—a pretty imitation of the grown-ups. Oh, it is so beautiful here! She could plant nasturtiums here, by the veranda, she could work on her ideas for a documentary—perhaps about mothers, single mothers. She can see, up here, how terrible it is for children not to have mothers and fathers, a whole house, a whole family. She waited for Dinah to come up to her, to hug her, say hello, take some attention, but Dinah was in love, this morning, with Josh. Ruth addressed herself to her coffee, her English muffin. Her coffee was gone, was it worth it to get up and get some more? Should she ask Dinah to do it, did Marc ask Josh to do such things? The cement of the steps is warm against her back. No, she'll wait a minute to get her coffee, and watch Marc, who is still reading the paper.

"Come on, give me that!" Josh reached for Dinah's muffin, and shoved his whole body against her, laughing.

"No, quit it!" She held her muffin out away from her.

"Come on!"

"Josh," warningly.

Ruth got up and returned, stepping carefully past the children, holding another cup of coffee.

"You could have gotten me some."

"Oh, I'm sorry. Can't I get you some now?"

"No, no, I shouldn't have any more, I guess."

He stood up suddenly. What's going to happen now? (In his house.) But he told her.

"I thought I'd work for an hour in the garden, until it gets too warm, then I thought we'd take a ride into Nanaimo to show you a few stores, where you'll be doing your shopping later. Then we could come back here for the kids, and if we're not too tired we might drive down the island to Victoria for dinner. We have to return your car down there anyway, don't we?"

At home, she'd be at work by now.

"OK . . . well, if it's OK, I'll just go inside and tidy up a little."

But he was already striding off to the garden.

"Dinah," she said, "have you made your bed?" And the kids disappeared up the stairs.

Inside, the air was heavy with incense. She sniffed disapprovingly, what a stupid habit! She had already made the waterbed; she gave it another desultory tug. She picked up some copies of *The New Yorker* which had obviously been strewn by the bed for some time. Some of them were folded back to particular stories. Should she fold them back to their covers, should she stack them, should she leave them the way they were? She stacked them, but left them on the floor, still folded back to their particular stories.

Straightening up, she saw a blot of bright blood on the bare, paint-spattered floor. And then another. Shit! It couldn't be time for her period. Or could it? It couldn't be. Standing there motionless, she computed. There should be a week more, at least. Could it be all the sex? While she thought in the semidarkened room, a line of moisture ran down her leg. She roughly pushed her nightgown between her legs and hotfooted it to the bathroom. It never started like this. (But still she remembered once when it started like that, at UCLA, when she was on her way to a class, and once at an Andres Segovia concert, but that had been the start of a miscarriage. And her mother once had told her about meeting a woman socially whose stockings and shoes were soaked, and the woman had been very cheerful about it; the point of the story having been that one need never be socially damaged if one had poise enough.

She washed herself, folded a plug of toilet paper against the blood and walked quietly upstairs, past the children's room. "It's easy to entertain if you live informally." She and her husband had read that in a magazine the first month they were married, and joked about it ever after. Easy. Easy! (And how that had modulated into one of his favorite argumentative refrains: Nothing good is easy!) But nothing is easy, nothing, nothing. Where did the jokes go, family jokes of families that were not anymore?

Upstairs she took off her nightgown, pulled on some Levi's and a shirt, looked through her still unpacked suitcase for Tampax—there weren't any. She bundled up her nightgown, thought of her mother prescribing cold water against the stains, then tucked it down into a corner of the suitcase.

Outside, in the sun, holding the keys to her rented car, she said, "I think I've got to run into town right away. My period's started and I don't have any Tampax. I'd better get some." Old as she was, she was a little embarrassed. She wished she knew him better. She doesn't know him at all, really.

He had been on his hands and knees weeding between rows of squash. His brown face was shiny in the sun. "But I said we'd be going into town in an hour."

"Yes, I know, but . . . it *really* started, you know? In kind of a rush. Ordinarily, it doesn't . . . I just think I'd better make a quick trip right now. Because if I don't, then, when *we* go in, we'll have to make those extra stops . . . " She had a picture in her mind, all too clear, of bleeding on his Mercedes.

He crossed over to a corner, picked up a garden hose,

130

turned it on. He moved the hose quickly, fretfully even, up and down across the vegetables. A corner of her mind remembered that vegetables should be irrigated, really, never watered from above. Her mother used to say that. Because the sun burned the leaves, was that it?

"What it is," she said nervously, "is that, see, it really started in a rush, so I don't feel too terribly secure right now. So I'll just go in and be back in half an hour and then we can have the regular excursion later." She was also embarrassed, as well as sad, that their wonderful lovemaking would be cut into by this boring, inevitable, biological accident. Couldn't she have managed all this better than to have this start—and so clumsily—on only her second day up here?

"Didn't you know it was going to start?" He appeared to echo her thoughts, still moving the hose, this way, that way, over the plants.

"Actually," she said lightly, "no. That is, I didn't expect it until next week." She could feel blood soaking through her makeshift wad of toilet paper. "Look, I'd better be going." But she turned to go back inside. She'd better fix it again. (Really, did she get the dates wrong?)

"You could walk to the general store right down the road. Of course, I don't know if they even *carry* that sort of thing. It's mostly for fishermen—beer and bait, and that sort of thing."

But she didn't want her first appearance, her first purchase, to be for that.

"Look, it's really easy . . . "

"*Didn't,*" he shouted to her as she turned toward the house, "didn't you think to bring something with you? I can't imagine why you wouldn't do that. It's not exactly a *surprise,* is it? It shouldn't be, it comes once a *month,* every thirty days, I don't see why a woman should be so *surprised* by that."

She turned around. She blinked. The sun was shining, the greens of the lawn, the garden, the vines covering the hotel, were as brilliant as ever, more so. He was still watering.

131

"I *told* you," she said, more lightly than before, "I didn't know I was getting it. It wasn't supposed to be until next week."

"I'm sorry, I just can't believe that. A woman has got to keep better track of herself than that."

She waited. He watered.

"Well, anyway," she said, "I'm going."

"Another thing. Another thing." His voice was shaking. "Why'd you come up this weekend anyway? You could have waited. Since you knew, you must have known, your period was coming . . . "

She considered answering, but the bitterness of having made the trip at all, using her own money—it was all right for *him,* his family was rich!—the bitterness of Reggie at home alone, if only for this preliminary weekend, the injustice of *him,* harvesting early vegetables, while she drove through heavy traffic tracking stories no one cared about; the bitterness, finally, of having been left by her husband, in every sense of the word, to fend for herself, of being, if not for this cluck, who can't even water his plants the right way, a woman forever alone with two children, choked her with rage. And this was only the first morning.

"Look, I can't just be standing here," she said. "Anyway, I'll just be gone a half hour." She considered arguing from a position of sweet reasonableness ("Look, Marc. Why are you *doing* this? Whatever is it, really, that's upsetting you so!") But she didn't care, she was as angry as he was, perhaps, maybe.

"Is that the way it's going to be with you up here?" he asked her. His voice trembled. He stood in what was now almost a swamp, his plants bowing, sinking, awash in rivulets of mud and moving water. "You're just going to come up here and do everything the way you want!" And he turned the hose directly on her, then flung down the hose and stamped away. She turned, went upstairs, snapped shut the

132

bag. She hauled it painfully into the kids' room and did the same to Dinah's little canvas carry-all.

She carried the two bags down the hotel's center staircase and into the kitchen, where the children were at the table, playing Scrabble. She saw them both smiling, their heads bowed, over their game. Then she spoke to them.

"Josh, Dinah, your father and I, I think we've made a mistake." But it was too ridiculous. Ruth was thirty-six, Marc forty. If they had been lovers for only three weeks, they had been acquaintances for over twenty years. Certainly they had a reputation as grown-ups to maintain. She raised her voice. "We seem to have made a mistake," she said, crying. Dinah, with terrible poise, got to her feet. Josh covered his face with his hands and began to sob. The world was crazy. Dinah looked at her mother, then bent over the boy. He didn't push her away but cried in her arms. "I'm sorry," Ruth said. "Come on, Dinah." It was still no more than eleven in the morning. What had happened? She couldn't even tell what had happened.

"OK. OK. Come on."

She walked with her daughter out to the front porch, on to the driveway. (How pretty it was here! What a shame to leave it! How pretty it is here.) Dinah got into the car. One suitcase in the trunk, one in the back seat. There. The sobs followed them out on the sunny air. Where was Marc? It would be appropriate to say goodbye. Wouldn't it? Wouldn't it be? She started the motor, backed out of the driveway, got on the pretty country road which would take them to Nanaimo, and then to the highway which bisected the island, going south to Victoria.

It was about twenty miles to the highway. Then an hour to the city. Then nobody could find her. She didn't hurry though. It was a beautiful day, horses grazed in the fields, a thin edge of ground fog was just disappearing off the line of the mountains. She couldn't think of anything to say to Di-

133

nah, and so she didn't say anything. She was waiting for Marc
to catch up with her, and sure enough, in ten minutes or so
she saw his Mercedes in the rear-view mirror. She sped up,
but he too increased his speed, and honked his horn repeatedly. She looked for a wide place in the soft shoulder and
stopped. He pulled in behind her.

"You can't do that, you can't do that!" He yelled into the
window at her. But there was all the difference in the world
in his voice, his stance. He was ordinarily angry because she
had done an ordinarily irresponsible thing.

"I can if I want to, you don't own me yet!"

Dinah began to sniffle.

"OK, get out of the car, let's talk about it."

They stood companionably in the sun, leaning against the
warmth of the car.

"That was terrible to leave Josh alone like that."

"But that was *crazy,* making that crazy *scene!* Over nothing!
And squirting me with that water. I can't *take* that, I'm not
going to take that!" All the while it struck her that this was arguing in a major key, that this was perfectly OK.

"I *didn't* squirt you with the water."

"Are you kidding? Are you kidding? Ha ha ha!" She shouted histrionically, but didn't really argue the question, since
he had refrained from mentioning, a second time, his son.

"You want to go back?" he offered, staring across the glit-
tering, steaming fields, to where horses cantered, snuffled,
sauntered, whimpered.

She shrugged, got back in the car. Dinah had geared up
her crying.

"Come on, kid, cut it out."

"But where are we going? What are we *doing?*"

"People fight sometimes, is all. It's nothing to worry
about." A blatant, immoral lie. Dinah dried her tears.

Marc followed them in his car, pulled up behind them in
the little circular driveway on the island side of the hotel. As
a family group they entered, together.

"I'm sorry, Josh, I'm sorry," Ruth said to the boy, but he looked at her wearily and went upstairs. Dinah followed him.

"I don't know, I don't feel too much like going for a drive right now, and I *certainly* don't feel like making it into Nanaimo." Marc giggled nervously. She giggled too.

"Look, I *have* to get to the bathroom, and I *have* to get to a drugstore."

"Look, well, ah, if it really isn't the right time for your period . . . "

"I swear it, I swear it!"

They laughed out loud.

"Maybe you'd like to get to a doctor . . . "

She saw no need for it but was glad to comply with one of his requests. And a country doctor told her that it wasn't her menstrual flow at all, but a piece of membrane, which having sloughed off in their energetic coupling, could be cauterized, and was. Once "home," she cleaned herself and looked forward again to the evening in a way that delighted, horrified her. (Because that must have been it, mustn't it? That sex, being irrational, could give rise to such irrational behavior? Couldn't that have been it? Mustn't that have been it?) Once home from the doctor's they met the children in the large kitchen and made four kinds of grilled sandwiches, taking turns using the little broiler which Marc kept on his sink. Josh didn't speak to the adults but he clowned and laughed with Dinah.

Ruth and Marc spent the afternoon walking by the bay. She thought that he seemed tense, but after all, she'd already left him once, before she'd been here even twenty-four hours. So naturally, he'd be tense. Wasn't that strange of her to do that? Strange of him?

And late, late at night she thought of this, or assigned herself to think of it, but he was sleeping so sweetly, so matter-of-factly; there was something so matter-of-fact about the back of his neck, his fine broad neck; so much more stable, in his body, than her husband ever was, that she couldn't think about it much. Her own body, so happy, melted against the warmth of him, of the waterbed. It wasn't so much; everybody quarrels. She planned to think about it, but she went to sleep. The crime against the children she dismissed. She'd trained herself for years not to think about that.

VI

It is easy to pass the town of Cedar Bay. It is an effort to get
to Vancouver Island in the first place; a plane ride, a boat
trip, a crossing of water and leaving of cities. It is vacation,
Vancouver Island, tourists eating store-bought cake in the
drafty, high-ceilinged tea room of the Empress Hotel; row
upon row of luggage in the lobby from Saskatchewan, Manitoba, Alberta, Quebec; from Burma, Brazil. The tag ends of
the world vacation for a day, or two, at the Butchart Gardens, the totem poles, the Empress. Then the trip is back, to
Tokyo, Rio, Alaska, Seattle. Only a very few, American hippies or middle-aged couples in search of a profounder life,
take the island highway north from Victoria to Duncan, Ladysmith, Nanaimo, and all that lies beyond. They're looking
for larger life, trees felled by hardy loggers, big fish hauled
up in handmade nets, a few chilly rounds of golf played out
on raw new grass.

Even the hardy traveler, heading as far north as the Camp-

137

Carolyn See

bell River for the salmon fishing, may miss the turnoff to Cedar Bay, miss it because there is no sign, among the roadside stands offering fresh strawberries or tire repair, no clue at all that a simple turn to the right leads away from Mill Harbour (where a trailer court overlooks a bay of its own, entirely filled, in summertime, with the split corpses of freshly felled trees) north to Cedar Bay, where nothing at all is happening—if you discount the yacht landing at the south end of the bay and the lumpy little peninsula to the north, where a few cement houses cluster together to form a town so new it doesn't have a name. The shrimp boat sails out from the no-name dock before dawn every morning, and returns each afternoon about four, its cargo already cooked and ready to buy, tentacles tangled together in boiling, stinking seawater.

Between the yachts and the cement houses, twenty miles from the main highway, lies the town, or at least the old hotel and grocery store, of Cedar Bay. There is more here, certainly, than these two enterprises; a line of houses along the cliffs above the strand, lost among dogwood, pine, the ubiquitous maple. No one can tell just who lives here; these houses, like the yachts at the bay's south end, are empty as often as lived in, all rocking silently in waves or trees, open maybe a month of the year, or six months, or a week. Down on the narrow shelf of flatland between cliffs and shore a few houses pack together, newly built, raw stucco, concrete block, fitted out with the newest in storm drains, concrete ditches, screen doors, and plastic trikes, the homes of loggers, or merchants from Duncan or workers in the new light industry some other place inland. A few living room windows sport stickers from the Chamber of Commerce in Nanaimo or Duncan, or even Victoria to the south. There is no Chamber of Commerce in Cedar Bay; there is no commerce.

But there is a main street, and on the street, between road and shifting, grayish shale, the grocery store, with its own floating dock. Church socials are advertised on the store's outdoor bulletin board (but the church, both churches, are

138

inland, in Nanaimo). School dances once a week (but the high school is south, in Mill Harbour, where the people are, where logs cram the bay like fiddle sticks). Vacuums are offered for sale or rent or trade; power mowers, power saws, hand lathes, outboard motors, skiffs, sabots, trailers, campers, mobile homes, motors, bicycles, rucksacks, pup tents.

It rains almost every day in Cedar Bay, even in the summer, and the ink on every card is running, weeping, in the cloudy, drizzly weather. No one answers these advertisements. The cards stay up from month to month; no one lives in this town, really. Fishermen come in for salmon eggs, a pint of whiskey, and crackers damp with salty fog. They hire one of the two boats which lie bobbing at the far end of the grocer's floating pier. The fishermen come back in the afternoon, buying Jergen's Lotion for their cracked and chapping knuckles, and another pint against the weather; they stow their gear and their few fish in back of station wagons or campers or pickup trucks, and make it home before dark. The one or two wives who come into the store to buy groceries for dinner ignore these fishermen, and the fresh filets of fish which pretty nearly always stock the butcher's counter. They head instead for the meat in "frozen food," each anonymous two-pound slab wrapped like a gift in old-fashioned waxed paper. The fishermen head for Duncan or Nanaimo and rum and Cokes, a big steak from the mainland, and a baked potato, with sour cream.

The road to Cedar Bay winds right from Nanaimo toward the sea through bright green hills. Ground fog races down pine-dotted slopes, obscuring Kelvin Creek Ranch ("Ranch house accommodations on working ranch. Smoking indoors discouraged. Dean and Dede Zerk"). Kelvin Creek widens, thickens, requires a bridge ("Silver Bridge Inn. Color Cablevision. Sauna. Putting green. Frank and Elsie McWhinnie"), and unwinds, with steady purpose. The road turns left at Silver Bridge, as if it were going somewhere; north, all the way to the Campbell River. The road continues a quarter of a

139

mile, a half, and stops short up against a cliff. Cedar Bay. At the top of the cliff stands a national monument, with whitewashed signs, two benches, and a tiny cannon imbedded in cement, pointed belligerently at the mainland. The monument cannot be reached from Cedar Bay; there is no sign, no clue, that the monument is there, eight hundred feet above. The road does not go up, or through. No, the road to Cedar Bay, which began so promisingly, simply stops; comes up short against shale cliffs. Out along the cliff's intersection with the sea, oysters pack, promiscuously, in layers. But there is no sign, no clue. The impulse is to stop the car (or carriage, or wagon) and *sit*, listening to the soothing lap of inland waves, the complaining wheeze of pine. It is trouble, too much trouble, to turn your car around. (The road *ends* here, stops short; there is no convenient cul-de-sac.)

Perhaps it was this which led someone, in the last century, to build the Cedar Bay Inn. He built it from cement, even in those days, disdaining the trees that grew on three sides of him. Good gray cement, mixed on gray shale beaches seventy, a hundred years ago, indestructible, sheltered from north winds by the cliff, from hostile armies by the lonely cannon eight hundred feet up. Did soldiers come down, on weekends, lonely evenings, and huddle on cement benches, drinking beer or Lemon Hart? Was there mining, or the thought of it? Why is this place here, when Cedar Bay has no river, no currents suitable for logging, where industry is nil and pleasure the same? Kelvin Creek is a "working ranch," with genuine, if stringy cattle. Frank McWhinnie found a flat place and a need, and put in his putting green. The builder of Cedar Bay Inn had no such enterprise. Perhaps he was afflicted by apathy rather than ambition, and coming, unexpectedly, to the end of the road, simply laid about him, rather than turn around.

The Cedar Bay Inn may give the town its name. Its history is shrouded in conjecture. Or perhaps the inhabitants simply won't tell Marc Mandell about it. They appear to hate him, and no particular wonder: ("Cedar Bay Inn, twenty miles east of Duncan. Sleeping rooms, most with private bath. Balcony overlooks Cedar Bay. Cocktail Lounge. Beer Bar. Bathing. Marc Mandell, Linda Blue Eyes"). Five miles north, thirty-six settlers have chattered countless times about incorporating; shouldn't they be Shrimp Bay, Shrimp Cove, Shrimp Harbour? But shrimp live in every cove and harbor on this island, and there is only one Cedar Bay Inn. The grocery store, on the grubby counter by the cash register, by the salmon eggs and ChapStick and ancient cardboard stuck with trout flies, carries a small box of postcards done in pen and ink. *Cedar Bay Inn,* the facsimile handwriting reads, *1927.* The building is charming seen like that, long and low, with a porch facing the road, an arcade to shade the weary traveler, and huge shade trees above, to complete the design. Who lived there then? Who managed it? So far the grocer hasn't answered Marc Mandell's questions. He spoke neither to Mandell nor to Linda Blue Eyes, who two years ago had her picture taken in front of this same store, naked, her only garment an American flag wrapped around her slender body, to celebrate the Fourth of July.

"I told her we shouldn't do that," Marc Mandell said, "I told her we should get married, or at least say so for the tourist directory. But she wouldn't do it."

"Which?"

"She wouldn't tell a lie, she wouldn't get married. Either one. We didn't get a single customer. We put up a sign at the grocery store and somebody took it down the very same day."

It was by now another Fourth of July. A month since Ruth had seen Reggie. Two weeks since Ruth had phoned the station turning her vacation into something else. (And spoken to Ed. "Okay, babe," he had said laconically. "See ya.") Six weeks since that first weekend. Now the sun came out each morning, rain fell in the afternoons. Dinah and Josh played by themselves, to her fear, along the rasping gray shale beach

141

where they might drown, or in the pine-shrouded gloom of endless forest, where they might get lost. A hundred yards away, in front of the grocery store, some kids from Cedar Bay played, on bicycles, their heavy shoes grating on the ground, scraping loutishly on gravel. Dinah and Josh stayed away from them.

"Don't you know those kids, Josh?"

"Sure. I know them from school."

"Aren't they nice?"

"Sure. They're nice."

"I just thought, if you . . ."

But there was enough for her to do, to think of. The inn itself, intractable and cold, potentially so beautiful. Last summer, Marc (and Linda Rat Eyes, God damn her undeveloped body, malnourished little ribs) had brought in steer manure, grass seed, rose bushes. There was no snow in Cedar Bay, to speak of; the Japanese Current took care of that, and around a couple of trees already growing on the ocean side of the inn they had fashioned a creditable garden—growing, the natives must suppose, entirely against nature—that soft green turf almost all the way down to the beach.

Ruth could turn her talents to the inside of the inn. The building was simple, perfect—a doll's house, the skeleton for a dream existence. A gravel drive sloped from the road to the inn's porch and old-fashioned front door. There was a tiny "office," a kitchen, and what might be a dining room to the left, and on the right, that large airy room which opened french windows onto the veranda, and then the lawn, and then the gray sea. "They have two kinds of bar here, we found out," Marc repeated hopefully. "Beer bars for young kids, where all you can serve is beer and tomato juice. And then regular cocktail bars, which they fix up like regular English pubs . . ."

"Have you ever been to England?"

"Well, *yes*, for a week, with Katherine. And actually, I never saw the kind of thing they've got around here. But they're very nice. Like I told you. I wanted to do that first, so we could start making some money. But Linda couldn't get behind it. She hated the idea of people drinking."

"What about the beer bar?"

"We didn't do that either. Well, hell! We've, we'd only been here a little over a year."

After the garden Marc and Linda had done the upstairs, and Ruth, in some pain, had to admit that it was beautiful. Six rooms, all with balconies looking out over the flat and luminous bay, the snow-covered peaks beyond. Four bathrooms. They had started—the two of them, during the bitter winter, at the far end of the upstairs hall, and papered, painted, cleaned, while Josh spent his time in school, and the natives of Cedar Bay had laconically gone about their daily work. Marc Mandell had renewed his acquaintanceship with his mother, had persuaded her to take a few walking trips through Beverly Hills boutiques which sold the best in French wallpaper. Flowers, paisleys, even some satin stripes. ("I got a thousand-dollar easel out of her once, like that. She tried to weasel out of it with some kind of chickenshit Akron thing. But I kept telling her I had to have it, I couldn't do my work without it. It was only a thousand dollars! Finally, she did it. She made a fuss, but she did it. I've done a lot of thinking about it—I used to talk to Patty about it, and I finally decided that damn business of my dad's took a big chunk out of my childhood, it took him away when I needed him, so it—she!—can damn well pay me off.")

Mrs. Mandell had found the money, had sent roll after roll of the finest papers to the post office in Duncan. Week after week, the forty-year-old Jewish dropout and the girl young enough to be his daughter had made the trip on muddy roads and picked up cylindrical packages and paste while suspicious clerks answered their greetings with the curtest of grunts and nods. Mandell had bought Linda a sewing machine, and the kid, who had quit high school but not before she'd taken Home Economics one, two, and three, had sewn

143

up curtains out of all her poor belongings—lace blouses, ribbons, patchwork. The three of them, on weekends, had searched the antique shops in Victoria for marble-topped bureaus and brass beds and old-fashioned washing stands.

Just as his money began to run out, Marc Mandell appealed to his father as one businessman to another, and his father, disgusted but dead game, had found (wholesale) four tubs, four basins, four toilets. Should there be shower curtains? Individual coffee machines? Television? *No!* Perfection was what they had worked for. They had it.

Why had Linda really left? It seemed that Ruth would never know until she asked, but now, in these surroundings, she didn't like to ask. Against each flowered wall in each spotless, perfect upstairs room, there hung a sewn picture—embroidery against paint. Linda's work. The one thing lacking in these rooms—the money really had run out, temporarily—was heat of any kind. Electricity was too expensive, gas unavailable. Marc Mandell had wanted coal stoves in each room but Linda had been afraid of tuberculosis, and polluting the environment. She had wanted wood fireplaces, Marc said, she had hated the objections he made. The rooms had remained perfect and unlived in, except for Josh's room, dark and quiet, banked with objects, cold as a tomb.

Every morning they woke, to trees, birds, the sun coming up over Canada. They heard the hushed voices of the children—Dinah's more loud by far than Josh's, but still quieter than Ruth had ever heard it. Every morning they had breakfast, fixed by Mrs. Heuser, a woman from the neighboring town Ruth had found to come and live with them, against the possibility of heavy domestic work. Well, at least, *I'm* here, Ruth would think vaguely, he can get this thing started if that's what he really wants to do, and she vaguely thought of helping him, getting some kind of show on some kind of road, but although it seemed clear to her that they would need, for instance, an island bartender, to bring in customers, they still didn't even have a bar. And when they went through mail-order catalogs to pick out furnishings for this bar, all Ruth's decisiveness deserted her. She leaned back, swaying on the waterbed, and said, stupidly, "Oh, go ahead. Whatever *you* like."

Up here, no one knew who she was. At home, in her life, the phone rang; she got telegrams, sometimes, just to go to parties. In stores people followed her with their eyes. If they didn't know her name, couldn't remember her, still they *knew* her, knew her from somewhere. At a hundred and seventeen pounds, she was accustomed to feeling somewhat heavier.

Here, in the mornings, after breakfast, she walked, with a string bag, up to the grocery store. (The children never made the trip.) She had stopped wearing makeup, stopped setting her hair. It hung, almost straight, and grew longer, noticeably, curling inward on each side, with a disconcerting tendency to meet under her chin. She wore turtlenecks against the cold, although it was the beginning of July, and jeans or the long demin skirt. On that first weekend, Marc had ordered a denim dress for her, out of the pages of *The New Yorker*, and it looked almost too authentic. Dressed in denim, holding her wad of string, she came in the store every morning, through the screen door, which every morning crashed behind her with a bang.

"Good morning!" In her best voice, the voice which had queried kidnap victims, society matrons, jockeys, even a governor once.

"Morning."

"What's good this morning?"

"What do you like?" With a leer she did her best to avoid.

"That . . . meat, in the freezer, where do you get it?"

"Around here."

"But is it . . ."

"Ask the ladies. Over to the church."

"Your vegetables really are quite nice."

Not even a nod.

"I think," she would say, "I'll make up some Spanish rice

145

today." (Or a stew. Or spaghetti.) And he would watch, the
grocer, while she picked out an onion, and some carrots, and
walked down an aisle to pick up a package of noodles, or
toothpaste. If she saw a woman in the store, which had happened four, five times in the month she had been here, Ruth
would nod, vigorously, and sing out, "Good morning!" to no
reply, or to a single, downward nod. Children ran from her,
teenage girls giggled, the boys merely stared. Once, leaving
the store, she took her courage and her groceries up to a
group of four or five young men who lounged at the shore
end of the dock, picking twigs off a nearby hedge, peeling
them with their teeth, flinging them, chewed, into the shallow water.

"You know," she said, "I'm from the Cedar Bay Inn. In a
couple of weeks my friend and I will be opening up a beer
bar there. We certainly would be glad to see you all there
some night."

In silence they stared at her, plainly as amazed to be spoken to as she was to have spoken. My God, she thought, with
the worst pang of homesickness she had known so far, they
can't be more than Reggie's age. Or Hollis's. She looked
longingly at their sweet faces. They looked at her, or out to
sea, or at each other.

"Of course," she said, "it wouldn't be for a few weeks.
Maybe even a month. But we sure would like to see you
there."

"Yes'm," one of them said. She turned around, the string
of her bag cutting into the palm of her hand, and walked
away, back down the road toward the inn. Blackberry hedges
grew by the side of the road, covered with berries, with
thorns. If the sun came out in July and August, there'd be all
the berries they could use, Marc had said. He and Linda had
taken two weeks off just to make jam last year. Ruth hurried
along. The damp ground steamed. Not a sound, one sound,
except the dip and sigh of inland wavelets, and her own foot-
steps on asphalt, then gravel, then asphalt. She thought of

146

the Mideast war, of smog, and traffic. How lucky I am, she thought.

She brought her bag into the kitchen. Should she put up the stew, or wait for Mrs. Heuser to do it? She looked out the window and saw Dinah and Josh playing in a tire swing which Marc had rigged in a giant oak at the far edge of the property. They were too far away for Ruth to hear their voices, but she could see that they were carefully taking turns. Marc had driven into Duncan for some paint thinner, some white enamel. The cocktail bar was next. Mrs. Heuser was . . . somewhere. Between meals she disappeared into the village. She was cordial and garrulous when she was in the kitchen, talking to Ruth, not of Cedar Bay but of her children, her daughter, who had traveled to Newfoundland for adventure and died there of TB and neglect, her only son, a railroad man, who'd died a few years ago on the mainland, in an avalanche. Mrs. Heuser was a refugee too, to this place. But she could talk, over counters, in church.

Ruth looked in the mirror which hung, tactlessly, over the kitchen sink. She saw an astonishingly old woman, with lines around her eyes, and a nice, nutbrown face.

Marc came home a little before noon. They ate lunch— apples and cheese and wine—out on the lawn by the beach, and stretched out, with the kids, to take advantage of the sun. Toward the end of the afternoon they swam, Ruth, at least, conscious of fifty or so possible eyes on them, from different corners of the bay.

After the four of them had cleaned up, they played shuffleboard on the veranda. "This is so much fun!" Dinah said to Josh. He nodded, and Ruth worried about the loudness of her voice. Josh gave her a push, a gentle cuff in the arm.

"Josh!" his father said warningly, and the four finished the game in near silence.

Dinner on the terrace, with candles, wavering, and the first of the season's mosquitoes.

147

"Tomorrow I'm going to get to the last of the papering," Marc said.

"Say, Dad?" Josh said.

"Yes."

"Can we go into Nanaimo Saturday afternoon? There's going to be a kids' matinee. I read about it on the bulletin board."

"We'll see. You know, Josh, we're trying to save money."

"*Ma!*" Dinah said, but as the three others around the table looked at her she said, "Nothing, this dinner is good."

"Dad?"

"Yeah."

"When are we going to get to open the place?"

Marc Mandell only looked at a full moon which had risen with incredible rapidity, like a helium balloon, straight above Cedar Bay.

"Marc," Ruth said, "I don't think I ever asked you. How did you find this place anyhow?"

"To tell the truth," and he laughed out loud, a harsh noise against the acoustical silence of the deep, cushioned pine forest, the saltwater pond in front of them, the islanders who must be listening, in their cement houses and hidden aeries all round them, "I don't know. Josh, Linda, and I were out driving and we took a wrong turn."

At night, because there was no television, and if there had been, Marc wouldn't have allowed it, he read to them. They had finished *The Saturdays* for the children and *The Four Story Mistake*. Now safely braced in the waterbed against the wall, while the kids rolled on the floor in blankets as close as they might get to the Franklin stove, Marc read *For the Union Dead*.

Marc's voice broke as he read it, and Ruth felt tears sting her own eyes. After they had put the children to bed, after they had made love, Ruth lay there, warm, cushioned in warm water, listening to silence.

"Marc," she said.

"Yes?"

"Do you know anybody around here?"

"I knew you'd say that, sooner or later."

"I'm sorry!"

"You know what my father said? He said you'd last up here six weeks. That you couldn't stand it."

"It's beautiful up here."

"To tell you the truth, Ruth, I don't want any friends. If I wanted friends I could go down to Beverly Hills."

"It's beautiful up here . . ."

"But you want to go back, right?"

"No!"

"Listen, Ruth. I do know some people up here. But I just don't think you'll like them, that's all."

"Friends of Linda?"

"Sort of. Not really. Friends of both of us."

He turned over. The bed stormed.

"Listen. You don't think you'd mind? They're a little young."

"*You're* older than I am! Listen, Marc, anytime you . . ."

"No!" He turned over again, to her. Together they rode out the waves. "You're the one I want."

"OK!"

Since this morning Reggie's ghost had walked noncommittally beside her. She was the same height as Ruth but twenty, thirty pounds lighter. Her eyes were fine porcelain; she would cost thousands, oh, millions, in any art store. She was sick, perhaps; she was unhappy. Ruth had sent her one letter, received one letter in return. She might have the flu, a summer cold. She was allergic to bee stings, and during the summer bees nested between floors in their canyon cabin.

"But could we just . . . go out to dinner then?"

"Over to Nanaimo, and maybe take the kids to that show?"

"Marc, I want to see some *people*."

"You won't like them," Marc said.

* * *

Five miles south of Cedar Bay, past the yacht landing, another shale cliff rises. Above the town, on the bluff between Mill Harbour and its northern neighbor, lives a tiny community of Americans, leftovers from the sixties in tarpaper shacks, or lean-tos made of logs, or geodesic domes with one or two panels missing. Many of the homes are empty now; the money has run out, the winters are too cold, the neighbors not exactly welcoming. The settlers shopped, if they ever shopped, in Mill Harbour, Marc explained to Ruth, who sat primly in her turtleneck on the far side of the Mercedes. Mostly they try—tried—to live off the land.

"Some of them had a rock group up here for a while, called One. I let them rehearse out on the veranda at the inn. After a while they broke up and reformed, *re*-formed, they called themselves Two. I was going to be their business manager. I got along with them real well. Of course Linda did too. They loved Linda."

"Why'd they want to use your place? When they had all this room up here?"

He seemed slightly embarrassed. He was wearing a shirt, out of style now, from the late sixties. Pink and appliquéd with ribbons which traveled vertically the length of the shirt and hung down beyond in a sort of fringe, it reminded her sickeningly of the shirt her husband wore the day she found out he was screwing Jennifer. She saw Marc didn't want to answer; his ordinarily affable face tightened into an embarrassed, lying grin, an expression she recognized, knew too well from her own husband, that lying two-timing bastard.

"So," she pursued, "why'd they use the inn? Was it just because of Linda?"

"Ah, there was some feeling for a while that she might be singing with them."

"You never told me she could sing!"

"She can't! Couldn't."

Ruth looked down at her hands folded in her lap. Wrinkles. Thin fingers. An old wedding ring on her right hand.

She touched her necklace. Amethyst. Marc had bought them for her in Victoria. He *said* he bought them for her but he already had them around the house. Didn't he? Didn't he just pull them out of a drawer one weekend, and say they were for her? Well, what the fuck. Stones are stones.

They turned off the lonely bare road, onto a dirt path which headed out to the very lip of the bluff. He parked in front of a log house surrounded by junk of every kind, cars on concrete blocks, boxes which she guessed to be beehives, wavering lines of broccoli and cabbage and chard, a wood pile, neatly stacked, a refrigerator with the door off. As they got out of the car a gust of wind blew her nearly off balance.

"It was the piano!" he yelled into her ear, as he took her arm to guide her through the garden.

"The *what?*"

"A piano we had in the big room. They needed to use it. So they said they'd give Linda a chance to sing if I'd let them use the piano!"

"What'd you say to that?"

"I said *groovy*, of course," and the wind died down as they walked through onions, chard, potatoes, which grew like the sea itself right up to the front door of the little house. "What else *could* I say?"

"Hey, Marc! Hey, how are you, man!" A boy stood three feet above them, framed by his front door, peering down. "Hey, man, come on up!" There was no porch, no step, and so he reached out his hand, pulling mightily so that his visitor might climb into his home. "You too, ma'am, just step right on up."

Ruth cocked her foot and knee, stood trembling in a tiny room. An easy chair. Another easy chair. An easy chair next to that. The young man, stooping under the low, flat roof, his eyes glassy, his smile unbearably wide. A shelf of preserves, green things in what looked like water, the green stuff having risen to the top, the murky fluid left below. A tiny sink. An enormous cat. A basin, with more greens. A shelf,

151

crammed with preserves, unmatched saucers, chipped cups, heavy plates. A table—lace-covered. A chunky girl in a see-through blouse, enormously pregnant. Engorged breasts, nipples like boils. Another chair. Tapestry hangings. Ceramic knickknacks, what-not shelves. Day-glo paintings, soiled and torn. A double bed under a cloth alcove. Pictures upon pictures, of dew-covered daisies, dandelions in rye grass, pine-cones covered with more dew, nasturtiums, in bloom and dying. Nude studies, of the pregnant girl, of genitalia. Oriental rugs. Dust. The whole room not more than twelve by twelve feet.

"Hey, man!" Marc Mandell said to the widely smiling young man. "You really fixed up the place since we've been here last!"

"I'm Jason, ma'am," the young man said, "and this is Rainbow. I'm pleased to make your acquaintance, and glad to welcome you into my house. Rainbow, can you get a drink for Marc's friend here?" And then, to Marc, "Hey, man, how you been doin'? Still groovin'? Still truckin'? Still painting those pictures?"

"Ruth," Marc said, "these are my friends, Jason and Rainbow. We met them last year down in Victoria."

"Yeah, it was Marc who turned us on to this place," Jason said affably. "He said there were lots of places up here on the bluff where nobody lived anymore."

"Went back to the States," Rainbow said spitefully, and pushed a tall tepid glass of something green into Ruth's hand. "Couldn't take it."

"Well, I couldn't take it either if it wasn't for Rainbow. She makes it so we can live off the land, don't you, honey? People talk about it, they used to talk about it, but Rainbow really does it."

"It's true, Ruth," Marc said. "She really does it."

"Anybody can do it if they want to," Rainbow said truculently. She was a thick-faced girl, no more than sixteen. "Try it," she said suddenly to Ruth. "Don't just *hold* it."

Ruth sipped her drink. She saw that she was the only one in the room who held one.

"Very interesting," she said. "What's in it?"

"Weeds!"

"Sit down—Ruth, will you?" Jason said. "I have to go out and tend the bees for a few minutes. I've been meditating all day—Rainbow gives me that space—so I haven't got any chores done. Come on, sit down."

"Can't I come with you?" But already she was sitting, in a huge purple chair, her knees pushed dangerously up to her shoulders and chin, and no table anywhere in reaching distance to put her slippery glass.

"They hate strangers, the bees. I talk to them sometimes, I pray and chant, but they aren't the most evolved creatures to come down the pike. You sit here, and be welcome in the Spirit's name. As soon as I get back we'll have supper."

He put on a beekeeper's hat and scarf and gloves, and opened the door.

"Be careful!" she said.

"The bees never sting me, never. Not since I began to pray."

He shut the door. She held her glass and thought. Ordinarily, in the very recent past, she would have thought in terms of a story, not running to more than four minutes. Survivors of a movement; outcasts or pioneers? But male chauvinists were right in that one thing they said; it had taken only a month, one good long fuck, to paralyze her mind. Without a wrinkle of curiosity, she listened to Marc, talking now to Rainbow. She might have joined the conversation, but it would have meant getting up out of this chair. She peered into the green depths of her glass, as if it were the sea itself, and listened.

"Kale? *I* didn't know they grew kale around here!"

"You better believe it. Acres of it."

"But how could you afford it?" Her lover's broad back moved. He gestured energetically toward the preserve shelves.

153

"Afford? Buy! Come *on*, that's not part of my religion!"
"But where'd you get the jars?"
"Behind the general."
"What?"
"The general store."
"But *Rainbow*! Don't they ever catch you?"
"Oh, a guy caught me right with those jars!"
"What happened?"
"Oh, I was wearing *this*, you know, this shirt, and I told him the situation. I said I was the sole support of a saint, and I'm going to be a mother, and needed food, and we were starving, and how in native countries they said you needed sex all the time to build the baby, and my husband was always out chanting."
"So what happened?"
"We did it right behind the produce department of the general. He threw in a dozen grapefruit that were going bad. He came around for a couple of weeks. He was a dumb-ass son of a bitch. He brought me ten pounds of sugar for the grapefruit, can you imagine? I told him it was poison to your system and he brought back a twenty-pound jar of honey, I mean, can you *dig* it?"
"I can't believe it!"
"Jason was getting bugged, the guy was around all the time. Jason's not into sex right now, because of his spiritual development, but I was getting these terrible *sores*. The guy brought me a bottle of Vitamin E, but that was the end, I'd rather do my own work for my own food, you know what I mean?"
"How'd you get rid of him?"
"We asked him out to the house and turned him onto some acid, except it was nine-tenths something else, my own formula. But by the time he split—that was about two or three weeks ago—I had enough staples to take us through the winter. Enough flour, salt, lard, stuff like that."
"Lard? I wouldn't think . . . "

Good for Mexican cooking, Ruth thought dully, and looked at the two figures, no more than three feet away from her and ignoring her entirely, except for the public quality of their conversation. I am like her mother, Ruth thought. Naturally! She thinks of me as if I am her mother.

"What's this orange stuff?"

"Just poppies and goldenrod. Can you believe it?"

"And this?"

"Dandelions. They say you can get botulism from them real easy."

"And this . . . gook?"

"Pollen and rose hips mixed in with honey. I rub it on my stomach and my boobs every night. I try to do it every hour." She took hold of one of her gourdlike breasts. "If you *massage* them, see, you probably won't get stretch marks and you'll have more milk. With vitamins."

Sitting, as she was, at eye level with Marc's crotch, Ruth was not surprised to see a change in the profile of his trousers. But the door opened, chilly, and Jason came in, his net-swathed head ducked down against the ceiling.

"How were the bees?" Ruth asked.

"God's creatures!"

"Sit down here, can't you? And talk to me?"

"Sure."

"Marc said you're a musician." She spoke as quietly as she could.

"I only used to be one. And not very good. We were just kids, then. We didn't know what we were doing."

"Why'd you stop?"

"I got to a point where I felt bad every day I woke up. I went back home to see my dad once, and he said, real sarcastic, 'What are you going to be when you grow up?' I said, 'All I want to do is stop suffering.' I said it like a joke, but I realized it was the truth. So I found Rainbow and came up here."

"But didn't you like being a musician?"

"I *loved* it. But we weren't very good."

155

"Do you play now?"

"We tried it, a while ago, over at Marc's place. But all the old problems came back. And there aren't any good musicians on this island."

"What instrument did you play?"

"Guitar. Like everybody. But I composed some."

"Jason!" Rainbow called. "My boobs are leaking real milk. Want to see?"

"Jason made a record, before he quit," Marc said.

"What was that?"

"Oh, nothing—it came out of New York. Only a few copies."

"But what was it?"

"*The Cellophane Take Off,*" he said shyly, but she burst out, "I *have* that! I have that record! Why, I love that!"

"You're *kidding,*" Jason said.

"No, *no!* I love it. My daughter loves it too, of course, but I'm the one that even bought it!"

"I composed two of those songs." Jason sat down opposite her. "Do you remember any of them?"

"*Be-Jeweled Lady,* and there was something about a harpsichord—"

Marc and Rainbow were silent. In sweet, controlled excitement, Jason—who she saw by now was no kid, was thirty at least—who had lines around his eyes and might be someone you could talk to, said, in quiet excitement, "Those are the two songs I wrote."

"Dinner's ready," Rainbow said, and wiped at her nipples like a kid with a cold. In a haze of recognition of the possibilities of life, of the beauty of finding a possible friend, Ruth ate kale soup and kale casserole, she ate a salad made of "plants you can find right here on the bluff." She sighed with happiness when Jason, between salad and sweet, unpacked a hash pipe from behind the chipped china shepherdesses on the whatnot shelf, saying, "I try not to do this so much, since I've been chanting, but tonight's an occasion, isn't it, Rainbow?" Just as the sun was about to go down, it came out from under a harsh, heavy roof of summer clouds, and flooded the tiny room with perfect, rosy light. "Would it be all right," Ruth said, "to ask you to play?"

"Jason never plays," Rainbow said, but he stood up, and reached under the bed for his guitar.

The sun went down, a light going out. In the twilight, over Jason's head, a picture, a painting, glowed. It was a tree trunk, with squat roots, in a forest. It was a valentine, upside down, in a border of heavy lace. It disappeared, when she looked at it, like a faint star in mysterious heavens. When she looked at Jason it appeared again, just above his head. Or like . . . a tree trunk, with squat roots.

Sitting, legs apart, arms folded underneath her heavy breasts, Rainbow followed the eyes of the older woman, even in the dark, and began to talk.

"If there's anything I wish, Marc, I wish you'd come over here when I have the kid, and do some drawings. I really mean it. I never seen anyone make pictures the way you can. You made me look at nature for the very first time."

It was true, Ruth thought, drugged, happy. Look at that afternoon on her dry canyon hill. How many times had she attacked that hill, hoed it and shoveled at it. But not until Marc had she looked at those leaves, tremulous, trembling, alive as anything, alive as the kids . . .

"When I think of how you worked on those pictures of Linda. Man, she used to laugh about it, she thought you were cracked. Naked in the yard, naked at the store, naked on the porch, you were *cracked* on that girl's bod! But naked at the piano! Sometimes I think that's what broke up the band. I ask Jason to throw out that picture often enough, but *he* won't part with it. And he says what do *you* want with it, now that you've got an old lady of your own again. What I like is the way her butt goes flat there, right along the bench. And it leaves that little hole. It's a real art object. I've been trying to get Jason to let me trade it for something, to some horny bastard, that guy at the gas station up at Duncan . . . "

"OK," Ruth said.

"Going so soon?" Rainbow asked, in a perfect parody of what must have been her mother. She smiled widely for the first time that evening. She was missing two teeth. Outside, on the window, drizzle gathered into rain.

"Do you know what?" Ruth asked her, in tears. "Do you know that for every baby you have, you're bound to lose another tooth?" She ran out, crushing vegetables, and flung herself into the car.

Marc stood at the door, talking to the couple in the door, and came after more slowly, keeping to the paths between carrots, beans. He got into the car beside her, shut the door, turned on the radio.

"That was a lousy thing to do," he said dispiritedly, and started the car. He backed up, turned around, and started slowly back across the bluff to the road which would take them home. The radio came to life, and with horrid clarity, as the car plowed through dust which was turning to mud, Van Morrison began to howl, "*Oh, I can't ignore, those TB sheets!*"

"I can't stand it," Ruth said, sobbing, "I can't stand it up here. I want to go home."

"It's starting," he said, holding onto the wheel, ducking his head, peering up out of the windshield at the rain.

"How could you have taken me there?"

"I told you you wouldn't like them."

"That's not even what I *meant*! Oh, how could you be so corny? How could you keep *doing* it? Is that your only means of self-expression? Taking nude pictures of some secretary?"

"She's not a secretary!"

"Some jerk," she amended bitterly. "What I want to know, *Marc*, is why waste your time coming after me? Whyn't you just drive on down to John Marshall High School, pick one of them off the *bus*?"

When he didn't answer, she said, to herself, to him, "My God, that *woman*? That *chest*! My God, Marc, how do you live up here? How do you stand it? My God, Marc"—and again she addressed herself to her husband—"how can you *live* like that? What do you talk about? Don't you die of boredom? Didn't you feel like a fucking *fool*, following around some knock-kneed teenager with a pad of construction paper and a lot of felt *pens*?"

He stopped driving, in the middle of the muddy road. "Please, for God's sake. Don't say those things. I loved her." He laid his head over on the steering wheel, cradling his head in sheep-gloved hands. "She wanted to sing, to be a singer. I would have done anything for her. By that time."

"*It's all right*," Van Morrison whispered to his dying friend. "*It's all right, it's all right.*"

She sat in the car, looking out at blaring night. "*He* was nice," she said.

"It was interesting that you knew his music."

"You didn't think it was part of my generation?" she asked sadly.

"You made her mad."

"I did, didn't I?"

"In her own way, she's OK."

"What's going to happen when the baby comes?"

"They'll get money from the government. They already get money."

"Relief?"

"Aid to the totally disabled."

They both laughed. He put out his hand to start the car, but she stopped him with a hand on his arm.

"Marc, I'm just getting too sad."

"Do you want to leave?" He seemed no more surprised at that than at the rain.

"No!"

"Well? Then? What?"

"Couldn't I . . . visit . . . Reggie for a while?"

"Jesus!"

But she observed that he hadn't said he didn't love her, or accused her of not loving him; nor had she, even with the talk of Linda, suggested that she didn't love him, or that he didn't love her. She considered the past month. Scenery as

159

beautiful as summer camp, days full of useful projects, nights as beautiful as she'd ever known. No yearning for that nervous thing she called a "job." Only in the mornings, early, if she wakened before the sun came up, a horrible foul hole, right under her ribs.

But when the sun did come up and she could have breakfast, it went away, or faded, or filled with English muffins, something. But, to go back, to give up this, oh, she couldn't! Why should she have to? Couldn't she have her pleasure, her fun, her happiness, like . . . Jack, like anybody else? *You son of a bitch,* she addressed her absent husband, out of habit, *if it hadn't been for you.* She leaned her head against the closed window of the car.

"We're going to get stuck if we stay here much longer," Marc Mandell said, and still he seemed reluctant to start the car. "Look, there wouldn't be any point in asking her up here, would there?"

"Oh, Marc, do you think we could? Just for the rest of the summer?"

"Didn't I *say* so at the beginning?"

"She'd just be coming for a visit! But I'm not sure she'd come without Hollis."

"Well, why not?"

In an instant the couple in the cabin was blotted out by another pair; the boy far less talented, the girl an elegant little lady who saved her money from baby-sitting and allowances to buy brooches of real jade.

"Oh, Marc, I thought you only got homesick when you were a *kid.*"

"There isn't really very much to see up here, you'll find that out soon enough."

"We thought we'd spend the afternoon here in Victoria, show you the sights, before we drove up to Cedar Bay. Is that all right?"

"Of course it's all right. How can they say it's not all right? There isn't much to see though."

"We thought we'd take you to the Butchart Gardens, they have some great flowers, things you'd never see in California, and then maybe look in some antique stores . . . "

"Do they have many antique stores up here?"

"Lots. Really nice stuff. And then we thought we'd take you to the Empress Hotel for tea—that's another big thing up here—and then they have some waxworks on the other side of the bay. By that time . . . "

"I just took Reggie to the Movieland Wax Museum, in Los Angeles, for a joke."

"I told you! They don't want to do anything so dumb as a wax museum."

"They just went to one! Hollis, did you have any trouble with your mother about coming up?"

"Oh, no. She said she thought it might do me good. That's what she said anyway. She wanted me to get out of Topanga Canyon. She wanted me to quit my job."

"What was your job?"

"The hash pipe factory."

"Oh, yes."

"There was good money in it. Where are we now?"

"Coming into the city. But we thought we'd take you to the Gardens first."

"Isn't it kind of cold up here?" Reggie asked.

"I told you to bring warm things," Ruth said.

"Say," Hollis said, "where's the kid? Where's Dinah?"

"At home," Ruth said, "with Marc's little boy."

"I wish she could have come to the airport."

"She had a little bit of a cold."

"Would you rather go to the Gardens now or later on tonight?" Marc had stopped the car at the turnoff to the Gardens. He had an air of triumph, as though he had presented them with a question which he knew to be unanswerable.

"*I* don't care," Reggie said negligently.

"What's in those gardens anyway?" and apparently lest this sound too contentious, Hollis added, "I mean, when are they better, the day or the night?"

"Isn't it going to be freezing if we wait until tonight?" Reggie asked.

"The Gardens *now*," Ruth said. "Then tea, and then the stores and then the waxworks, and then home."

"Home?" Hollis whispered ironically to Reggie, but once in the Gardens he gave his girl a playful shove. "What's this?"

"A hedge?"

"You got it! And this?"

"Your average flower?"

Marc Mandell walked on ahead. Ruth hurried after.

"Are you all right?"

"Sure."

They walked further, in silence, and heard Reggie's squeals of laughter behind them.

"Glad to see her?"

"Of course, of *course!*"

They stood in line for tea at the Empress for almost an hour.

"Linda and I came here in January. It was different then."

"Lot of people here *now*," Hollis conversationally remarked.

They stood in line, four abreast.

"What *is* it, just cake?" Reggie asked.

"Well, it must be the thing to do," Marc said cheerfully, "because everyone is doing it."

"If places for two come up instead of four, shouldn't we just sit down separately?" Reggie said.

How easily she talks, when she wants to, Ruth thought, looking at her daughter, so delicately animated in her peach chiffon, as they drove north from Victoria, and pale silvery rain came down like spun glass. How well she does! How beautiful she is! And Hollis, smiling now, said, "Say, I can see snow from here! Can you ski now, even in the summer?"

"Say, buddy, I brought you up here to work!" Marc Mandell essayed, and they waited, in the car's closed-in breathlessness for Hollis's reply.

"Oh, *man*," Hollis wailed. "You got it all *wrong!*" But the conversation that followed as they turned off the highway to the final turn and the final dead end, was about the inn. The painting, the papering, even the loneliness.

Dinner was a success, and although Marc declined to read, the kitchen was filled that night with human voices. Dinah kicked and shouted like her old self, poor chimpanzee; and even Josh spoke. "Do you like *rocks?*" he asked Hollis quietly. "I can show you some rocks."

"Yes, I've worked here, been on my own, since my son, my favorite, was killed in an avalanche," Mrs. Heuser said, while Marc spooned in dessert.

"Why, this is a wonderful place," Reggie said severely. "You could do a *lot* with this!"

At eleven o'clock, when Hollis said, "Well, where do we sleep?" Marc left it to Ruth to say, "Upstairs, third door down."

"Do you know what they're *doing?*" Marc whispered later, as they lay exhausted, awash in his familiar waterbed. "If I'd ever tried that in my house!"

"I know, I *know*."

Reggie and Hollis had spoken to a couple sitting next to them at the Empress. A vacationing couple, looking for an out-of-the-way place to stay. Upstairs Dinah and the little boy slept, safely. In the room beyond them Reggie and her friend. The darkness was pushed back fourteen feet.

VII

The weekend after the four of them had taken tea at the Empress, the couple that Reggie and Hollis had met drove by. They stopped, and looked in at the completed upstairs rooms, the downstairs rolls of carpet and plaster dust. They enthused over the view from the veranda, were pleased to let Mrs. Heuser fix them lunch, and left her a very good tip. They were bound north, they said, to the Campbell River, but would be back, undoubtedly, at the end of the summer, when they might spend a few days. Did the Mandells have plans for summer boating? That would be great fun! They drove away, in their aluminum trailer, a dream made flesh. Reggie looked composed.

Reggie and Hollis often borrowed the car—not the Mercedes, but a pickup Marc had bought cheap, to carry building materials. They plainly thought the digging of a vegetable garden, or a morning spent in pasting paper on cement, was madness. They took long drives, to Cowichan and

164

Ladysmith, they ate lunch in loggers' restaurants over in Mill Harbour, they even took a picnic up on the bluff. Two or three days after each of these forays Ruth or Marc would be startled, almost frightened, by a knock upon their massive front door. "Is the place open, then?" a young logger would ask. "No offense, but is it open yet? Can we get a drink here, after work?"

Embarrassed, proud, Marc would explain that the upstairs was finished—except for the heating—that there would be a beer bar, within days, and a cocktail lounge for their parents. So they ought to come back. They should definitely come back. The young men, hands hanging apelike from scrawny arms, shirts open to show pale chests covered with tattoos, would stand in the doorways of the wide, unfinished rooms, and push each other in the ribs, and laugh. "Could we go up-stairs then?"

"Go right on up," Ruth or Marc would say, and listen, amazed, to the thud of heavy boots, the muffled hoot of some bad joke.

"Who's going to be serving in the beer bar?" Reggie asked one morning, as she stood elegantly, dressed to go out, watching Marc paint a corner of the public room ceiling.

"Oh, Marc, or even me, I guess," Ruth said. "Wouldn't that be something?"

"My God," Reggie said, to no one in particular. "*No, I think,*" she said, addressing them both, "that you need some succulent teenager."

"Succulent teenager?"

"Those guys want to see some girl in a lowcut *dress*," Reggie said patiently.

"What about you?" Marc asked.

"I don't think I'll be here."

"Couldn't you?" Ruth said. "Please?"

"The thing to do *now* is start looking around. Find a girl with a bad reputation."

"Sure you don't want to try out for the job?"

165

The french windows were open, fresh air, salt and sunny, poured into the big room. The smell of paint and sun and salt. Ruth loved Marc, but sometimes she had to admit to herself that his behind was rather large. Today, standing as he was, on that sawhorse in his loose, paint-stained jeans, she had to admit it.

"On the other hand," Reggie said, speaking to her mother, "you need to find some guy for in here."

"Marc was going to be in here."

"Someone they can joke with."

"I don't want to do that," Marc Mandell said stiffly. "They can joke with me if they want to."

"Well, then, you've got to get out and meet them!"

"How do we do that?" Ruth said sourly. It's so easy, she thought, so fucking easy to be sixteen.

"Join a club. Maybe go to church."

"Come *on!*" Ruth said. Marc painted silently.

"That would be getting into everything I've tried so hard to get away from," he finally said.

Two obvious questions hung in the air. Why had he tried so hard to get away? And why hadn't he done the simple things that Reggie had suggested? Made some effort . . . But the picture, as unpleasant as it was by now boring, of the slender, doped-out teenager, revolved once more into her mind. That little girl, wrapped in a flag, her brains and body boiling in acid. Because he was fucking his brains out, she thought again. And in the sun, even with her daughter there, the loneliness set in, like fog, like blight, like soft rotten spots.

"Well, then," Reggie said, after a silence, "we'll be going out. Don't fix us any dinner."

They came back, after dark, stoned and triumphant.

"Show them," Reggie said to Hollis, giggling, as they stood in the door of the upstairs room where they had finally moved the stove, the waterbed, the Mucha posters.

"No," Hollis said, inanely. "*You* show them."

How is it, Ruth thought, I was always afraid of my friends' parents?

"No, *you* show them. Oh, God," she said, laughing soundlessly until the tears came, bending double. "Oh God, it's too much."

Hollis removed his jacket. He was wearing a new T-shirt. "Will you look at *this*?"

Marc read aloud, from the youthful chest, "Cedar Bay Drinking Club. Where'd you get that?"

"We ordered them!"

"Who said you could do that?"

Reggie's lip went up. "Don't you *like* them?" she said vapidly. "We had them made just for you."

"Yeah, we've got six dozen of them out in the car."

"But who ever said you could do it!"

"They have a Mill Harbour Drinking Club," Hollis said, "a Duncan Drinking Club, a Cowichan Drinking Club, we saw the samples when we went in to order these. And all the kids, the logging kids—are wearing them. Hell, there isn't anything to do up here *but* drink!"

"I've lived up here a year and a half before you people ever got here," Marc Mandell said furiously, "and I never saw a shirt like this anywhere up here, anywhere!"

"But that's because you never went anywhere, isn't it?" Reggie's face was pale. "Or just that your friends never wore anything?"

Dinah, playing Monopoly with Josh in the far corner of the room, said, "I think I want to buy a utility. Don't you think that's better than real estate?"

Hollis appealed to the older man. "Mr. Mandell, Marc, we could see, driving all around here, that all the guys were wearing that stuff. And you can see it's true, really, because they don't have anything else to do. They don't go to college, they don't get behind sports—"

"There's the gymkhana," Reggie said. By her posture, she

167

had ruled Marc out of the room. He stood, handsome, but gaining weight, by the side of his own shifting bed. Reggie and Hollis stood confidently in the middle of the room. Ruth could only guess about the boy, but she knew Reggie's smooth belligerence was genuine and hard won. Marital discord, geographical upheavals, neighborhood fights had polished her like a natural gem, a perfect speckled pebble. When, after the divorce, well-wishers, or whatever it was people became at such moments, had phoned to speak to Ruth, she had stayed in a darkened bedroom with a damp handkerchief her only companion, attempting to perfect an imitation of her own heart-busted mom. It had been Reggie who had spoken, secretarylike, into the phone. "She's . . . asleep right now, could you call back later?" It was one thing to have a dad who sniffed coke like smelling salts, but to watch one's mother (frail boat, frail anchor) stray off, was another. Ruth remembered herself, at thirteen, on weekday afternoons, having swept the floors, and washed the morning's meager dishes, and having followed a recipe on the back of a box of Chef Boy-Ar-Dee, pacing the long hall of their silent house, waiting for her mother to come home, waiting in a good dress, with her hair combed, and lipstick, since if her mother had to be the man in the house, why, then, it was no more than her unnatural share to become the woman . . .

"Look," Hollis was explaining, patiently, "it's not just taking advantage of a fad, it's advertising. You get a few loggers wearing these to work, whether it's up-island . . ."

"Up-island!" Marc interrupted scornfully.

". . . up-island or over there in Mill Harbour, people are going to know there *is* a Cedar Bay Drinking Club. Why, there are people up here, never heard of this place and they live five miles away!"

"The one thing to do," Reggie said, "is to *start*—when are you going to open, really open?" Again she spoke to Ruth, not directly avoiding Mandell, but simply taking it that she and her mother were alone in the room.

"August."

"Then the thing to do is get out now, a little bit every day, and talk about this place. Put up signs—little ones—" she hastily said, "tack them up on phone poles. Go to some churches, some restaurants, young people's clubs, go somewhere. *You* don't have to go if you don't want to, *we'll* go around, for as long as we're here . . ."

"Where," Marc interrupted her stiffly, "do you suggest that we start? There aren't too many people around here, you may have noticed."

"That thing. The gymkhana. You take a stack of shirts, and cheer for the winners, and *you* know, just *do* it. Enter the games . . ."

"My God," Marc said bitterly, "I came all the way up here for that."

"What's a gymkhana?" Dinah asked.

"*I* don't know! You . . . hit the bell and ring it if you're strong. You . . . sack races, potato races."

"Can *we* go?" Dinah said, her voice rising.

"We'll see."

"Yes," Reggie said directly to her sister, leaving her mother out. "Josh can go, if his dad will let him, and Hollis and I'll take you."

"Can I be in the sack race?"

"We'll be hitting the sack right now, ourselves," Hollis said diplomatically, and they were gone.

"Well," Marc said. "Does anyone want another chapter of *Then There Were Five?*"

"No," Dinah said rudely. "We want to finish this game."

The rain came down. The whippet scratched on the balcony screen and was let in. Marc Mandell read to himself, *The Forty Days of Musa Dagh*. Ruth read *The Picture of Dorian Gray*. Around ten the rain intensified. They could hear—if

169

they were listening—the pines moan. The insistent sea speeded up, scratched on gravel, and scratched again.

"Aren't you guys about finished?" Ruth asked once.

"In a minute," Dinah said testily. "I'm winning."

"She's not winning," Josh said.

"Josh!"

"She's not," he whispered.

"Leave the game now," Marc said.

"Ah, *Ma!*" Dinah said, in a voice which might have seemed loud to some, but which her mother heard as pounds lighter; light-years away. Well, maybe that was good.

Josh was already picking up the game, putting it away in the box. His father favored neatness; the game would remain unsettled.

Alone, in bed, Ruth reached out and took Marc's arm. He rolled over, put his arms around her. "She's right, you know. I want this place to be perfect. Do you ever look at those rooms? The ones we finished, Linda and me? They're perfect. I know there's a whole part of me that just wants to be up here, with you—and the kids, of course. I'm not sure I even *want* anybody else."

Ruth lay beside him. He always pulled the drapes and closed every window before he went to bed. They were in a black cave.

"I hope I didn't hurt her feelings."

"Oh, no."

They made love, sadly.

But next morning, the storm clouds had cleared away. The sun poured generously in, through sparkling french windows onto spotless linen, while, at three separate tables for two, the six ate their breakfasts, chatting about the work ahead, like jovial acquaintances, strangers. Nothing was said about the T-shirts, but Marc suggested that—if Reggie and Hollis wanted to, of course—they might drive on down to Victoria and see about the shipment of equipment for the beer bar. They left right after breakfast, making two heavy grooves in the gravel in front of the inn. It seemed only natural to send Dinah and Josh out with leaf rakes to repair the damage, remake the pattern. The place, she looked at it from outside, was beginning to look wonderful. The small hotel of the song. A dream house full of rooms where all the debris of the past might be put in order. Or was it only that the weather was better?

Marc was already at work in what would be the lounge, sawing lengths of wood for the bar. They had finished painting, and the white woodwork, almost hot with clean brightness, was still tacky to the touch.

"What should I do?" she asked him.

"I don't think there's anything much *to* do, until the first coat gets dry. Why don't you just take it easy for a while?"

But she was too old for that. She helped Mrs. Heuser in the kitchen with what was left of the dishes, went upstairs and made Dinah's and Josh's beds. She stood in the door of what was now Reggie and Hollis's room, and saw that their bed had already been made, that clothes were hung up, and that her shoes, his shoes, toed a line outside the old-fashioned armoire. She went to where she slept with Marc, made up the waterbed, brushed a few ashes back into the Franklin stove, closed its doors. The room was clean, in perfect order. But she couldn't yield yet. She walked down the dark, narrow, back stairs to the kitchen. (They still had to do something about those stairs!) And told Mrs. Heuser to make up a list, she would be walking up, soon, to the store.

"You don't have to do that, I'll be glad to go."

But you had to do something, even on a morning like this. So if Mrs. Heuser would decide what she would be cooking that evening, Ruth would take the list and go on up to the store.

"Would stew be all right?" Mrs. Heuser asked. "And some bang-belly. Do you know why they call it that? Because of the way it hits your stomach!"

But Mrs. Heuser was in an expansive mood. As long as

171

they were having *that* dish, why not skip the meat for once, filthy stuff, God alone knew where it came from, and buy a couple of lengths of salt cod, and she'd put it to soak right away. And a few potatoes, to boil along with it! And some onions, and butter, and a lemon, if they had one, up there, this time of the year. And spice.

"Spice?"

Yes, spice. No, it didn't have a name. It came in brown paper bags, she knew they had it up there, for bang-belly.

It may have been the changes in the list; the cod instead of meat, the fragrant, stapled, paper bag of "spice." It may have been the simple fatigue of having been rude too long, or the inexorable beauty of the day, but the grocer said, as he rang up her supplies, "Nice day we're having."

"Yes."

"Fixing cod tonight?"

"*Yes!*"

"Place is looking good down there . . ."

She had the wit to say *thank you.*

Then, miraculously, "Going to the gymkhana, are you?"

"We thought we might."

"Good for the young people. My boys go."

"Do *you?*" she said, emboldened.

"Most times."

She dumped the groceries on Mrs. Heuser's sink. The little kids were down at the end of the road, playing in the swing. She went back into the lounge, called against the sun-filled air, "You want to go swimming?"

"Not now. You go."

OK. She went upstairs, changed into her suit, padded self-consciously downstairs and past the kitchen, across the veranda onto the wet, chilly, tender grass, which grew almost down to the water's edge. She spread a blanket in the narrow no-man's-land between grass and water. Across the bay, snow-covered mountains on the mainland lay complacently, like baked alaska. To her left, underwater, oysters reproduced.

172

She walked down into the cold water, past the few, unterrifying waves, cautiously, like the middle-aged woman she was—and swam out.

To give up everything, for nothing—that was folly. To give up something, a little life, a portfolio of obligations, for *this*, for beauty, pure and simple, better than a postcard, great, unfolded scrolls of beauty everywhere you put your eyes, was simple sense. "I consider that Marc has given me the few golden moments in my life," Patty had written her once, from Catalina Island. "Golden moments," Patty had written on a card decorated with handmade tiles, and at the moment there had not been a thought, Ruth knew there hadn't been a thought, of risks taken, prices paid.

Alone, on her back, having stopped swimming for the moment, Ruth relaxed as far as she could, looked straight up at pure blue sky, turned her head one way as far as it could go. She checked out the mountains, the little hotel, majestic monument of nature. She turned her wet face to the south, where along the far edges of the bay, a tangle of hedges, weeds, vines, trees, turned prematurely yellow and red, a harbinger of winter. Would they have snow? Icebergs? How could anyone think, imagine, her stupid or ill-advised? On the one hand there was "this"; on the other there was Pico Boulevard, tire repair shops, refrigerator trade-ins, streetcar tracks which the government had not seen fit to remove. There were rapes and murders. There were studio previews, and people (intelligent people!) kissing their own hands, and blowing their own kisses across the theater, to other people who were doing the same. There were vulgar businessmen, Gentile and Jew, lining up at seven-thirty in the morning once a year, to take advantage of the sale at Carrolls in Beverly Hills.

To give that up; hot sidewalks, singles bars, palm trees with rats, burritos with fresh sauce; to give up houses, husbands, quarrels and phone calls; to give up awards which never ran to more than $500 dollars, to give up friends, drowning in circumstance and melancholia, to give up chil-

173

dren even, if it came to that, was nothing much! Like an anchorite who gives up the world, because he doesn't like it anyway. OK? OK?

A boat, far out, poked by. She felt it not in waves, but ripples. The sky tipped, and the ice cream mountain. The yellow ribbon of russet leaves bowed and dipped along the southern shore. A big, black, spread bird sailed down and across and through the sky.

"Hey, *Ma!*" Dinah shouted, from the shore. "You want some lunch? Reggie's back and they want some lunch." Ruth did her cautious crawl toward shore.

"We picked up the tables and chairs," Reggie said. "We ordered some posters—very small and nice. And there's going to be an Elks meeting in Cowichan this Thursday night . . ."

"Look," Marc said, "I might as well be straight about this. They hate Jews at Cowichan, they hate Jews in the Elks. That's part of what's been holding me back."

"Oh, man," Hollis said.

"And *Saturday,*" Reggie continued, flushed, "the gymkhana in Duncan. From ten in the morning until five, every kind of sporting event you can imagine. The things for the kids and a bicycle race that starts first thing in the morning and doesn't finish till dark, and sprints, and a long-distance race they come from all over Canada for."

"And belly dancers," Hollis said. "The whole thing."

"And arts and crafts, and high jumps."

"Gosh!" Dinah said. "Wouldn't it be great if Dad came!"

The next four days it rained. Reggie and Hollis left every morning, their stock of Cedar Bar Drinking Club shirts reduced a little more by the end of each wet, pleasant day. Ruth planted a row of stock along the front porch and potted some fuchsias for the back, the seaside view. She drove into Victoria one afternoon, with the kids, to check the price of Japanese lanterns. She stopped off at a farm just north of town, and asked the farmer's wife if she might buy a couple of feed sacks, while the children cowered shyly in the back of the truck.

"What are those for?" Dinah asked, tired from the morning's errands.

"Sacks," her mother said, and congratulated herself. Sacks, in case the participants at the gymkhana were expected to bring their own.

On Saturday morning they were all up early, getting dressed. They were all to go in the pickup, even Mrs. Heuser. Ruth put on a sweater and a long skirt but Reggie insisted that she go back and put on her best pantsuit.

"There's no use not being what you *are*," she said. All very well and good, Ruth thought, if I could just get a little information on that subject. Her long loose hair looked straggly and homemade against the expensive lines of the suit, so she hauled out her curling iron for the first time in weeks. And eye shadow. In forty-five minutes her broadcasting face looked back at her from the mirror. Not bad! she thought. *Pas mal!*

Josh wore a clean Pendleton; Dinah, obeying some instinctive knock-em-dead theory, wore her best jeans and a sweatshirt with an owl worked on the front in tiny stainless steel beads. Beverly Hills's finest. Reggie wore a pantsuit of wine-colored wool, peach chiffon blouse, close-fitting turban. Hollis put on a Cedar Bay shirt. They went downstairs, the four of them, met Mrs. Heuser, dolled up in a polyester pantsuit of her own.

"Far out," Hollis said. "We're beautiful!"

"Umm, yes," Reggie said, and fingered the tiny clip she wore, of coral and old gold. A sixteenth birthday present.

"I hope we're doing the right thing," Ruth said.

"We *are* the right thing," her older daughter told her.

"Just a minute!" Dinah yelled, and they waited. She came out of her room wearing a pair of miniature dark glasses.

"OK?" she asked.

"OK!"

Their nerve, their gaiety, dampened considerably as they approached the outskirts of Duncan.

"Do you know what this thing *is*, exactly?" Hollis asked.

"It must be, well, like a military exhibit," Ruth said. "Parades of soldiers, polo games. They used to have them in India."

"Then what?" Hollis said.

"I don't know. The Commonwealth isn't so much now, is it?"

Reggie and Hollis looked blank. They were a long way from Encino, and Low Riders, and scoring a little coke.

"Here we are," Marc said. "This must be it."

This was a Saturday, and the town of Duncan, which usually bustled with trade, showed closed doors to the world. There was traffic, however, even at this early hour; the streets were filled with family cars, pickups like their own, and farm carts pulled by horses, the rigs waxed and polished and garlanded in ribbons. Young loggers gunned the motors of their souped-up coupes.

"You know," Ruth said, "this could be very nice."

"I hope to God," he answered.

They passed motels with no-vacancy signs already up, the usual roadside stands doing a brisk business in berries, and a girl already working at the local McDonald's, on her knees with an old-fashioned scrub brush. "I'm just not sure where to go, I'm just not sure what to *do,*" Marc said. A tacked-up sign asked them cryptically, "Good Times? The Cedar Bay Inn." Under that, another sign, more permanent, pointed to Fairgrounds, and under that, handwritten, *Gymkhana.*

They parked, finally, in mud.

"Oh *boy!*" Dinah shrieked, as she vaulted out of the truck's back. "Look at that, Josh! I bet they have an arcade! I bet they have pinball! Hey, Ma! Can we have some money?"

Mandell fished in his pocket and found a five-dollar bill for each of them. "Oh, boy! Gee thanks! Come *on,* Josh! Let's see what they've *got!*"

"Is it OK, Dad?"

"Sure. Meet us in front of the Ferris wheel in an hour."

"Don't spend it all in one place," Ruth felt bound to say.

The children moved off, Dinah in delight, hauling on Josh's arm, Josh setting a deliberately slow pace, holding his crumpled bill, smiling.

"This is going to be fun," Ruth said, holding Marc's arm, "this is going to be great." She thought fleetingly of the story it would make. You didn't make fun of it, the Island National Guard, marching twelve abreast, in a very short parade. You didn't photograph heifers or hogs or pickle relish, you just looked, and maybe, at a much later date, brought around heifers or relish of your own.

By the time they reached the fairgrounds, Reggie and Hollis had gone off by themselves, leaving Ruth and Marc standing by themselves, outsiders, old folks, alone.

"Well, what'll it be, pardner? The livestock or the country games?"

"Let's just walk around," Ruth said, a little timidly.

As they walked, people who Ruth had only seen once, or only thought she'd seen, nodded cordially and said hello. Loggers. Young women pushing baby carriages. Other visitors like themselves, city slickers from the yachting slips. In front of a sculpture of wired blackberries, dripping, in the balmy summer shade, they came upon the proprietor of the Cedar Bay General Store.

"Mr. Mandell," the man said, inclining his head, including the woman on his own arm in the greeting, "Mrs. Mandell . . ."

An honorary title. Perhaps he believed it. Perhaps he was only signaling that if these . . . *Mandells,* held on, held out, they might be let in.

But past the grocery man and his dumpling wife, hunkered down between lemonade stand and corn dog booth, camped on damp, unhealthy grass, she saw—heard—what at another time in western civilization might have been gypsies, some of those last holdouts of what might or might not be a dying culture. Women in gypsy clothes, past their prime at twenty. Degenerate mountain men from Florida or Kansas.

177

Children with twin streams of green trailing from nose to upper lip. Children on acid, children with tattoos, children on the breast at three, four, five, six. The men, having brought their instruments, formed an impromptu, terrible band. The regular residents of Duncan, Ladysmith, Cowichan, Maple, Cedar, and Brainerd Bays steered clear.

"I wonder if Jason and Rainbow made it over here today," Marc said.

"Why don't you go and find out if you want to. I'll stay here. Or I'll meet you later."

No, he didn't want to. But she could feel the sigh in his arm as they walked, the yearning for dirt, and good times. She was constrained to wonder bitterly for the hundredth, thousandth time in her life, what "they," the men in her life, the forty-year-olds, saw in all that. She was the first to salute the drug experience, but it wasn't just that; would her husband—or her lover here—have run off with Aldous Huxley? What is it they *see?* In these fifteen-year-olds, these unwashed functional illiterates, that swollen bitch with her jars full of weeds? Jack had run off with a relatively old person—twenty-five, with pantyhose, and a steady job. It was grim comfort to know that he'd made Jennifer, now, into another "wife," that he deceived her with a fleet of ladies much less than half his age, ladies with hair on their legs and under their arms, and live things in their pubic hair. Well, OK! Each man to his own taste! But what did they *see* in it?

Could she trust the man whose arm she was on? Probably. Maybe. His current project included her. It's only *after,* she thought bitterly. It's only after that they pack their bags and leave; after law school, medical school, dental school. After the kids are in college or the room added on or the greenhouse installed. Only after the hydroponic tomatoes are growing satisfactorily in their baths of vitamin water and sand, do the boys sally out to find one of those girls, itching and dripping. She'd opened her husband's doctor bill—a gypsies' warning—one Tuesday night, along with a Swanson

TV dinner. But it happened all the *time,* she'd found out, all the *time!*

A ruddy man reached out to shake her hand. She had been introduced again as Marc Mandell's wife. She came back to what must be reality.

Dinah ran up, from somewhere, and tugged at her skirt. "Hey, Ma! I *know* some of these people!" She waved in the direction of the musicians, the scruffy women and their kids.

"Oh, dear, I don't think so."

"But I do, I do, I *know* I do!"

She ran off, and Ruth smiled apologetically at the man who had looked doubtfully at the little girl, at them.

"My youngest," she said. "Do yours ever do that? That need to . . . recognize, to be part of things . . ."

The man looked at Marc, but he smiled too, just a nice rich kid from California, trying to make it a new way, you know?

"You two got the hotel, over in Cedar Bay, then?"

"Yes."

"First time here?" And Marc said yes again.

"Used to be a *real* gymkhana, when *I* was a kid. The Queen's Birthday. 'The Twenty-fourth of May is the Queen's Birthday. If we don't get a holiday we'll all run away!' Have you seen the displays?"

"Very nice!"

"The best part's this afternoon. The games and races and feats of strength. Your little girl might like it, Mrs. The weight lifting, all the loggers come from miles around. And the big race."

"What race is that?"

"A twenty-miler, combination cross-country and obstacle course. I ran in it a couple of times myself, twenty years ago."

"How interesting!"

"It's not just a local matter," the ruddy man said, as if guessing her thoughts. "People come from far away to run this. From Manitoba and New Jersey . . ."

Reggie and Hollis came up and were introduced. "Do you

179

think we might all go and have something to eat? Hollis and I have found the most marvelous booth you can imagine, fresh cornbread, and homemade beans, and roast beef they cut off for you right while it's turning on the spit!" A wind ruffled Reggie's loose blond hair; she clapped a pretty hand to her ridiculous turban.

"Oh!" she said, appealingly to the wind, and looked askance at the ruddy man. But he was greatly excited.

"Say!" he said. "That's my *wife's* booth!"

"You're *kidding!*" Reggie said, surprised by this wonder into unrefined language.

After lunch came the sack races, Dinah dying to be in them, Josh hanging back. But it was Josh who won, and Dinah who came in, crying and swearing, next to last. (Never mind, the last five children, all little girls, cried, sobbed, swore desperately into their mothers' skirts.) In the egg race Marc Mandell broke an egg but was a good sport about it. Word came through that the obstacle race had started. But it would be close to two hours before the finish in Duncan, and there was still an hour or more of games. More and more, whole families took to the soft warm grass. After the race there would be dinner to eat, and after that dancing in a tent.

The sun was on its way to going down, when far off, a man's voice wailed, "Here they come! He-ere they co-ome!" Families, couples, picked themselves up to hustle over to the finish line. Marc and Ruth, Reggie and Hollis, Dinah and Josh, were lucky or fast; they found perfect places, just a little to the front of the stretched white tape. Directly across the track from them, a group of the hippies, gypsies, stood rapt, waiting for the race to finish.

"I *know* them," Dinah insisted, "I know two girls."

"Where *from?*" Ruth said impatiently. "Where from, then?"

"I don't know."

"Ah, clam up, kid," Hollis said, and lifted Dinah up onto his shoulders. "How's that?"

180

"Just fine," Dinah said. "Oh, I love this!"

But the runners were coming. The first three, very close together, running in the colors, presumably, of their towns, their sporting clubs.

"Come on, *Jim!*" the crowd yelled. "Come on, Tom!" But there was a curious emptiness in their cheering, a hollow echo of puzzlement, of surprise.

"Come on, *Jack!*" a girl across the track began to squeal, her naked breasts under thin net constituting a whole separate cheering section, and another girl—Mexican or just filthy?—shouted, "Jack! Jack, I love you, I love you!"

"I *know* those girls," Dinah triumphantly shouted, and coming down this last stretch in a terrific burst of speed, his blond kinky curls covered with a soiled handkerchief knotted at four corners, his scrabbly legs whisking away like blender blades, arms flailing, thin chest heaving, foam sliding away from armpits and withers, came the figure that haunted her dreams, lived permanently in her nightmares, sat sneering next to her when she drove on freeways, or even here, on quiet country roads. That man, that man.

"Holy *shit*," he breathed, and broke the tape, with thin bones.

Over polite applause, the two girls shouted, "Oh, Jack, oh, Jack, oh, baby, oh!"

Hollis let Dinah down from his shoulders.

Jim and Tom came in, to applause and encouragement.

"Nice race," they said to each other.

The winner ran one crescent circle in the rough dirt beyond the finish line. He leaned over in agony, he shook out his legs.

"Holy shit," he said, "I got a cramp."

"Oh, Jackie, *baby*," the two girls wailed, and ventured out onto the track, half-naked, to embrace him. But he held them off with skinny arms.

"Where's my kid?" he asked the crowd. "Where's my little girl?"

"Oh, Daddy," Dinah said brokenly, "I missed you so much!" and weeping, she hugged his sweating body, his thin waist. Over her head, Jack looked at the rest of them with spiny triumph. "Hi, Reg. Hi, Hollis. How's it going? Ruth? It's nice to see you all."

A week later he had gone. It was raining again. Each morning they all ate breakfast in the breakfast room in promising sunlight, but by ten the sky had clouded over. All last week and into this the rain had come down, placid and silvery. This evening, as on the seven before, the rain came down.

Just before dinner, Jack had driven his van up in front of the inn's front veranda to say goodbye. He had been parked, for seven days, down at the dead end of their gravel street.

"I can certainly park here," he had smiled at Ruth, who on the morning of the second day had walked down to the van to ask him to leave, go away, somewhere, anywhere. "You don't own this property down here. I already checked that out." Jack had sat on a set of pull-down steps at the rear of his van. He was wearing jeans, and a fur coat over his bare chest; he had just washed his hair and was fluffing it out with a battery blow dryer. The two women with him had been sunbathing in the nude, but at a word from him had walked off, trembling in breast and butt, behind the van.

"Jack, you know what you're doing to me!" (The old tone; martyred, histrionic, helpless.) And he took his cue.

"Doing?" he muttered fiendishly. *"Doing? I'm up here to visit my daughter. Would you keep me from visiting my daughters?"* And his voice rose in volume, a really prodigious voice from such a delicate frame. It echoed—*daughter, daughters,* into the dark pines, along the watching cliffs.

"How long do you plan to be staying?" (Icy contempt, the second step, which worked about as well as it always did.)

"Oh, a week or so," he said, grinning broadly. "Say, want to

182

turn on? I bet you don't get much of a chance with old lard-ass down the road."

She left then, walking back down the gravel path, hearing the gravel crunch beneath her, hearing her husband's voice, full of glee she recognized from happier times, saying, "OK, kids, you can come out now," and she reached the inn and went in the side door, where Marc Mandell waited for her.

"What'd he say?"

"He's leaving in a week."

"Well, he can't stay down there!"

"Why don't *you* tell him!" she said, went upstairs, and cried.

But Marc didn't tell him, didn't go near the place. Dinah went down there every day, to play, although Josh was strictly forbidden to go. Every afternoon Jack walked up to the store, in a crushed velvet tank top, holding Dinah by the hand, or carrying her across his delicate shoulders. When Ruth went up to the store, she was greeted by icy silence, icier than before. When she came back she was greeted by more silence. When in the evenings, Dinah returned, boisterous and happy, her voice, loud for the first time in days, fell into icy ponds of silence. Josh spent his evenings reading; he was tired, his father coldly said, of spending all his time with a kid younger than he was, and a girl at that. Reggie and Hollis played cribbage or gin, in whispers, in a shifty adolescent stance which Ruth found increasingly repugnant. During those seven nights she and Marc continued to make love. It would have taken more than an ex-husband to keep them apart, but afterward they fell away from each other and one night, the fourth night, he remarked out of black silence, "Do you have to keep turning over and over like that? That's a very inconsiderate thing to do, in a waterbed."

Now Jack was gone, not omitting the formalized farewell in front of the hotel. He had driven up in front and parked until Ruth had come out. "But I want to say goodbye to *every-*

one," he said charmingly, from behind his steering wheel, and the two little ladies beside him, dressed this time, had nodded and smiled. Except for Reggie, they had all come out and said goodbye. When Dinah had begun to cry, standing alone, halfway between the motel and the car, he had smiled sweetly. "Don't worry, kid. I'll be back to visit in just a couple of months." And he had driven off, down the road, past the grocery, and turned inland.

Tonight they sat in the room upstairs. Marc Mandell went over his accounts; he had just received another check from his father, who had asked in his letter when this venture might be getting started. He had not asked for a return on any of his money, had only stated that soon he would like to stop giving his son money to live on, since his son was, come to think of it, almost forty-one years old. Marc had asked Ruth about money. She had handed him a two-hundred-dollar check.

Now she sat on the couch by the window, reading *The Last of the Just.* Hundreds of pages of penance for the concentration camps, and for her ex-husband. Reggie and Hollis played cribbage. "Fifteen two, fifteen four, and a pair is six." Dinah colored for a while, rambunctiously, so that her crayon strayed onto the rug. Marc pointed this out to Ruth, who went downstairs for detergent and a rag. After her crayons had been taken away, Dinah laid out a jigsaw puzzle, right in front of the door to the hall, so that people had to step over it on their way to the bathroom or down to the kitchen for a snack. She talked to herself as she worked on the puzzle, rhetorically addressing the group or an empty room. "Let me see, does this piece go *here?* Or does it go *here?*" Her voice was raspy from previous weeping, her eyes were swollen and red. Marc looked up, every time she spoke, from his accounts, and sighed. Dinah began to sing. Marc looked up from his accounts once more. "Ruth, she'll have to be quiet, or she'll have to go in the other room!"

Now they pursued the time in silence. Reggie and Hollis

counting off their score silently, no sounds escaped their moving lips. Ruth turned her pages. Josh fingered his collection of crusted pebbles. Marc self-consciously put numbers on his page.

Once again, a wheezing hum. Ruth felt the ghastly apprehension her mother must have felt when *her* new husband had belted down his twenty-third Bromo-Seltzer of the day and suggested strongly that she, Ruth, might really do better in boarding school. Marc looked up, ferociously, waited for her to act. She put down her book and looked at her two daughters. Reggie looked "like" her, playing cribbage, had taken her "side" in the divorce. Dinah looked away from her, three-quarters away. Ruth saw the jaw, the hair, the brittle legs that came directly from her father. She saw the delicate wrists, the same wrists, hands, she had first seen, admired, loved in Jack. It wasn't true, of course, that he would be back in two months, as he had said; and that accounted for the furtiveness, irritability, despair, at large in this cozy room. He was here, God love him, he was here now.

"Well?"

VIII

Even Canada has a summer. All across that chilly country, the land swells and grows sluggish. Mosquitoes big as grasshoppers laboriously take to air, flap and flap, then settle on a body to suck. In Toronto ten people die of encephalitis. On Vancouver Island the logging mills shut down for a few weeks. One spark at this fragile time, one electrical sputter, one fiery exhalation, one unsupervised birthday candle, will send the dusty island sky high. It's hot; oh, hot. The dogs, on porches, fitfully pant.

Toward the north a hint of smoke, a car wreck, nothing more. Southward, fretful tourists pack by the busload into Victoria and the Empress Hotel. In Cedar Bay, the street is empty. Five-thirty, six this evening, some few islanders will drive from Nanaimo, from Busbury, out to where the shrimp boat docks.

Ruth thinks of sending Reggie and Hollis up there; it is too hot to cook, but she thinks better of it. They are upstairs in their room, Room Six, taking a nap; she doesn't like to disturb them. Upstairs in Room Three, separated from Hollis and Reggie, Ruth and Marc, by spotless, painted, empty rooms, Dr. and Mrs. William Pomeroy of Los Angeles, California, sleep or talk or make love in clean twin beds. He is asthmatic and handsome, she is quiet and drawn. They have four children, Mrs. Pomeroy said at breakfast, all in high school or college in the States. Yes, four. All in school. And this is the first vacation the two of them have taken in over five years. Dr. Pomeroy devotes himself to his patients and his children. This morning the Pomeroys walked out to the north beach, the doctor's trousers folded up to the knee, picking up oysters along the jagged gravelly bed. They returned, asked ˏMrs. Heuser for bread and a knife. Hollis, making sandwiches for his own and Reggie's lunch, looked sideways at the crumbling display. "You eat a lot of these up here, young man?" the doctor asked, and wheezed.

"Only for the pearls," Hollis said. He took up his own tray of salami, cream cheese, five ripe peaches, four thick slices of bread, and holding a six-pack of beer against his side, slid past the doctor into the dark hall and up the stairs. The doctor remained in the doorway, holding the knife. The butter and crackers waited on the sideboard, already warming in the torpid air. He carried a paper bag, damp, dripping, which must hold the oysters.

"Here," Ruth said, "let me do that."

"Thanks, thanks. I don't know much about it. But I sure love oysters. How are these anyway?"

"Oh, very fine." She took an oyster, set it on its side on the chopping block, slid in a knife, hit down, hard. The oyster fell into two halves. How easy, really, this real world.

"Would you like a little lemon with these?"

"Thank you very much."

Another oyster, another, another.

"Are you having a nice time up here?" And when the doctor looked at her, startled, she added, "in Cedar Bay. On your vacation."

"Yes, oh, yes! It's very beautiful!"

187

"Do you miss L. A.?"

"The weather's pretty terrible down there right now."

"I know. I come from Los Angeles myself."

"Really?" He seemed disappointed. "What part?"

"I used to live in Topanga Canyon."

"Lots of fires up there."

"Yes."

"Well, that's fine, really, what you've got there, that'll do fine. I'll just do the rest upstairs myself."

"What part are *you* from?"

"*Oh!* Oh, Westwood, West Los Angeles. Wilshire and Barrington, that's where my office is. Say, you did a real good job with these. I want to thank you very much." Nine oysters skidded across the flowered dinner plate which she handed him. Bits of shell flecked their smooth genital surfaces. They looked dirty.

"Wouldn't you like some ice under those?"

"Oh, no indeed, this is fine."

"Well, at least some beer."

"If you have some cold, that would be very kind of you."

"Would you like me to help you with that?"

"Oh, no. I've been enough trouble as it is." And he climbed the stairs, holding the oysters, the bread, the butter—the beers, three of them, against his chest, making a damp stain against his soft shirt. He was cute, the doctor. He disappeared from the top of the stairs, she heard him walk down the hall to number Three, kick the door shut with his heel. What would they do in there, after the oysters, after four children? Would passion come back to them, in a twin bed, against sheets laundered and folded and sorted by Mrs. Heuser?

Ruth had cut her hand. She noticed it on the fourth oyster, but continued her work, hoping only that the blood wouldn't discolor the oyster's soft tints. She wishes now that the doctor will find one, one thin red string, soluble, in his . . . oh, God, it's hot! She needs to lie down. She has been putting up jam this morning, the blackberries from across their own road, and up along the highway. She and Marc had sent out the little children for two full days. Then Reggie and Hollis went out with buckets; Reggie efficient and giddy, Hollis languid but bringing back the most berries. Finally, last night, in twilight, she and Marc, with the same stained buckets, under thorny shelves. He had been stern about color, and the matter of size.

"Remember now. All the berries have to be black, dark blue, dead black. If you pick a red one it's going to be awful."

"Even in a jam?"

"Yes."

The berries were plentiful. She didn't have to pick the red ones. And this morning, when Marc went to work in the new bar, she closeted herself in the kitchen with berries, pots of them, and scalded clean glasses, and paraffin, and sugar. The difference between doing a story and being one. Reggie and Hollis had left early on Marc's instructions, and in Marc's pickup truck, to pick up a load of chairs for the beer bar. They had been back by noon, she'd heard them laughing. And going upstairs. Ruth's legs ached. She walked out of the kitchen, wiping her hands on a dishcloth, pressing her hair over her ears with her fingers. That finger, on her left hand, kept bleeding. She opened the double doors to their new bar, their bourgeois pride. Six upholstered chairs, two polished coffee tables, three floor lamps, white net curtains against the french windows and the view of the bay. A game of electronic tennis still in the mail, even now making the trip up from the continental United States. While the loggers, the young bloods, disported in the far drinking room, taking their quantities of draft beer and tomato juice, the town's gentry, please God, and if there were any, might lounge in here, taking Irish coffees and golden gin fizzes and tequila sunrises. And might they come, these winter evenings coming, from as far away as Victoria, as far away as the good doctor Pomeroy himself. It was a beautiful place they had here.

Marc was at the far end of the room, in the octagonal wet-bar he had constructed, an indoor gazebo against the British bulk of the rest of the drinking room. Inside those eight plywood flimsy walls, fitted according to homemade plan, coated with padding and red vinyl, studded with dull clamps and nails, was a tiny stainless steel sink with running water, a plastic partitioned tray with green and black olives, red and green cheeries, pickled onions. While Reggie and Hollis drew beer, dispensed it nervously to kids their own age, Marc Mandell, lately of Los Angeles, and Betty Coed of Hollywood had stood, these past five evenings, behind this bar.

"Yes, yes, a brandy alexander, how is that made, then?" Aping the prevailing almost British accent. "Just wait a minute now, till I look it up in my book, oh, it's a *blender* one, is it?" Tall and exotic, Californian and rich, lounging behind shallow leaves of plywood and vinyl, veiled and elusive, a sloe-eyed six-foot-three beauty, perfect looking in the indirect bar-lights which he seemed to have rigged for the sole purpose of making himself beautiful.

Five nights they had done this, in their little enterprise, their castle. Five nights: Friday night, their grand opening, not very well attended; Saturday night, when there had been some unpleasantness down at the beer bar and Reggie had run upstairs weeping. And Monday, Tuesday, Wednesday. So-so nights. Now they waited for the weekend. Marc knelt within the confines of the diminutive octagonal bar. Oh, those shelves! Each one cut to order in a neighbor's miter box, hammered with slim and perfect nails. Bottles of liquor still unopened; Campari, amontillado, aguardiente. Very beautiful! And their own.

He bent under the sink, fixing a very minor leak. The carpet, bought by the yard from Victoria, continued into the bar and out the other side. Thinking to protect it, he had ordered, not plastic or rubber mats, but raised wooden slats made for restaurant kitchens.

Ruth lifted the opening in the bar, stepped inside. He

straightened back on his haunches, still looking at the sink. She moved to stand just behind him and put her hands on his shoulders. Just to touch him was right now her greatest pleasure in life. One morning, after a night of delicious excess, while they still lay in bed, she stroking his back, rubbing his perfect neck under his perfect, miraculous hair, he had said, abrupt, embarrassed, "Look, I had a dream last night, about my car. I had it in the filling station and the guy was filling it with oil, quarts of oil. We were standing in a big circle of oil. And I was saying to the guy 'That's enough, fella!' and then I woke up. And I know enough by now, after all those hours with the shrink, that the Mercedes is, well, it isn't purple for nothing . . ."

"Oh, sure, *sure*," she said hastily. "I know, I know, you're right."

"Yes, it's dumb, I know, but a dream like that . . . Say, would you mind just touching me underneath my ears there?"

And the tips of her fingers disappeared up under this thick curling black hair and pretty soon she moved over enough just to put her lips against the delicious bumps where his neck modulated into his spectacularly perfect spinal column, and in a few minutes, she couldn't help it, she took one hand away from just beneath his ear and reached around his substantial, muscular, perfectly manly waist, and there they were.

He leaned back, still on his haunches, still facing away from her and put his weight against her legs. His head, his heavy head, pressed back against her thighs.

"Oh, it's fixed," he said, "I got it taken care of right away. I'm just worried about what the pipes will do this winter."

He pressed his head against her, moving slowly, a bear scratching itself against a tree trunk.

"Hey, cut that out."

"Why?"

"I'm trying to be more ladylike with you."

191

He turned, up on his knees.

"Hey?"

"How do you take these off?"

"Someone might come in."

"Don't you want to?"

"*Yes.*"

"Come on, get down here. They won't see us."

She came embarrassingly quick. *Cheap!* her mother whispered from twenty, twenty-five years ago. *Cheap!* her mother reiterated, but he was continuing, as solid, as calm, as unhurried as any bear, any elephant, any whale, and she came again, played out, just before he finally allowed himself.

She hadn't even remembered to shut the little door to the bar. Oh, who cares, she thought, and considered the possibility of moving to retrieve her T-shirt, her shorts, even moving an arm to that purpose, but he said, "Don't, please," and she didn't.

She only moved her eyes, up at the trays, ah, the jars, the bottles, the perfect patterns of late afternoon sunlight which glanced off the huge, perfect, potted Boston fern which hung from their porch roof, swung softly in the late summer breeze, created patterns on patterns which sifted through the front door's beveled glass panels and the thin curtains she'd hung just a week or so before—we live in paradise, she thought—the light creating the barest sensuous shift against Marc's tanned calf, turned down, still against, adjacent to her own. She heard a bird's soft cooing. Too much, she thought, you'd never hear that, not where I come from. Not even in the canyon.

"Over here, Dave."

"What?"

"Over here. Move it over here a little."

The pattern on her beloved's leg shifted. Violently.

"We don't even have a fern," Ruth said. "Marc! We don't have a fern! Marc, there's someone out on the porch!"

"Say, what is this?" Marc Mandell said angrily, in his own

doorway, adjusting his belt, standing between the intruders and his brand-new cocktail lounge.

"Mandell?"

"Yes?"

"We were told this was the place to come."

A little man, swarthy, in his fifties, his shirt open to his tired waist, stood close in on the front porch. Behind him, a crew of middle-aged men worked, tacking up plants, training plastic vines across a hastily erected trellis. The men were patient, but hurried. Two enormous trucks had pulled up in front of the inn—or rather they had passed the inn and were parked now where Jack's panel truck had parked the month before. Why didn't we hear them? Ruth thought. My God! She smoothed her hair back, as she stood (what she hoped was) out of sight at a french window, and watched as two men collaborated to set up a stand of lights in the drive, and two more men set up a reflector. One of the trucks hummed audibly. Wires came to and went from it, straggled through bushes, up on the steps of the front porch. They attached to lights, dollies, cameras. Out along the road, a man by himself poured sand into buckets and hung them on yet another machine; bucket by bucket his crane dipped. He hung on a smaller bucket, the crane swooped halfway down. "OK, Al?" he yelled across their fresh, vulnerable lawn, and the man in the open shirt looked back over his shoulder and bawled, "Yeah! Keep it like that for now," even as (Ruth saw, from the window) the skin on his chest flushed purplish-blue, and broke out in gooseflesh.

"Well," the man said, in anxiety, a frenzy, "isn't it all right? They said it would be all right."

"*Who* said it would be all right?"

But the man only said, consulting his clipboard, "Cedar Bay Inn, for two days, maybe three, at five hundred a day, and we don't go inside the place under any circumstances."

"My name's Mandell," Marc Mandell said, extending his hand.

193

"Mitchell Gampson," the shivering man replied, and extended his own. "Christ! it gets cold up here. They didn't tell us that."

"Only in the afternoon," Mandell courteously said. "Come in, and have a drink. What is this anyway, what's it going to be for? You want to use this place for a movie?"

"Just a commercial, a very simple commercial. We'll be out of this, we'll be out of your way in two days—three at the most. If we go on into the third day," he said hastily, over Mandell's rising breath, "we pay you the *full five hundred!* Now that's fair," he said, "that's very generous!"

He stood, holding his clipboard and shivering, between their front door and the bar.

"Can't you come in, sit down a minute?" Ruth asked him. "Would you like a sweater from the kitchen?"

"No . . . ma'am, thank you very much." He looked at her sharply. Ruth held herself ready to be recognized—at the very least the obligatory "You look so familiar to me . . ." but Gampson's eyes went immediately back to Marc Mandell's. So much for "fame," Ruth thought sadly, so much for television.

"How'd you find this place?" Mandell asked, putting a scotch on the rocks on the bar. "Where'd you find out about us?"

"Research crews, out of Victoria," Gampson said nervously, downing the scotch in an instant. "I don't like to drink on the job. Dulls the reflexes. You have to be ready for anything in this business."

"Just what . . ." Ruth said, hesitantly. It was strange how, in two and a half months, ten short weeks, she had learned all over again to shut up, to let someone else ask the questions. But he answered her anyway.

"Independent producer, ma'am." (Why did he talk that way! Couldn't he see they were city folk, inhabitants of Beverly Hills, Santa Monica, Century City, Venice, even as he?) "Independent producer of commercials. With those trucks

194

out there, I can go anywhere, do almost anything, and come
back with a finished product, and bring it in under the cost it
would take to make it in a studio."

"This place is pretty much off the beaten track," Ruth said
doubtfully . . . And shut up when both the men looked at
her.

"I'll have another, if you don't mind," Gampson said. "Say,
do you know what you got here? You got yourself a potential
bundle. You got all the water commercials, all the, I don't
know, the small hotel commercials, you got your *forest* here,
and this whole early American setup. Actually," he said judi-
ciously, "I could do more than one up here. I got the hot
dogs, I got a dirt bike. I got a terrific speed boat account. You
think that guy up the road would rent his dock?"

"It's starting to rain," Ruth murmured.

"Rain! Jesus!Does it do that all the time up here?"

"Only in the afternoons," Marc assured him, but Gampson
was already running to the door. "Strike it," he bawled, "but
leave the vines and plants! We'll be working out of here the
next couple of days."

"Say, if your . . . boys would like to put up here at the hotel, you'd be welcome," Mandell said shyly. "We have some
rooms upstairs, two with private baths. And we can give you
a real country dinner."

How beautiful he is, Ruth thought. How perfect in every
detail. I love his lips. I love the way he speaks. I love his teeth,
perfect square, decent white teeth . . .

"Oh, no! Thanks! This is great, all right—great stuff! But
you know the boys, here. I got them all rooms in that big motel over in Duncan. They'd be lost without their color televi-
sions. But this is some terrific place you got! I really mean it!
I think the guys are packed up already. But we'll be back tomorrow, first thing. You're welcome to watch! I think you'll
find it interesting. *You'll* be welcome to watch, ma'am."

And he ducked out the door, and trotted across the lawn
to the first of the trucks. Its motor was already running.

195

Marc Mandell was very happy. He went to his bar and poured himself another drink. "Do you realize, Ruth, that in our first real week of business we're going to be making more money than I thought we'd be making in the whole first summer?"

But the summer is almost over, Ruth thought. She was also thinking that the man from Los Angeles hadn't recognized her, hadn't known her face, her work.

"I won't have to ask my father for any more money!"

"A thousand dollars isn't going to get anybody through any Canadian winter," she said bitterly. She was thinking of her own slim savings, saved past marital debts and missed child-support payments and her own impulse buying; her savings, represented now in a few square yards of chintz, a long lonely roll of in-door, out-door carpeting.

"He isn't going to believe it. He won't be able to believe it. *Forty-one years old, he still doesn't know what he's doing with his life!* He won't be able to say that anymore."

"You worked," Ruth said vaguely, "you worked as much as anyone else."

"We worked hard, Linda and I, you and I, and it looks like it's going to work. It actually looks like it's going to work."

"Umm," Ruth said. Big deal, she thought. A lousy thousand dollars. I used to make a thousand dollars in one week. Well, two weeks.

"What are we going to do in the winter?" she said sourly.

"Why, Ruth," he said.

"Oh, never mind," she said. "Come on, be a bartender for me. I could use a drink." He didn't even offer me a drink when he was pouring before, she thought.

"We don't want to drink up the profits before we even make any," he said lightly, worriedly, and poured her a vodka on the rocks, then changed it by adding tonic to the very brim of the glass.

Dr. and Mrs. Pomeroy, showered and dressed up, came into the lounge. "We thought we'd go over to Duncan for dinner," he said, holding his wife possessively by the arm. "But look at this! Say! Isn't this nice! Can we have a drink here before we go?"

And Marc, blushing with pleasure, poured them two scotch and sodas.

"What was that commotion we heard this afternoon?" Dr. Pomeroy said. "Looked like it might be someone making a movie?"

"A commercial," the proprietor said proudly. "Dirt bikes, I believe. They'll be here for the next two days. Maybe three."

"Isn't that something!" their first customer said. His wife stood, composed, by the bar, sipping her drink, listening? No, not listening, Ruth decided. Not even listening. Just standing there, after wading, oysters, probably love, with her hair combed, listening?

Ruth picked up her drink from off the bar, walked over to the windows which faced onto the sea. This already is a beautiful room, she said to herself, a quite remarkable room. This is really a beautiful place.

Outside, on the veranda, outdoor furniture, as much as they had been able to afford, trembled in the wind. The bay, barely visible in the black twilight, showed fitful whitecaps. Pebbles grated against each other. In the dark window, which in spite of every melancholy she didn't lean against, so that she, or Mrs. Heuser, wouldn't have to wash it tomorrow, she saw her face, aging and sad. No! Her mother's face. "Ah, gee!" she said out loud, to this dark, outlandish country. "Ah, shit!"

Next morning, out on their front porch, an enormous man in full leathers strode across the swept cement, fondly touching plastic vines. "Takahashi takes you *wherever* you want to go," he addressed the camera, "even if it's home to see your ma." Recorded birds sang loudly, and from behind a constructed bower he drew a tiny old lady in flannel robe and slippers, her hair done up in curlers and covered with a fluff of net. From out on the lawn, her breath clouding the brisk

197

morning air, Mrs. Heuser watched, sipping a cup of coffee, wearing flannel robe and slippers, her hair done up in curlers covered with an insignificant fluff of pink net.

The giant in leathers stepped on the old lady's foot.

"Get off me, you nit!" she snarled, then saw her observers through the glass curtains.

"Mitch"—she waved gaily—"we've got company! Come out," she told them, waving and gesturing, but when the others obeyed her, sheepishly, Ruth went back upstairs to change, into jeans and a shirt at least. She couldn't bear that professional people, even if they never knew or cared who she was, even if she never did anything again, should see her, scuffing in the wet lawn, in slippers and a robe. Would she look like Mrs. Heuser in twenty, ten, years? Standing in her jeans and shirt as she brushed at her hair she thought no, she would be seen in something like this, inevitably, daily, walking up to the store and back again; driving the pickup down to Victoria for supplies.

She came out through the side door in the kitchen, past a hedge, around the side of the generating truck. The sun was still very low, the sky itself spotted with clouds very satisfactorily turning silver and pink. From a distance she heard an ominous boom and grumble; from down the road by the grocery store she saw the hiss of gravel flying, watched with terrible apprehension as the motorbike groaned down the road and swooped into their perfectly tended front yard. The giant in leathers dismounted, began his stride toward their little white hotel, which Ruth had to admit looked terrific in the rosy morning light, everybody's dream of home.

"Not on the flowers, Duke! You're not the kind of guy who steps on his own mother's flowers!"

Mitchell Gampson, having surrendered to the elements and wearing a huge fur coat which buttoned up under his chin and beyond, paced halfway across their lawn and shouted. Then he stopped, apparently overcome by the futility of it all, and turned right, toward the south side of their modest little spread, to where a catering table had been set up.

"Again," he said forcefully, peering into the middle distance, holding his coffee so that its steam matted the expensive fur under his nose. "Again. It's early yet."

The giant boarded his bike, skidded off in a shower of pellets, disappeared at the left turn by the store. Silence. Ruth turned her attention to the people waiting. The old lady, in full makeup, lurked tensely in her vine bower. Ruth, who had been used to crews of two or three, to lights you could carry in a suitcase and cameras that fitted on a shoulder, gazed with awe and interest at the big black truck which quietly hummed beside her. The reflector was up, adroitly taking light from the sun and directing its light into the recesses of their porch. A fleet of extra lights. Only one camera, but an enormous one, on tracks, tended by four or five men pushing, pulling, muttering to it and to each other. A young girl, with a gold chain around her waist, and a clipboard in her hand. The crane, whether for camera or sound, she didn't know, parked unused beside another truck for the cast and crew.

Again, after expectant silence, the groan, the whine, the roar. This time Duke ran his dirt bike into the hotel's picket fence and lay in the dirt, dazed.

"Again," Mitchell Gampson said, gazing as one who loves nature, past the south rim of the hotel and out to the placid sea.

"I think I skinned my knee."

"Do you think we have all *day*?" the director shrieked. "Don't you see the sun is coming *up*?"

Sulking, the actor remounted his bike, thrummed off. "It's all right," the director explained to himself, to the little crowd still dressed in sleeping clothes, gaping. "We got another one to work on later. When the sun comes up. Even if it rains. If it's a light rain."

Again the man on his dirt bike swerved around the corner.

199

Again he pulled up in front of the inviting little "home," strode purposefully across the lawn in his heavy boots, and climbed the stairs. Again he pulled the fragile lady to him, looked out into the camera's eye.

"What am I supposed to say?" he asked.

The four or five men on the camera dismounted their black machine, resignedly began to push it back.

"Again," the director murmured, pouring more hot coffee into his cardboard cup, picking a doughnut from one of the cartons, a doughnut which left red jelly in his moustache and a dusting of pure white sugar on his already fouled fur.

"This'll be the last time for today, Duke," Gampson said. "You see, man, the climate is against us. OK?OK? *Takahashi takes you wherever you want to go, even if it's home to see your ma.*"

Favoring his knee, Duke drove off on his bike. He returned, parked his bike, embraced his mother, said his lines, still sulking.

"OK, man, we'll try it tomorrow, OK? No sweat. We'll see you at the hotel tonight." The giant strutted, looking neither to right nor left, got on his bike, gestured to the girl with the clipboard, who trotted across the lawn, got on behind, held onto the broad black leather back, shielding herself from the Canadian wind, as they skidded dangerously away.

"*That* should have been the commercial," a man on the camera remarked. "They put real feeling into that one. Takahashi takes you where you want to go."

"Holy Jesus," Gampson said. "What happens now? For this next one especially, we absolutely *cannot* do without a script girl. What about you?" he said abruptly, turning to Reggie, and Hollis pushed her forward, like a recalcitrant child. "Thirty a day, deducting the two hours the other girl's already worked, of course."

Four or five of the elusive inhabitants of Cedar Bay had come down the soft shoulder of this dead end road, stood now, staring vacantly at the clump of exotic city people. Ruth felt the grocer's eyes upon her. Not ever again, you bastard,

200

she thought, tossing her head, giving the director and her daughter her best attention. But Reggie was shaking her head. "I couldn't do it," she said. "I wouldn't know what to do."

"But it's simple, *simple!* All you do is keep track of the scene, see? And this is a simple one. We're going to use a dog. We're going to have this guy sitting on the steps eating a hot dog and patting his own dog at the same time. Well, all you've got to do is see, basically, in this one—he's *holding* the hot dog, he *takes* a bite, he *calls* his dog, he *takes* a bite, we *zoom* in, he *pets* his dog, he—"

"I couldn't possibly do it," Reggie said firmly. "My mother could, though."

"*Who?*" The director stared at her. He had taken enough already, his posture said. More than any man should have to. He couldn't take much more.

"My mother. Over there. She used to work in television."

A frown crossed Marc's usually good-natured face. The grocer looked over at her, differently, as did his wife.

"Oh, but it isn't the same thing at all," Ruth said, but she had already crossed the lawn and was talking to Gampson. "I only did the news. On a local station."

"No kidding," the director said with surprise. "You know, I thought I knew your face yesterday but I couldn't be sure. Come on, what d'you say?"

"I don't know . . ."

"Twenty-five *over* union scale? That's as much as we can do."

She looked at her family. Reggie nodded, Dinah grinned, Marc had gone back into the house. She looked past them at the grocer's dull, suspicious face.

"Sure thing," she said. "How do I do it? What do I do?" From out of the second truck a couple of men unpacked cartons of hot dogs which steamed in the cold morning air. They brought out a cage with a Dalmatian who yapped excitedly and bit at the bars which imprisoned him. "God damned

201

dog," the director said, but climbing businesslike up onto the huge, dormant crane was a figure, a medium-sized man with a sweet familiar face, covered down to his melancholy eyes with a knitted yellow stocking cap. Edward.

She walked over to him, legs unsteady. "What is this, some kind of cheap trick?"

"My dear," Edward said, peering not at her but up at the angle of his crane.

"What are you doing here?"

"Little extra money."

"But what are you doing *here?*" It was one thing after another; she would never be able to run away, the world was not small enough.

"Location work. I don't mind a little location work."

"Look, what is this? I want to know how . . ."

"Hey, you want to work or you want to work? I've got my own stuff to do here." He straightened up, looked at her, past her. "It's a big ocean, I don't know what to tell you. This isn't my idea of the best time in the world."

She knew he wouldn't tell her anything else, and anyway, the press of events was upon her. It was not like being the star, it was far from being the star, it had nothing to do with her regular work, but she fell into it, slid into it, made the acquaintance of the man on the camera and the boys on the track, was introduced to the advertising men from the east— locked away as they were in the truck. They would not come out until the three spots were in the can, they were taking no calls, nor sending any. She held the clipboard that the previous, the real, script girl had left.

She spent the rest of the day holding the dog, checking the level of the soft drink, and watching with awe as the actor consumed three cartons of hot dogs.

By three in the afternoon the rain had begun to come down. The crew voted to stop; Gampson heatedly refused. "Not until it pours!" he shouted. "Besides, I like the light."

The actor sat on the porch, unwrapped a hot dog, took one bite, one chew, called for his dog, who bounded with increasing hysteria across their once-smooth lawn. The actor playfully cuffed the dog, and with his left hand anchored firmly in the dog's collar, said a few words and took another bite. The camera trundled forward during this, and back, defeated, as the actor couldn't or didn't swallow, or the dog growled unexpectedly, or ran to Ruth or to the camera, or lay, simply, on the lawn, and wagged its tail.

It took them three full days. The script girl didn't come back. By the second day, Ruth had begun to speak to Ed, or he to her. On the morning of the third day, standing against the catering table, he told her what it had been like to make the Volkswagen commercial with Zsa Zsa Gabor's mother. Laughing, she looked up and saw her lover peering at her from behind one of the hotel's net curtains. She composed her face, but later, while she held the dog against the hotel's mashed turf so that its trainer could force a tranquilizer against its stubborn teeth, Edward told her (and the rest of the company) about the Nazi trainer in town with his repertory company of trained wolves, and she laughed again.

Late in the afternoon of the third day Mitchell Gampson handed her two checks. "This one is yours," he said. "This one is for your husband. Say, it's really been swell." Bird loops, unnoticed, shrieked above them. The check made out to the Cedar Bay Inn was for six hundred dollars.

"Listen," she said, "this isn't right."

"Yeah?" Gampson said smiling. "Two hundred a day, that's what I told him."

"This isn't right, you know," she said, and went to find Marc.

He was outside, on the beach side of the hotel, planing a door to fit. He looked at the check she handed him, and walked, without a word, through the hotel. In the middle of their new cocktail lounge, where they had first heard their

203

visitors drive up, they now heard them drive away. A rumbling, and another rumbling, and when they opened the
door, in the uninviting twilight, they were alone.

The lawn was rubble, the fresh new flowers smashed, their
painted picket fence hung at a crazy tilt. The ferns they had
been promised were gone; they had been ripped, along with
their brackets, straight from the walls and porch ceiling, leaving raw brown holes in the clean white paint. Only the artifi-
cial birds remained, on record, chattering aimlessly.

"Marc," she said, but he had gone into the house.

She stood for a while, looking at the ruined little land-
scape. It was no good saying that it could be fixed, that she
could plant it all over again, that winter was coming anyway,
that really this wasn't a business. Because if it wasn't a business, what was it?

She saw that either the dirt bike or the Dalmatian had not
only tilted the fence but unbalanced the mailbox. She walked
through the yard's brown mush, to see if there was any mail.

Under a thin stack of circulars and bills she found a letter
from Connie. Ruth took it back to the porch, and sitting in
the dark, sheltered from the rain, she turned the pages of
the letter from her friend:

And so, you see, what with Howard in total hysterics,
and his parents hiring what have to be the very best at-
torneys, and nasty men waiting behind every palm, as it
were, well, I know Marc isn't going to be too crazy about
this, but I can't stay in town, I have to have a place until
all this blows over . . .

Ruth folded the letter carefully, got up from the steps
where she had been sitting, and went inside.

She paused at the foot of the stairs and looked up to where
the door was closed against the cold (and her). She thought
she heard faint music—a show tune, their only customers
must have a radio. To her left, past the dark breakfast room,

the light was on in the kitchen, but the door was closed. She turned right, into their cocktail lounge, black for the night, CLOSED. They were closed, all right.

"Reggie?"

"Yes?"

Reggie sat on a love seat across a coffee table from another love seat. Ruth sat down opposite her. Her daughter looked away from her, outside, at the window. Rain spattered against dark panes, a branch or two scratched at the thin surface.

"Where's Hollis?"

"I don't know. Upstairs, I guess."

"Dinah?"

"*I* don't know."

Ruth got up, made her way to the bar, poured herself a long draft of brandy. "Do you want anything?" she called across the darkness.

"No."

She came back, sat down. Her knees touched the table that her daughter's knees were touching. The table was bare. Her daughter was wearing white pants with a wide black belt— Ruth, although she couldn't see the belt, saw her daughter in two halves—and a sheer, white, long-sleeved blouse. As always, Ruth thought, she was perfectly dressed, perfectly calm. Only her hair, her pretty hair, missed it. Meant to be coiled back into a sophisticated twist, it stayed severely back behind her ears, schoolmarmish, or when it strayed, as she saw it was doing now, it turned her into an untidy child. (Was it the dark or her imagination that she saw Reggie as she used to be—eight years old, nine at the most—as young as, certainly more fragile than Dinah?)

"OK, kid." And Reggie shifted warily, pulled her knees up almost to her breasts, locked her white arms about white legs. "Why'd you do it?"

"Do what?" Reggie asked haughtily.

"Call Edward. Ask him up here."

"Who says I did that?"

But Reggie, like her mother, was a practical liar but not a good one.

"There isn't any other way he could have gotten here. Is there? *Is* there?"

No answer. The silence hung between them. (Questioning Reggie when she was six: "Did you get into my makeup? Did you? *Did* you?" Reggie, declining to answer, her nose literally up in the air, chin at a haughty unapproachable angle, pointed away from her mother but at her at the same time, tears trembling in her eyes, cheeks scarred with slashes of Revlon pink, lids slashed with Max Factor blue.)

"No." Then no answers after that.

"Is there? Reggie?"

"Did you walk home in the creek?"

"Oh, no. No."

"Then why are your boots wet?"

"Fell down in the water."

"What water?"

No. No answer.

"And Connie wouldn't have written a letter like this on her own. I'm not a fool, you know."

Reggie let that lie there.

No? Poor foolish lady, buying two-piece bathing suits after you're thirty-five, suffering first love again and again and again, pretending, in the most inept way, to be a grown-up?

"Because," Ruth said vaguely, "it's really rotten."

Her daughter's face was featureless, a moon, a blank. Only if Ruth looked at the dark beside her could she see Reggie's face at all, out of the corner of her eye. (Her own mother: "Get that look off your face, get it off, get it off." Even as she, little Ruthie, used all her effort to make her face expressionless, to void it of any, all trace of expression.)

And later, after the divorce, her mother a whirlwind, a dervish around the room, a blur: "You've got to take shit in this world, oh, *you* don't think so, not *you!*" Meanwhile shak-

ing out white double bed sheets like sails in a hurricane, biting pillow ticking, shaking and pushing pillows *in in into* the
slip until, her mouth free again, she whacked down the ferociously clean pillow and slip onto the bed with bitter glee,
hair waving in the back bedroom *take shit take shit!* While Ruthie, silent, put her nose up and her chin out and away from
her mother, silently, saying, not me! No I'm not! And ended
up with this instead.

"If you've blown this for me," Ruth announced formally,
"I'll never forgive you."

Syllables from her daughter.

"*What?*"

"Big deal."

"Look. Reggie. Your father and I have . . ."

A laugh from the other side of the table.

"Jack and I have been separated four years now . . .

"When you grow up you're going to have a life of your
own . . .

"I raised you kids for four years by myself . . .

"This could have been—could *be*—a wonderful thing for
Dinah. She could have a *family*. There's room for *everybody*
up here." It was true. Room for the rich man (he lived here),
the poor man (he came in his van), the kids by every previous
marriage. There had to be, in fact, room for everybody. Unless there were room for everybody, by now, there couldn't
be room for anyone.

"OK, so Reggie?"

Silence.

"You know Marc wants you to stay up here . . . *I know!*"
Ruth said suddenly to the dark. "You brought Jack up here
too! You got Connie to send this letter!"

"She's having that trouble right now," Reggie said distant-
ly. "Wouldn't you want to help her out?"

"You know he's not going to want her up here! He hates
her!"

Silence.

207

"You listen to me, Reggie! For four years I've worked like a dog, I've done what I was supposed to do, for fourteen years before that I lived with a maniac, a nut, an incompetent, a tyrant . . ."

The moon moved. Into a smile.

"And now I'm going to do what I *want* to do. And you're not going to keep me from it. Because I *want* it!"

"Supposed to do?" a voice came out of the dark, with loathing. "You did what you were supposed to be doing? Is it so great to come in the living room and see your father strangling your mother? Was that what you were *supposed* to be doing?"

"Oh, that," Ruth said, but silently.

"Is it so great to sleep every night with your little sister because she has nightmares and then she wets the bed and you can't do anything about it because your mother's gone out and taken the car and there aren't any more sheets and the washing machine doesn't work?"

"Wait!" Ruth said, but Reggie continued.

"Is it so great, is it so great to come home from school to a woman who's been crying all day and there's your little sister sucking her thumb and she's *four*?"

"It was hard," Ruth said, defensively, "but I got through it!"

"Is it so great to get up in the morning and your mother's on the phone, and you get home from school and she's still on the phone and you get to bed at night and she's still on the phone, and the only time she ever talks to you is when she's on the television telling you the news?"

"I had to make a living! Your father left. . ."

"And you're not even sure about that! Because your mother and your mother's friends are all boy crazy except they're all forty years old? So if your sister wants a glass of water in the night you get up and get it yourself so she won't meet some weirdo in the hall with his balls hanging out!"

"All right."

"And then she's a big success, see? And she calls you from

Phoenix. Only you're already asleep and she wakes you up—
*Oh, I'm having such a good time! Wouldn't it be wonderful if you
were here!* Except there's no way you're going to be there, because she's there on business, see? And you can't go back to
sleep and the kid wets the bed again. But you can't do anything about it because there's nobody there!"

"*OK!*"

"And then it's a big *deal,* see? Because the kids say, oh, *your
mother!* And she's going to the hair stylist, and she's buying
the clothes and she gets some stupid boyfriend to take you
out to Scandia for your birthday and they put a candle in
your soufflé grand marnier and the candle melts right in,
and they laugh, only it's *your* birthday they're laughing about.
And when you get home the kid is crying and the baby-sit-
ter's stoned out of his mind! It's one o'clock and the Grateful
Dead are playing!"

"I *know.* I know that."

"And then if she's not a success her heart's broken! So she
never answers the phone. She's lying on her bed crying, she
can't be disturbed. She's in the shower, now, she's working
now, *she's working now!* And the phone is always for her! So
cute, so full of fun!"

"Please!"

"And you know what you eat? You eat Swanson's frozen
TV dinners! You eat Spaghetti-O-S. You're fifteen years old
and you're eating Spaghetti-O-S. You're eating sandwiches
she picked up from the store. You're eating chicken from the
Colonel!"

"Well, Jesus Christ!" Ruth said furiously.

"You know what Dinah did one night? When you were
out? Again! With some creep? She went outside, while I was
watching television, and she stood on the patio. She stretched
her arms out in the dark, all by herself, and she was crying!
She said, 'Daddy, come back! Mommy, come back!' "

"And what had *you* been doing to her that night! You're
not such a queen, you know!"

"Oh, no," Reggie said, sobbing, her hair falling down over her eyes. "I'm not a queen."

"Look," Ruth said, "if it was so awful, why don't you let me leave? Stay with Hollis, stay with your *father!* Stay here if you can *stand* it! If it was so terrible, if you say it was so terrible, why can't you give me a chance?

"Because if it's so terrible," Ruth went on, "I don't see what you want me around for. If it's so bad" (and she heard her own mother saying, low and vicious, *why not go live with your father?*) "why not let me leave and be done with it?"

"Because of Dinah."

"But if I'm so *bad,* if it's so *bad . . .*"

"This is the only thing I can think of that is worse."

Ruth stood up. "Well, Reggie. I don't agree with you. I think, although it's been difficult, I've done the best I can . . ."

"Fuck you," Reggie whispered.

"I don't know if I can repair the damage you've done," Ruth said, "but I'm certainly going to try."

"Fuck you." It was the second time Ruth had heard her say it.

"I guess you won't be wanting to stay . . .?"

"Fuck you!" A little girl running too fast down the hall, dropping her bottle. Getting slapped for it. A little girl in a rocking chair, with earphones, singing to no one, without a tune.

"I've had about enough of you," Ruth said to her daughter, and meant it with all her heart.

"Fuck you," Reggie said hopelessly.

Ruth jumped up, ran around the table, stood above her daughter with her arm raised.

"Get away from me, will you?"

Ruth left. With her friend's letter in her hand, she walked upstairs and opened the door to the family room. The little kids weren't there, they must be outside. She wondered if they had sweaters. It was furiously cold in here, even with the fire.

"Marc, you're not going to like this, but I've got a letter here from Connie. She's desperate, there's some kind of custody fight, and she wants to come up with the kids."

"Ruth. I made a mistake asking you to come up here . . ."

"I thought you'd say that."

"You're *not* like Patty . . ."

"Wait a minute . . ."

"I can't *stand* you around here."

"Was it the work? Just two or three days of work?" (No, she thought, it was what made her husband leave, the mark on her back she couldn't see.) "Because if it's that . . ."

"It's not that!"

"But I know you . . ."

"No! No! No! I made a mistake! You've got to get out! Tomorrow."

"No *way*," Ruth said, and shut the door, walked over to the Ben Franklin stove, where green twigs whined and cracked, and sat down.

IX

"What it is, Ruth, what it is, is that you have to have everything for yourself. You know that, you know that. I'm not interested in that!"

"That's crazy!"

"*Your* kids, *your* husband, *your* work, *your* friends!"

"I don't know what you're talking about!"

"Just the way you had to go to the store that first morning. The way you want to go to the movies *you* want to go to. Never the ones *I* want to go to!"

"Don't any of your friends talk about where they're going to the movies?" she said loudly. (They had been to two movies since she had come up here.) "Don't they talk about that? Do you mean to tell me that your father tells your mother *where they're going to the movies?*"

"Of course," he said desperately, "of course my father tells my mother where they're going every evening. It's always been that way, except from maybe where *you* come from. It's always been that way. The man decides, because someone has to decide. It's just like if we were to go camping, see? You can't have someone saying I want to go down this trail this morning, this would be best, and the other person just saying—and she probably doesn't know anything about it!—you just can't have her saying *I'm going to go down this trail* and she doesn't even know anything about it!"

"I know about movies," she mumbled.

"Oh, you! You and your *friends*! You think you know about everything because . . . You drive around, and your dumb face up there on television, well, you aren't there now! And you don't know nearly so much as you think you know!"

"Well, what do *you* know?"

"I read," he said, sadly. "I read the important reviews. I read *The New Yorker*. I read it every week. I subscribe to all the important magazines. You don't subscribe to any one of them, I *know* that. Patty told me. She said you never read anything. Your kind of people think you're too good for that . . . !"

"Wait a minute," she shouted. "You didn't *tell* me! Your father comes home at night. And they want to go out. To a movie, or anything, anything like that, she might want to go to a wedding, or to visit a friend, I don't care, I don't even care what it *is*." She was screaming. "But I just want to hear you say it, you rotten Jewish bastard! He comes home, and he tells her where he wants to go, and they do it, just like *that*?"

He smiled prayerfully, put both his hands flat on the table, then clasped them together. "Yes," he said. "Yes, they do. It's always been like that, believe me. He just decides, at work usually, where they should go that evening, and he tells her, and she . . . gets dressed, and they go out. Just like that. They never fight about it. It's your kind of people that fight, gentiles, divorced people, I don't say you can help it, you were raised like that."

"Would you say," she said carefully, "would you say you want to be like your father . . . when you grow up?"

"You bitch, you stupid bitch. I really hate you, you know

213

that. I don't know how a person like Patty could be your friend, she was a good person, she—"

"Of course," Ruth said, "so good you left her flat, with four kids, but not before you broke up her marriage."

"Connie, now that's something else. You're like her, you're just like her, shapeless mouth, shapeless cunt, I used to screw her in the ass sometimes, you know why? Because I hated her fucking stupid face! Just like I hate your fucking stupid face! OK? OK? I couldn't stand to look at her, just like I can't stand to look at you!" He was crying. "Got that? Got that, you dumb gentile shit? Got it?"

"So. What do you want me to do?" That airless pause, that nothing in time, no breath, no breath; the abyss. Again, the same boring abyss. The room was black now, she couldn't see furniture or the outside. His face faded, and swam into view again.

"So I want you to leave, you . . . *old* . . . you only have a few good years *left*. So why should I have to keep you after that? What it is," his voice spinning farther and farther out in the dark, a fragile spidery thread, "what it is is that I asked you up here, I thought we might have some chance for some kind of life. I tried to disregard the fact that your marriage had failed . . ."

"Marc," she asked, "didn't you have a marriage that failed once?"

"I'm a widower," he said. "A widower. That's not the same thing."

"You were divorced once, you hypocritical bastard."

"That didn't count."

"It *did* count."

"No! Because it didn't! I'm not like you."

"No," she said. "No," she said, echoing her mother, tearing up a birthday check and wafting it, disdainfully, into her step-father's cornflakes, "no, you aren't."

Silence. The dark. The children somewhere in this building. It's not so bad in this abyss. You spin, you glide, you soar. Fish learn to live at great depths.

214

"So will you just go get your suitcase and pack it up and *leave?*"

"No," she said, "you smarmy little bastard," and it was true, she thought, never really in her life had she met such a smarmy, chicken-shit, rotten bastard. "I'm not leaving. You can't get me to leave, you smarmy bastard. OK? OK?"

Marc put his head down on the table.

"My marriage," he said, "it wasn't everything I said. At first we quarreled a lot. You could say we used to fight. I guess I wasn't so nice, I don't know. We used to have a garden. While I was still in the army we grew all our own vegetables, you've seen those pictures. When we were in the army, we had a pretty good time. We were away from the folks, that was pretty good. I'd come home from the base, she'd be ready, we'd go somewhere. But I have to tell you, when I got out of the army, it wasn't too hot. We had to see her mother once a week, we had to see my father once a week. At first, when we were first married, we'd sit on a couch and we'd hold each other's feet and rub them, me at the one end, her at the other. But then it got so she just rubbed my feet, that was it. I used to play baseball, you know me, since high school, I've always loved baseball. I used to play every Saturday with the guys I went to school with, Dutch Van Burkleo, Bruce Willock. When she went in the hospital to have the baby it was Saturday, I asked her, what should I do? She said, go on out and play baseball, and I did it, I was *right* to do it, I would have been waiting and waiting there in the hospital, what was the point? The first two weeks the kid was home, I slept on the couch with earplugs. Well, I was in graduate school, I had to get to sleep! Anyway we got through that. Years. But then she *died*, Ruth! I was left alone with a child to bring up. You can't possibly know what it was like! Oh, I see you laughing, I see that smirk on your stupid face, but you can't know what it was like. For one thing, I was glad. I was in my thirties, I was feeling kind of old, I thought *now*, I know what I'm doing, I can find myself the *perfect wife!* Someone real young and terrific, someone to take care of Josh and me,

someone like Katherine, only *more* so! I was back at my father's house, everybody was being nice to me. My mother was
taking care of my own baby, I couldn't stand it. I met this
girl, she was a clerk in my father's factory, a Ukrainian girl,
real blonde, she, I asked her to marry me to take care of the
baby. My dad was asking me where I was going at night. I
couldn't tell him I was out with a clerk. I took her out one
night, I took her to a motel, she said she would marry me. I
told my dad, Jesus, he was furious, he always loved Katherine so much. Marya wanted to be married in our house, we
have that beautiful house, but Dad wouldn't do it. She was an
awful woman. I came home one night, she made a shrimp
dish with curry gravy, I told her I didn't like curry, she threw
it right on my head. I went into the shower and wouldn't
come out. Another time she threw boiling coffee on my *foot*.
She said it was lukewarm, she said it was cold, but it was boiling hot, Ruth! Another time she hit me in my pitching arm!
So I left her, I left her after six months. She was always wanting to go out and always putting up her hair, and she hated
the kid!

"I had to find somebody for the kid, so it came to me. What
I really needed was someone more my own age, someone
with kids, a divorcée. My friends knew a million of them. I
met Connie the regular way, some friends of mine told me
they knew a nice divorced woman with kids. I called her
up—I kept on calling up this woman I didn't even know. She
put me off right away because she asked me how old I was
and I wouldn't tell her. Why should I tell her how old I was?
Then I asked her how old she was and she wouldn't tell *me*.
We went around and around about it, 'Why should I go out
with you if you won't even tell me how old you are?' I finally
hung up on her. Then I called her back. We went out for
dinner, you know about it, to Trader Vic's. We ordered rumaki and she ate all the rumaki. She ate *ten* of them—I only
got *two*! When I said something about it she said I was cheap.
I took her home, I wasn't going to see her again. I went into
her back bedroom to pick up Josh where he was sleeping—if

you knew, in those years, how many dates I went on with my kid in the back seat! How many drive-in movies I saw with him right back there in his pajamas! So I picked him up and carried him out to the back seat—I've told you this—I leaned back in there to get him settled, I got the blanket up around his neck and then I backed out of the car and straightened up and she was all over me. I was between the front door of the car because I'd already tossed my coat in there, and the back door where the kid was. She was leaning up against me, biting my neck. I turned right around and got the kid and brought him back in the house. Then the whole thing just started. I couldn't get out of it. I'd call her at work in the morning, she'd be real sexy on the phone, so I'd go over there that night and she wouldn't be there, not even a note. So I wouldn't call her again and a couple of days later she'd call *me,* crying all I wanted to do was screw her, I didn't have any feelings, I didn't care about her feelings. So I'd go over there again and there'd be a couple of other guys there already. We'd all sit there and she'd get on the phone with somebody else and we'd watch her rotten kids run through the living room with their trucks and trains. Josh would be in the back somewhere by himself. Finally, the other guys would leave and she'd ask me why I never brought over any groceries or wine or beer or dope. I'd be so mad I'd try to leave but she wouldn't let me. When we were fucking she'd scream like a banshee, I'd be afraid Josh would hear. I know he *did* hear. Then one day I went over there during the afternoon, there was a big gray car in the driveway. The kids were playing out in the back, the dogs had knocked over her trash cans in the front yard. I started to pick up the trash off the lawn and I got so mad, I thought why do I have to pick up after her, for God's sake? Then I heard that sound, I'd actually thought it was one of the dogs, it was that awful howl, so I stepped through the bushes and looked in the front bedroom window and there she was, her dumb legs up in the air, oh God, I hated her, I wrote her letters every day, she read the first one and sent all the rest back. Then I sent her telegrams they'd read to her over the telephone. Then I stopped. My shrink made me stop. Then she started writing me letters. She was sorry, she really loved me, she didn't know what made her do it. So I called her up. I called her up the day I got the first letter. To tell you the truth I was crazy about her! Then I came over one night for dinner. She was out doing the shopping, the kids were out in the yard playing. I went into the kitchen for a beer then I went into her room to lie down. There was a letter on the nightstand, in her handwriting, to some guy, telling him how much she loved him, and how she was wasting her time with some jerk, while *he,* the guy she was writing the letter to, got around to leaving his wife.

"So I left. I was still living in the big house, with my folks. Every time I tried to move out they'd say, 'What about Josh? What are you going to do with Josh? You know what happened the last time, don't you?' So I'd go out every night, I'd take him with me. I took him to museum openings. I took him to the movies. I took him to the park, I took him on dinner dates. I took him down to San Diego to the Zoo. I took him to Sea World. I took him to my friends' houses for dinner. I took him out for walks. I bought him a dog. I took him camping. I tried to teach him to shoot, but I didn't even know how myself. I took him to Hawaii, I bought him a surfboard. I took him skiing. I got him those collections. I took him to the synagogue, it was so dumb I never went back. I took him to the Self Realization Fellowship, he went into Sunday School and came out with a gold star pasted on his forehead. I took him to Synanon but he got scared in the games. I thought of joining Alcoholics Anonymous but I don't even drink. My mother said he was the best boy, the sweetest boy, she'd ever brought up. I tried to enroll him in lessons for gifted children on Saturdays, they tested him and found out he wasn't a gifted child. I went out with every Jewish girl in the city. I still get postcards from them. *He* still gets postcards from them.

"Saturday mornings I'd wake up, I'd go out in the backyard, I'd do a dozen laps in Dad's pool. I'd go inside, the maid would have my breakfast ready. My mother would be up already, calling department stores on the phone, getting a couch covered. The maid would be cleaning out the refriger- ator. My dad would be at work, naturally. Josh would come down in his pajamas and he'd be sitting up at the table for breakfast. Carmen would bring him his breakfast. He'd look at me, he'd say, 'Hi, Dad.' I'd be pretending to read the pa- per. My mother would say, 'Marc, if there's something you'd like to do today, I'll be glad to take Josh along with me.' I'd look over at him and he'd be looking at me. I'd say, 'No! We're going to the Museum of Science and Industry!' And my mother would say, 'If you'd only tell us ahead of time what your plans are! It's so hard on Carmen!' And we'd go out.

"Then I went to a P.T.A. meeting, on a Thursday night, when Josh was in the first grade. Not even an open house. Just a P.T.A. meeting. I talked to Josh's teacher. She was pretty, about twenty-eight. Oh, Josh was so bright! Josh was so good in mathematics! He didn't have a mother? Well, wasn't it wonderful how well he was doing! Here were all these compliments from a girl who wasn't coming on to me. She just *said* it, because of Josh. I loved her, I asked her out. Nobody gave me her phone number or said she was a nice girl, I just asked her out. We had coffee that night, we went out the next night and the next. It came to me that what I re- ally needed wasn't a selfish single girl who only thought about herself, or some divorcée who was only out to get all she could—and that's the *truth,* Ruth—but a *career* girl, an *in- dependent* girl, a girl who wouldn't make a lot of demands on me that I couldn't come through for! Our first weekend together I wanted to go somewhere with her and Josh, but she said no, that would interfere with their relationship in school. So for the whole semester we never went anywhere, the three of us. Oh, she was full of scruples! She wore nylon blouses and high-heeled shoes and pantyhose. I loved her. I really loved her! She was like my wife, only I couldn't even

219

remember, was my wife more beautiful? Was Jeanette more beautiful? I was happy. We went to restaurants and plays, and poetry readings. My friends didn't like her very much, I was in heaven, she was *mine.*

"I found an apartment for me and Josh, so she could spend the nights. But she was real wrapped up in her job! She had to work on Sunday nights to be ready for Monday mornings, and Friday nights she was too tired to go out. Then she had to work on Wednesday nights to get her papers caught up with. Are you getting it? Do you get it? It took me a long time to get it. She was giving me the brush. Me. *Me!* You don't *know,* Ruth, I couldn't *tell* you the women who loved me. I couldn't even tell you the women I took out after Katherine died. The lady photographer with the bleached blond hair and the dark roots. The secretary—the *other* secretary in my dad's office with the enormous tits. All the Jewish English majors, all the girls my mother knew about, honest girls with big noses! Bad girls with nose jobs! Good girls with glasses! All those girls from Synanon fucking for their mental health! They all loved me! They wanted to marry me. They sent Josh presents! What the hell, they knew I was rich, they knew about my dad. I even told the teacher about my dad, she said she just got very tired on Saturday nights. So would it be all right if we didn't screw? If we just lay there? She liked to feel that her life was her own. She didn't like to be railroaded. I parked outside her house, I watched her, I looked in her windows, I waited and waited for the other guy. There wasn't one. She sat there, in her living room, all alone, reading, looking at papers. Once I watched till after midnight, she was making a *feltboard.* What do they want a feltboard for, in the first grade? But I never got to ask her because by then she wasn't answering the phone.

"But by then I'd met Patty. Oh, I know she was your friend, but to me she was *the married woman!* The doughnuts! The fresh fried doughnuts! The cakes in seven layers, each one in a different color! The drinks with eight different liqueurs she gave us after dinner! The sauces, pancakes, the piroshki, the blini, the preserves, cream filling, egg filling, *meat filling*! The crêpes she made and kept in the freezer, stacks of them, with waxed paper in between each one! The German chocolate cakes, in layers, with fudge! The tortillas, my God! Homemade! Ruth, I tell you! You aren't even on speaking terms with a stove compared to her! A stove wouldn't even *talk* to you. The salads, the shrimp salads, avocado salads, the crabmeat and papaya salads, the aspic she poured over everything! The stuffed tomatoes! And I'm not even talking about her garden, or that she upholstered her own chairs, or went to every single game of her boy in the Little League, and saw that he had flute lessons besides. Or that her daughter went to gymnastics and her other son spent his summers working in a computer center even though he hadn't hit fifteen. I'm not even talking about the geraniums started from slips and the ivy from cuttings. I'm telling you that when everyone started to smoke dope, she grew that too, in damp newspaper, out on top of the dryer in the back porch. I'm not talking about the loom in the living room, and the dish full of wool to be carded that she kept by her bed. I'm not talking about the knitting, crocheting, tatting, embroidery! Well, *you* know it! But not so well, believe me!"

"No, I was really . . ."

"She subscribed to *Sunset* magazine, she made her own mayonnaise in a blender because she said it was quicker. She made her husband build a sundeck, then she made him build a greenhouse because she said she wanted to raise orchids. She *did* raise orchids. She made him build a roof on the sundeck, and a storage closet for all the power tools she made him buy. She wanted raised flower beds, he raised them for her. I shared an office with him, poor schmuck, he asked me home to dinner one night, she thought he wasn't making enough friends at work. Then it turned out we'd gone to the same high school, she'd even known Katherine. She *said* she'd known Katherine. It was a Tuesday night, we had fresh fruit salad with curry-flavored yogurt, we had sauerbraten the way her German mother taught her, homemade potato pancakes, and I don't mean from any mix! She grated those fucking potatoes. Then fresh peach ice cream, homemade, in her fucking *ice cream* maker! She found out I had a son and invited us back the next night, we had Chicken Kiev, homemade, and none of the butter leaked out until you cut into it. The five kids sat at a separate table and had hot dogs and hot fudge sundaes.

"The next night was Friday, Jeanette was too tired. She said she just couldn't see me, so I was going over to my folks with Josh. Three-thirty my friend gets a call from his wife, she made this simple little stew, but she's made too much, would I mind coming over and helping them eat it up? And bring Josh, of course? *Of course!* It was ragout, with baby onions and white wine. The kids had chicken wings marinated in soy sauce and strawberry shortcake; we had crêpes suzette. Afterwards she got her kids to teach Josh how to play Monopoly. We went out in the backyard and played badminton. Then we came back in the house to eat some leftover peach ice cream. I went into the john and when I came out poor Dan was waiting for me. 'How about the three of us go out somewhere? Patty can get a sitter, *she'd* like that, she stays home so much of the time.' I said yes. So she phoned up a sitter, she had a list, alphabetical, right up on the wall by the phone. We went out to a topless place. Patty's sitting there with her hands folded in her lap, she wouldn't look at the girls, she wouldn't order a drink, she wouldn't even order a 7-Up. Did I say she was gorgeous? *You* know it! She had this tiny waist because of her yoga, and this terrific complexion because she rubbed fruit peels on it every time she made a salad, and she had this terrific chest, boy! She was wearing a tweed skirt—in a topless joint, can you imagine! And a beige sweater with full-fashioned sleeves! Patty's sitting there with this *look* on her face. She didn't say one word while we drove home and she didn't invite me into the house. She went in to get Josh from the sitter while I waited on the front porch.

222

When she came out he was still sound asleep and the tears were running down her face. She didn't say one word. She just gives him this tremendous passionate kiss on his neck and hands him to me. Then she slams the screen door and goes in the house.

"The next day, I called her. I had to use the pay phone in the hall at work and even then I waited until Dan had gone to lunch. She answered the phone.

" 'Hello,' I said.

"She said, 'Hello.' Then she was crying.

" 'Oh!' she says. 'How could we have *gone* to a place like that?'

"So then I'm telling her it doesn't matter, and it certainly doesn't matter to me! Remember, I'm Jewish, I'm a kid, and I have a kid! I'm sailing around and around those three-bedroom houses in the Valley with broken-down divorcées! This date, that date! One woman doesn't want to give me a goodnight kiss, the next one feels rejected if I don't fuck her before dinner! I go home and there's my mom and my dad! Either that or I live alone in some shitty apartment! And everywhere I go there's that God damned kid! Every time I move I've got more stuff—it's never my stuff, it's always *his* stuff. First it's those sets of Carter sleepers, then wood blocks, and then Lego blocks and then trikes and now bikes and all his collections! Coins! Insects! Bottle caps with riddles on them! And here's this lady sobbing away on the phone, what am I supposed to do? *Look,* I say, don't *do* that. *Look,* I say, is it all right if I come over tonight? Then she says sure, but only if I bring Josh. That night it's blanquette de veau and homemade butter brickle.

"Actually I felt pretty good about it. Jeanette even called me a couple of times to see if I was OK. From her point of view she'd been dropping me and here it was she was the one staying home grading papers and nobody breaking the silence. Then after about three weeks there's poetry reading up in Malibu. On the cliffs, at a place called Positano's. Patty wanted to go. But Dan hates poetry. He says, why don't the

223

two of *us* go, he'll go where he wants, we can get a sitter, we can all be doing what we want to do. So, OK, we went. After the poetry reading we walk out, we're in a trance. She's not saying anything, I'm not saying anything. She's wearing that tweed skirt, and imitation pearls, those oxfords. She's got all this beautiful hair down her back. The moon is shining like a bastard. And all of a sudden I take hold of her hand and all of a sudden I kiss her. Then we get back in the car and drive home without a word.

"The next morning Dan comes into the office, he's breathing funny, he leans over my desk, he takes a punch at me. Can you believe it, actually? He's six inches shorter than I am, half my weight, I didn't even *do* anything and he takes a punch at me! I told him I didn't even *do* anything! Then he tells me—he's got ahold of my collar, I couldn't believe it—that Patty, that beautiful, industrious, virtuous girl, moved out to a motel in the middle of the night, and he's home with those four kids and what the fuck do I have to say about *that?* She's spent hours in the night telling her husband she *loves me.* Can you understand what I'm saying? That friend of yours, that good friend of yours, is as mad as a fucking hatter. I'm horrified, I'm terrified, I don't understand what the fuck is going on. Meanwhile I'm trying to figure out how I can find out what motel she's in. And pretty soon he goes home—he's got to find someone to take care of the kids—he's got tears streaming down his face—the guys in the office are looking in at us, I'm living in a crazy world. As soon as he leaves, the phone rings, it's like she's been watching the place.

" 'Hello,' she says.

"I say hello.

" 'Can you come over?' she says.

"I say yes.

"And in five minutes I'm out, I don't even care if her husband's out in the front, I'm driving down Little Santa Monica like a madman, and there she is, across from the Mormon Temple in the Brigham Young Motel, and we spend the rest of the afternoon screwing our brains out. She loves me, she tells me, she can't help it, she doesn't care what happens, she's in this for good, oh, she loves me, she loves me. And she *loves Josh!* Afterwards, or between times, I ask her what she's going to do. She's gone, for good, she loves me. But what about the kids? Oh, she'll *keep* the kids, she *loves* the kids. But what about Dan? Well, she doesn't love him. I'd had it, I was in a vise. But meanwhile, here's this beautiful woman, this really gorgeous woman— not a speck of makeup on her face, this beautiful hair spread out all over the pillow, a body beyond my wildest dreams. And she's so pure, so *good!* She never mentions that I have to do anything—she'll keep the house, of course, and get alimony. After all, the kids are too young for *her* to work, nobody would want her to go to *work.* Oh, she may go into teaching eventually, or social work, or politics, she's always been interested in politics! Meanwhile, she loves me. To tell you the truth, the sex is not so hot, but oh! She loves me.

"So. Dan transfers out of the office. Josh starts looking at me like I'm some kind of monster. My mother is crying all the time. Dan's living with his married sister. My folks will never have us over for dinner, and when they do they won't speak to her. Her kids *hate* me, and the feeling is mutual. We're just maybe getting it on at night—she's draped the whole bedroom in madras bedspreads, she's lit enough incense to keep us sneezing for a week, she's put on one of her simple white cotton nightgowns, there's all these fresh flowers put around everywhere there's room for a vase, she's lit all these candles, we're really just about to get into it, she's put some records on, some—God, I don't know, could it have been the Beatles yet? No, some Brahms, some Beethoven, she'd always say, 'This is his fifth concerto, do you mind?' There we'd be, a real magic evening, and little Anthony rushes through the door, crying and choking, and throws up on the bed. I don't mean he did it once or twice or three times or four times but he did it a dozen times! All the oatmeal cookies and marinated chicken wings and Scandinavian

225

finger sandwiches all over the bed, once all over my feet! And the oldest had nightmares and the youngest was asthmatic. Patty would jump up and put her hand across whoever it was, and he'd howl and retch, and the light would come on in the kids' room and they'd all come to the door, Josh too, of course, in pajamas she'd made for him, homemade pajamas, and they'd stare in at us with the kid throwing up and the clouds of incense billowing out, and me sitting there, or struggling into my pajamas with puke on my feet, I tell you, I was in a noose! I was in a trap! I didn't know what to do. I'd be driving to work, Dan would pass me in his car and turn his head. And Patty! She was working so hard and working so hard and working so hard, she's given up everything for me, well, why didn't I do something about it! Well, I didn't *want* to do anything about it! My shrink told me I didn't *have* to do anything about it. But meanwhile Patty catches Dan at the bank where he's trying to draw all the money out of the joint checking account and she can't meet the house payments, and the kids are beginning to get peanut butter sandwiches and blaming me for it, and Patty's losing weight, and there's that whole feeling she's giving me now that when we're fucking it's only fucking, not making love, that I'm *that kind of a guy!*

"So one morning I'm coming to work and I'm coming in late so I won't pass Dan in the car. I park down the block and I'm walking to work, and this girl in front of me steps right off the curb and falls right over. She's real yellowy pale, no more than eighteen. She's wearing a boy's undershirt, not a T shirt, but an undershirt with this little lacy stuff around the straps. I can see her ribs under the shirt. She's lying in the gutter holding her breath like little kids do, trying not to cry, you know, holding her breath for as long as she can, then letting out and starting it all over again. People are just crossing the street around her. Her wrist is swelling up and turning blue before my eyes. I get out of the car and pick her up— believe me, it wasn't so easy, I'd gained a lot of weight!—I put her in the car and drove her to an emergency room. She didn't say two words to me. She gives her name to the guy at the desk as Linda Blue Eyes. I thought she might be an American Indian or something but no, she just picked out that name, she was some runaway dropout from the Thousand Lakes in Minnesota and no, she didn't have a job, and no, she didn't have insurance, and they were going to kick her out, but I said I'd pay, what else could I do? The guy behind the desk gave me some kind of fishy look, but did I give a shit? I *lived* on fishy looks by this time, I was the origin of fishy looks, I could care less, I had this big belly, I gave him a fishy look right back. 'Any relation?' the guy said. 'Father, uncle?' I just gave him my fishy look.

"I stayed while they put on the cast. Then I sat by her for a while in this ward, she's talking to me, crying, babbling, calling me her daddy. She's shaking and sobbing, I found out later she was stoned out of her mind which is why she walked off the curb right into the air. Right off into the air! She says please don't leave! She doesn't have anybody. So I stayed a couple of hours, what else could I do? When I finally got to work I passed Dan's new desk, he gives me a funny look, a different kind of look. And there's a message waiting for me on the desk, call Patty *right away*! I called her and she was crying. Why didn't I tell her, how could I do this to her? And of course, she's got to have not just one friend but *two* friends in this hospital, the intern who was learning to put on the cast, and the candy-striper who came around with the magazines.

"I'm holding the phone, listening to this voice on the phone. I know what Patty looks like now, all gray under the eyes from not eating. No more candles, no more incense. I'm sitting there, on the phone, listening to her cry! My shirt buttons are pulling across my belly. It comes to me I'm thirty-eight years old! I hung up the phone, I drove over to Josh's school and got him out of his classes, and then I drove back to the hospital. They'd given her some kind of extra drugs. I said, 'Come on, come on, we're getting out of here.' She said, 'What?' I said, '*Come* on, I don't give a shit, come on.' Josh is standing there, right behind me. Linda's just lying there. A nurse came in and said, 'What are you doing? What is this?' I said, 'Don't worry, I'm *her father,* I'm taking her away.' I turned around and gave Josh a look. He gave me one right back. Meanwhile, the girl's out of her *cabeza,* lying on the bed, saying, '*Oh darling, darling!*' It was the one heroic act of my life, I went over to the bed and scooped her up and said, '*Come on!*' I picked her up and walked out of there. Josh held the car door open so I could shove her in. Then he ran around and jumped in the back seat. 'Hold her head,' I told him, because she's so dopey she's sliding all across the seat of the car. So he sat in back and held her head, one hand on either side of her head, while I drove around and tried to think. I drove out to Santa Monica, to the Surfrider Motel. I went in, I said, 'Listen, I've got my daughter out here, she's been in an accident, and I'll be frank with you, she's had some drug or other. I don't know what. I've got my son with me, too, but I don't want to take this girl home to her mother.' I carried her to a room and turned on the television set. Josh sat right by her. 'I like game shows,' she tells him. 'Do you like game shows?' I left them there and got in the car, I drove home. By this time I was living in an apartment up in the Pacific Palisades. I ran over to the manager's apartment. He was a paraplegic from the war. 'Look,' I told him, 'something's come up, I've got to leave town. Nothing's wrong, but I don't want you telling my folks *anything,* OK? And that woman? You know? I don't want you to tell her *anything.*' I packed two suitcases, one for Josh and one for me. Then I stopped by Pup 'n' Taco and bought six tacos, and stopped at the liquor store and got some beer. When I got back they were still watching game shows. When she saw the beer she said 'Oh, I don't drink that! I'm not into that!' 'Come on,' I said, 'that's what I got! You're drinking it.' So she just laughed. She started eating one of the tacos, and drinking out of the bottle, the beer hit the lettuce and foamed up, like peroxide when you put it on a cut. She poured a little more into her mouth, making fun of me, doing what I said but not doing it. The beer came out of the side of her mouth, just a little stream of it, down her neck, down her chest. She was still wearing a hospital gown, and she more or less blotted her breast with the side of her hand. 'Josh,' I said, 'we've got to get her out of that gown and into some pajamas.' 'Sure,' he said, 'you wanna use mine?' 'No!' I said. '*Mine!*' She's looking past us at the television set. We undress her, one of us on each side of her. I undid the strings of her hospital gown, and put on the pajama top. Josh sat in front of her and buttoned her up. 'Josh,' I said, 'we've got to have some stuff for tonight.' I took out all the money I had left, I handed it to him. It didn't come to more than seven or eight dollars. 'But you've already got the tacos!' '*Never mind!* We need stuff for breakfast. Get some granola. Get some milk, get some grapefruit. And don't make phone calls, you hear me?'

"'I know,' he said, and started to leave. 'How about if I hitchhike over to the house and get my bike?' He knew I never let him hitchhike, but I told him OK, this one time, and he left. I pulled the curtains on the windows and turned around to her. She was just sitting there looking at me and she reached in the fly of my own pajamas and starting touching herself . . .

"I found out later she had *no energy*. She'd get in the bathtub, for instance, with her washcloth, and I'd hand her a bar of soap, and she'd sort of rub the soap on the washcloth and kind of listlessly rub the cloth on her arms and then her hand would sort of fall back on the water and lie there, while the dirt floated up. Pretty soon I'd get mad at her and grab the washcloth out of her hands and start scrubbing her back and the back of her neck and she'd flinch the way a kid does, but she'd let me do it, just the way a kid lets you do it, because she *has* to let you do it, and she'd just open her legs a little bit and the next thing I'd be out of my clothes and in the water with her—luke warm, you know?—with all that soap. I'd be in there thinking, oh, *God!* she's letting me do this to her! This little *kid*. And then afterward I'd be sitting in the water, feeling like a jerk, and she'd reach up and pat my face."

"Did she have any parents?" Ruth asked.

229

Carolyn See

"In a couple of hours Josh came back with his bike. He started riding it around and around the pool. It was still only maybe four in the afternoon. Nobody knew yet that I wasn't coming back. I was never so happy in my whole life. I looked out at the ocean, with my kid and this little girl and I was never so happy. I told Josh to look out after her and not let her go anyplace! Then I went up to Tex Sporting Goods and bought three goose-down sleeping bags, and two little red nylon tents, and three goose-down jackets. I bought three dozen packages of Top Ramin and a pan, and some beef jerky. I put it all on my American Express, my dad ended up paying it. That night I put Josh on the couch and Linda in bed with me. She kept saying, 'I have what you want,' and I believed her.

"The next morning we took off. Do you know what that means, Ruth? Do you know what that means? You can't pos-. sibly know what that means. We drove north and north and north, on credit cards, no money in our pockets, and camped out every night. Linda would panhandle sometimes and bring me money and put it in my hand. We found this place and I went home to get some money from my dad. You can imagine what he said to me. I called up Patty. She said, 'I don't care what you've done! I forgive you, I love you!' I was in town ten days, she stayed with me every night. I told her, I told her! She wouldn't even believe I'd been *gone*. Did you know my father is co-owner of this hotel? I never told you that. He's co-owner of this hotel. There's nothing on earth I can do to get away from him!

"We found this place. Josh went to school. Linda stayed home with me. She was careless in the house. She didn't do things the way I wanted her to. She wouldn't make the bed in the morning until I'd asked her three or four times. She wore the same Levi's and the same shirt, over and over. I'd read to her at night and she'd go to sleep right while I was reading. I told her that Katherine used to rub my feet at night and that I wanted that, I *needed* that. She'd do it, if I'd ask her, but she didn't have any strength in her fingers. She'd

230

take ahold of my feet, and pull at them, but not in any reasonable way! Just this dumb grip on my feet! I couldn't stand it!

"She was afraid of everything. She was afraid when I raised my voice, when I yelled at Josh. She'd disappear for hours upstairs with him, I wouldn't know what they were doing up there. Once they were upstairs all day, I didn't even get any lunch. I finally went upstairs and they were bent over on the floor, working on a jigsaw puzzle. *Every Animal in the Jungle,* with about five thousand pieces in it. They looked up and asked me to help but I wouldn't do it. I went downstairs and they wouldn't come downstairs! I didn't even get dinner until nine that night! Another time I went up I thought I smelled pot up there. I was afraid to ask her. She had all this cocaine, she carried tabs of acid in her shoe. Once she *shot* some acid up into her foot, can you imagine? I watched her do it. It made me sick, that little dirty foot, and I watched her face change as it came up her leg, into her back, into her brain. Then she got right up and went across the room and sunk right down on the floor and put her head between my legs.

"She was afraid of everything. She was afraid of floods. She was afraid of getting married. She was afraid of big dogs. She was afraid of black guys, she'd been raped once by a black guy when she was stoned. She was afraid of earthquakes, she read all those hippie papers and for a while all you read in them was that there was going to be an earthquake. She made me get that waterbed, and if I'd turn over in the night without telling her about it she'd start to cry, she thought the earthquake was starting. Because this was it, Ruth, this was it, I came home one day from sawing wood— the whole top floor was finished, and Josh was doing OK in school, and she'd made me realize I didn't have to answer my parents' letters and that I didn't have to write them at all except to ask them for money. It was getting real cold up here, *real* cold, and I borrowed a chain saw from a neighbor to go out and saw wood for the winter. The first day she came with

231

me and watched all day long while I cut the wood. The second day she said she had a cold so Josh went with me. We came home about seven at night, it was freezing cold and rainy and she'd let the fire go out again. There was a note on the table but I couldn't read it. I said to Josh, 'You read it!' He picked it up and read it.

"I made a fire in that Franklin stove, and I pulled a chair over to the fire and held my face into it until my skin was burning hot. Then I picked up the letter and read it. She'd left, she said, she left because she was afraid the island was going to fall into the ocean.

"So I can't have it. When I say squash for dinner you *have* to make squash for my dinner. *My* pictures have to be up on the wall because I have to have them up there! I have to live, I have to go on living, I have to make Josh into a grown-up, I have to work, I've got to have a little fun, and I can't take much more. So if you won't do it, you have to leave. *Right now.* You can't get my hopes up again, because I'll die, I'll kill myself, I'll certainly die from all this because I can't take any more!"

Silence.

"It's hard to know how all this got started," Ruth said finally. "Jack had all those suits when I married him, he took me to the bank . . ."

"I know exactly how it got started. Exactly how it got started! You think I went to school in the east. I didn't go to school in the east! I went right here, to USC. Do you think USC is any place for a Jewish kid with a big nose and a big ass? Do you think belonging to either one of those two fraternities was anything so hot? Can I tell you about the Saturday mornings when whole troops of gentile guys in khaki shorts would hiss through their teeth as they walked by our house? Hiss like a gas chamber? Calling the roll in class and they smile if it's not a gentile name? You think they don't know a Rose from a Rosenberg? They *know*, that's all they know.

"My folks had a girl all picked out for me, a nice Jewish girl, with long black hair and a nose job and straight teeth.

232

But I wouldn't do it. Instead, I joined the French Club. Can you imagine the *French Club*? I thought I'd be the only guy there. But there were others, with the same idea. Big guys with frizzy hair like mine, some of them in pre-law, they've already bought those awful suits, those vests . . . I wanted a blond girl, you know? Not a bleach, but a real soft blond. Because I wasn't very smart myself. *J'entre dans la salle de classe. Je regarde autour de moi. Autour de moi* was Katherine, from Marshall High. She didn't know one damned thing. All she did was laugh. I thought at first she just did it to be popular, but she really had a sunny temper. I went out with her—she arranged it, some kind of double date where we went up to the snow—and we were stuck in somebody's old-fashioned rumble seat for fourteen hours. She didn't stop smiling once. I brought her home to meet my folks, my father fell in love with her, even though she wasn't Jewish, my mother took her off into the den to show her the old family pictures. You had to love her. She was really a nice girl. The nicest thing that ever happened to me. We got married, in my father's house. She danced with my father, I'll show you the pictures . . ."

"I've seen them."

"I was never so happy. After I graduated we went into the army. I was a soldier. After I got out I should have gone into the business right then, but I couldn't do it. So you know what I decided to be? Well, you know! A *sociologist*. My dad was heartsick. After I started graduate school he didn't give us any more money—except what he gives my mom to give us on the sly. *Her* mother is helping us out. I enroll at UCLA, we get a house, a little house, down by the beach. Katherine wants to get a job full-time. I can't let her do it. So she works up at school typing file cards for an old professor. I'm getting up in the morning, I'm driving a Volkswagen, the back seat is full of *my* cards, the well behind the back seat is full of *her* cards. We drive up to the university in the morning, we drive back at night. Katherine decides she's pregnant. She *is* pregnant. We have dinner once a week with my folks, once a week with her mother. My brothers are looking at me—why don't

233

I get a *job,* drive a decent car? What are they working for *me* for, putting me through college? Nobody in the Mandell family ever heard of sociology! I work on my cards every night, I'm going to be a sociologist. Poor Katherine comes home, her shoulders ache. I wanted a hobby, and I got the idea to make my own beer. I got Katherine to bring home all the beer bottles she could find. We'd been married almost five years, the kid's learning to walk. Oh, *God,* it was boring. I'd never screwed another girl in my whole life except once in the army. That summer I took a seminar in statistics. The guy next to me asked me one day if my wife and I swung. Can you imagine? *Katherine* swinging? She still used Noxema! I went straight home and took her to bed. Before dinner! She felt terrible about going to bed so early. Because the bed had only been made since that morning, it had about six hours more to go before we usually went to sleep. Should she get up, right afterwards, and make up the bed before we went back to bed? Should we just lie in bed and watch television? But then I wouldn't get any *work* done. Should we have sex again? But she didn't really like to do it a second time. Only that's not what she *said,* she said if you really loved each other and had been able to *show* it the first time, then you shouldn't have to do it a second time. So we were lying in bed at a quarter to eight, and I told her what the guy in the seminar said. She'd already gotten up once to put on a nightgown—and she gets up again and starts picking up around the room. She had this perfect American face, I can't even tell you what kind of face, no lines, these perfect blue eyes, and those blond curls, she's crying down into her nightgown and wiping her nose on her sleeve. I really couldn't tell what part of it bothered her the most. That I was trying to reject her? Believe me, a six-foot Jewish guy with a stomach and a bad game of tennis was not going to reject Katherine McMasters. And why was I asking her anything anyway? Why didn't I just have an affair? Listen! I got to be the freethinker in our house. About how we did it and when, and why we couldn't do it with other people. I knew there was something wrong

234

with her because she'd married me in the first place. So I'd sigh, before I'd go down on her, or I'd manage to come too quick and then say, gee, it's too bad you don't ever want it a second time, and I always talked about *it* instead of *her*, so that way she could wonder about whether it was it or her I cared about, right? And also if she began to detach *it* from her or me or *us* maybe we'd be in business."

"Didn't you think you were taking a big risk?"

"I didn't think about anything. All I knew was if I saw Cantor's another night or Du Par's another night, if I ate another chicken pie or cheese cake or talked to my parents or made it another single time with my wife wearing that same nightgown I couldn't stand it."

"Why didn't she do something?"

"What *could* she do? She couldn't go to school, she was *already* in school. She couldn't go to work, she was already typing those cards. She couldn't get a better job because I wouldn't let her. She couldn't quit because we needed the money. She couldn't talk to anybody, I hated all her friends. A wife is supposed to get along with her husband's friends, but I didn't have any. So it went on like that for quite a while. And the kid is driving me nuts. Then one night, in her little nightgown, she starts crying. OK, she says, since I don't like her anymore *that way*, maybe some of my friends can teach her how. By that time I've got it in my mind no one could teach her *anything*. She sniffs all the time, she's beginning to gain weight. So when I sat next to the guy in the seminar next Thursday afternoon, I said yes. He said yes, what? I said, my wife and I *do* swing, sometimes.

"I gave him my phone number but he didn't call for about a week. Katherine was really awful, especially at night. 'Here's something you might like to do?' or 'I suppose it might be *boring* if you were to just touch me a little bit first?' And her girlfriends began to give me some real funny looks. It's getting *hot*, I forgot to say we were in summer school. After dinner she'd sit out on the steps, in her cutoffs, we would have had a meatloaf, and oven-browned potatoes, and a tomato and lettuce salad with that red french dressing. She'd be watching the kid. I'd be sitting up at the card table where we'd had dinner. It's not like we didn't have money—we *had* money, my dad had money, we could have had money. I don't know what we were doing! There was that bright light on over the table. And she'd be out on the front steps, she'd take the phone out there, talking to her girlfriends about me . . .

"One night I was out in the back porch fiddling with my beer. There were bottles lined up all along the washtubs, all along baseboards, there was this green smell. I'd bought a capping machine, I thought I'd try bottling some of the stuff. The kid was out there getting in the way. I went back into the living room and I heard the popping out on the porch, all the bottles popping. Katherine heard it too and she came out on the porch, she was helping me clean it up when the phone rang. It was the guy from the seminar. I went back out to the porch. 'Katherine,' I said, 'Hurry up with that! They want us to come right over.' She didn't even ask me who it was. She went into the bathroom and took a shower, and came out wearing a white blouse and a cotton skirt and sandals. It was like we were getting ready to go to school in the morning. She sat in the living room and waited for me to get showered and dressed. We drove all the way from Venice where we lived up the coast to Malibu. Katherine didn't speak to me all the way up there, not like she was mad, but just like she was putting on her lipstick, or looking out the window. She took out a handkerchief and got something out of the corner of her eye.

"It was this house right on the beach, between the ocean and the highway, there were already some cars there. I'd been afraid we wouldn't be dressed right and I was right, she wasn't. She had that cotton blouse. The guys were in slacks and shirts and the women had long dresses with stockings and high-heeled shoes. They were all drinking highballs. One woman even said to me, 'You want a *highball?*' We sat around the living room, I was on the one couch, Katherine

236

was on the other. I was sitting next to this girl, she had a nice little face with her hair brushed back, she worked at Van De Kamps Coffee Shop four nights a week. Her husband was a chef at a fancy restaurant further in town. She told me all about the living room furniture they were buying, white, sectional pieces, you could buy it piece by piece. She asked me what I did and when I told her she said, 'Oh, how interesting.' She didn't know a sociologist from your grandmother. There were just these four couples, in the living room. We're drinking along—and this was a *school* night, I couldn't believe it. Then one guy reached over and turned off the light on the end table. But there was still some light in the kitchen. I looked over and here was this guy, he had one arm around Kate and he bent his head over to kiss her. His shoes, he was wearing those big police oxfords, turned sideways on the floor. Katherine just leans back like in high school, she doesn't move, she just sits on the couch with her ankles crossed, and pretty soon she reaches up her left arm and puts it up around his shoulders.

"And right next to them on that couch is another couple, the guy is doing the exact same thing. The woman, she's wearing a skirt and high-heeled shoes, she's leaning back the exact same way. This little woman with the black hair says, 'Do you like my perfume?' And I say, sure, and she says, 'It's Mitsouko,' and leans over and kisses me, with those very soft lips. Someone's put on a record, Lionel Hampton playing *Midnight Sun.* Boy, when I think, Ruth! She says, 'Do you like my shirt?' She's wearing black velvet pants like Juliette Greco used to wear and she has this sort of soft silver silk shirt. I say, '*Do* I?' But then she says, 'I have a hell of a time getting it dry cleaned,' and takes my hand and puts it on her breast. Winona had all these bras, all kinds of lace and straps and bones. This was blue lace, I found out later. We're all just lying there on the couches, necking, and necking. Then one couple gets up and says they're going in the other room. Then the other couple on our couch gets up and does the same thing. Then the guy with Katherine gets up and says *he's* going into the other room. Katherine just walked past me with her head down. Winona was whispering to me about her self-beautification program. She got up in the morning at six, before anyone was up, and put an egg on her face and waited until it dried. She did twenty-five situps in the morning and twenty-five at night. She'd named her little girl Lennie, after Lennie Tristano, the jazz piano player, the blind guy. I told her all I cared about was Gerry Mulligan, she said, 'Oh, I went out with his drummer, one of his very first drummers.' Then she kisses me again. I'm not kidding, Ruth, I still count those nights as some of my finest nights. She said, 'I'm glad we got to keep the living room for ourselves, because we get to keep the fire.' And she starts to get undressed, she has these little breasts that don't sag, even though she's had a baby, she says it's because she keeps doing the exercises. We lie down on the floor and do it. It's great for me and it looks like it's great for her, then I look down at her face. I say to her, 'Was it all right for you?' She says, 'Actually, not,' and puts my hand *right there*—and keeps telling me, like I'm scratching her back. 'Just a little further *up,* now just a little to the *left,* now slowly, slowly! That's right, now a little further down, no *down,* toward the *rug*!' It's the first time a woman has ever given the slightest hint that she wants in the slightest way to really *feel anything*! And the word love hasn't been mentioned once. Not once! I couldn't believe it. It was like heaven. There wasn't one *book* in that living room, and not one mention of love. And by the time she finally came, there I was again, and we did it again. Then she gets up and puts on her clothes and goes out into the kitchen and makes a big pot of coffee and digs around in the refrigerator and finds some sweet rolls. And pretty soon everybody else comes out and we stand around in the kitchen and drink coffee and then we pretty much say we have to go home.

"On the way back in the car, the first thing I looked over at Katherine, she looks over at me, we both burst out laughing. And we laughed all the way home. We'd think we'd be over it and then we'd start laughing again. Little Katherine McMasters, you dig? And that nice Marc Mandell. Before we went to sleep I asked her if she had a nice time. I can't say it enough to you, it was so funny, we were back in our own bedroom, we had our back porch full of beer bottles. A couple of them popped off in the night. The next morning, I went to school and worked all day. When I came home, she was already there on the front porch, she had dinner on the stove, she was sitting there in her shorts drinking a coke. I said, 'What's happening?' and she said, 'Oh, *your* mom called, and *my* mom called, and Joan called . . . and Jeff called.' Jeff was the guy in the seminar. He was the only one besides me who went to school. 'Jeff says would we like to come over.' I said, 'I don't know, what do you think?' She says, 'Well, what do *you* want to do?' It's like we're deciding whether or not to go out to dinner. Finally she says, 'Well, it's all right with me if it's all right with you.' So we went.

"The next night we went out with my folks. Brisket of beef at Cantor's and my dad saying again he doesn't know why I'm wasting my time in school. The next dinner with Katherine's mom, she had a new boyfriend, some thin old guy in his fifties. Katherine's real nice to him and makes her mother kind of mad. On the way home, I ask her, 'You know what you were doing, don't you?' She says, 'No, what was I doing?' I said, 'You're a real P.T., you know that?' I'd have never ever said a thing like that in my other life, never. And the next night we went back."

"But didn't you ever talk about it?"

"What was there to say? It wasn't like today. There wasn't any dope, nothing like that. There was Winona and Faye and Phyllis and Katherine, and every once in a while another couple. The seminar ended and we had the last part of August and the first part of September before school started. We went over there maybe three nights a week.

"Then the last part of September, Katherine found out she was pregnant again. In those days you still couldn't get an abortion, but we didn't want an abortion. We already had the one kid—Katherine's mom had been baby-sitting for us so we could go out—and he had to have a brother or sister sometime. We took a lot of kidding in the group but to tell you the truth we felt great. We felt like we could do anything we wanted. Everywhere we went was funny. To see my mother-in-law's boyfriend eating flanken and then think of him doing that other stuff. And we finally had something to talk about. Katherine was a wonderful girl but she wasn't too smart. I knew she would have probably liked it better if I'd gone in the business. But now we could talk a lot. She'd say, 'You know what that new guy did, wanted me to do?' and then she'd tell me. It was like dreamland. I'd never been so happy in my life."

"So what happened?"

"We decided to go ahead and have the baby. No big deal! We'd beaten the rap, we had a real double life, we were happy. I was going to get a terminal M.A. and be a social worker. Because who was I kidding? What did I know from sociology? My dad would help us buy a house. I wouldn't have to go into garments. And the thing is, I wasn't that *smart!* The changes we'd gotten in our lives, that was just as much of a change as we wanted."

"You didn't mind . . . ?"

"I didn't really *think* about it, you know that kind of time in your life when you don't think about it? I went back to school, it was my last semester. Then two nights before Thanksgiving Katherine woke me up. She had cramps, she said, she was spotting some. I told her to go back to sleep and I went back to sleep. Maybe an hour later she wakes me up again and she's bleeding quite a lot. I call the ambulance over at UCLA, it's a rainy night naturally, and my own car is in the garage. But no problems, they say they'll be right over. She's crying, she says the pain is terrible. Some of my friends' wives have had miscarriages, I don't remember that it's so awful as this. So you know what I do? I go back to sleep. She wakes me up again, she's crying, she says, 'Marc, are you sure they're coming? Don't you think you could call my mother?' I call the emergency room again, they say their ambulances are out

240

someplace, but hang on, they'll be right over. I look at the clock, it's after two in the morning, I hate the thought of calling Katherine's mother. What's she going to be able to do? Katherine's crying into the pillow, she's apologizing for keeping me awake. I turn off the light again, she says do I mind? Couldn't I keep the light on? I'm a prince, I keep the light on, I go back to sleep. About a half hour later she wakes me up, 'Would you mind calling the ambulance again?' She's so *considerate* I figure I have to do the right thing. I say to her, 'Look, while we're waiting, honey, can't I rub your back?' '*No!*' she says, and I reach down and the whole bottom half of her nightgown is soaked in blood. I call the emergency room, the guy says, '*Look* you bastard! We're coming there when we're *coming* there, and not before that, and if you keep calling, we're not coming there at all!' Something like that. I got out the telephone book and looked in the yellow pages, under A. By the time I got to an ambulance that was really going to make the trip out to Venice she was unconscious. By the time they got to the house she was dead. I never did call her mother."

"Jesus."

"Yes, *Jesus. Jesus,* what was it for? Was it for screwing? No, that was too dumb. Was it because I loved her? That was ridiculous! Or didn't love her? I heard about a guy who backed out of his driveway and ran over his wife, I heard about a guy who smashed right into a bar with his car and killed somebody drinking and the guy on the next stool said, 'Say, look, this isn't a drive-in!' When the ambulance came I sent it away and sat there looking at Katherine. I put her arms across her chest and fluffed out her hair. I even put some lipstick on her mouth. Then it came to me I heard this crying. It was the kid. Katherine always took care of him, she was the perfect mother, I don't think I'd even picked him up more than ten times in his life. The minute I heard him crying I knew he'd been crying for a long time. The neighbors must have heard him crying and they'd heard the ambulance, don't you think? They would have had to have heard it. What if I called

Katherine's mother, she'd find out from the neighbors that the kid had been crying, maybe all night. But if I called her mother, maybe she would call *my* folks, so I wouldn't have to. I remember I read in a book about a woman who bled all the way through the mattress when she had an abortion. I got down on the floor, it was about seven in the morning. I didn't see any blood. I got up and went over and turned on the *Today* show. Then I turned it off. What if somebody heard it? The kid was screaming his brains out. I went back over to the door, opened it, looked into the room. You know how sometimes they mess their pants and get into it and more or less paste it all over everything? He'd got shit into his hair and on the walls and down between the bars of the crib. For God's sake, Katherine, aren't you going to do something about cleaning this up? But she just lay there like in the old days, prim, like when we were first married. 'Don't you love me, Marc? Say you love me, Marc, oh, I just love you, Marc, honey.' I thought, could I kill this kid and get away with temporary insanity? But they knew I'd called those ambulances. The neighbors would know. And how could I touch the kid? How could I put my hands on him? He's screaming, he's dripping, he's purple in the face. I close the door and go back on the edge of the bed and turn the *Today Show* back on again, real low. It's the old days, Frank Blair's still on, and that guy who died of cancer. And pretty soon I called up my father and told him what happened. He was furious.

"From then on it's been Josh and me, Josh and me, *Josh and me.* And all those women either like him or they don't. They send him presents, they draw him pictures, or they hate him or they say he's repressed. But I have to tell you, Ruth, that I really don't care about that! What I'm saying is that it has to be me up here, me, me, me, me, me! Now, I don't mind your kids, *up to a point.*"

"Sometimes I think I don't even like kids very much . . ."

"I don't even mind your crappy husband!"

"It's like you have them before you know any better . . ."

"What I *can't stand* is your trying to be the center of things."

"Of course, with Dinah, I was thirty years old. But I knew Jack was fooling around. Actually, I didn't *quite* know . . ."

"I *don't* care! Can't you understand that?"

She understood it perfectly. "I'm thirsty," she said. "Do you think there's any beer in the kitchen? Not in the drinking room, Reggie's in there."

They went downstairs.

"Don't turn on the light," he said, and wiped his face. "How about some wine instead?"

"Yes, please."

He crossed over to the refrigerator, opened the door, holding one of the good glasses from his marriage, and filled it up to the top. It was too full, in fact, for him to walk, so he stood inside the door, holding the glass out to her. She came over, and examined him in the cold, intimate light. We all have our stories, she thought. He just tells his with a straight face.

"But do you see how it started? It started exactly when he asked if we ever swung, and I said, yes, *sometimes. Well?*" he said.

She reached up and kissed his cheek. "I don't even *care.*" He pulled away, then looked sideways at her, exhausted and flirtatious. She smiled. They kissed and kissed again, until the bang of the front door indicated Dinah and Josh coming in with the dog.

X

Once again they were back at the house in Topanga Canyon. Their family—what there was of it—together. Ruth, gaunt, tan, gray, and wasted under the eyes. Reggie, dead white, quiet as the tomb. Dinah, sucking her thumb, sucking it, sucking it.

But what the hell? Isn't that the plan? Make new friends and ke-ep the o-old; one is silver and the other is gold! "It's not as if we're giving anything *up*," she'd explained to them all on the way down, "because we're not. What we're doing, don't you see, is *widening* everything. So that we'll have two homes, or three, instead of just one. So Dinah, it's like when you go and visit your grandmother, or your other grandmother, and then you can come home after that."

"I hate my other grandmother."

"No, you don't."

"I *never* go and visit her."

"Yes, but what I'm getting at is you *can*, can't you?" Ruth cried out. "If you wanted to you *could*, couldn't you? That's

244

all I'm saying. That you don't have to stick to one place, one time, one life! My *God*, your *father* . . . !"

But Reggie cut her off with, "She knows all that," and Hollis said slyly, "Yeah, Ruth, cut it out, huh?" *You jerk*, she thought furiously. *You punk!* How had she gotten herself to this place? Where kids could . . . She thought back to the night when she and Marc had clung together on the balcony, and whispered together while that . . . person escorted her daughter downstairs to lust. How could I have let them do it? (So that they'd let me do it.)

They had crossed three days before on the island ferry to the American mainland, rented a station wagon in Seattle, driven down the coast through Washington and Oregon, turned inland at San Francisco on Highway 5, still heading south. She drove with a car full of children down the center of the state, watching clouds of dust skid in beige wings from either side of the car in front of her, thinning into nothing as far as the eye could see. A world without horizons, an impressionist nightmare. Silence, except for *suck suck suck* beside her in the front seat. In back, two sulking teenagers. What do they want, Ruth thought. What do they *want*?

The plan was this. Ruth would be staying at Cedar Bay with Marc. Since she had never really *moved*—only left—she would have to take care of that technicality. Dinah would stay with Ruth; little girls stayed with their mothers. But Reggie would not be deprived of her last year in high school. She was a teenager, an American; California girl. She would return for one school year to Canoga Park High. Living with friends or in the canyon house, whatever. Living with Hollis was what she and the boy said now. And who was Ruth to say no? Since that night she had hated both their faces; deciding, with familiar logic, that he had put her up to it, that her daughter would never be "leaving" if it weren't for him. In a year . . . there was a university in Victoria. Next summer things might be better. But for nine months Ruth would be almost free.

The trip had been long, arduous. There had been a flat

245

tire; she had been grateful for Hollis then. While he had
jacked up the side of her car she had gone over to Reggie,
and once again, in clouds of dust, with only the far sounds of
cows together, mooing, had put a stiff arm around her waist
and said, "Look. Why don't you just stay up there with us?
You like it there, I know it."

"Can Hollis stay too?"

"Honey, can't you see where all that gets kind of ridiculous? The summer's *over*. He's supposed to live at his *own*
house." She tried a humorous tone. "It's bad enough that *I'm*
running off without . . ."

"It's OK if you do it, it's not OK if we do it."

Could I have gotten away with anything like this, she thought
wildly, *with my own mother?* "When I was growing up, the kids
moved where the parents moved."

"I don't want to go where you go!"

"Well," she said carefully, "you *are* seventeen by now. I
guess that's not so bad. I was living by myself when I was seventeen." (Because my mother asked me to leave, and it was
awful.) "Do you think you'll want to stay in the canyon?"

"I don't know. I wrote a letter to Debbie and she said it
might be interesting to find a little house of our own, so we
could have a garden."

"But a house is a lot of work," Ruth started to say, when Dinah, who had been listening, broke down. "You mean you
aren't even going to stay in our own *house!*"

"Honey," Ruth said, "it's still your *daddy's* house, see? We
each own half of it. So if Reggie moves out, he would just
move in, or maybe even if she doesn't . . ."

Reggie leaned down to look in Dinah's face.

"Don't you like Debbie? You could come down on visits to
see us. That would be every—well, on Easter, and . . ."

Dinah wrenched away, stood by herself for a minute,
looked at Hollis as he bent close to the car, looked north at
cars coming toward her in the dusty light, and south at the
cars going away, and marched straight through the space be-

tween her sister and her mother, off the road to a barbed wire fence. She pressed her face into the wire and cried.

But that had been yesterday. They had gotten here, gotten home, in late afternoon, found the cats still alive by the neighbors' kindness, found a few stacked plates and cups as evidence of Jack's visits. The canyon parched under foul September sun, example of the desert Los Angeles really was. Yellow, sere, glazed overhead with metallic sun and smog; this was hell, Switzerland after the H-bomb. Every flower that Ruth had planted here during the years of her marriage was dead. Every marigold, every nasturtium. What would Jack do with the place, once he got it for his own? Maybe he would finally buy her out, maybe she would use the money to put in a new floor at the inn. Wide boards, pegged and grooved. Did anyone do that up on the island? But the shrimp boat, little bowl-shaped bay, were far away.

Ruth woke at ten the first morning, pressed against Dinah, wet with sweat. She heard Reggie and Hollis whispering below. She drank coffee in the patio, sweating, and waited for them to come up. She'd been right. It was too late to save any of the plants.

By noon they had more or less decided what to do. Hollis had telephoned his mother, told her he was in town, announcing he would spend the following year with Reggie, staying at Reggie's house. He couldn't exactly support himself, he'd said reasonably, he'd work part-time but would expect his mother to pay at least half his expenses. His mother wept in tones which Reggie and Ruth could hear through the receiver and across the room. Even Dinah lost her forlorn look and began to look cheerful, listening.

"No! No!" he said. "No! I'm not coming home, I know that much. I won't do it. I'll run away again, and you'll never find me!" Actually, Ruth thought, there was no need for such a fuss. Hollis had written several postcards to his mother in the short time he had been up in Cedar Bay.

After a few minutes of shouting, Hollis jumped up with

247

the phone, shambled out on the balcony, where he shut the door behind him. When he came back in he told Reggie that he had decided, after all, to live with his mother. "But I'll be over here every night, kid, you know that. And I'll bring the guys over, we're going to be forming the group again. And Mom says if I live at home for this year, she'll pay for at least my first two years at Berkeley. So isn't that a good thing? Isn't that the right thing to do? What do you think, Ruth? Don't you think it's the right thing to do?"

She at least knew better than to answer him. "Reggie, *please!* Why don't you change your mind? I hate to think of you alone down here."

But Reggie got up, took the phone from Hollis, and took her own time out on the balcony. "Debbie says it's OK with her if we live here for a while. She doesn't want to live at home because of her step-father, and if we stay here we won't have to pay rent, so we won't have to get jobs. Isn't that right, Mother? I mean, can you give me enough to live on, if I don't spend too much money?"

"Oh, shit, Reggie!"

"So. Now that it's all settled, the best thing to do is just get started, isn't it?"

"Listen, if there were any other way . . ."

"One other way might be if Marc were willing to move down here." A high voice pitched sweetly.

"You know he's not going to do that."

"Another way might be if you stayed down here for one more year, just until I got out of high school."

"Oh, could you do that?" Dinah shouted. "Could you, could you?"

"No," Ruth said with hatred, "I couldn't."

"OK, then," Reggie said, tossing her hair back over her shoulder. "You'd better get started. This is going to be quite a big move for you, isn't it? How many years have we lived here? Since before Dinah was born, isn't that right? Dinah, did you know that you were not only born when we lived in

248

this house, but that you were conceived here? Do you know what that means? In the back seat of Daddy's car. That's because Daddy's mommy was visting in the house, can you imagine? So that's a long time, you know? Almost eight years. Did you know that this is the oldest house in this part of the canyon?"

"As old as the Indians?" Dinah asked.

"No! They were here hundreds of years ago. A *long* time ago. But there's a place on the cement part of the foundation that says it's been here since 1916. Did you know that? Come on, let's go and see."

Twelve-thirty on a foul September afternoon. Almost eight years to the day since they had moved in. She and Jack and all the friends they had, trudging like African bearers up this winding path, carrying boxes, trophies, armloads of clothes. Jim Stockwell with a sack full of hamburgers. Paul Ficus marching through the picture window of the old valley house with a bureau drawer in his arms. Shattered glass. Deviled eggs. Canyon living. Their late, great experiment in the counterculture.

She poured herself another cup of coffee, started to make up the bed. Ah, Dinah had wet it. Ruth hauled bedding out onto the balcony, breathing urine, dust, hottest sun. What will they do when the next fire comes? But Reggie was right. This was the oldest house in this part of the canyon.

She thought of her rented station wagon. It was a small one, and she hoped not to be back again this way for months. She would have to be careful what she packed. Six or seven empty cartons stood in the back porch, against the possibility of ordinary errands. The stacks of newspapers, for winter and the Ben Franklin stove. She took a handful of papers, and a first carton, and dumped them on the living room couch. She picked up a huge ceramic cat from Tonalá, Mexico; dun-colored, with painted whiskers, covered with flowery scrolls. She and Jack had bought it years before, even before Reggie was born. They fought about it during the divorce.

("I've always thought of it as *my* cat," Jack said, high-minded. "*Did* you? Because I've always thought of it as *my* cat!") Later they settled that each of them would keep the cat for six months of the year. It was perhaps the one reasonable decision of their divorce. She wrapped up the cat.

She picked up a pre-Columbian figure of a man and woman in bed, embracing. It was genuine, and hers—a birthday present from her in-laws, but broken. She wrapped the pieces and put them in the box. There was some "family silver," not much of it, an embarrassingly thin box. A wedding present from her mother. She took it.

She took three stumpy figures made by Dinah in different primary grades—all of these things so far from the bamboo étagère, which she would not be able to take. Two rocks glued together with epoxy and painted to make a face. Another face, of plain brown clay, with deep holes for the eyes and mouth, and a long, painted column of a nose. The third figure, a white rabbit, painted to a high gloss, with a glob of absorbent cotton glued on for a tail. The cotton was dusty and gray.

She went into the kitchen, bent down, peered in the hot dark cupboard for a soufflé dish. She had told Marc that she made good soufflés; he had asked her to bring the soufflé dish. Actually, she wasn't sure she remembered how, or if she would be able to do it again, but she wrapped the dish, which almost filled this carton. She picked it up, and, going outside and round the house, started to carry it down the path to the car. She found Reggie and Dinah coming up from the basement. "Do you think we might take a couple of cartons from off the porch?" Reggie said. "I thought I might help Dinah pack some of her toys."

"Do whatever you like," Ruth said roughly. "Dinah, you'd better call your father at some point. Tell him we're in town, and tell him we're leaving."

Reggie tossed her head, sauntered into the house. Dinah

followed, her head down. Ruth took the carton down the hill and stuffed it into the back of the station wagon.

The walk back up the path tired her. Three months away from this canyon had left her out of shape. She picked up another carton from the porch, another couple of Sunday papers. Reggie and Dinah were downstairs, she could hear the thin, chittering ring of their voices.

A wooden vase full of dried acacia bossoms. Leave it. A ceramic cow someone gave to Jack and her. Ugly thing. A dead potted plant in a macramé holder which Patty had made for her. Well. She removed the holder, wrapped it in paper, put it in a corner of the carton.

She sat down, bent her head to her knees. There was so much here! If Jack would have only *taken his things* when he left, but no, no, no, no, he couldn't *do* that! All the stuff, all his old trophies, all his sweat clothes for twenty years, his worn-out Adidas shoes, his baby pictures, ski sweaters, skis, weights, dumbbells, even his old Navy uniforms! In bottom drawers, in closets. He wouldn't take any of it. All the arguments about community property, and what he ended up taking was the good Mexican rug and both tennis racquets and all the balls and all the good records. Sneaked into the house when she wasn't there and took the old Charlie Parker seventy-eights from when they were first married, and the brand-new Sergeant Pepper because the old one had worn out, and that one she'd never been able to find again in any shop—*Pearls Before Swine*—took them and waited until she asked him where they were, and then said, "Those? *That* one? Why, you must not need it very much, I've had that one for—it must be six *weeks* by now!" And meanwhile, his uniforms, heavy blue flannel and moldering braid, rotted in mothballs at the far end of her closet, staking out what was left of his possession.

Pictures. One small carton. To remind her of home. A Japanese print of a peasant couple in front of a mountain, the

251

woman holding a stick, the husband with his hands clasped over his mouth. Jack's from the war years. Supposed to be valuable. She'd take it. And let him yell. Into the carton, between thick sheets of newspaper, an original painting by Kenneth Patchen (but Marc would say it was second rate). A print from years ago by a friend of theirs: *Still Life with Baby Peacock* by Wesley Daimler. Ten years ago Wesley had gotten drunk at a poker party they had given, spent the night on their living room floor, entwined in Connie's twinkling, willing limbs. Jack had been furious, hearing their groans, but the print had come as an apology for the night. Take it. Hurry up. Her father painted—a hobby between ladies. Oh, Daddy, fooling around like that, what did it get you? How many couches did you buy, how many sets of fitted and unfitted sheets? She packed four of his pictures away, charming, rustic oils. Further up on the wall, a larger, more sophisticated watercolor of the old man himself. He'd left this one with her when he took his powder, how long? Twenty-six years ago. She'd slipped an eight-by-ten fan-club glossy of Frankie Laine in over the smiling face; Frankie, his greased hair gleaming, his secretary's pure hand having spelled out *Thanx* beneath his air-brushed, puffy lips. He stayed there, framed, for three years, partly to spare her mother's feelings, partly because the child Ruth had loved Frankie Laine.

She took the second carton into her hands, lurched it up and against her aching chest, hauled it out of the house and down to the station wagon. The trunk full of clothes, she thought, the back seat full of cartons, a few big pictures in the back covered with blankets. A few kitchen things up in the front seat with Dinah and me. *And I could take some cuttings.* But the only things alive now were succulents. Her succulents had died once, by the hundreds, the undiscovered thousands, just after Jack had left, when the temperature on a frosty night had gone down to eighteen degrees. She'd wept when Jack had left, she'd cried, but she'd saved her real tears for the bright morning with its cold and angry sun, when she'd gone out on the patio to find the whole world weeping. Plants with leaves like little children's fingers, burst from within by the cold, weeping brown mucus onto the cheap brown dirt! Ah, shit! Why was she crying? It was just that starting the one project made her remember the other. "I'll be perfectly frank with you," a PR man had told her once while they worked together to set up an interview. "I consider that I've had it. I just don't have the guts to get one more apartment, or install another phone, or buy another *cat*."

She was running in it again; the human race—with the women who typed, their children held hostage in transparent lucite squares. She'd be planting flowers again, well, she'd done it all summer. She'd be picking up Dinah from school, waiting patiently with other parked mothers on blank deserted asphalt, for the afternoon bell. Maybe she'd have another kid.

Trudging up the path, her head down, she passed Dinah and Reggie both holding onto a cardboard box.

"In the back seat, *on* the seat," she called after them. "Do you hear me?" But they didn't answer.

OK. Open a beer. Stand in the kitchen and put water on your face. Pull down the Sunset Garden Book. God! The dust. The Adelle Davis, all three of them, inscribed, from when she'd been on the show. But Ruth had asked her to inscribe them to Reggie! Shit! The Julia Child, just Volume I. The collection of dinner plates from twelve different states. She loved them, no one else—no, Jack loved them too, Reggie loved them too. She picked up Dinah's baby plate and cup, roughly wrapped them in paper, crammed them in by the books.

Enough! She was ready to go. So tired of this house, this tiny, messy, impractical, drafty, ill-heated, ugly, boring, inconvenient—she'd take her clothes, and Dinah's—all she could carry. No more than four more trips down the path and the car would be full, there would be nothing she could do about it, she'd have to go. She was done with this city, this

253

house—let Reggie make her own arrangements! Ruth would send the money. Tomorrow, from wherever in California she happened to be. Even this afternoon, if she got out in time. She'd take an envelope, address it to Reggie. Ms. Reggie Parker. P.O. Box 1802, Topanga. Send her the money. How much? Shouldn't they talk about it? What about Jack? Would he give her any money? Maybe Reggie would have to work after all. Had she thought of it? It was a mark of how Ruth had brought up the children that she was sure Reggie hadn't really thought of it.

Ruth went into the bathroom, voided. God, she thought, that noise, that smell! She thought of how she and Marc might look to strangers. Two middle-aged people, fucking. Two bellies undulating, like the psychedelic wave-makers they used to sell in department stores. Hair growing damply where it shouldn't be; not enough hair where it should be. She thought of the postscript to Connie's letter; she hadn't shown it to Marc:

And if that weren't all, screaming queens, bull dykes, raving loonies, custody quarrels, gallery conspiracies and other considerations, Luke bored a *hole,* can you believe it, in the doorway of my bedroom, just the level to see, well, just the level to see. I told him, look, I'm laughing, *but stay out of my sex life.* You want to know about sex you ask me. But he said he knew all about it, *the cock goes in the cunt thump thump and it's a real good way to spread pin worms.* Frankly, I don't know why I—

She got up, washed, splashed her face, returned to the living room. Dinah was on the couch, away from it all, sucking her thumb. Reggie, beside her, bolt upright. "You're taking everything in this God damned house!"

"Reggie, that's not true, how *could* I? The car can't take more than five cartons at the very most!"

254

"You're taking every good thing. There's nothing left here. You're doing what *he* did."

"Well, I'm *moving out* of here! That's what we've been talking about. That's what I've been telling you! What did you want? What do you expect?"

"Nothing."

"Well?"

"Nothing!"

Silence. The sound of Dinah sucking. Of flies. Of cars whizzing, far down in the canyon.

"Reggie? If you moved out, you'd take your things, wouldn't you?"

Silence.

"Reggie? Wouldn't you?"

"Yes."

"Look. I asked you to come along!"

"Sure."

"I want you to come along."

"Sure."

"If it's going to be your house now"—but it would never be her house—"don't you want to be able to put your own things, where you want them?"

Silence.

"Look, Reggie, you're not going to do this to me. If you don't want to come along, that's your problem, not mine. I've put in sixteen years . . ."

Reggie answered the last sentence but one. "Not your problem?" she asked, and got up, tossing her hair, and left the room. It was so hot that her hair in that familiar gesture, instead of tossing, lay stuck, much of it, against her damp cheek.

Fuck you! Ruth whispered to her disappearing back, and went out into the kitchen for another carton.

Underwear, sweaters, scarves, jewelry, pants, so angry that when she came out in the living room to find Jack on the couch in a flamingo matte jersey shirt open to his waist, and baby conch shells around his neck, wrists, and ankles, she had no more room for reaction. Jack sat by his sleeping daughter, smoothing her pale hair back from her damp face. On every third or so stroke, seashells caught in the fine yellow threads; he carefully disentangled them as they talked.

"Jack, I'm moving out, I'll be staying up there for a while."

"What about Dinah?"

"She'll be going with me."

"But when do I get to see her?"

"I'll be coming down a lot, you've already been up there once . . ."

"Before, I used to get to see her once a week." *And before that you saw her every day,* but she didn't say it, looking at his old face, his gray hair, his thin little hands, his hard-kept skin rippling across his ribs. ("You know when you're in shape? When you can pick up the skin, like *this,* and there's not a bit of fat there. If your skin's just like a dog's, that's when you're in shape!")

"It's very beautiful up there. Didn't you say once that . . . Jennifer wanted to live in a planned community in Oregon? That wouldn't be too far away . . ."

"Ah, I can't stand that crap, that macramé, that silversmithing. I want to *run,* Ruth! And sail my *boat!* That's all I want to do."

"Well?"

"So what's going to happen to the house?"

"I thought Reggie could stay here, for the year, until she finishes high school."

"But what about *me!* It's half my house!"

"You could live here with her," Ruth said, with cruel naïveté.

"Are you kidding! I'm not going to have my life-style messed with!" Then, seeing that he *was* being kidded, he subsided. "One year then. But no way am I going to live with her, I'm not responsible. And what's going to happen about the money? I'm only working part-time, you know."

"*I*," she said smugly, "am not going to be working at all."

"You can't do that! How's the kid going to live?"

"I don't know. I'll send what I can. But Reggie may have to get a job. *You* may even have to get a job." On this undeniably good last line she got up to finish packing her clothes.

"Bitch!" he whispered. "Cunt!"

She turned back to him, shaking. "What's the matter, can't you . . ."

But the front door opened, interrupting them.

Four young men appeared first in the doorway, and then lined up on the couch. They were chubby, well fed by their mommies, their bellies lay comfortably over their metal jeans buttons. One of them, with the sweetest smile, had wavy, fresh-washed hair which lay not down to his shoulders but parallel to them, long crimpy yellow stuff which continued, horizontal, to his shoulders' ends and past them. He looked like a human feather duster.

"Hi," he said companionably, in answer to her stare. "I'm Ronnie. Friend of Hollis's."

"I'm Ruth Parker, and this is my husband, Jack."

The two freaks looked at each other in disgust. But the young man had been well brought up. "This is Jake, and this is Freddie, and this is Jordo. We left our instruments out front."

"Oh?"

"Hollis says it's OK to use the house to rehearse. That's real nice of you, Mrs. Parker. We've had a lot of gigs this summer—we kind of missed Hollis though—and if we work real hard, we might be able to make this into a dynamite group." He spoke loudly, patronizingly, as if to the deaf.

"Well—Ronnie—I suppose you, it's all up to Reggie, she's going to be living here now."

"Oh, yes, ma'am!"

Four pairs of dull eyes shifted to Hollis, lately returned, lounging in the doorway, who put on his most docile smile and said, "Oh, it'll be all right with Reggie, I already checked it out with her. And don't you worry, Ruth, we'll take good care of everything. Don't you worry either, Mr. Parker, we'll be sure to leave everything just the way we found it."

"If you *think*," Jack began raspingly, but another sallow young man cut him off.

"Say, this is some pad you got here," and his neighbor on the couch dolefully whispered, "Far out." Their legs, long and insentient, shod with hiking boots, reached halfway into the room.

"Good vibes," the fourth volunteered, nodding as he said it. "I sure like these canyon houses."

Hollis smiled in the doorway, tall and charming, and Ruth said in her most social tone, "How was your mother, Hollis? I imagine she was glad to see you," and was rewarded by a look of pure hate.

She excused herself to go past him, went downstairs, passed Dinah's room, where she and Reggie were stuffing toys in a box.

"Only two boxes of toys," she called in harshly. "We'll get the rest later." She heard Dinah's voice, a high pale twitter. "I'll take this," Dinah said, "and this," reaching out at anxious random to her shelved walls crammed with animals, dolls, games. Ruth heard a clatter, the slim thud of a plastic chicken dropped to the bottom of a cardboard box.

"Now wait a minute," Reggie said reasonably. "You want to be sure to take things that you can really *play* with. Like the Old Maid cards. Or the Clue. Does Josh have Parchesi? How about Scrabble?"

But Dinah said, "Can't I take this?" And Ruth heard the thin, pathetic clack of something else flimsy, something plastic.

I can't *stand* this, Ruth thought, and dove into her closet, pressed heavy winter clothes on each side of her ears, breathed old wool; I can't stand the pain. She was appalled to hear everything so easily from Dinah's room. How much did they hear from Jack and me, she thought, how many fights, the night I found out about Jennifer, the night I told him to leave?

She scooped a line of clothes from her closet, winter things, heavy pants and suits, and blundered, in tears, out into the living room. Jack was still there waiting.

"If you think I'm going to put up with this," he hissed at her, quietly so Reggie wouldn't hear. "If you think I'm going to let every freaked-out baby from the San Fernando Valley . . ."

"Talk to *her* about it," Ruth said spitefully. "Talk to *them* about it." Then she said, "Take some of these clothes, will you?"

"Why should I?"

"God damn it, Jack! Help me for *once*. Help me!"

For once he did. He went to her bureau—after years still knowing how and where her things were kept—opened the drawer with the heavy sweaters, shawls.

"You'll want these, won't you?" And they made another trip down the hill.

On the way back up, trudging, sweating, she said, "If you keep on giving Reggie your hundred a month in child support, I'll do the same from up there, OK?"

"OK."

"And she can get your medical benefits? Don't you still have some insurance?"

"Yes."

"And you'll come up and see Dinah?"

"Your boyfriend isn't going to like it."

"I . . . don't care. You'll come up, won't you?"

Soon her clothes were packed in the trunk of the station wagon. There only remained Dinah, and Dinah's things. She and Jack, working together now, went together to Dinah's door.

"I want *this*," Dinah said desperately, and dropped a torn comic book into the carton. "I know I'm going to want it."

"Dinah," Reggie said, "don't you want to take some dolls?"

"Don't take too many things," Ruth said. "There'll be plenty of things to buy up there. Plenty of things to do."

"Come on, Dinah," Jack said. "Why don't you come out on the patio and talk to me for a while?" He scooped his child off the rumpled bed and took her outside, in his arms, her face hidden against his thin neck. He called back in the room, "Reggie can help you with that, can't she? There's no use taking too much time with this."

So he'd agreed to it. He was going to let her do it. It really was going to happen. She was going away.

"Just the one carton of toys, and a small suitcase, and everything hanging up in the closet."

"She'll need winter clothes," Reggie said, and opened up small pink bureau drawers.

"Listen, Reggie. Thank you for being with Dinah like that."

But Reggie didn't answer. Upstairs Hollis and his friends began tuning up.

"Look. You don't have to put up with all that—music—unless you want to. Because it's your own house. You'll be the head of it here. Of course, if you *want* to, that's another thing. Another whole question. All I'm saying is . . ."

Reggie packed stacks of cotton underwear, Levi's folded in thirds, hand-knit caps and sweaters. Kept her head turned away.

OK, Ruth thought. OK, OK, OK, OK. "Are you finished with that?" she said coldly. "Because if you are I'm almost ready."

"Yes. Just a minute."

Ruth went into her own room, wrote a check for two hundred dollars, made out to Reggie. She looked in the mirror, ran a comb through her hair, thought about changing. What's the use? As hot as it is here, it will be hotter on the Ridge Route and up on Highway 5. If they drive all day they may hit San Francisco by eleven or so tonight. Tomorrow morning the trip across the Golden Gate, that wonderful tunnel at the beginning of Marin County with the rainbow colors painted on gray concrete. Then up, up, through Oregon, Washington, across on the ferry, toward that lawn, that harbor, that toy steamer on the far horizon. See? It is happening! She can take a shower and wash her hair tonight in San Francisco. She picked up her purse and the check, and, going back into Reggie's room, laid the check down on the bureau where her daughter could see it.

"This is just for now. If you need any more, just let me know. I'll send you some more in a couple of weeks, anyway . . ."

Reggie nodded.

"Look, I think it's just as well if I go now. Everything's ready . . . there's no point in prolonging this. Are you going to walk me down to the car?"

"I don't think so."

"Well, at least come outside and say goodbye to Dinah, can you do that?"

Reggie picked up the suitcase, Ruth the stack of half-size clothes on hangers. They walked upstairs past teenaged blockheads, muttering, picking on their guitars, lost in blue smoke. The hot air in the living room was thick with it. Hollis sprawled on her couch.

On the patio, Jack sat with Dinah on his lap. She was crying. He spoke earnestly to her, words Ruth didn't hear. He got up when he saw his wife and other daughter, took the suitcase from Reggie. For a few seconds the four of them stood there, caught in time.

"Reggie thinks she'll say goodbye right here," Ruth said. "Dinah, give your sister a kiss goodbye." Dinah hugged her sister around the waist, weeping.

261

"Come on," Reggie said to her. "It isn't so bad. We'll be coming up there to see you, Hollis will take me, and you'll be coming down here, to see your dad, you still have your room here . . ." She had bent down and was talking straight to Dinah, looking into her eyes.

"Come *on!*" Ruth said. "We've got to get started. This isn't doing anybody any good. Goodbye, Reggie. Write me." She leaned over, put her arms around her daughter. Reggie turned her pale cheek to be kissed.

"Goodbye," she said, and went back into the house.

The others walked down the dusty path to the car. The last time, Ruth thought, past the two eucalyptus trees, the place where she once saw the rattlesnake, and finally, the last two homemade steps, the canyon street, glare of the car, the sizzling secondhand shell.

"Say goodbye to your father, Dinah."

But they had already said goodbye. He gave her a last kiss, put her in the front seat. It was hot as a sauna in there.

"Be good," he said to her. "Write to me." But she was already curled up, her thumb in her mouth, eyes closed.

They stood together now, by the door to the driver's seat. For the first three years of their marriage she hadn't even known how to drive. She had never written a check until the year that they divorced. "I'll write," she said. "Jack, I think this is a good thing."

"Yeah, sure. Take care." He didn't look at her, but away. His fierce look concealed a terrible shyness. (Didn't it? Didn't it?) He took a step forward and put his arms all the way around her. The first time in years.

"Oh, Jack," she said, in tears, "I hope you win all your races!"

Then she was in the car, driving (the last time) through Topanga Canyon, toward the San Fernando Valley and the Ventura Freeway, which would take her to the Bakersfield turnoff and out of the city, over the Ridge Route and onto Highway 5. She drove past the place where all the lupine grew in the spring, past the Community House—when they first moved here it didn't even have any walls—past the American Legion, past kids hitching this way, and—across the street—that way. At the top of the Topanga Crest, the little summit that looked down into the hundreds of thousands of houses in the valley, she started to cry. Crying, she drove past trailer parks and tract houses, down the hill into the smoggy, valley floor. She pulled into a Mobil station.

"Hot enough for you?" the attendant said, and stopped when he saw her face.

"Fill it with Supreme, and would you check the oil and tires, please?"

Ruth got out of the car, rummaged through her purse, called her own number.

"Reggie?"

The voice was clear, musical. In the background an incredible din.

"Reggie, baby?"

"Oh, Mommy!"

"Reggie, I hate to leave this way."

"Oh, it's OK, it's *OK*."

"I can't lose this chance . . ." and to the sound of sobs, "I love you, honey."

"Oh, I love you."

"I'll call you every week."

"Sure."

"I'll write you every day, will you write me?"

"Sure!"

"Look . . ."

"No, no, it's *OK*. I know you have to. It's . . . probably even good." Reggie spoke, in her clear voice. Ruth saw her baby, running down the hall, falling; the glass, and milk, and blood. God, did I . . .

"Oh, Reggie . . ."

"No. Let's get off. Oh, I'm so glad you called."

"Me too," Ruth said, but heard Reggie's voice, "Goodbye,

goodbye," and then the rude buzz. The attendant peered curiously at her, she saw him, she held the phone to her ear; a fly was closed in the booth with her. She couldn't leave, she couldn't leave this booth. Finally, she clicked for the operator.

"Operator," she said, "I need to make a long-distance, person-to-person phone call, to Marc Mandell in Cedar Bay, on Vancouver Island. It may be listed under the Cedar Bay Inn."

His voice was soft, and full of honey. She could hear the ease, the comfort, the money there.

"Oh, Marc," she said, "Marc?"

"Well, hello there, Ruth . . ."

"Marc, I have to, you have to, just talk to me for a few minutes, oh, Marc, I just left her there all alone."

"But didn't you get in just last night?"

"*Yes,* I drove all night, all day, I got in last night. Oh, *Marc!*"

"Isn't that pretty fast? You sure you got her *set up* all right?"

"It was so awful there I had to leave. I just got up this morning, and stuffed things in the car. Jack came up to the house—oh, Marc, she wouldn't speak to me when I left!"

"Did you remember the soufflé dish?"

"What?"

"Did you remember the soufflé dish?"

"Yes . . . I think I have it here in the car . . ."

"Because you *said,* Ruth, that you'd bring it before. Remember? The first time you came up for that weekend, and the second time, the beginning of the summer. But you *forgot it both times.* Even though you said you'd bring it. I really considered it an omen of what our life was going to be together."

"Marc! I'm trying to tell you! I'm calling you from a gas station, I've got Dinah in the car."

"You should have stayed a few days longer."

"Oh, I *know.* But she didn't seem to want me to stay. She seemed like she wanted me to leave."

"Did you make adequate arrangements for her care?"

"What?"

"Someone to stay with her? Money for her in the bank? I don't like this, Ruth, I never did. I never kept a secret of that. I don't like the idea of her living down there alone."

"But, Marc. We agreed. Didn't we? She didn't want to stay up there with me. And there are people down here—Hollis—"

"And what kind of use is he?"

"Where are you?"

"What?"

"Where are you now, in the hotel?"

"Out on the terrace. I just got in from sailing."

"What kind of day is it?"

"Beautiful, why?"

"It's hot down here."

Silence.

"Marc?"

"*Look,* Ruth, I'm glad you called, because there's something I've got to call to your attention."

She thought of the money she would have to pay for this call, of how often he used her credit cards for gas instead of his, of how he chose ground turkey instead of beef in the co-operative market down in Victoria, because it was the cheapest protein available. And at that moment the operator said, "Your three minutes are up, please signal when through."

"Yes?"

"You know how when you left, Josh and I gave you a ride down to Victoria? You know how we all went down together?"

"Yes."

"Well, Josh and I decided to get the car lubed. We stayed there all day, waiting for the car to get done with. I bought Josh lunch, I ended up buying him dinner. Then we decided

265

to stay in town for a show, Ruth. To tell the truth, we felt
pretty much at loose ends without you. We didn't get home
until after midnight. A good deal after midnight, you know
how long it takes to drive from Victoria to the Bay."

"Yes."

"Do you remember, when we said goodbye?"

"Yes?"

"We were all outside, in the driveway?"

"Yes, sure."

"I'd told Josh to lock Whisty in the kitchen, and he did?"

"I guess so."

"Well. Just *after* that, Dinah decided—*again*—she had to go
to the bathroom?"

"Well, *yes.*"

"Dinah, *Dinah,* went upstairs, *through* the kitchen, came
down again, closed the kitchen door, but she didn't *look,*
Ruth. She locked Whisty into the cocktail lounge. Do you
know what that means?"

"Did he tear up a lot of stuff?" Looking at the car, hoping
Dinah wouldn't wake while she was on the phone, watching
cars go up, down, up, down, from the canyon, to the valley.

"The poor dog couldn't go to the bathroom in the proper
way! She kept him from . . . he had to go, right there on
the floor."

"Look. Can't we talk about this when I get up there? I'm
sorry about the dog, but people are waiting for this booth."

"Not only that. She *locked* Whisty *away* from his food. The
dog was crying there, Ruth, crying for over nine hours. We
heard him the minute we parked the car in the garage. He
didn't have one thing to eat. It was just terrible."

"I'm in this booth, Marc. I just left my *daughter* down here
so I can be with you . . ."

"You're bringing the other one with you. Now I don't *mind*
that, I don't *object* to that, I told you that would be all right
with me, as far as I'm concerned that's OK. But certain rules

266

have to be obeyed in this house, and that has to be understood. Right now."

"Marc." She saw him in her mind's eye, not at Cedar Bay, not on the terrace with the lawn and the boat chugging in the distance. That was gone now, along with the woman who served breakfast, and told about losing her son in the avalanche, or Dr. and Mrs. Pomeroy wading for oysters, their trousers rolled above the knee, or the inland sea of the waterbed and Marc kneeling on it, walking on water: *I love your body!* It was gone. Like *I Love a Mystery* when she was eight. Like taking the train when she was five. Like her mother's pretty face. But Ruth remembered, clearly, her first afternoon with him, in the dusty, snake-infested brush on the ridge of the canyon behind her house. Marc Mandell, from her high school, his soft shirt pocked with foxtails, his arms folded across his chest, bent over sadly as if he had a cramp. "I feel very good about this, Ruth."

"Marc, do you know what you're doing? I don't know how to answer you . . ."

"What do you mean?" he said shrilly, but before she had a chance to begin to answer, went on, his voice high, trembling, "Oh, I know what you say about her. You take the position that she's just like any other kid. Maybe she *is,* or *was.* But with no one to look after her, no one to take care of her, no kind of even ordinary decent care, it's no wonder she doesn't do what she's told, hasn't the least concept of discipline . . ."

"Marc?"

"Yes?" His voice teetering, the man on the string between two skyscrapers.

"You can take the question of Dinah's good manners, and how well I take care of her, and all the money I'm going to pay for this fucking phone call . . ."

She could hear expectant breathing, in the north, on his veranda.

267

Carolyn See

"And you can change the whole thing into one-dollar bills, and stuff them up your ass."

"Ah, God."

She heard the relief in his voice, the disgraceful, sickening relief, and then hung up.

And before she had time to think about it, or to start again to cry, or think about hauling all that stuff back up the hill, or think of her life, in fact, in any aspect, she dialed a number more familiar to her than any.

"Hello, may I speak to Mr. Nichols, please," and "Hello, Mr. Nichols, this is Ruth Parker. I hope you . . . didn't take what I said last April too seriously. Because. Because," through boring middle-aged tears. "Oh, Mr. Nichols, can I have my job back? Or some job, something?"

"I'll see what I can do."

XI

A house, a room, a car. In the morning, work; in the evening, brandy; at night burglars or the fear of them, the late show, or its absence; the light above her head, a magazine, the sound of one, lone, insomniac bird. Reading magazines because books were too heavy. Once or twice she went to sleep with a book clenched in her hand and woke up to that, the printed word, under glare, and remembered, knew, what it was to be her mother.

Books took you to another world, Mr. Kurtz upcountry, the road to Kuling seen from a sedan chair. OK, OK, but what was the point? The world was *this,* narrower every day, every minute. This was fear, the adventure, such as it was.

She had taken to sleeping with Dinah. The bedrooms were far away, she feared burglars. Time and time again she reviewed the situation; there weren't any burglars, how could there be burglars? She had never seen any—except once, twenty-two years ago. Twenty-two years ago. She was a middle-aged woman. She had friends she had known for twenty-five, twenty-seven, thirty years. She slept with the light on, she creamed her face, she slept with a book—no, magazines were better. She would develop her mother's picture at least that much; that generational polaroid. Dinah slept soundly. Didn't she? Didn't she? Devout in sleep, her thumb still in her mouth, submerged in blankets, a golden dolphin, hard not to touch her. In nine years she'd be sixteen, what then? "She'll leave you," her own mother said, over the phone. "Younger than that, probably, you'd better get used to the idea. What are you going to do then?" That would probably be easy. One thing or another, one way or another. She found pleasure with women friends—getting stoned, exchanging confidences. Already the confidences had changed. They happened in the past tense. ("Al wanted to be a millionaire before he was forty . . .")

She had two thoughts about her own mortality. She would live a very long time; she would show them. Or she would die, soon. Her children would be orphaned. She thought about this in the night. (Estelle had died, telling jokes. Her husband remarried. They said he was happy.) But what if Ruth died when Dinah was ten? And she tried to picture her own mother, whose mother had died when she was eleven. Poor little girl, Ruth's mother. In middy blouses? Who ironed them? Who bought the skirts? Who changed the sheets? Listen. In Ruth's mind it was three-thirty in that house—after school. Her mother had come home, through the back door, to oilcloth, a dripping icebox; poverty, poverty, and a sound of coughing in the back room.

Some days Ruth worked, sometimes not. Three-thirty in the afternoons, Dinah came home. Who knows, who knows? Caught in time, walking down a dark hall to her sinking mother.

* * *

She was back again, in hell. Pico Boulevard—hell must be Pico Boulevard, choked in yellow haze. A Mexican restaurant, and the "world's largest game store." The broken cement effigy of an enormous chili bowl. Waiting for a stop sign, at a crowded intersection, three cars back. The couple to her right fighting bitterly, while the kids in the back seat cried. The man to her left, waiting to turn, picking his nose. To the north on Westwood Boulevard, first-run movies, the university, the best *pâtisserie* in the city. To the east, Beverly Hills; to the south, the blacks. Out west, toward the sullen, yellowish sea, Nick, Dick and Clara's Television Repair. The light turned green, but no, she didn't make it through the intersection.

It seemed to her that she had done something good in her life. Sacrificed something she wanted for her children. How odd, how pretentious, how silly, and maybe in the long term, how ill-advised. September. Back home, surrounded by boxes, weeping; cashing in on friends. Asking her pediatrician for tranquilizers, since she didn't have her own doctor, telling her dumb little story; the pediatrician literally sobbing in sympathy: "Your children will thank you for this! You've done a noble thing!" She, palming her prescription, turning to leave, finding the door blocked by the pediatrician himself, wide, tall, nervous, fifteen years younger than she, winding her up in a fumbling embrace. "Say, I'm not sure I dumped that guy," she mumbled. "I think he dumped me." The pediatrician's kiss, damp and soft as a baby's washcloth. "You've done a noble thing!"

Which means, the three of them, any morning, waking up in the living room. Morning sun breaking the canyon into slanted cracks. Ruth getting up, after a token argument, to make the coffee. Reggie jumping at a chance, leaping up from the couch and into the double bed with Dinah. Coffee for Ruth, who sits now on the couch, drawing Reggie's sleep-

271

ing bag up around her knees. The couch already sags here in this one place, is it time for a new one? Someday, when the kids are older . . . but Reggie is already seventeen. Dinah grumbles, "Couldn't I have some coffee, you could have gotten me some coffee, God damn!"

"Don't swear," her mother says.

"You know what happens to you when you drink coffee?" Reggie says, delicately sipping at her own cup. "Remember when you had that iced tea when we were driving down Highway 5?"

"Yeah," Dinah says, with satisfaction. "I was *awful.*" She, sitting at right angles to Reggie in the bed, kicks out at her sister's legs. Reggie spills coffee on the sheet. "Hey, *watch* it," she says, and Dinah prepares to howl, but thinks better of it. Soon it will be time for breakfast, *quesadillas* on paper plates with chili sauce. Throw out the plates, wash up the skillet, then what? The house is not exactly clean, the refrigerator not exactly full. Ruth doesn't have to go to work today. She works less since she came back, they have her on strictly human interest stories now; even she can recognize their irrelevance. She has covered Jack Benny's funeral since she came back, and two other funerals of old movie stars, one of which didn't get on the air.

The truth is that in the short time she has been gone, the station has changed. There is a woman now as anchorman, or anchorwoman, a hefty girl in her twenties. She wears silk shirts and pearls, and competes directly with the girl with harlequin glasses on another channel and the girl with bleached blond hair on yet another. The situation is better now for women. But Ruth's pieces are fewer, more far between. The proper sort of thing for a woman pushing forty. What the hell, it's harmless, really, a way of filling an hour, of killing an afternoon, of regarding the present, recalling the past, a good way to make a living. They won't fire her.

Reggie sits up in bed.

"Dinah! You rat!"

"Hmm?" Dinah looks immensely pleased.

"Oh!" Reggie says. "Oh, oh, oh!"

"Watch out for the sheet, now," Ruth says. "Don't pull it out." She is the one who will end up making the bed.

"Mother! Do you know what she did? You rat!" she says to Dinah. "You little shit!"

"What *is* it, Reggie?"

"She farted! In secret! She *farted* under the sheets!"

"Why, *no*," Dinah says between giggles, drowning in giggles, "I didn't, I wouldn't, I *couldn't* do a thing like that. It must have been *you*, Reggie!" And falls over on her side, laughing, laughing, laughing, while Reggie puts down her coffee and smothers her sister with a pillow.

"Well," Reggie says finally to her sister, "you're sure lucky. You couldn't have done that up there with that bastard."

"Don't say that, Reggie," Ruth says.

"He is a bastard, Mom," Dinah says. "He *is* a bastard."

"Don't say that, Dinah, please."

"He is, Mom," Dinah says, and then shuts up.

The letters from Cedar Bay began to come. In his beloved handwriting. Five to six pages. Onion skin paper. "I don't know whether I hate or despise you most," but she read to the end, weeping, and answered in kind.

The letters came two, three, four, five times a week. Finally, one afternoon at work, when she should have been out on assignment, she held one, unopened. "I don't know what to *do*," she wailed, sobbing, to Mario. "I can't stand it anymore, I can't stand it, I can't stand it!"

"Just send it back! Don't open it!"

"I *have* to open it!"

Silence. Then, "Well, OK. *Steam* it open. OK? Get a teapot and steam it open. Find out what he has to say. Then paste it back and write a very dignified letter—you just can't take this anymore, your feelings are—whatever. Then put his letter, in its envelope, and *your* letter into another envelope and send it back to him."

"Another envelope?" she said blankly.

"Ruth," he said slowly, "a slightly *bigger* envelope."

She spent the rest of the afternoon at home with a teakettle. The envelope, which she had expected to open easily, was stubborn. She was clumsy, and held the envelope closer to the stove's flame than to the spout. Parts of the envelope turned brown and began to curl. Parts remained stuck shut, despite her best efforts. She tore these, finally, impatiently and ripped the contents from their sheath. The letter, as usual, made her cry. She looked through Dinah's toys until she found some glue, and put his letter and envelope back together. It was a dreadful job. Then she sat down with pen and paper.

"For the past two months I have taken this pointless, unjust abuse," she began, and continued for three pages; no cross-outs, no blots. She searched the house—for a slightly bigger envelope—and made a special trip down to the post office.

He answered by return mail, a large, official-looking, manila parcel. *Special Delivery,* it said. *Certified. Special Handling. First Class.* Hands trembling, she opened it, there in the post office. Her own medium-sized envelope fell out, still sealed, together with three closely typed sheets. Powerless, her hands picked up the fluttering papers. "You bitch," the letter began. In the post office's waning light, she read his last letter. She dropped the disgusting record, the handwritten mess, into the wastebasket, drove home and called up Edward.

"Home so soon?" he pleasantly inquired, and within a day or two, they spent a night or two a week, at home, with the children, eating barbecue from paper plates. And when the children were in bed, and the news over and the late show over (or during the news or the late show; because who cared, who paid attention to such amenities?) there was some pleasure.

Another afternoon Ruth stayed home. She had bronchitis and the people where she worked were very nice about her taking time off. It was late November, the prettiest season in Southern California. A temperate sun beat down through smogless air, catching leaves in radiant lacy patterns outside each window. Ruth sat on the couch, drinking hot lemonade and icy beer, talking to her friends on the phone, watching color television.

Late in the afternoon, a friend of hers appeared on the screen. A friend she had known twenty-five, twenty-six, twenty-seven years. And her friend's husband. They were on a game show and the game was this. Three Hollywood couples, answering questions about married life.

Ruth knew her friend right away. Her hair had not been brushcut. It hid, sorrowfully, under an expensive scarf. Her husband, under his burnished swatch of hair, pinched his face into a smile. His series had been cancelled. Their marriage, people said, was not going well.

"If one of you were to buy a *car*, without telling the other one . . . !" "If your mother-in-law came to visit . . . !" Gales of laughter. Outside Ruth's room, oak trees caught the sunlight. Not entirely unpleasant, to be sitting here with a cold.

"If there's one thing in the world that your husband worries about that you do, but he's too polite to ever say anything about it, what would it be?" The two other women answer with innuendo, brash confidence. Harlots, speaking harlotry. Ruth's friend answers, "Oh, maybe, when I arrange an outing for the kids, and forget to tell him anything about it?"

When it is his turn to answer, her husband smiles and answers the question. "I'm too polite to say anything about her

275

weight." The show is ending, the women sit on their husbands' laps. Ruth's friend seems to float an inch above her husband's dancing knees.

Twenty-seven years ago Ruth's mother took her downtown on the streetcar to see Nellie Lutcher at the Million Dollar Theatre. The opera, too, a few times, the ballet sometimes, with two or three other little girls in tow, but Ruth and her mother saw Nellie Lutcher alone; four hundred pounds of her, singing in a high, don't-care voice, *"Fetch it on down to my house, daddy, ain't nobody home but me."* And then the two of them came home, through the violet Los Angeles afternoon, to the empty house, the bourbon, the racing form, the silence, the Lady Esther Four Purpose Face Cream, and in the night, her mother's helpless sobs, stretching to every corner, every horizon, as far as life itself.

Autumn. In the Rosarito Beach Hotel. Mexican shoreline close to the border. Once hostelry to Rita Hayworth and Aly Kahn. Now serving Margaritas by the pool to social workers and secondary school teachers. Ruth took Dinah; Connie brought her oldest daughter. The children swam and ran by the pool, the women drank Margaritas and smoked in their room, while the children clucked nervously and made dark remarks about Mexican jails.

One afternoon, puffing, sighing, they heard a commotion outside and went to the window to look. Below the line of ocean, the brave line of tiny triangular flags which still flew over this broken resort, in the lanai beside the enormous pool, a table of drunken Americans had asked a trio to sing. The trio strummed out old favorites and the Americans, two by two, began to dance. A fellow in his twenties with a girl in a wide straw hat; a chunky young man with a girl in a yellow dress. There was left another young man, in kakhi shorts and shirt, across the wide round table from a woman who was much older (mother, perhaps, to one of the girls), dressed in a black top with new white beads (Ruth had that same week bought the same white beads). The young man nodded his head to the music, tapped his fingers on the table. The woman gazed out to sea. The young man pushed himself to his feet and carefully, through chairs, made his way to her side. Would she dance? And, his arm against her waist, her arm against his neck, they step together, he in the style of the sixties, she in the style of the forties. Another step. And the young man stops dancing, drags her to the side of the pool and throws her in. She can't swim.

She spoke to Jack often, more often, on the phone. "You've got to help me," she had wailed to him when she came back. "This is worse than what I went through with you. I don't want to put it on the kids! What am I going to do?" They met for lunch, in dark restaurants. He sipped Chablis while she wept, into Kleenex, cocktail napkins, her sleeves. "Hang on," he had said, vaguely, "hang on." Now he called her every day. "You'll never guess what happened," he would say. "I shouldn't tell you. No, I won't tell you."

"Come on," she'd say, at home, weeping; or at work, rocking in her swivel chair. "Tell me."

"I came back from this track trip, it was two or three in the morning, I told Jennifer to meet me, well, she didn't mind, it's not like she's got anything better to do with her time . . ."

"Three in the *morning?*"

"Ah, well, *shit!*"

"So?"

"*What!*"

"What happened?" Swimming up out of grief.

"So I get off the plane, I'm dead to the world, and there at the gate is Joanie!"

"Joanie?"

"Another girl! An entire other girl! She's there to surprise me. So she surprised me!"

"And how old is she?" Beginning to smile, rocking in her swivel chair. "In high school yet?"

"Ah, *shit!*" And come to find out, in a week or two, she barely was.

Patty called to say that she had heard from Marc Mandell, wintering somewhere farther north and inland—far from his family, his father, and Ruth, who, he wrote Patty, had betrayed him sorely. Patty read the letter over the phone, laughing. "It is without excuses or alibis, or, I hope, any sense of guilt, that I have come to the conclusion after some years and some misadventures, that I made a mistake, dear love, when I ever let you go. In my fantasies I have always been with you, and I ask you—think about it at least—to let me try to make this a reality for both of us. In my deepest thoughts, Patty, whoever I have been with, I had always wished it were with you."

Still, it came as a surprise to hear, some weeks later, that Patty had bought a goose-down parka, left her kids with her ex-husband, and taken a plane to the north. She came back once, to buy provisions, and took Ruth to lunch.

"You have no idea what it's like up there," she said. "The wind howls at night and shakes the house, you have to be very careful of fire. There's no real work to do, because the house is so ugly you can't worry about making it beautiful, and all the food all comes up from the States in cans. You can't make a good meal so you don't worry."

They were sitting in Denny's, across from the station where Ruth worked. Ruth had ordered a hamburger, Patty the diet special. "It's the last one I'll have for a long time," she said, looking out the window to the traffic of Hollywood Boulevard. "How do you stand this, Ruth? Going to work every day? I mean, don't you think it's a *crock*, this stuff about careers?"

"What about the children?" Ruth asked her friend. "How are they taking it?"

"Oh, they're upset," Patty said, "but they'll get over it. The

278

way I see it, I've put in fifteen years being the best mother I can, what more could I do for them anyway? Oh, they're upsct, but"—her face broke a little—"don't you think I would have lost them anyway?"

No woman Ruth knew had ever left her children. The only place she had seen it done was in TV movies, and then only on ABC. Nobody she knew even watched those movies.

Why, *I* could have had him if that's all it was, she would think, desperately, in the night. Just kiss off your kids if you can *do* that! And she heard, to her anguish, that Patty's children were doing very nicely indeed, that they loved living with their father, that they wrote their mother every day, and were enrolled in excellent schools. You can do that, yes, and it doesn't even matter. She thought about Marc all the time, with hatred. She remembered how often he had told her that Patty was sexually unexciting, and did not doubt at all that Patty heard the same—nightly—about her. Dully she knew that they were happy, that any fight she conjured up for them in her mind, the butane running out, the . . . butane running out; the equation didn't work because there was a larger one, were larger ones, problems in geometry, overwhelmingly simple.

How could she *do* that? she wailed in the night. I know *he* could do it, the bastard, the prick, but how could *she* do it? She found she was addressing her mother, not the poker-playing senior citizen in the trailer, but the trembling young divorcée on the streetcar downtown, who behind her red eyes took care to sit up straight and look out the windows, who shepherded her little girl past murmuring Mexicans into the Million Dollar: *Ashes to ashes and dust to dust, come on baby, you must, you must!* OK, Ruth thought wearily, again, again, OK.

At last, in the night, on the freeway, it came to her. As simple as cornflakes. If most forty-year-olds, the "kids" she had grown up with, preferred children twenty years younger, well, then, like geometry, the rule must hold true in every circumstance. She opened her eyes, at home, at work. She looked for the old guys.

She spent evenings with men like puspockets, stuffed full of grease and gin. They told her the stories of their lives— stories which because of simple arithmetic had to run half again as long as the ones she had been used to. Sixty years of defeat, of wives upon wives, affairs upon affairs. She couldn't remember the details. Their faces blurred, fading at the edges, while she said, "Wait a minute. Was that your first wife, you said?" And those men, old enough by definition to be her father, recounted over and over their wretched tales. "So I went over to *her* house, see, with *my* wife, and *she* was already married, and I think already pregnant at the time. I followed her out into the kitchen when she made the first round of drinks, and she said, you know what she said? She didn't look at me, she looked straight into the refrigerator, and she said, *'You bother me! You bother me!'*"

"And that was . . . your second wife?"

"Her? Hell no! Oh, *she* was something!"

Drama in sex; in lost identities. "You should have seen me then, I could do it five times in an hour. I wanted it everywhere! There used to be a rocking chair out there in the kitchen, we'd sit in it, she'd be on my lap, her husband must have known, he never said a thing."

Baked potatoes, with sour cream. Imitation gritty bits of bacon, moistening, spreading. Lettuce, yellow at the edges. Olives, with red guts, piling on wet napkins. "You ought to see me down at the farm! Oh, I can carry a bag of manure as well as any man *your* age!" But men of her age were already too old to carry bags of manure, and she would never see the farm in question; he lived there with his wife.

If they were twenty years older than you they were married. If they were twenty years older than you and *not* married, they were generally already dead. She heard, from time to time, of men on the other side of that all-important time gap who were not married. (And white; she felt in terms of dignity and principle that they had to be at least fifty-five *and* white.) She heard of them, from time to time, from reliable sources, as Sherpa guides might speak with dreadful certainty about the *yette,* those Abominable Snowmen. Apt name! One afternoon she met one, in her own office, out from Washington to cover an election. "My wife has passed away," he told her solemnly. "Could we? Might we? Could you pick me up at my place?" Why not? Were we not in a new age? She found him standing at his curb, dapper and well-pressed, full of the cynical newsman style she once had found—still *did* find—so attractive. She got out and walked over to the passenger seat.

"Oh, no," he said, smiling, ruddy-faced. "*You* drive. I lose consciousness from time to time."

She became the recipient of "gifts." A couch. The second-best double bed at Sears. A wrist watch. An "antique" ring whose stones fell out the first time she washed her hands. A pantsuit and a pair of boots. Where she had resented being supported by her husband, she relished these gifts. They were concrete. (I am worth, at the moment, ninety dollars' worth of suede.) Am I, to these men, a *chick*? She met a surprising number of wives, in hallways, in restaurants. Slender, agreeable, well-kept. Spending whole nights with those guys, they had the worst of it.

She remembered her own mother coming home from dinner dates; snapping, sparkling; a live, fallen wire, twitching, smoking, on wet cement. "Dogs! They're like dogs!" And as she paced, her high heels clicked along the polished floors like claws. "They only want that one thing—"

Ah, if they could only get it! Couldn't they stay home with those well-kept women in silk blouses? Couldn't their twenty, twenty-five, thirty, thirty-five years count for something? Hadn't they got it together in all that time? Could *they* enjoy

281

these dreary dinners? Didn't they tire of meals eaten in smoke?

"I took a bike ride today," one man told her fatuously. She was amazed. Those feet, pushing down on pedals, pressing, right, left, right? That face, stuffed from within, out in the fresh air? Like a dog out for a ride, pressing his snout into the wind? The years fell from his face, and she saw the boy up on the bike. Poor wretched bastards! They only wanted the one thing; and sex was just a metaphor for that one thing.

Dinah came home one afternoon and saw the couch.
"What's *that!*" she cried.
"A couch," Ruth said.
"Jeez Louise," Dinah said, "that's *awful.*"
"Where'd you get the ring?" Reggie asked one day.
"Just got it."
"Is it real?"
"That's his story."
"You don't even know if it's *real* or not?"
"Well," Ruth said defensively. The next Saturday, as she was doing errands, she had the ring appraised. Genuine stones, gold-filled setting. She had the missing stones replaced. Three dollars apiece.

Some mornings, when she got up, she felt funny. She went to a gynecologist. Nothing was wrong. The pain—if it was that—shifted up. She went back to her psychiatrist. "I think you're coping as well as you can, under the circumstances," her psychiatrist said. *I am falling apart,* Ruth thought. *Am I falling apart?* Jack came over and spent some Saturdays with her and the kids.

"Where'd you get the couch?" he said, once, and when she shrugged he shrugged too. "Pretty *weird,* isn't it?"

Reggie moved out. One morning in December, four months after their return. No hard feelings. Just to be closer

282

to school. No hard drugs. Just time to try it. She moved all day, up and down the path. Jack was there and helped. He and Hollis carried Reggie's bed down the hill, her bureau, her bookcase, her framed posters from *Vogue,* her autographed photograph of Fred Astaire. Ruth fixed lunch. The four of them ate, played cards. Ruth broke out a bottle of champagne. *Good luck,* she said. The room was filled with smoke. Hollis shuffled the cards one last time, cut them, cut them again, stood up. Reggie, in French T-shirt, a turban, wide French pants, stood up. "I love you both," she said, and turned around and left. Hollis left, head down. Jack said, "Well, bye," and walked out after them. Dinah biked and shouted at the bottom of the hill.

That night she and Dinah watched a movie, on television, alone. Dinah broke down and cried. Ruth patted her and said, "It won't be so bad."

What had she ever given Reggie? Not her beautiful figure—that was from Jack's mother. A sense of humor? That was Jack's, damn his shifty eyes. A love of martyrdom? *Bien sur.* A good recipe for prune roast? Don't ask.

Connie took up with younger men. A Jamaican bicycle rider. One of her other friends took up with a woman. Ruth stuck rigidly to men, white.

Her mother had used Four Purpose face cream. Her mother had read at night. Her mother lay awake, reading, waiting for prowlers all night. Their dog, an undersized German shepherd, would lie, asleep, at the end of the long, tiled hall. Once in an hour he would get up, woof once, twice, then walk the length of the hall in awful silence, only the click of his claws against the night.

Ruth was rarely alone. Jack called every day. Edward called every day. She went to work most days, some days. I really ought to be able to live my life alone, she thought. But

283

an acquaintance of hers, a married woman, said, "When they tell you you ought to be able to do it alone, that it's something you can do for yourself, dear, that's when you go home and shoot yourself."

Her luck changed. She met, interviewing doctors during a doctors' strike, some handsome doctors. She set herself a limit. No one under fifty. To one doctor, over lunch, she said, "I feel funny. Not sick. Like I'm falling apart." He was a nice man, divorced, with seven children.
"Well, come on over to the office," he said.
"You're on strike," she said.
"Ah, *hell*," he said, mildly.

She went weekly to the China Palace and saw her past. Jack, with a different woman every week. Sometimes Edward, with another date. Her psychiatrist. Her husband's psychiatrist. Her high school friends, graying. One night, with Connie, she saw Marc Mandell's parents, and two customers from what must have been out of town. Ruth and Connie sent the kids to the ladies' room, with instructions to check out what they were eating. Hysterically laughing, they came back and reported: Lion's Head, Peking Duck. Mr. Mandell did not acknowledge the attention. The next week, they saw him, in a suede jacket over a wine-colored turtleneck sweater, dining with a woman considerably his junior. Chicken with Peppers, the girls gleefully reported; Mushi Pork.

The spring rains came. The lion-colored canyon sent up brisk new shoots. It's not so bad here, Ruth thought loyally, defensively, it's really quite pretty.

She met a silver-haired scholar. He wore tweeds and a moustache and spoke five languages. And he was sixty, that was the wonder of it, sixty! They went to a verse-play; he drank six martinis before the performance and stayed awake for the full two and a half hours. That night, after walking her up the canyon path, he bowed from the waist, and disappeared, into the brush. "Is this him, *he*—the man of my dreams?" she asked herself, her friends. "What do you think?" "Isn't he a little old?" Connie asked her, sardonically, on the phone. "How's his heart?" her psychiatrist rather tactlessly asked, and Mario, at work, still smarting from his own divorce, asked, more cannily than most, "Does he have any dependents?" Ten days later, at his place, he shucked his saffron silk pajamas.

"Oh, my *God!*" she breathed.

"Is something wrong, dearest?"

"Not likely!"

Picnics. Parties at the office. Museums with Dinah and her friends. Banks.

A plastic horse, carrying within it a hidden inland sea. The weeds grow up around it. One or two prickly pears fall close to it, or are kicked in that direction. They take root. Ceanothus, California lilac, spreads toward it, and Spanish Broom from the place farther down the hill. A yucca springs up just underneath, encounters the fragile, plastic shell, makes half an S around it, and keeps on growing.

Early March in the sharp bite of spring air. The alarm. Dinah in bed beside her. Cold. God damn it. The sun up over the canyon wall. Well. Get up, no slippers, no buttons to her robe. The sound of her mother's angry slippers against cold linoleum floor. *Crash* down the door of the broiler, *slam* in the toast! Slap, slap, slap, slap. But her own mother always made fresh orange juice in the morning. Get out of bed, put on the water for coffee, light the oven for extra heat. Back in bed, turn down the sheet, the fresh, yeasty taste of a child sleeping.

"Hey, get up."

"Absolutely not."

"What is this absolutely?" Blowing in the back of her neck. Two hundred and twenty volts of love into a tiny 110 socket.

"Absolutely not, is all."

Seven-fifteen, the kettle boiling. "Oh, if there were some good little boy or girl," Ruth wails theatrically, "if there were only some good little boy or girl around here to get up and get their poor mother a cup of coffee!"

Still dark outside. So lonely without Reggie.

"Forget it!"

"Oh, if only . . . " But it's getting to be seven-twenty, they have to hurry. "I tell you what. I'll get the coffee, you get the clothes out of your room."

"But it's your turn. I did that yesterday."

Ruth feels her face stiffen.

"OK, OK!" Dinah says hastily. "I'll do it. Gee, it's cold!"

"Stand by the oven while you get dressed."

In the end she ends up half dressing Dinah herself, standing by the stove, sipping her coffee, jerking pajamas off with angry fingers, pushing the T-shirt (boat-necked, like Reggie's, French, from Paris) into the oven, waving it there, skimming it over the kid's head, the Levi's are cooking in there, the zipper is hot. "Ouch!" Dinah says. *"Ouch! Watch it, will you?"*

Breakfast side by side on the couch, watching cartoons. Ruth hates cartoons, Dinah hates the news. The alternative, the *Today Show,* is worst of all; the successes of the world, important men and charming women, well-dressed, up at six AM and talking to the world.

At five minutes to eight, Dinah jumps up and stands by the television. Turns to Channel 2 to hear Hughes Rudd tell the last "human interest" item of the news. As every morning, Ruth stretches her arms toward the television, calls out, "Hughes, I love you, do you hear me? Don't you want to get married?" It's true, he is the man of her dreams, honest and plain , not like that prick up north.

Only a few more minutes. "Brush your teeth, wash your face, comb your hair," which some mornings, to Dinah's great delight, comes out "Brush your face, wash your teeth, comb your hair" and the kid is gone, out, her hood up against this last cold weather, her spelling book in hand. Oh, corny! Norman Rockwell! Ruth remembers a cover of the *Saturday Evening Post* when she was a girl. A suburban house. In the foreground, two little boys walking to school. Spit and polish. Perfect. American. In the background—how *did* he draw it anyway?—the mother, hair in curlers, standing in their room. Total chaos. Unmade beds, pennants, ball bats, clothes thrown up against the wall and somehow sticking there, boots, shoes, hockey pucks. When Ruth was young (but it must have been only for a week, her mother threw out magazines once a week), she'd loved that picture; this was how the real world did it. After the kids went off to school, the mother went out to the kitchen, her husband would already be off to work. She'd sit at the table and leaf through the paper where he'd left it, then she'd get up and make all the beds and do the dishes and get dressed, and go out to do the shopping. (She would make a list.) She would come home, make herself a sandwich, she would make a nice dessert for that night's dinner, she would do some work in the yard then, or sit talking in the kitchen with a friend. She would be home when those two boys got home, she would be home for her husband, maybe in a long dress. She would never be tired.

Goodbye, Dinah. That little life. Was it programming, pure and simple, or did parents actually love their children?

Turn on the shower. Turn on the television set, high, so she can hear it in the bathroom. Makeup. Dress. She needs to buy some clothes. The phone rings. She hesitates, she's late, she answers.

"About those tests. Your pap smear was all right, your cardiogram was OK, all the rest, but there's one reading here, your liver, well, you're drinking too much."

"But I love to drink, doctor!" Sprightly, her public voice.

"Stick to pot," the doctor says, and she can hear the daring in his voice. He is plain but cute, and over fifty.

"Say," he says, and his tone shifts again. "You're a nice woman."

"Thank you," she says, and waits.

"Maybe some night we could go out for a drink?"

Down the path into the car, warm up the engine, this is what men go through, this is where the husband went on the cover of that *Saturday Evening Post*. She is late but not too late. She'd like to do a piece on . . . on old people, not how sad they are, or ill used, but what really goes on, do they have sex? Do they fall in love?

She shifts up into second, and into high, automatically pushes the radio button. She thinks to improve her mind and turns to the classical music station. It's violins, she switches. The nasal pain of Bob Dylan lasts less than a second; she moves the dial again, watching the road.

Speeding, just up against the speed limit, she settles in, happily listening to bad news.